Novels by
C. S. Friedman
available from DAW Books:

The Magister Trilogy
Feast of Souls

The Madness Season

This Alien Shore

In Conquest Born
The Wilding

The Coldfire Trilogy
Black Sun Rising
When True Night Falls
Crown of Shadows

Feast of Souls

C. S. Friedman

DAW BOOKS, INC.

DONALD A. WOLLHEIM, FOUNDER

375 Hudson Street, New York, NY 10014

ELIZABETH R. WOLLHEIM

SHEILA E. GILBERT

PUBLISHERS

http://www.dawbooks.com

First Printing, February 2007
1   2   3   4   5   6   7   8   9

To Paul Hoeffer.
For his many labors of love.

Acknowledgements

THIS BOOK would not exist without the contributions of one very special person. I regret that I can't give you her real name. She lives two separate lives, you see, and the one I needed to learn about was a thing of shadows and secrets, so different from anything in my own experience that I did not feel that reading books about it was enough. I needed a real person, someone willing to share the darkest moments of her past with me, someone insightful enough to understand how those moments shaped her life.

Her clients call her Anna.

With rare candor and boundless generosity this lady opened her heart to me, sharing her memories freely—good ones and bad ones, triumphant and troubling, from the desperation that first drove her to sell her body to the rare moments of empowerment she snatched from a world of exploitation and abuse. Though her I came to understand the social and sexual dynamics that had molded my main character in her youth, and to make her real. Without Anna's counsel, such a project would have been nigh on impossible.

So thank you, Anna, for helping bring Kamala to life.

Thanks also to my agent Russ Galen for his creative input into this work, and David Walddon as always for being my most insightful critic (and most enthusiastic cheerleader). Also Paul Hoeffer and Carl Cipra for outstanding commentary upon the work in progress. I couldn't have done it without you, guys.

Feast of Souls

Prologue

IMNEA KNEW when she awoke that Death was waiting for her.

She had been seeing the signs of his presence for some time now. A chill breeze in the corners of the house that wouldn't go away. Shadows that seeped in through the windows, that didn't move with the light. The icy touch of a presence upon her skin when she healed the Hardings' little girl, that left her shuddering for hours afterward.

The mirror revealed little. Of course. It wasn't the way of witching folk to age and die like normal people. The fuel within them was consumed too quickly, like a fire into which all the winter's wood had been placed at once. What a blaze it made! Yet quickly gone, all of it, until it smothered in its own ash.

How long ago had the dying begun? Did it start in her youth, when she first discovered she could do odd things—tiny little miracles, hardly worth noting—or not until later? Did Death first notice her when she made tiny points of fire dance on the windowsill, with a child's unconscious delight (and how her mother had punished her for that!), or not until she reached deep within herself with conscious intent to draw strength from her very soul—from that central font of spiritual power that mystics called the *athra*—and to bend it to her purpose? When and where was the contract with Death sealed, and what act marked its closing? The healing of

Atkin's boy? The calling of rain after the Great Drought of '92? The day she had cleansed Dirum's leg of its gangrene, so that they wouldn't have to cut it off?

She was thirty-five. She looked much older.

She felt eighty.

Soon, Death whispered, his voice disguised as the whisper of falling snow. *Soon. . . .*

With a sigh she fed some more wood into the stove and tried to stoke its dying embers to more radiant heat. It had been more than a year now since she'd last used the power. She'd hoped that if she stopped, some of her strength would return. Surely whatever internal energies created the athra in the first place could restore it to strength, if it was no longer used for witchery. But even if that were true, how much of her life was gone already? Each time she had used the magic to heal a child, cast out a demon, or bless a field against the onslaught of locusts, she had drawn upon her own life force for power. The supply wasn't endless. All the witching folk knew that. Just as the flesh became exhausted in time, so did the fires of the spirit bank low, smolder, and finally extinguish. Use the fuel for things other than staying alive and the fire would be extinguished that much sooner.

Yet how could you have the power to heal, and not use it? How could you watch a child turn blue before you and not clear out its lungs and give it life again, even if the cost was a few precious minutes of your own life?

Minutes had seemed like nothing in the beginning. What do young people know of time, especially when the power is pounding in their veins, demanding expression? By the time you became aware that minutes combine to make hours, and hours add up to days, and days to years . . . by then Death was already knocking on your door.

No more witchery, she had promised herself a year ago. Whatever time she had left, it would be her own. She had let the village know she wouldn't be able to do healing for them anymore, and that was the end of it. Let them hate her for it if they wished. It would be a poor answer to her years of service if they did, but she wouldn't be surprised. Human nature was remarkably ungrateful when it came to expecting sacrifice of others.

And already it had begun. She had heard the whispers. Every child that died of the pox now died because of her inaction. Every injury that led to death now was due to her callousness. Never mind that illness and injury were a natural part of life that only costly miracles could defy. Never mind that for two decades she had expended her own life-energy to provide those miracles. Never mind that Death was breathing down her neck now because of those very acts. This year she had turned them all away, and that was all that anyone seemed to care about.

Human nature.

She leaned forward over the fire, trying not to ask herself the question that all the witching folk did, in the end. *Was it worth it?* Too much danger in that internal dialogue. Answer no, and your last days would be filled with regret. Answer yes, and then your dying was your own damned fault.

Suddenly a knock on the door drew her from her reverie. Who on earth was visiting her in these final days, when all the town was treating her like a pariah?

She walked to the heavy oaken door and pulled it open. By the dying light of the winter day she could see two figures standing outside. No need to ask what they'd come for. One of the figures held a small bundle in her arms, and from its size and drape she guessed it to be a child, swathed in blankets. A pang of emotion stabbed her in the heart, guilt and anger hotly combined.

Isn't it enough that I refuse you in the marketplace, in the temple, in the very streets? Must you bring your sick ones to my very door, to be turned away?

For a moment she almost shut the door in their faces, but a lifetime's habit of hospitality proved too strong to overcome. Grunting, she stepped aside for the two to come in. By the stove's dim light she could see them better: a tall, gaunt woman, peasant-born, who had clearly seen better days, and a young girl by her side, hardly looking better. The kind you healed and sent home knowing that Death might claim them the next year anyway, from starvation or abuse or any one of the thousand things no witching power could heal. The girl had a hard edge about her, as if she had already seen the rotting underbelly of the world and become inured to its stink; it was a frightening look, in one so young. The woman . . . looked merely desperate.

"Mother," the woman began respectfully. "I'm sorry to bother you. . . ."

"I don't do healing any more," Imnea said curtly. "If you want a cup of tea to warm you before you set on your way again I'll give you that. I might have a scrap of bread. But that's all."

She expected the woman to argue with her and she was braced for it. Gods knew she'd been through this before, a hundred times over, it seemed. But instead the woman said nothing, merely lowered a corner of the blanket wrapped around her child. The glimmering green pustules on his fevered face spoke volumes in that moment, before she covered them up again.

Green Plague. Imnea had seen it only once, years ago. That was after it had claimed half a town. The witching folk had banded together then— an event as rare as the Red Moon that had shone down upon the effort— trying to burn away the infection not only from a handful of bodies, but from the village itself. It was said there were times in the old days when the Green Plague, sweeping through the land, had killed two out of every three people. That time it didn't. Maybe their efforts had helped stop it. Maybe the gods had seen so many witching folk offering up years of their own lives to heal others that they decided it was time for a single act of divine mercy to be granted. Or maybe Death was just too busy gathering up all the new contracts the witching folk had offered him that night to worry about spreading the convulsive disease further.

She didn't need to feel the boy's skin to know he had fever. Or to read his future to know the terrible suffering that awaited him if the disease went unchecked. It was a horrible way to die.

"I don't do healing anymore." The words lacked the conviction she wanted them to have. Damn these people, why did they have to bring the boy here, into her home?

"You have the power. They say you've healed this sickness before."

"And I don't anymore. I'm sorry. That's the way it is." Each word scored her throat like a hot knife as she forced it out. Didn't the woman understand what such a healing would cost her?

What gives you the right to demand my life?

The Plague would force the boy into seizures soon, terrible seizures in which he would scream out for water, but vomit up anything that was given to him. It would go on for days, if his family didn't put him out of his misery. And they wouldn't. They'd pray and they'd make offerings and they'd ask the gods to please, please make this boy one of the few who were strong enough to survive the Plague. And so he would suffer, endless days of agony, until all that was left was a desiccated husk from which the human soul had long since departed, begging unheard for the final mercy to be granted.

And then others would follow. The whole town, sooner or later. Maybe even Gansang itself, if the infection spread far enough. Very little could check the Green Plague once it had taken hold in a place.

He was still in the early stages. If she healed him now, if there were no others infected yet, the town might be spared.

Imnea turned away to stoke the fire. The new log wasn't catching. The embers were growing dim.

"Please," the mother whispered.

No bribes. No threats. No promises. Imnea was prepared to counter all those. But the simple heartfelt plea was none of those things, and all of them combined. Guilt stabbed like a hot blade into her heart.

I should give her a knife and tell her to end it. For the child's sake. If she doesn't handle the body fluids when she kills him there's a chance it won't spread.

With a sigh she turned back to face the pair. They deserved that much, these villagers, that at least she would meet their eyes while she shattered their hopes. But it was the girl's eyes that caught her own this time, not the woman's. Clear eyes, remarkably so given the hollows of hunger and hardship that hung beneath them like dark moons. Green eyes, flecked with gold as if with fairy dust. Yet it wasn't color or clarity that made the girl's gaze so arresting as much as an indefinable *something* . . . as much out of place in these dim surroundings as a gleaming star would be.

Such depth, in that gaze. Remarkable in one so young. Imnea wondered briefly if she had the Power . . . but only briefly. She had no time to worry about matters of Power, least of all to appraise the potential of some fledgling witch who would probably die of hunger and cold in the gutters of Gansang long before she ever found a suitable teacher.

Perhaps it was that thought which plucked at her heart like a harp string. Perhaps it was the memories of the ones she had taught, and the children she had borne, and all those people who had turned to her for healing or counsel or simply comfort, in her thirty-five years of life. Maybe it was something about the power that made her hear their voices now, begging her to help this woman . . . or maybe it was Death playing tricks on her. Trying to hurry her along, so that he wouldn't be late for his appointment with the next witch on his list.

Damn you to hell, she thought. *My life you can have, that was mine to give up, but not this boy's. Not yet.*

In a voice as harsh as winter ice she said, "Give him to me."

The bundle was given to her wordlessly. It was lighter than it should be, she noted; mostly blankets. The child hadn't been big to start with, and the early stages of the Plague had probably stripped his bones of what little meat they'd had. Her own bones ached as she shifted his weight in her arms. *Poor child, poor child, at least if you live through this you can tend to any others who get sick. There's comfort in that.*

For a moment she shut her eyes. Just resting, gathering her spirit, letting the aches and pains of her premature aging settle into the background so that her rational mind was foremost. The gods hadn't taken that away from her yet.

I wouldn't want to live through another Plague year anyway, she told herself. *One horror like that is enough for anyone.*

She began to hum softly, a focus for her witchery. She could sense the woman and the girl watching, fascinated, as she prepared herself. If only she could show them what it felt like! If only she could share with another person—any person—the pain and joy and fear and exultation of such an act! For one of them to understand what the power was like, how terribly it cost her to use it, that would be worth everything. Because then her sacrifice would be understood. Then she would be loved for what she had given up, not hated for all the times she had failed.

At last, when the music was ready, when the room was ready—when the child and the mother and the time and the night outside and all the world were ready—she reached inside her soul to where the heart of all power lay. It was faint these days, so very faint, not the resplendent beacon of power she had discovered in her youth, but a much older soul, nearly exhausted now. It wouldn't have lasted another year, she told herself. And it would have been a cold and lonely year to live through, with all the villagers hating her.

Are you sure? Death whispered in her ear. *Very sure, Imnea? This time there is no turning back.*

"Go to hell," she whispered to him.

The warmth of her living soul filled her flesh, driving out the chill of the winter night. Then outward it flowed, into the boy. Clean, pure, a gift of healing. She shut her eyes, trusting to other senses to observe as it bolstered his own failing spirit, feeding strength into his athra, giving it focus. Fire burned along his veins and the boy cried out, but neither the mother nor the girl flinched.

The disease was strong in his flesh, rooted in a thousand places; she burned them all, drawing upon her athra for fuel and the boy's own soul for focus. Some witches said that a disease was like a living thing, that fought back when you tried to kill it; she thought of it more as a thousand living things, or tens of thousands, that might fight or hide or burrow deep into the flesh for protection from such an assault. You had to find them all or the disease would come back later with renewed strength. How much of her life force had she wasted in her early years, learning that lesson?

The log in the stove hadn't caught; the fire was dying. Winter's chill seeped into the cabin and into her bones, and she let it. There wasn't enough power left within her to keep her flesh warm and heal the boy as well. Not that any witch with a brain would waste power on the former task anyway . . . not when there was wood to be burned. The power was too precious to waste on simple things. If only she'd understood that, in the youth of her witchery! A tear coursed down her cheek as she remembered the hundred and one little magics she could have done without, the tricks performed for pleasure or show or physical comfort. If she could undo them all now, how much time would they add up to? Would they buy her another week, another year of life?

Too late now, Death whispered.

Dying. She was dying. This is what it felt like, when the embers of the soul expired at last. She could feel the last tiny sparks of her athra flickering weakly inside her. So little power left. How much time? Merely minutes, or did she have all of an hour left to wonder if she had done the right thing?

"It is done," she said quietly.

The mother leaned down to take the boy, but hesitated when she saw his face. "He looks the same."

"His soul is clean. The pustules will drain within a day or two. He will be safe after that."

And you, his mother . . . if you have caught this thing too, I am sorry, there will be no one to beg for favors when the first signs show . . .

She tried to rise, to see them out. Hospitality. But her legs had no strength, and her heart . . . her heart labored in her chest with an odd, unsteady beat, as if the drummer which had guided it for thirty-five years had stopped his music and left it to flounder.

She was cold. So cold.

"Mother?"

The eyes of the girl were fixed upon her. So deep, so hungry, so very determined. Drinking in knowledge as if it was the fuel her soul required. *See, child, what the power can do. See what happens to you when you use it.* There was no wonder in the child's eyes, or even fear . . . only hunger.

Heed this lesson well, my child. Remember it, when the power beckons. Remember the price.

"Come, child." It was the mother's voice, nearly inaudible. Imnea's hearing was growing dim; the world was an insubstantial thing, all murmurings, windsong and shadow. "Come away now."

Are you ready? Death whispered to her.

Imnea clung to life for a moment more. A single moment, to savor those dreams which had guided her . . . and to mourn those which had gone unfulfilled.

Then: *Yes,* she whispered. Voice without sound. *Yes, I am ready.*

In the stove the last embers of the fire sputtered and died, leaving the room in darkness.

Beginning

Chapter 1

THE MARKET in Royal Square was always busy, but this day in particular the crowds were so dense that it was hard to get from one end to the other without being jostled nearly to death. Some said it was because the weather was perfect, a fine spring day flourishing beneath a nearly cloudless sky, inviting one and all to leave behind their winter solemnity and come squeeze fruit and prod chickens while dreaming of the best of summer feasts. Some said it was because the harvest had been good last year, which meant there were many things to sell, and many farmer's wives with money in hand ready to buy foreign delicacies.

Some said it was something else entirely.

The stranger stood at the edge of the crowd and watched the people for a long moment with a practiced eye. He was taller than most of the locals, and thin, with jet-black hair that hung down to his shoulders and eyes to match. His features were aquiline, cast in an exotic olive tone that spoke of foreign shores and mixed origins. More than one woman turned to watch him as he stepped forward into the crowd, which was only to be expected. Tall, lean, graceful in his movements, he had always attracted women.

He was dressed in a simple black shirt and breeches, and might have been judged a peasant in his Sunday best, or else a nobleman who had tired of all the extra layers which the display of rank required. A quick look at his fingernails—fastidiously clean—removed the peasant interpretation from consideration. Seamstresses might notice the shirt was of unusually fine cloth, but it took a practiced eye to determine that, and the cut of his garments was not so expensive as to attract undue attention.

Sometimes even peasants wore black.

There were some who said that the crowds in the Royal Square gathered today not for gossip, not for trade, or for anything so mundane as market business, but simply to *be* there. For it was whispered that today a Magister from Anshasa would arrive at the palace with full retinue, and this was the closest that the common populace could get to the main gates to watch him arrive.

Anshasa. How many of the men here had fought in the great wars against that southern kingdom, how many of the women here had mourned the loss of father, husband, son in those conflicts? Though a tenuous peace had endured now for several years there was no love lost between the two nations, and the gossips who had so fastidiously digested and disseminated the news of the Magister's visit were at a total loss to come up with a reason why it was taking place. Surely it was all but suicidal—even for a Magister!—to journey to the heart of enemy territory with no more than a brief truce in an eons-old conflict to safeguard him.

The stranger gazed out upon the crowd, studying them as if they were all foreign beasts, and he a forester learning their ways. A gaggle of young maids in the livery of houseworkers passed him by, their bright eyes full of curiosity and flirtation; he smiled, which set them to giggling even louder. Predictable beasts.

He picked up a piece of fruit from a nearby wagon with the passing intention of eating it, then saw the bruised surface and put it back. Strangely, the woman behind him who picked it up in turn found it undamaged.

The wind had blown the blacksmith's fire into itself, and filled his tent with smoke. It shifted as the stranger passed, and soon the air was clear.

A chicken about to be beheaded died an instant before the blade struck its neck, and was thus spared both fear and pain.

A minstrel's mandolin, painfully out of tune, discovered its proper notes.

A pickpocketing child tripped and went sprawling in the dirt, his ill-gotten gain splayed out upon the ground for all to see.

A woman who, unbeknownst to her, had started the day with the seed of a deadly cancer in her breast, returned home without it.

The stranger's journey brought him to a tent that was set apart from all the others. Talismans strung from the tent poles tinkled like windchimes, and a small but colorful sign invited visitors to enter and receive advice from a "true witch." He hesitated a moment, considering, then ducked slightly to clear the low door flap and entered. A heady incense filled the small space, which was decorated with richly embroidered throws and rugs. A woman sat behind a low table, upon cushions of silk embroidered with moons and stars, in front of a tablecloth of the same. Showmanship. There were cards laid out before her, and a sphere of flawed crystal, and a pile of runic stones.

"You wish your fortune told?" she asked him.

"That depends," he said. "Are you really a witch, or simply a performer?"

She smiled. She was young—she looked young—and a small bit of gold had been set in the surface of one of her front teeth. "That depends on what you pay me, sir."

He drew forth a handful of coins from his pocket as if he neither knew nor cared what they were, and cast them down before her. Gold glittered in the lamplight and caught the banners of afternoon sun that streamed through the tent's entranceway. She gasped in surprise and he smiled despite himself, certain that such a consummate performer normally prided herself on keeping such emotions to herself.

"Is that enough for the real thing?" he asked her.

She looked up at him, as if seeking understanding in his eyes. Another day he might have indulged her, but today he didn't, so he made sure that any witchery directed at him would slide off him like water from oilskin.

"What is it you wish to know, sir? And do you care which medium I use?"

Ah, the paraphernalia, the paraphernalia . . . was it just part of the show for this one, or a genuine focus? Some home-grown witches were ignorant enough that they thought they actually needed tools to draw upon their own soulfire. It never ceased to amaze him.

"You may use what you wish. And my question is . . ." He glanced out of the tent, to where the gossiping villagers milled and mingled. "The reception that the city has prepared for its foreign guest, is this a welcome in good faith? Or something less benign?"

She had been reaching out for the deck of cards as if she were about to use them, but as his words settled into warm scented air that hand withdrew, and she leaned back and studied him.

"You know I can't answer that, sir," she said at last. "If the king is keeping secrets then his Magisters are protecting them, and all the cards and crystals in the world won't get past their safeguards. And if I did learn such secrets, and passed them on to strangers for a handful of coins . . . then I wouldn't last very long in this city, would I?" She pushed the coins back towards him. "I'm sorry. Please take them."

There was hunger in her eyes, he noted. She wanted the truth but she dared not ask. It was always that way with the witching folk, for they could sense on a visceral level his true nature, yet did not trust their own instincts to name it.

"Loyalty has its own value," he said quietly. "Keep them."

He left the tent without further word. He was sure that as soon as he was out of sight she would pick up her cards again and begin asking questions about him. He did nothing to stop her from finding the answers this time. If she was willing to waste precious moments of her life searching out who and what he was, who was he to render that sacrifice meaningless?

Towards the far end of the square was a place where the merchants had not been allowed to set up their booths and tents. Drawing near to it, the stranger could see why. From this place the palace itself was visible—or more to the point, this place was visible from the palace. Gods forbid King Danton should gaze out his window and see dirty peasants going about their daily business! No, this close to the palace there was a promenade where the clean and well-dressed might take the morning air, while the local princelings gazed out of their windows and admired them from afar. Maybe one would even spot some young and tender lass dressed in her Sunday finery and sweep down from the palace to take her away to a life of wealth and leisure. So did the comely maidens hope, no doubt, as they strolled along the promenade on the arms of awkward youths in which they had no real interest, dreaming of the day they would be noticed by someone better.

Today the press of crowds along the promenade was no less than suffocating, as peasants and tradesmen both strained to catch some sight of the great road beyond that led to the palace gates. That was where the foreign Magister would ride, swathed in black silks, upon a black horse, and accompanied by the gods alone knew how many dignitaries. There had not been a state visit from Anshasa in as long as anyone could remember, and the gossips who thrived on royal trivia chattered as they made ready to receive him, ready to read meaning into every detail of his retinue's number, attire, and behavior.

It never changes, the stranger mused.

He watched for a while, but had no lengthy interest in the matter. After all, it was rumor, not royal announcement, that had gathered the crowd. There was the possibility that no grand retinue was coming at all. Hard for the peasants to grasp, with their innate awe of royal pageantry, and of course King Danton was known for putting on a great show at the slightest excuse, but that was not the custom in all places, and for one whose daily business involved the wealth and power of nations, such a procession might well seem a tedious display. Not to mention a hot and sweaty one. A true Magister was unlikely to relish such a show, the stranger thought, though he might send his luggage on ahead with all the trappings of royalty, to amuse the peasants and perhaps give vague offense to the king who was his reluctant host.

He continued his wanderings, across the great road and beyond. A packet of dried venison from one pocket stifled his noonday hunger, and when he reached a place where food was served he bought a flagon of mead to wash it down. He could have made it taste like a king's feast if he had wanted, but he was rarely so self-indulgent. As for his clothes, black though they were, they had accumulated by this time a patina of dust and sweat and would never be mistaken for a Magister's attire.

He could have cleaned them, of course. He didn't.

Around the back of the great estate, beside the great fence that guarded the king's property, he paused. It was quiet here, for the thickly forested hunting grounds beyond offered no good view of the royal habits. Fine for him. He called a bird to him—a hawk responded, strong of limb and elegantly feathered—and he whispered instructions into its ear, gave it a fine silver ring he had been wearing, and set it free. It soared over tree and stream and quickly was lost in the distance, winging its way toward the palace.

Minutes passed.

Half an hour.

He ate the last of his dried venison and reflected that he should have bought more mead.

At last there came a change in the air that he could sense before he saw it. A shimmering, a shivering, that echoed in his own soul, stirring the fires within. When the air began to ripple before him he was prepared, and when the field of ripples was large enough and steady enough for his purposes he stepped into it—and through.

On the other side was a vast, shadowy chamber, filled with black-robed men. The windows were narrow arrow slits that let in little light, and the vaulted ceiling and dark stone walls drank in the meager offerings of the only lamps in the room, a single pair set along the mantle of a man-sized fireplace.

The Magisters stood about a long table of dark wood, their chairs pushed back behind them. They were all ages, all races, all shapes . . . and all men. Of course. The nature of women didn't allow them to join such company.

The stranger looked about him, studying each in turn. The few whom he knew received a nod of acknowledgment, but there were not many. Those who frequented Danton's court were unlikely to visit the southlands, and Magisters of the southlands rarely braved these hostile latitudes.

"I am Colivar, Magister Royal of Anshasa, bound in service to his Majesty Hasim Farah the Most Merciful, scourge of the Tathys, ruler of all the lands south of the Sea of Tears." The northern language felt harsh on his tongue compared to the liquid resonance of his accustomed dialect, but he spoke it well enough to make himself understood. Little wonder the northerners did not revere poetry as his own people did; one could hardly scribe paeans to love in such a guttural and unsatisfying dialect.

"You are welcome, Colivar. If a bit early." The speaker was a man who had chosen to appear in the guise of a white-haired sage, though of course that did not necessarily have anything to do with his real age. His long beard was impressive, and as snowy white as the fur of a meticulously groomed cat.

"My luggage will be here on time."

A soft murmur of amusement that did not quite become laughter coursed about the room. Only the sage's eyes remained cold.

"The king might deem such levity offense."

Colivar shrugged. "I made no promise of pageantry for his amusement."

"And we made you no promise save safe passage to and from this place. Be wary of offending the one who rules here."

The one called Colivar laughed. It was hearty, heartfelt laughter that echoed freely in the vast chamber and set the dust to shivering off the window sills. "The king rules here? Truly? Well then you must be cutting the balls off your Magisters, for I don't know another city where men of power would stand for such a thing."

"Hush," one of the locals said, glancing toward the great oaken doors that guarded the room. "He has got ears, you know."

"And servants."

"And all of them have minds as malleable as clay," Colivar responded, "and we are the potters."

"Maybe so," the white-bearded Magister allowed, "but here in the north we pride ourselves on discretion."

"Ah." Colivar brushed at the dust on one shirt sleeve, then the other. "So do you plan to tell me why you have asked me here, against all the tide of morati politics, or does this mean I have to guess? Mind you," he said, his eyes growing hard for a moment, "you won't like my guesses."

The white-bearded Magister studied him for a moment, then nodded ever so slightly. "Perhaps introductions will make things a bit more clear. I am called Ramirus, Magister Royal of King Danton." He introduced two more men by his side, both members of the same company. "And this . . ." he indicated a swarthy man wrapped in a black burnoose and turban, "is Severil of Tarsus."

The sardonic essence faded from Colivar as quickly as it had possessed him. "Truly? A Tarsan? That is a long and arduous journey, even for one who commands the soulfire. I am honored to meet one who has come so far."

"And Del of the Crescent Isles."

Colivar's brow elevated slightly as he nodded, acknowledging silently the distance and effort involved in that journey as well.

"Suhr-Halim of Hylis. Fadir of Korgstaat. Tirstan of Gansang."

The list went on. Names and titles in two dozen languages, from as many nations. Some of them were from places whose names Colivar didn't even recognize, and he had thought himself well schooled in all the known places of the world.

"Quite a collection of visitors," he said, when the introductions were done at last. There was no longer humor in his voice; it had given way to something colder. "I have never seen so many of us, from so many places, brought together. We do not tend to trust one another, do we, my brothers? So I assume there must be some pressing business that is truly extreme, for our brother Ramirus to have called us all here."

"If I said a threat to our very existence," Ramirus said quietly, "would that suffice?"

Colivar digested the words with the somber care they merited, then nodded.

"Very well," the Magister Royal said. "Then you shall come with me, and see for yourself."

And without further word he led his wary guest out of the dark chamber and into the heart of the palace.

Chapter 2

E THANUS REMEMBERS:
    Whoever is at the door will not go away. He's ignored their knocking for some time now, preferring not to be disturbed, but time after time they keep coming back. The knocking is soft but insistent, not harsh enough to anger him outright, and the attempts are spaced far apart, as if their purpose is not to force him to obey so much as to remind him that the visitor has neither left nor forgotten him still.

At last with a sigh he rises from his studies, leaving behind the Chantoni hieroglyphics he has been working so hard to decipher, to confront whoever it is that thinks that he has time to waste on visitors.

It's a spring day (*he recalls*), and as he opens the door a gust of pollen-laden air sweeps into his sanctum. Fresh, sweet, and brimming with life. He should have built the place with more windows, he notes mentally, and not been constrained, as he was, by concerns over heating it in the winter.

On his doorstep is a girl. Not quite a child, but thin and scrawny enough to be taken for one at first glance. That she's has a hard life is nothing he needs magic to discover; it is etched in the very outline of her features, in the way she moves, even in the way she breathes. So is the fact that she has defied her environment and thus far come out on top. Her eyes gleam with the cold determination that the poet Belsarius once called "the diamond glare," meaning that nothing can scratch its surface. Her face and hands are meticulously clean—probably scrubbed not an hour before—but the rest of her has the faintly weathered patina of one who is not truly intimate with cleanliness. Peasant stock, he guesses, city born, and not raised gently or treated well yet trying nonetheless to present herself politely. Interesting.

Briefly he toys with the notion of binding enough Power to know more. But the habit is long gone and the temptation passes.

"Master Ethanus, Magister of Ulran?"

His expression darkens, and the passing interest he had in her quickly dies. "I no longer lay claim to that title, girl, or any other." His voice is gruff, as befits her question. What, is this some little chit that wants a spell cast for her, and has trudged through the depths of the forest to find him here, in this place he built for himself precisely so that he might live undisturbed? Of all the things he might be interrupted for, that is by far the most annoying. "Go find a witch if you want help, there are plenty about."

He closes the door in her face and goes back to work. At least, that is his intent. But her small foot is in the doorway, and to his surprise he finds that he is not quite callous enough to crush it.

He glares at her. Diamond eyes, indeed.

"So it please you sir," she says—and she bobs a bit, in what might have been a curtsey had it been done properly—"I have come to learn the ways of magic."

"Then like I said, go find a witch. I'm not a teacher."

Again he almost slams the door shut. He is hoping that if he looks like he really means it she will pull back her foot just in time, and he can close it. But she doesn't move, and he is not willing to cripple her—or to make the commitment to healing her—so with a sigh he resigns himself to finishing out the conversation.

"I don't wish to learn from a witch, sir. I wish to learn true sorcery."

With a sign of pure exasperation he says, "Well, you're a girl, so you can't. Now may I get back to my work?"

But the chit doesn't budge. Nor do the diamond eyes so much as blink. "And pardon my asking, but why won't you teach girls, sir?" The words are polite but there's a hard edge to her tone, as if that isn't the answer she wants and damn it all, she's going to stay here until she gets a better one.

With a sigh he opens the door, and crouches down slightly to meet her at eye level. "Because women can't master the power, girl. That's simple fact. You think others haven't tried? Their nature is not compatible with the demands of true sorcery. Many have tried, and they master the power as witches do, and die as witches do, of their own exertions. So it will be with you if you follow this course." He stood again. "Forget the Power. Live a long and happy life. That's my advice for you."

"Men do both."

"Yes. Men do both." But even the majority of those men who seek to become Magisters fail, he thinks, and are never more than witches. To try to do it alone, without training, all but guarantees failure, a short life grasping after a dream that only a precious few are allowed to attain, prematurely exhausted as the soulfire expires. Or sometimes, in the worst cases, success is attained . . . and brings madness in its wake.

To become a Magister is one thing. To understand what that is, and what one has become, and to accept it and go on living, that is another.

"So what is it in me that makes it impossible?" the girl demands. "Some female part? I'll cut it out."

At another time he might laugh at such ridiculous audacity, but her tone makes it clear she is deadly serious. "What," he challenges her, "take a knife to your gut and gouge out living flesh? At my command?"

"No," she says evenly, "I'll go to a witch and have them take it out, so that I don't die of it. And then I'll come back here and show you. And if you say there's another thing that's got to go, then I'll have that one taken out too. Until there's nothing left of me that a man would not have, and you are willing to teach me."

He steps back a bit, into the shadows of the small house, and gestures to the walls surrounding. "Look at this place, child. Do you see magic here? Is there one brick here laid with the soul's power, one piece of furniture sculpted by any vehicle other than human sweat and toil? I built this place myself, with my own hands, every inch of it, choosing it to be that way. Now you come to me for lessons? *Me?*" He shakes his head. "I admire your determination, but you've come to the wrong place. Go to the courts of Selden or Amarys and ply your arguments there; perhaps the

Magisters will listen to you. Ethanus of Ulran is not Magister any longer, and he does not teach. Not boys, and not girls who would cut themselves up and make themselves into boys."

The girl points quietly to a far corner of the room, near where the wall meets floor. "There."

"There what?"

"Power. You said there was none." The slender finger, with delicate crescent moons of dirt under the nails that have somehow escaped both soap and water, is insistent. "Right there."

He turns and looks where she is pointing, ready to deny the allegation, but with a start he realizes that she's right. Down there, in that very spot, the year of the great rains . . . all his fledgling masonry skills had proven unable to hold the groundwater at bay, so at last he had sealed the inside of the house against leaks. Just in that one place. The rest had been adequate as it was.

"And I'm not a child," she adds.

He looks back at her. Studying her more deeply this time than before, weighing not only her outer appearance but the fire in her soul as well. It is strong, very strong. A witch with such athra might last many years. A man with such athra . . . he might risk madness and death to join the ranks of the Magisters, and perhaps succeed.

And she has the Sight. That is rare in anyone.

"What is a child?" he asks her.

The diamond gaze does not flinch. "Creatures that are sold on the street by their parents, to get the coin to make more children." She paused. "Adults sell themselves."

So cold. So very cold. Was it strength he was seeing in her, or an outer shell containing a battered soul which would shatter at the first real trial?

"Is that what you have come here to do?" he asks. "Sell yourself?"

"If I must," she says evenly.

If I were to imagine a woman with the spirit needed to become Magister, he thinks, *to survive Transition and the aftermath, this is what she would sound like.*

He lowers himself before her again. Eye to eye. Searching deeply for the things that are hidden behind flesh, hints of a soul so sheltered from a stranger's view that a man might search for years, he senses, and never catch sight of it.

"Have you ever made a flame dance upon a windowsill?" he asks softly. "Or called a lightning bug to your hand on a summer's night? Have things ever happened because you wished they would, or those who would hurt you gone away suddenly and no one knows the reason?"

The crystalline gaze is steady. "No, sir, because those things bring death. And I do not mean to die."

Yes, he thinks, *that is what is required. A hunger to live, at any cost. That is the first thing and the last, besides which all other requirements are superfluous.*

"And if I said that to cheat Death we must embrace Death?" he asked her. "What is your answer then?"

A flicker of a wry smile plays across her lips—plays there, and then is quickly gone. "That a lifetime of whoring prepares one for such bargains," she says evenly.

Yes. Yes, I suppose it does.

He stands straight again, noting that her foot is no longer in the door. There is no need for it any longer. She has intrigued him and she knows it. Maybe a city Magister would turn her away, having more important business to attend to, but a hermit in the woods who has devoted himself to study and reflection, who has sworn off all Magister's business till the end of his time on earth, and therefore has very little to do with that time, such a one might well be tempted to take on a girl apprentice, just for the challenge of it. Just for the mad, improbable, and utterly pointless challenge of it.

There are no female Magisters. Never have been. Never will be.

She waits. Silently. It is a good sign. Discipline is always a good sign.

Imagine if there could be one. What a stir it would cause! What a project that would be, to make it happen!

"What is your name, child?"

Her eyes flare a bit as she bridles at the title—as he intended—but her voice is still formal and calm as she answers, "I am called Kamala, sir."

"And if I turn you down, Kamala?" His voice is equally formal, equally calm. "If I say to you that I have sworn never to take on another apprentice—which in fact is quite true—and if I then say to you that there are reasons no woman has ever succeeded in mastering sorcery, and I know what they are, and you will be no exception, and I will not waste my time on you . . . if I say to you all those things, and then close the door in your face, what then?"

"Then I will make my camp outside your house," she answers. "And I will serve you in whatever ways I can until you change your mind. I will be as an apprentice would be, paying for his lessons. I will split wood for your fire, I will weed your garden, I will carry you fresh water from the stream every day by my own hands—by my own sweat and labor—and not use witchery to do those things, even though I probably could, until you agree to teach me how to use the power without dying. And every day you'll see me labor for you, and you will know in your heart that I won't ever give up on you, and in the end you'll teach me what I wish to know."

The diamond eyes sparkle defiantly.

Slowly he draws himself up to his full height, many a handspan over hers. Then he turns away from her. No smaller footsteps follow, nor is protest voiced. Good. He goes to the place where his tools are and chooses a heavy ax, one that only a large man might wield comfortably, and returns to the door. She is still waiting. Silently. Good.

He drops the ax at her feet, head first.

"Woodpile's in the back," he tells her.

Her foot is no longer blocking the door. He shuts it and returns to his desk. Turning up the wick on his reading lamp, he opens up the next scroll of Chantoni writing, pinning its corners down with river stones.

He does not start reading again until he hears the sound of wood splitting.

Chapter 3

THE PALACE of King Danton was of ancient stone, hung with tapestries that might have been bright and cheery once had age not bled their colors into one another, and sunlight faded the lot of them. No doubt they had some historical value, or perhaps were of sentimental importance to His Majesty; those were the only excuses Colivar could think of for allowing the dismal things to remain as they were a moment longer.

He stopped at one, a battle scene, and Ramirus allowed him the indulgence. It was a vast tapestry with hundreds of soldiers depicted upon it, and though the flags of the opposing armies had faded greatly, their colors could not be mistaken.

"The Battle of the Coldorra," Colivar mused.

"I believe your people lost that one?"

Colivar shrugged, ignoring the bait. "They were not my people at the time."

He fingered a place in the tapestry where moths had nibbled at it; the faded and frayed threads had already begun to separate around the tiny hole. "And you do not repair this because . . . ?"

"His Majesty wishes them left as they are. He likes it that they 'look old.' "

"Ah." Colivar nodded. "I see. I shall advise King Farah of that, should he wish to send him gifts in the future." He waited until Ramirus turned away and then tapped the flawed spot with his finger; the section of damaged cloth became whole again. *My gift to you, King of Coldorra.*

Ramirus brought him finally to a wing that was cheerier than most, with windows of human proportion that admitted a modicum of sunlight. That they looked out upon a courtyard could be assumed; Danton's penchant for defensive design would allow no openings so large in the outer walls. The whole of the palace was a strange mix of social center and fortified keep, as if the men who built it had been unable to decide what its true purpose was. Or perhaps it had simply existed for so long, and been used for so many different things, that its various purposes were layered over one another too thickly to make any one out clearly. Not unlike its royal master, Colivar mused.

Briefly he wondered what vast security measures that he had so casually sidestepped were present at the main gate.

A servant girl curtseyed as they approached, not daring to raise her eyes to meet theirs. "Magister Ramirus. How may I serve you?"

"Is Prince Andovan in?" Ramirus asked

She nodded.

"Is he well today?"

She hesitated, then nodded.

"We would like to see him."

She looked at Colivar. "Who shall I say—"

"That I have a guest is all you need say. He expects me."

She curtseyed again, then again while moving backward to a pair of wide oaken doors, and dipped again while easing the nearer door open and slipping inside.

"Prince Andovan is a young man yet," Ramirus said, "third in the line for the throne and therefore unlikely to inherit it. Nonetheless his health is of great concern to His Majesty, who has told us to spare no expense or effort in seeking the cause of Prince Andovan's current illness, or in affecting a cure." The Magister's eyes glittered in what might have been either disdain or amusement. "It was that command which allowed us to request your presence, and because of it he had no safe ground upon which to refuse us."

Colivar raised an eyebrow in curiosity. "You brought me here to cure the son of my enemy?"

"No. I brought you here to confirm what ails him." His expression was grim. "If it is what we think it is, no man can cure him."

The heavy door swung open. It was the girl again. She curtseyed. "If you will come in, Master Ramirus, His Highness will see you."

Colivar started forward, but Ramirus caught his arm. "Don't you think you should dress appropriately for this?"

"Does it matter?"

"Perhaps not in your realm." The word *uncivilized* was all the more apparent for not being voiced. "It does here."

Colivar shrugged. His own patron didn't much care what he wore so long as he got the job done, but the northlands were notorious for their love of "proper" protocol. With a sigh he passed a hand over his own garments, weaving enough of his soul's power into their substance to clean them, press them, and—more significantly—exchanging the faded and weathered product of the clothier's art for that perfect shade of black that only magic could provide. Oh, the dyers' guild had tried to produce such a color many times over down through the centuries, but even their best efforts could not provide a black stain permanent enough to stand up to sunlight without fading. Only magic could do that.

When his shirt and breeches were as dark as black cloth could possibly be, when the midnight perfection of them was so well set that not even the high noon sun could compromise it, he thought to himself, *These cheap tricks are the coinage by which life is bought and sold. Who shall pay the price for this one?*

Together they entered the prince's chambers.

The young man inside didn't look particularly ill so much as restless and annoyed. Prince Andovan was blond, unlike the king, and had clearly inherited his good looks from somewhere other than his hook-nosed, eagle-browed father. Colivar guessed he must have been a robust youth before the mysterious illness took hold of him, and an active one as well. The Magister made note of the hunting tapestries that lined the walls, the customized crossbows that hung beside the spacious window, and a collection of claws and teeth that were framed over the bed. *Likes to be outdoors, with the wind rushing in his hair, chasing down some poor animal that only wanted a quiet noonday meal.* Colivar looked at the young prince again, more discerning this time. *That being the case, he is very pale, even for one of northern blood.*

"Is this the southerner?" the prince asked. He brushed back a lock of golden hair from out of his eyes as he spoke. It was the kind of gesture that maidens doted upon. "You spoke of bringing one here, but I still don't understand the reason."

Ramirus bowed his head slightly. "Master Colivar is especially accomplished in the healing arts, Your Highness. Your father gave me permission to bring him in as a consultant."

"I would think one of Farah's Magisters would have more interest in encouraging my death than delaying it."

"Highness." Colivar offered his most respectful bow. "Our countries have been at peace for years now. I am a messenger of that peace."

"Yes, yes, yes . . ." The young prince waved aside the argument as casually as he might have swatted at a fly. "Magister business, I'm sure, and I won't poke into it, but you will excuse me if trusting you about my person comes hard. Most of your countrymen would as soon stick a knife in my back as measure my pulse, I'm sure you know that."

As would I, Colivar thought, *but as you said, this is Magister business.*

"I have told him nothing of your situation, Highness." Ramirus' tone was the very essence of formality. "I did not wish to prejudice his inspection."

"Yes, well. My father trusts you. He knows the customs of Magisters better than I, so I will respect that. So." He looked up at Colivar. His eyes were a pale blue, clear in color, but the whites were faintly bloodshot; the color of sleeplessness. "What do you need from me, Magister? I warn you I've been poked and prodded by the best; you'll be hard pressed to come up with anything new."

"A few questions first. May I?" he asked, indicating a chair near the young man. He knew Ramirus was glaring at him as he sat down, but that was his problem. Colivar hadn't come many hundreds of miles to play standing courtier to the son of his country's great enemy. In Farah's domain he sat when he wanted to; he would not honor an enemy prince with greater courtesy than he offered his own.

"Tell me of your symptoms first," he said quietly. And he settled in to listen not only to the young prince's words, but to the shadow play of memory behind them.

The young man nodded. His expression made it clear that he had told this tale many times and was wearying of the repetition. "It began a year ago, nearly to the day. I had just returned from riding. Suddenly there was a terrible weakness . . . that is the only way I can describe it. Like nothing I had ever felt before." He paused. "My father was most upset. He called in Master Ramirus to look at me, but by then it was as if nothing had ever happened. My strength had returned in full, and the Magister said there was no sign of any illness or bodily damage to correct."

"Tell me about the weakness," Colivar directed.

The prince drew in a deep breath and leaned back in his chair. "It was as if, all of a sudden, I was very tired. Not only in my limbs, but in my very soul. Not that I lacked strength per se, but that I lacked the desire to use it. I know that seems strange. It is difficult to describe, especially now, after so much time has passed. But that is how I recall the sensation.

"There was a servant who gave me a flagon of ale. I remember holding it, and being unable to bring it to my lips. Not that it was too heavy. It was too . . . pointless."

Colivar's expression grew progressively darker as the story was told. "Go on," he said quietly.

"That was all that happened the first time. Father made some offerings at the temple to assuage any gods that might be displeased with me, and said not to worry about it otherwise."

"But it happened again."

He nodded. "Yes. It was not nearly as dramatic, the second time . . . or the third." He sighed heavily. "These days I do not recover so quickly. The spells of weakness, the days of normal strength . . . they bleed one into the other, till I cannot rightly sense the border between the two. Sometimes the sun shines in my soul, and all seems well with the world. Sometimes . . . sometimes I cannot get out of bed. And I wonder if the day will come when I truly will never rise from it again."

Colivar could feel Ramirus' eyes upon him. He pointedly did not look up to meet them.

"Others have said it is the Wasting," the prince offered. He managed to say the word without fear, which said much for his courage. The mere name of that terrible illness would have most men wetting their beds.

"It may be that." Colivar kept his tone noncommittal, his own emotions under lock and key. "Or it may simply be some disease with a random pattern of remission and recurrence. There are many of them in the south-lands."

Ramirus offered, "That is why I called Magister Colivar here as consultant."

The prince spread his hands wide in invitation. It was a graceful motion, infinitely polished, that almost disguised the fear lurking behind it. *Almost.* "What do you need from me?"

Colivar held out his hands. After a moment the prince realized what he wanted and placed his own in them.

Blood flowing through warm flesh, heartbeat steady, pulse weak but regular . . . Colivar let his senses flow into the flesh of the prince, tasting the essence of his life, assessing the purity of his mortal shell. There was no disease there, he noted. No sign of it at all. Yes, he had suspected that would be the answer, but it was such an undesirable answer he'd been hoping he was wrong.

Diseases could be cured.

Drawing more power from within himself, he looked deeper into the prince's flesh, seeking anything physical that might cause such illness: parasite, infection, unnatural growths, unseen injuries . . . but there was nothing. A broken bone that had healed long ago, with fragments of memories adhering to it: a fall from a horse.

And then, only then, he looked where he did not wish to look, for the answer he did not wish to find.

At the prince's soulfire.

It should have been bright, in a man this young. There was no excuse for it to be otherwise. To say that his spirit's fire was banked low and dying was the same as saying that this youth, this attractive and energetic prince, was in fact a doddering old man.

And yet it was so.

No disease could explain it. No injury, no tumor, no parasite.

Only one thing.

He looked up at Ramirus. The man's expression was dark. Now Colivar understood why.

"Well?" the prince asked. "See anything useful?"

Colivar let go of the young man's hands. And yes, now that he knew what to look for, he could see the signs of the Wasting all over him. It took everything he had to keep his expression neutral, so that the prince could not read his emotions. That was for his own protection, of course. If he knew for a fact what was killing him, there was no telling how he would react. Or how his father would react, learning of it.

You did not exaggerate, Ramirus, when you said we were all at risk.

"I must confer with my colleague," he said slowly. "There are some diseases in the south with like symptoms. We must speak on them before I can be certain of a diagnosis."

The prince exhaled dramatically in frustration, but nodded. One did not argue with Magisters. How like a young lion he was in his aspect, Colivar thought: bold, restless, independent. If a human enemy had struck at him, no doubt he would answer the offense as a lion might, teeth bared and claws unsheathed. Yet this illness was not a thing of leonine conflict but of secrets and shadows and mysterious causes; clearly it assaulted his pride as much as his flesh that he had not yet declared victory over it.

If the answer is what I think, my prince, there can be no victory.

Colivar was silent as Ramirus led him from the room. He almost forgot to bow on the way out. When the door was shut behind them he stood there for a moment, still as a statue, trying to absorb what he had observed and its implications.

"You see," Ramirus said quietly.

"He is doomed."

"Yes."

"And we—"

"Shh. Wait." Ramirus gestured for Colivar to walk with him back the way they had come. This time Colivar did not notice the dust or the faded tapestries. His thoughts were too dark and too focused for such trivia.

When they were far enough away that neither Andovan nor his servants could possibly overhear them, Ramirus said, "Danton suspects the truth. But he trusts me to provide a diagnosis, and I have not yet made it official."

"If it's the Wasting . . ." Colivar breathed in sharply. "There is no cure."

"Yes." Ramirus nodded grimly.

"And that means one of us is killing him. A Magister."

"Yes," Ramirus said. A muscle along the line of his jaw tightened. "You see now why I brought you all here."

"When Danton finds out the cause—"

"He will not." His expression was grim. "He *cannot.*"

"But if he does—"

The Magister Royal raised up a hand to warn him to silence. "Not here, Colivar. This business is too private for open spaces. Wait until we have returned to my chamber, where there are wards to keep away eavesdroppers. The others wait for your input."

"And you?" Colivar challenged him. "Do you wait for my input as well?"

Ramirus looked at him. The pale gray eyes were unreadable. "The enemy of my king would not be here if I did not value his opinion," he said quietly. The narrow lips quirked into something that might, ever so briefly, be called a smile. "Do keep it from going to your head, will you?"

Chapter 4

ETHANUS REMEMBERS:

She stands in the doorway, an amalgamation of opposites. Fiery red hair like a corona of flame framing a face whose strength has seeped out into the night, leaving behind the visage of a ghost. Slender frame, wiry and strong, now moving with the hesitancy of age, as if every step takes effort. Motions that are normally lithe, like the motions of a cat, now made uneasy, as if somewhere between mind and body a vital connection has been severed. Every step is conscious, now. Every movement takes effort. The sheer strain of living has marked her youthful face as it marks the face of ancient peasants. A welcome mat for Death.

Soon, he thinks. *It will be soon.*

"I looked within myself as you taught me," Kamala says softly. "Even that is harder, now."

"What did you find?"

"A faint spark, barely alight. Heatless. Dying."

He nods.

"You are driving me to my death."

"Yes," he says. "That is the process."

"Yet you tell me nothing of what I am to face."

"Experience has shown that telling an aspirant the truth gains him nothing, and puts secrets at risk unnecessarily. Therefore you will proceed in ignorance."

"Don't I need those secrets to survive?"

Her gaze is the one thing about her that never changes, never weakens. Diamond eyes. He meets them with brutal honesty. "No book learning can help you now, Kamala. The part of your soul that is to be tested soon is a creature of instinct, that will not benefit from intellectual knowledge. Giving it facts will gain it nothing. Some believe it even hinders the process, by distracting it from the business it must focus on.

"I have prepared you as best I can. Soon you must go off alone, to that place where Death will seek to claim you. The key to defeating him is something you must discover on your own, else it has no value." He paused. "Trust me. All other ways have been tried by Magisters, and this has proven the best for training."

And no woman has ever won that battle. Or chosen to come back, once she knew the price.

"This is how it is always done, then?"

"Yes."

"With you?"

He tries to remember that far back. "Yes. Though I was not as headstrong an apprentice as you, and I probably annoyed my Master a good deal less."

She gives him a wry smile; for a moment her face seemed young again. "Not like your house hasn't benefited from my presence."

Fair enough, he thinks, and he smiles despite himself. In his quest to find new things for her to work on he'd let her have free rein with the house. The walls veritably vibrated now with the residue of powers awakened and bound to their substance, and the result was something far more elaborate and refined than the crude stone structure he had built for himself so long ago, if not always to his taste.

If you die I will need to start chopping wood again.

"No woman has ever survived this," she says quietly. Her tone makes it clear it's a question . . . and it's the first time she has ever asked such a thing directly. He is about to give the easy answer when he hesitates and thinks suddenly, *No. She deserves the truth. At least that much, to take with her into Transition.*

"No woman has ever been presented as a Magister." He picks his words slowly, carefully, not wanting to say too much. That is always a danger. An apprentice who learns the truth might react badly. There are a few on record from the early days, when teaching was different, who bolted and ran as soon as they were informed. One almost got away before his Magister hunted him down, and was going to spill the precious secrets he had learned to all the townsfolk, as an act of misguided philanthropy. It was a wake-up call to the sorcerous community. No one takes such chances now. "It is generally said that none of them survive Transition. I am not so sure anyone knows this for a fact. A percentage of those who gain the power of a Magister are driven mad by the process, and must be destroyed by their teachers. It may be that women have gotten that far. No one speaks of failed apprentices."

"Why are they driven mad?"

He shook his head with a faint *tsk-tsk* sound. "Now now, Kamala. You know I'm not going to tell you that."

"That's on the list of things I'll understand when I get there."

"Yes," he says.

Soon. Very soon.

She sighs, and the unbrushed corona of her hair sends a few red tendrils down across her eyes. She pushes them aside with a careless hand, not much caring what it looks like as long as it stays out of her way. Her casual disregard for her own appearance should have resulted in a less appealing creature than what stands before him, he reflects. But Nature is cruel that way, and will resign the princess in her ivory tower to a lifetime of paints and curling irons trying to mimic that natural beauty which, in a moment of whimsy, she granted a peasant-born whore. Kamala's lean and athletic frame might not please men seeking dumplings in the cheeks of their women, but any man who values the spark of fire in womankind, whose desire to possess is aroused by independence, who is drawn to fierceness rather than languid beauty, will surely find her maddening.

If she ever walks among mortal men again, he reflects darkly. *That has yet to be seen.*

"So what is my lesson today, Master Ethanus? Or does it even matter anymore? Shall I simply move the clouds about, back and forth, until my athra is exhausted?"

She voices the question lightly but he does not answer her lightly. His eyes fix upon her with a sudden and disarming solemnity. Her tentative smile flickers out like a candle flame in a gust of wind.

"Yes," he says. "Move the clouds."

He sees her tremble, but she voices no questions. Good. She understands.

She goes outside. He follows her. Twilight has come and the sky is a resonant blue, agonizingly beautiful, that shivers black about the edges. The clouds are misty ghosts that gather about the face of the full moon just above the crowning of the trees. A perfect night for such an exercise.

He watches as she takes her place in the center of the clearing, facing the moon. He can sense her reaching inside herself to the source of all power, a process she once described to him as "turning one's soul inside out." He can see how much effort it takes her to do it this time, and how weak the result is. Her life force is nearly exhausted, burned out in a handful of years by magical exercises designed to empty her soul of all its natural strength at an unnatural pace. She is young still, strong in body, but almost lacking in that inner fire that keeps a human body alive. Tonight . . . tonight that last precious spark will go out. And if she is lucky, if she is strong, if she is above all else *determined* . . . something else will take its place.

Whether she can endure living with that *something* is another question entirely.

With a grace that seems more ghostly than human she raises up her hands to the heavens, as if she would implore the clouds to move of their own accord. It is not an easy task he has set her, for despite the showy tricks of witches in drought season, weather is hard to manage. One must take the power in a single human soul and weave it into the very substance of the earth and sky, until no star shines and no breeze blows without that soul shivering in resonance. Then, and only then, can one alter small parts without unbalancing the whole.

He sees her take a deep breath. He wonders if it will be her last.

He did not plan to watch her any more closely than this, using the eyes of his earthly body and no more. But the bond between apprentice and master is strong even in mundane arts, and a thousand times stronger among those who share the secrets of soulfire. Without need for conjuring a Magister's sight he can see her power arching upward into the heavens, a blast so pure, so brilliant that for a moment it blinds him. What potential she has, his fierce little strumpet! He watches with satisfaction as she weaves her power into the substance of the wind, noting the skill with which she binds each separate layer of the heavens to her will, so that when she bids the clouds to move there will be no single wisp left behind. How well she has learned the arts of the witching folk! If only she would give way to reason, and save herself while there was still time. . . .

But it has been too late for that for a while now, and even as he forms the thought he sees her falter. Only a shiver at first is visible, along her outstretched arms, but inside her he knows it is as if ice has suddenly filled every vein. He remembers it from his own Transition. He remembers what kind of panic takes hold of a man's soul when the spark of life that has burned within him since birth sputters like a dying candle. He remembers the prayers one voices—useless!—as if any god who has watched one squander one's power for years will feel sympathy for such last-minute regrets. The heart clenches in one's chest like a fist, as if fighting to keep hold of those last few precious drops of life. But by the time that moment comes it is too late. The mortal life has been consumed, and the figure of Death hovers over his newest charge, pausing but for one precious instant while the fires of the athra sputter into darkness—

He hears her scream. Not a sound voiced by her flesh, but an agonized howling of her innermost soul. It is at once defiance, fear, determination—raw stubbornness, which has always been her strongest trait. Yet even that is not enough now. *You must be willing to leave behind what you are,* he thinks, *and become something so dark and terrible that men would cringe in horror if they knew it walked among them. And you must choose that course of your own accord, without being shown the way; you must want it so much that everything else is cast aside.*

Does a man truly cast aside everything? he wonders. A woman must. Nature has prepared her to bring life into the world and nurture it, and the very essence of her soul is shaped to that purpose. Such a soul cannot manage Transition in its natural state, nor survive the trial of the spirit that will follow. Can Kamala strip herself of all that the gods gave her in making her a woman, can she hunger for life so desperately that the lives of others are as nothing to her? It is a trick men are born to,

for Nature has fashioned them for war, but women must learn it un-
naturally.

You were meant to bring life into the world, he thinks. *Now, to survive, you
must bring death.*

She is on her knees now, shaking violently as spasms of dying engulf
her soul. Ethanus can hear her desperation screaming out across the heavens. He even hears his name, voiced as a prayer—a plea for the information she needs to survive—but he makes no answer. Each student must
find his own way to the Truth; that is the Magister's tradition. To do otherwise may bring weaker students through Transition safely, but it cannot
make them fit for what comes after.

*Forgive me, my fierce little whore. And forgive the gods, who have decreed
that all birth must be agony.*

And then—

He can sense it in her. A sudden awareness of something outside herself. Beyond the clouds, beyond the wind, beyond the parts of the earth
that man has given names to. A source of power outside herself, like but
unlike the athra whose flow trickles to a stop within her soul. She grasps
at it but it eludes her. *No!* she screams. *I will not fail!* Another spark takes
its place and she focuses her will upon it, desperate to lay claim to it before her flesh expires. Ethanus can taste her determination on his tongue,
the sudden elation of understanding. This, this is what she was meant to
discover—this foreign spark that is not soulfire, but might be bound and
made to take its place. Why did Ethanus not simply tell her that? Why
has he not taught her the tricks she needs to tame it? Now she must wres-
tle with Death even as she races to weave a link between herself and this
distant power, so strong that no force wielded by man or god can ever
sever it.

And he knows it before she does, when she has won. He knows because
he has watched other apprentices expire at this point, consumed at the
very threshold of immortality. In them the final sparks within their own
souls had died before they could claim this new power, and Death had
dragged them screaming into oblivion. In her . . . the ice within her veins
cracks . . . the strangled heart dares a new beat . . . the breath that has been
all but choked off by the force of her trials draws inward once again, bringing warmth to her lungs. He knows before she does because he knows

what signs to watch for. She . . . she knows only that awareness of a foreign power throbs within her now like a second heartbeat, and that her flesh draws strength from it, easier with each passing breath.

When she is sure of what she has done, and sure it cannot be undone, she looks at him. There are tears in her eyes, red tears, for her body has squeezed forth blood in its exertions. *How appropriate,* he thinks. There were tears in his own but he wiped them away before she could notice. He does not want her thinking to question what emotions spawned them.

"I live," she says, and in that phrase are captured a thousand things unsaid. A thousand questions.

"Yes," he responds. Answering them all.

"I am . . . Magister?"

He gazes at her for a moment. Loving her, as he had not expected ever to love. *Look one last time upon her in her innocence,* told himself, *for you are about to destroy that innocence forever.*

"You may use the power as you will," he says quietly to her, "for whatever purpose you like. You will not die. You have learned to draw your athra from other places, other sources. So it shall always be for you. When one source fails, you will find another. No Magister who truly desires life has ever failed to do so."

"Then what?" she said. "What's wrong? You spoke of a trial. Is that over?"

For a long moment he just looks at her. Fixing in his mind the picture of what she is now, before the Truth makes her into something else. A creature of legend, by virtue of her sex. A creature of darkness, by virtue of her choice.

"But one more thing," he says. "One final lesson."

She waits.

"Know this, Kamala: that there is no source of athra in all the universe which can sustain you, save that which is contained within the souls of living men."

The distant clouds move across the face of the moon. The clearing is dark and silent.

"Now," he says, "you are a Magister."

Chapter 5

698O," RAMIRUS said. His voice echoed in the vast chamber like a ghost's cry in a crypt. "Prince Andovan is dying. And a Magister is responsible." He spread his hands broadly to indicate the room, its occupants, and all that their presence implied. "You see now why I have called you here."

The one called Del made a sound in his throat that might have been a cough, or it might have been derision. "I see that the gods have played a cruel joke upon your royal patron, Ramirus. But truly, are you so surprised? Transition doesn't give a devil's ass about race, age, or station. It stands to reason that sooner or later a member of a royal family would be chosen. For myself, I'm only surprised it didn't happen sooner."

Ramirus' voice was low, as a wolf's warning growl is low. "You do not understand."

Colivar expended considerable effort not to smile. The subject matter was somber, true, but it was still a pleasure to see the Magister Royal of his enemy scorned in front of so many witnesses. A small reward for a long and dusty journey. "If I may . . ." He awaited Ramirus' nod with the gallantry of a courtier. "The issue here is not if Andovan is dying, which none of us truly cares about, or even if a prince of Danton's realm is dying—which *most* of us do not care about—but rather, what men will do in the course of that dying. Yes?"

"Precisely," Ramirus said. He nodded toward the two lamps on the mantle, forcing their wicks up higher. It was minimal compensation for the loss of the day's sunlight, which could no longer manage the narrow angle required to work its way into the chamber. In truth, the dark wood and unpolished stone of the room's vast interior made it feel as if night had already fallen; Colivar could not have guessed what the hour was. "We all know what the Wasting is in truth, and we know how hard the Magisters have worked to obscure that truth from outsiders. How many of us have not contributed toward that goal, at some point in our careers? Not granted an extra bit of fever to a sufferer, so that he might seem to be in the grips of a true disease? Or given him pockmarks or festering wounds or something else that might cause men to attribute his loss of strength to some more *natural* cause?

"Centuries of such tricks have caused men to believe that the Wasting is exactly what we say it is—a fearsome disease, no more, no less. Even doctors, while mourning the failure of their most effective concoctions, do not search for other causes . . . they merely waste their days seeking some new philter or paste that will grant the sufferers comfort. While we, knowing the true cause, know that there is no comfort to be had. Once the soul of a Magister has begun to drain a man of his mortal energy there is no end to the contract that is possible, save his death."

"Well," Colivar said casually, "there's also the option of his just not using the power any longer, but it's unlikely any Magister would agree to such a thing, merely to save a life."

Ramirus nodded. "Precisely. And in this case it is no peasant we are talking about, content to die in obscurity in some mud hut while the world goes on about its business without him. This is a royal prince. He is guarded by a cadre of doctors as fierce and determined as Danton himself. There is not a cure on earth that will not be tried on him, and its effects cataloged in minute detail. There is not an expert on disease who walks this earth who will not be found and brought here, whether of his own free will or against it. Already his sire has said that there are to be no limits in money spent or risks taken to save the boy—and that may well be our undoing."

"Money can't buy a Magister's secrets," Kellam of Angarra said dryly. "And without that, they're not likely to guess at the truth."

"Are you so sure?" Ramirus demanded. "Are you so very sure? Thousands of years of folklore and superstition have attended this disease—witches on their deathbeds have been less than a hair's breath away from discovering the truth—ignorant and drunken louts offer up paranoid ramblings in their cups that sound fearsomely accurate to peasant ears—how much will you wager that now, with a king willing pay for every stray rumor, those things will not gain a patina of respectability, and perhaps be investigated?"

"There are natural creatures that feed upon the athra," Del said. "No reason for anyone to think men are involved."

Ramirus' eyes narrowed; the snowy brows gave him an oddly feral expression, like that of an owl whose territory has been befouled. "Your education is lax, my brother. There is only one creature that is known for a fact to feed thus . . . and none of *that* species has been seen in the lands of men for centuries. The rest are tall tales we have created, attaching them to illnesses and conditions that have other causes, to obscure our own nasty habits. How well will those tales hold up, once a man of Danton's estate directs all his wealth and power toward investigation?"

"Sickness attacks the body," Lazaroth muttered. "A Magister attacks the soul. Any witchling worth her salt can tell the difference—if there's reason enough for her to be looking for it."

"So," Colivar said. A smile flickered across his face before he could stop it. "Kill the prince. Problem solved." He glanced at the fading sunlight. "Just in time for dinner, too."

"Not an option."

"Why?" His dark eyes narrowed ominously. "Danton needs him? The country needs him? Those are mighty *political* concerns for a Magister, Ramirus."

Ramirus scowled. "And your suggestion isn't? What kind of bonus do you get from your royal master if you come home with word of Andovan's death, Colivar? Much less the news that you caused it."

"Gentlemen." It was Kellam. "No offense, but we *are* discussing the survival of all our kind, yes? I myself don't give a rat's prick who sits on what throne or how many sons he has, in the face of that." He turned to Ramirus. "Colivar may annoy you, Ramirus, but that doesn't mean he's wrong. Tell us why the boy can't die. And by the way, dinner isn't a terrible idea. Most of us have been traveling since daybreak."

Ramirus scowled, but he did go so far as to reach out to the bellpull that hung by the fireplace. Hospitality was hospitality. He waited until the faint, fearful knock of a servant sounded upon the heavy oak door and called for him to come in. A young boy did so hesitantly, clearly fearful of entering the Magister's domain.

"A cold supper for my guests," Ramirus told him. "Have the bell rung when it is ready." He raised an eyebrow in Colivar's direction as if curious whether he would trust the local food, or the local servants, but with a dry smile the Anshasan bowed his graceful acceptance of the offer. There was even a faint arrogance about the move, as if he were daring Ramirus to do something unworthy of a host, that he might be caught at it.

Don't dare me to kill you, Ramirus thought. *No man is proof against that much temptation.*

Not until the door was locked again and the boy's footsteps had faded from the hall beyond did Ramirus speak again.

"The problem," he said quietly, "is this. Should we move against the boy openly or even covertly now, the chance of discovery is great. Danton already has witches attending him, and several are marginally competent. How much effort does it take to trace such action? Any one of us could do it. Odds are one or more of them can do it."

Colivar shrugged. "Kill the witches."

Ramirus glared. "Have you no better advice than this? That all should die?"

"Magisters. Magisters." It was Del. "This is unseemly." He turned to Colivar. "Your tone ill befits a guest, brother."

"The manners of the south," Ramirus muttered.

"And *you.*" Del's eyes narrowed as he turned to the Magister Royal. "You let this go on way too long. We should have held this discussion *before* Danton brought witches into the picture. Then we could have killed the boy with no repercussions and chalked it up to some accidental cause. Now . . ." he glanced back at Colivar, then to Ramirus again. "Now things are . . . complicated."

"Exactly," Colivar agreed. His eyes gleamed darkly in the lamplight.

"Heed me well," Fadir said. He was a husky man, broad-shouldered and muscular; not for the first time, Colivar wondered if he had been a warrior in the days before he found his power.

"In my lands this would never have happened. In my lands I never forget the line we walk, that we must never stray from. If someone threatens Magister secrets, they die. That is the Law." He met Ramirus' eyes straight on. "I agree with my brother. You waited too long." Then he looked at Colivar. "But what's done is done, yes? Now we must deal with this mess as it stands. And perhaps, when it's over with, set guidelines for our brotherhood in the future that such things will not happen again."

"Agreed," Colivar said.

"We must find out who is responsible," the one called An-shi mused.

"Perhaps," Kellam said quietly, "it is one of us."

"No." Ramirus shook his head decisively. "Do you not recall upon my invitation to you, I asked if any had claimed a new consort within the last two years? Even allowing for those who might have lied in their answers . . ." a faint smile flickered about the corners of his mouth ". . . none were even close."

"And better to lie about a more recent Transition, if one is to lie at all." Colivar mused.

"Exactly."

"So it is none of us," Fadir said gruffly. "What do you propose, then? Use the power to trace the link, find out who's eating the boy? You know that can't be done. Anyone trying to work his sorcery on a consort risks being dragged into the link and eaten himself. A piss-poor way to go out of this world, I say. Not how I intend to end my life."

"And what if we do find him?" Del asked softly. "I will not kill a brother for the sake of any morati." The reference to those who lacked the power to extend their own lives brought sneers from several around the table.

"Nor I," others agreed; a chorus of rejection.

"Gentlemen." Ramirus' tone was even and firm. "That is why I brought you here, yes? So that the greatest minds that have ever mastered the athra might seek a solution together, and perhaps come up with better answers than a single Magister could manage."

In the distance, muted by stonework corridors, a bell rang.

"I believe, gentlemen, that is your dinner. I suggest we take refreshment and then retire, and meet again on the morrow to compare our thoughts, and seek a solution to this unpleasant situation together."

"Your servants seem impossibly fast," Colivar remarked. "Do you employ witches in the kitchen now?"

Ramirus glanced at him. Of the score of emotions glittering in his aged eyes, disdain was the most obvious. "I had food laid out in advance. Of course." He shook his head and tsk-tsked softly. "You would do well not to underestimate me, Colivar. For some day it may be more than dinner at stake, yes?"

———

The night was quiet, humid and warm but not beyond tolerance. The two moons held vigil at opposite ends of the sky, lighting a marketplace that would play host to its share of whores and wastrels until daybreak. A mere human could not see them from the palace, but it took little effort for a Magister to adjust his vision, making it possible.

Ramirus stood at the edge of the ramparts, staring out into the night. Colivar watched him from a distance at first, cloaked by the shadows of the eastern tower, then moved forward with a deliberate footfall, one meant to be heard. The white-haired Magister nodded slightly but did not turn away from whatever he was watching.

Colivar took a place a respectful distance away and gazed out over the ramparts himself. It was a pleasant view in the warm, sticky evening, shadows dancing in the woods surrounding the palace and the sound of distant voices carried faintly from stragglers in the marketplace beyond. The smell of trees was thick and lush, unfamiliar to his senses. Rain was a precious commodity in the south, with monuments of sculpted stone more common than this wet and wild indulgence. Colivar was not yet sure how he liked it.

When it became clear that Ramirus had no intention of addressing him, he spoke first. "You know what they would say about you in the south? 'He feeds camel dung to family.' "

Ramirus glanced at him. "I remember when you dressed in northern furs and spent your time cursing the habits of glaciers." He looked out over the ramparts again. "I liked you better then."

"The god of chameleons has blessed me with a rare adaptability."

"A fickle god, as I recall."

"He asks little for worship, save that I live each moment for what it is, and do not cling to the past. While you, my brother, never change." He chuckled softy. "Though the beard was very impressive during the Balding Plague, I must admit."

"And each night cost someone precious minutes of his life, that I might keep it." He stroked his beard lovingly, as if it were the milk-white skin of a courtesan. "I like to think it was a woman."

Colivar looked up sharply. "Can you tell when you draw upon a woman for power?"

Ramirus shrugged. "I like to imagine that I can. The natures of men and women are so distinct that surely it must be reflected in their athra. But how can one ever know for certain? As consorts they live and die anonymous lives, faceless to us even in their dying, and our best guesses as to who and what they are can never be confirmed. Sometimes I wonder if we could do what we do, if it were otherwise."

He looked at his guest with eyes that were remarkably young for being framed in aged flesh. That, too, was a lie. "Why are you here, Colivar?" He said it softly. "Why does the boy's life matter so much to you?"

"I told you. In our meeting."

"Camel dung."

Ramirus sighed and gazed out again at the night-shrouded landscape. "Your manners really are execrable. I don't know how King Farah abides you."

"You know the best road for us is one that ends in the boy's death. All your fancy northern words can't obscure that fact. So what, then? Why this song and dance to convince us otherwise?"

A muscle tightened along the line of Ramirus' jaw, but he said nothing.

"Shall I guess?" Colivar pressed.

"If it entertains you to do so."

"I think you are afraid."

Ramirus' expression darkened, but again he made no answer.

"Afraid of what, though? That's the question. Not physical harm, I'm sure. When is the last time anyone dared to assault a Magister? No, it must be something else. Something more . . . subtle. Politics, perhaps? Oh, but the great Ramirus would not stoop to get involved in morati politics . . ."

He said between clenched teeth, "You overstep your bounds, Colivar."

"I?" He bowed, a bit too expansively to be sincere. "I am but a weary traveler, traversing the dusty miles to give counsel to my colleagues. You are the one who summoned me here. Some might call it ill courtesy to do that, and then offer nothing better than half-truths and evasions."

"Some might remember where they are and guard their tongues, lest they give offense."

"My mere presence here is an offense and you know it. One can only imagine Danton frothing at the mouth when you first suggested it."

A faint, almost imperceptible smile quirked the corner of his mouth. "No, he did not quite . . . froth."

"You think I don't hear the guards slinking about my door like furtive rats, playing eyes and ears for him? I'd put on a show for them if it wouldn't burn out my current consort faster than I like."

"What do you expect? He is a king, you are his enemy's servant. Surely such actions do not come as a surprise."

"Does he really think that spies will help him? Does he really understand so little of what we are that he thinks he can sneak up on any of us?"

"Perhaps I play a more subtle game than you do, chameleon. Perhaps my patrons, unlike yours, are granted no more than a shadow of the truth."

"Perhaps."

"It is hard to kill a Magister, but not impossible. And I have known a few who were indeed 'snuck up upon,' when their attention was elsewhere." He turned his gaze to Colivar once more. "Do not underestimate Danton. Other men have done so, and they are feeding the worms."

"Magisters?"

"Not that I know of. But I have seen him drive a witch to her destruction. It was . . . disturbing."

"She must not have been very skilled."

"On the contrary, she was most impressive, while she lived. He played a subtle game with her, encouraging her to see enemies in every shadow. She burned herself out in a fortnight guarding against them, never knowing that he was the cause." He paused, then added thoughtfully, "I wondered if she might not make Transition, despite her sex. She had the spirit for it. Wouldn't that have surprised him!"

"Not likely the moons will shine upon such a day."

"No," he agreed. "There are some boundaries that nature will not allow to be compromised."

He turned back to the forest, clearly meaning to signal Colivar that the conversation was at an end.

"And the boy?" Colivar pressed.

Ramirus sighed. "Is a royal prince. With all the complications that come of such a position. Nothing more."

More out of curiosity than need, the black-haired Magister sent a tendril of power questing toward Ramirus, to taste the tenor of his lie. The power slid neatly off him, garnering nothing. Of course.

"I think you are afraid," he repeated quietly. "I think you fear that if Andovan dies you will be blamed. Not for having caused his illness, but for having failed to cure it."

"People die of disease all the time. The Wasting is notoriously difficult to cure. It would be no fault of mine."

"Yes . . . and I am sure Danton is the understanding type, who will respect that answer."

The muscle along Ramirus' jaw twitched again.

"And what if Andovan should die of some other cause? A stone falls from the ceiling of his room, let us say, and strikes him on the head. Why then, the blame would still fall upon you, wouldn't it? Surely the Magister Royal should be able to foresee such things and forestall them! That is truly why you won't let us act, isn't it? That is why we risk this dangerous course, wherein all our secrets might be laid bare."

"What if he does blame me? He cannot do me harm. Though he may imagine otherwise."

"Perhaps not, but you could loose this plush position of yours."

"Then there will be others. What Magister has ever lacked for patrons?"

"When you have failed Danton Aurelius, King of all the High Countries? His word has power, Ramirus, far beyond the reach of lesser monarchs. And if he were to condemn you now as a failure—or even worse, as a traitor—with all the volume attendant upon his rank, you would not be finding a perch as comfortable as this one for a long, long time. Of course," he mused, "there are always petty chieftains in the desert who might be willing to harbor an incompetent Magister. Provided he doesn't go too close to their sons. Or their goats. Do you like the desert, Ramirus?"

"Your tone is insufferable," he muttered.

"Of course, there is another solution. Kill the boy first, and then, if the father causes trouble, kill him as well. Ah, but then the kingdom would fall to his firstborn, that strutting moron Rurick, and revolution would probably soon follow—yet another fine thing to have upon your record as Magister Royal when searching for your next appointment." He chuckled softly, a dark and humorless sound. "No, Ramirus, I would not want to be in your sandals right now, to be sure. Your reputation is about to be dashed to pieces, and all you must do to save it is convince a dozen or two Magisters that they should hunt down one of their own kind for you. And then do what? Kill him? Lock him away for the decades it will take Andovan to die naturally? Or have you come up with some solution so novel that Magisters haven't yet thought to forbid it?"

"It is my hope," he said, picking his way through the words slowly, carefully, as if each one must be formed perfectly or it would fail in its purpose, "that once we find the one responsible, we will be able to find a way to break the bond between them. He will only need seek another consort then, and Andovan will be free."

Colivar applauded softly. "Excellent, Ramirus. You make that sound almost reasonable. Never mind that such a thing has never been done before—"

"It has never been attempted."

"But you will still need allies, to convince the others. Yes?"

A white eyebrow arched upward, incredulously. "You are offering that? Do I hear aright? Or did I drink too much mead with dinner, and it addles my brain?"

"Depends upon the price."

"Ah . . ." He nodded approvingly. "Ever the vulture, Colivar."

"We are all of us vultures. Else we would have died long go."

"True enough."

"The word of an enemy has especial value to you in this. For when the others see that even Colivar is backing you, even the one most likely to wish you harm, that will carry more weight than the tepid support of friends, yes?"

The corner of Ramirus' mouth quirked upward in a brief, dry smile at the mention of "friends." As if there could ever be anything between Magisters besides respectful rivalry at best, and at worst . . . at worst that rivalry gone sour, competition become something so dark and fearsome that the morati dared not even dream of it.

Anything to pass the centuries.

"So what is your price?" Ramirus asked. "I take it you have one."

Colivar spread his hands wide. "I am a reasonable man. Some minor favor, perhaps. A word whispered in King Danton's ear, at a moment when he seeks advice."

"A small enough thing," he said dryly. "I take it you have some particular advice in mind?"

Colivar stroked his goatee with lingering pleasure; in more sensitive company it might have been judged a parody of Ramirus' own mannerisms. "I was thinking perhaps . . . Auremir."

Ramirus breathed in sharply. "Now you do overstep your bounds."

"Such a lovely port city, don't you think? Apparently Danton does, for I hear he means to war against its masters and take control of it."

"Ah, so your master has interests there. Good to know."

"My *patron* is not at issue here."

Ramirus raised an eyebrow. "Indeed? Are you a player in morati politics now?"

"Men die. Even princes. It is always wise to have interests that do not depend upon the good will of a single monarch . . . or even of a single nation."

"Very true. If not traditional Magister philosphy."

Colivar smiled darkly. "You will find I am far from typical."

"So I begin to see . . . and this port? You will want it for yourself?"

"Not at all. It serves me well as it is now, a tiny free state surrounded by enemies. I merely have concern that if one of those enemies should upset the balance of power in that region . . ."

". . . it would be very bad for morati politics."

"Exactly."

"And one must always be concerned for them."

He bowed his head respectfully. "You understand my position, then."

"I understand you ask a lot," he said quietly. "Auremir is one of the most valuable ports in the Free Lands. If Danton were to have his eye set upon such a jewel—note I say *if*—it would be very difficult to dissuade him."

Colivar spread his hands suggestively. "Equally difficult to save a Magister's reputation, once such a powerful prince had fixed his royal mind upon his ruin. Yes?"

There was a long, long silence. Finally Ramirus turned away from the ramparts, away from Colivar. A rising wind whipped his black robes about him like bat wings as he moved. "I do not see that it benefits Danton at this time to claim Auremir," he said quietly. His voice was devoid of any emotion though his aura blazed with it. "I shall advise him accordingly." And with those words he strode toward the tower, willing its heavy door to open before he reached it so that his angry stride need not be interrupted.

For his own part, Colivar bound enough power to make sure that Ramirus couldn't hear him laughing as he left.

Chapter 6

E *THANUS REMEMBERS:*
  It is hard to concentrate on translating ancient runes this evening. Hard to concentrate on anything.

She is restless.

Sometimes he imagines he can feel her in his soul. It is a strange and disconcerting sensation. Intimate, on levels where he is not accustomed to intimacy. Is it this way because she is a woman, he wonders. Does the bond between master and student become something more when one half of the equation is feminine? Or is he just seeking excuses to feel close to her, to avoid admitting the truth for one night more: that she is a Magister now and will soon hunger for all the things that come with that rank. It is as inevitable as the summer rains and the winter snow.

"Master Ethanus?"

He looks up and sees her in the doorway. There is an odd stillness in her today; not a gentle stillness, but tense, anticipatory. He has seen similar stillness in a cat, while it paused to decide if it would eat a mouse or play with it.

Is this the day, he wonders.

She waits upon his pleasure as always, her habits as much that of servant as student. He rolls up the scroll that is before him and stands, stretching briefly. Outside it is twilight, with the moon already risen, and a faint chill that hints at autumn beneath the mask of summer warmth.

"Come," he says, "let us walk."

She falls in by his side easily, her long legs adapting to his pace. She follows him in silence down the path their feet have worn into the wooded brush on so many other nights, past deer that are just setting to their evening meal. Kamala has fed them often—a strange charity in one who now thrives upon the death of her own species—so they perk up their heads at her passing, as if to ask if today is a day when treats will be dispensed.

But no, tonight she is preoccupied, and he can feel the questions stirring inside her, as if fighting over which one will be voiced first.

Beyond the path, up the side of a rocky hill, is a promontory that gives a magnificent view of the sky and the surrounding forest, which he has used as the setting for many lessons. Now he leads her there yet again, and she stands beside him on the shelf of granite, while all around them the creatures of sunlight give way to the denizens of the night in a thousand rustling, chirruping exchanges.

They stand in silence for a few moments, sharing the beauty of nightfall.

"Why did you leave Ulran?" she finally asks.

He sighs heavily.

"If you do not wish me to ask, I won't."

"No, it isn't that. You have a right to know."

He sighs again, and rubs his forehead between two fingers. "The King of Ulran—Ambulis, his name was, Ambulis the Fourth—asked me for fireworks. You know, the kind that morati can make with black powder. Only he wanted something larger, something . . ." He shakes his head. "He wanted what black powder could not provide. A spectacle that would not only fill the sky with light but awe his people with its sorcery. A spectacle so beyond morati means that all would know that a Magister had created it, a Magister who served his will . . ." His voice trails off into the darkness.

"And you refused?" she asks.

"No." He says it quietly. "I did not.

"It is not so easy to deny a king when one is Magister Royal. One grows accustomed to the easy luxury of the life, and to the nearness of power, to the manipulative games that are possible from such a station, but there is a contract inherent in such a position, that one is there to do a king's will, and short of defying the Magisters' Law, one is expected to comply with all his requests.

"The Law sets its own limits upon us, of course. Morati can never discover the source of our power, for if they did they would war against us with all their strength, and the earth would soon be drenched in their blood. Therefore we strive never to use our power in ways that would draw attention to our secret, and the death of too many consorts in one night would do just that. So we set our own limits on how we will use the power, and we give kings false reasons for those limits. Ironic, is it not? For if it were not for the Law we could obtain all that we desired with a wave of the hand, and not need kings at all."

He shakes his head slowly, remembering that night.

"I could have said no. I did not.

"I told him to gather all the supplies he would need were he to put on such a show himself. That angered him, for it seemed to him that I was refusing to honor his command, but of course I wished everything done by natural means that might be, to lessen the cost. And so he gathered fireworks made by the masters of the art, the best that a king's gold could buy, muttering complaints about the cost all the while.

"I could not say to him, *Gold is cheap, lives are not.* I could not give him any reason he would accept, save that it was the way of Magisters, our custom not to do for kings what they could do for themselves.

"Those were tense days, filled with anger on his part, dissembling on mine. I remember wondering if I had made the right choice in coming to this position. Wondering if any convenience that a king might offer us was worth the price.

"Then the day came. It was the celebration of a military victory, and the streets of the capital city were thronged with people. Any roof that seemed strong enough to bear the weight of men was holding more than its capacity in spectators, and I admit that I strengthened more than one, when I feared they were about to give way. Several Magisters had come from the outlying lands and were offering entertainment to the nobles while I prepared myself, and I remember watching them like a hawk from the corner of my eye, knowing that any one of them would unseat me if he could, perhaps because he truly coveted my position, perhaps just for sport."

"For sport?" she asks.

It is rare she interrupts him thus. But he can sense the hunger that is behind the question, her need to understand this alien creature called "Magister Society." *As if the very phrase itself is not a contradiction in terms,* he thinks; words that attempt to conjure unity in the ranks of those who are too suspicious of each other to ever share anything, save what is necessary to guard their great Secret.

Soon, he thinks, *soon she will leave me.*

"We have no adversaries worthy of note outside our own ranks," he tells her. "The morati are creatures of death by their very nature and so they cannot be a challenge to us, merely . . . an inconvenience. A Magister need do nothing to combat a morati adversary, save wait. Choose another project, sit out a century, and Death provides certain victory. Where is the challenge in that? What is the point in indulging in such conflict, when the resolution is known from the start?

"And so the centuries pass us by, and we know that but for our terrible Secret we could have anything we want, without limit, and our consorts die in steady pageantry, paying the price for our power and we become cold, inhuman things, because Magisters who are too human perish of their own compassion. And in the end nothing really matters except those who share the same Secret, master the same power, and suffer the same dark restlessness.

"So I saw them all there, my brothers, my rivals, and I knew that any one of them would bring me down if he could, merely because it would be a challenge to try it. They knew what I had been asked to do, of course; the whole kingdom knew. They surrounded me like vultures about a corpse, watching . . . waiting . . . hungering . . ."

He shook his head as if to banish the memories.

"And so the festivities began. The sun set and it was a dark night with no moons; the king had scheduled it thus deliberately. There were so many drunk revelers in the great plaza and beyond you could become intoxicated just by breathing in the air that wafted up from them, bright spirits in parti-colored costumes that flitted in and around the visiting Magisters like drunken moths, and the king beside me, drunk on his own power, on anticipation of the spectacle to come, and all the glory that his reputation would accrue from it.

"And then it began. The morati explosions first, bursting upon the twilight sky. How magnificent they were! Yet still not enough for this king, who wanted men not only to celebrate his military victories, but to be awed by his sorcerous connections as well. And so after I had let the crowd grow accustomed to that spectacle, I lent my assistance to the efforts and increased the display tenfold in brilliance, in color, in motion . . . I conjured a thin mist throughout the heavens that reflected back the light of each explosion, so that color filled the skies as in the grandest of lightning storms. I wove the streamers of light into patterns that became something else, and then something else again . . . a woman's smile, a soldier's halberd, the coat of arms of the king. Night became day beneath my ministrations, yet even the most glorious sunset would have been hard pressed to compete with my spectacle, and even the drunken moths below stopped beating their wings, their beer and ale forgotten, as they gazed up in wonder at what their king had provided for them.

"And then . . . it happened. As I had known it would. You cannot redesign the heavens without great price, and even with a young and healthy consort such a thing would have been risky at best. As it was I was calling upon more athra than my consort could spare, and his death shot through me like a spear of ice, shattering my concentration.

"It is not normally such a sudden thing, or so disarming, but when one is in the middle of a major undertaking, it is quite terrifying. So much so that Magisters will go out of their way to drain an exhausted consort in privacy, in advance, rather than risk a new Transition in the middle of an enchantment. But that kind of murder had never been to my taste, and now I was paying the price.

"The light in the heavens was lost to me. My life nearly was as well. In desperation my soul struck out into the night—now made dark as my conjurations faded—seeking a new source of soulfire. In that instant, that terrible instant, all my rivals knew what had happened. Of course. They had been waiting for it, holding their breath with each new display, hoping that such a moment would come. It is the only moment a Magister is truly vulnerable, in which a man might take his life . . . or attempt something worse.

"I do not know the name of the sorceries that were launched at me then. Perhaps subtle things, that would only have left barbed hooks in my soul to answer to another's power in the future; perhaps less subtle things, meant to cripple or maim on levels no morati would ever see. We are a cruel people at heart, and nothing inspires cruelty more than a rival's helplessness. Meanwhile the morati world was blind to our drama, wondering only why the pretty lights had ceased, and when they would begin again.

"At last, gasping, I succeeded in claiming a new consort, drank in its athra like a desert traveler might gulp down fresh water, and drove back all those forces that were accosting me in the darkness. I think I won. Who knows? Maybe there is something still left in me from that time. Maybe some tie between myself and some rival remains . . . how can I ever know for sure? There is a reason we fear being around other Magisters when we change consorts . . . and reasons other Magisters wish to be there when it happens.

"That is why they had all come, of course. They knew, when they heard the spectacle advertised, what the cost was likely to be.

"At last I managed to come to my senses and take control of my body again. Blinking, I saw King Ambulis standing over me. There was rage in his eyes.

" 'Have you failed me, Magister?' His voice was pitched low so the crowds below would not hear it, but I knew that my rivals did. 'The sky is dark, and I do not remember ordering it so.'

"Wearily I got to my feet and turned my attention to the night again. Below me I could see the pale faces of the visiting Magisters watching my every mood. The crowd was drunk, oblivious, screaming for more pretty lights. My head pounded from where it had struck the railing when I fell, and inside me fear was like a coiled serpent in my gut. What might my rivals have done to me, in that moment of Transition? What might they do in the next one, if Ambulis drove me hard enough to necessitate another one?

" 'Well?' my king demanded.

"And so I drew the life force from my new consort, alighting the night with his soulfire. A glorious display of pure death, which only the Magisters understood for what it was.

"*Someone is dying for this,* I thought, as my conjured lights lit up the sky.

Not for martial conquest, or to create something for posterity, or even to conjure some minor luxury that I would like to possess. Someone is dying for this man's pride. Is he worth it?"

He pauses. "I left the next morning. And have never looked back."

"And have you found peace here?" Kamala asks softly.

He stares off into the night for a long time before answering.

"The woods are tranquil," he says at last. "My needs are few. My consorts die of old age, mostly . . . a bit sooner than they might have otherwise, but not so soon that people remark upon it. And there are no black-robed predators surrounding me, waiting for the first sign of weakness. Yes, I suppose that is peace, as a Magister measures such things."

Now it is her turn to be silent. He does not need to look at her face to know what she is thinking; it is thick in the air about her.

"It's not enough for you, is it, Kamala?"

She says nothing.

"It would not have been enough for me, when I was young."

Emerald eyes stared out into the night, unblinking. "I have had dreams of late. Strange dreams." She bites her lip for a moment, remembering. "I think they are . . . of my consort."

Ethanus stiffens. "That is not possible."

"So you have taught me."

"What do you see in these dreams? What makes you think it is him?"

"Not a face. Nothing that specific. I just . . . feel a presence. And I sense the link between us. I know what he is. But I can never make out *who* he is." She looks up at him. "Is there any way to make the dreams clearer? I try nightly, but with no success."

He whispers it. "You don't want to do that."

She does not argue with him—she never argues—but her eyes blaze with a headstrong defiance he knows all too well.

"Kamala, listen to me." He takes her by the shoulders and turns her to face him. "That way is death, do you understand me? The gods were merciful when they declared that our consorts should be faceless entities, their identities unknown to us. If they were otherwise, how could we do what we do?"

"Have you never wondered about the ones that sustain you?" she whispers. "It seems to me a natural curiosity."

"Kamala . . ." He chooses his words carefully, knowing her stubbornness for the iron thing it is. If he cannot make her understand the whys and wherefores of Magister custom it is unlikely she will respect them. "We are not human any longer, not as the morati measure humanity. We live on stolen energies, fueling a life that has long since gone cold within its own core. If there ever comes a moment when you doubt your right to claim those energies, when you regret what you must do, the link will break, and you will die.

"Do not ask for his name. Do not try to dream of his face. Please. You must trust me in this."

"Do you think the dreams are real?" she persists. "Do you think if I saw his face in them it would be the real thing? Or only a fantasy of the sleeping mind, conjured by my curiosity?"

Ethanus shakes his head, his lips tight. "I don't know. It is said that once some Magisters tried to gain knowledge of their consorts through sorcery, but all those efforts failed; no man has ever succeeded in discovering who he was bound to, by any means . . . but those were *men*." His voice lowers to a whisper, hardly louder than the night breeze, but as charged as lightning. "You are something new, that has never existed before. Maybe the rules will be different for you. Maybe a woman cannot kill a man without wanting to know his name. That doesn't mean it is a wise thing to seek it."

"Maybe that is why they died," she says quietly. "The other women. You said some of them might have come through Transition in the past, and died afterward."

"A speculation of mine, no more."

Her expression is grim, determined. "I do not intend to die."

"Then do not seek this knowledge."

"I have come this far already. Knowing a man's face will not kill me."

"Kamala—"

The glittering eyes are fierce. "Do you doubt me, my Master? Do you think I would give up this life—this *eternal* life—for fear of killing a single man? Do you think there is that much softness in me?"

He chooses his words carefully. "I think that when they hang criminals they put hoods on them for a reason. It is easier to kill a man you do not know."

"An executioner who falters loses a day's pay at most. A Magister loses his life. I know the difference."

How defiant she is! How sure of herself! It is a quality he has remarked upon since the beginning, the sheer stubbornness of one who survived so much adversity in her youth that she cannot imagine herself being bested by anything. It has been her armor against trials thus far, but it is a flawed armor. Those who do not acknowledge that dangers exist cannot prepare to face them.

You are not yet proven as a Magister, he thinks. *Not yet gone out into the world, to be tested against your peers. Until that happens you are no more than an exercise in potential, a Magister's odd experiment . . . and the gods alone know what will happen to you when the others learn you exist.*

"I am not your teacher any longer." The weight of the words upon his conscience is massive, but they must be spoken. "I can give you advice now, but no more. As you trusted me once, I ask that you trust me now. You have barely set your foot upon this new road and neither you nor I know where it leads. Do not let your soul be lost to distraction. Keep to the path that is charted and safe. There will be time enough later to take chances."

Her eyes blaze with fire but she says nothing. He sighs heavily, knowing the look. For all of her discipline and obedience in matters of apprenticeship, she remains at her core what she was the first day she arrived on his doorstep: an angry, abused child, determined to take the world by the short hairs and force it to give her what she wants. And now she has the power to do so.

Gods help you when you start demanding what the world does not wish to give. And gods help any Magister that tries to get in your way.

"For now," he says quietly. "Promise me that."

There is a long, long silence. Before her Transition he would have known how it would end. Now . . . now there is no way to predict her.

"For now," she says at last. Her voice is solemn, but the fire in her eyes makes it clear just how short a time *now* might be.

She turns from him and starts her way down the rocky hillside, into the shadows of the forest.

He lets her go, in silence.

Chapter 7

THE WIND picked up just as the market was shutting down; its touch set the talismans about the witch's tent to tinkling, an odd and random music to herald the coming of night.

The witch called Rakhel counted the few coins in her purse and sighed. She hadn't earned much today, but that was to be expected. People didn't come to consult an oracle when their lives were going well, and the recent rains and seasonable weather had made the locals more than content. Crops were rising high and spirits with them—what need had such people of a witch's prognostications? Even the usual diseases of harvest season seemed to be avoiding the city this year, as if all of nature were determined that the city's witches should go without work.

And so it was doubly fortunate for her that the foreign Magister had visited her a short while ago. His generosity would see her through a dry season and she was grateful for that, even if she did shudder each time she handled his coins. Dark omens clung to them in a faint patina that morati eyes would never see, but she had been gifted since her birth with the ability to see what others did not, and she could not mistake it. Was that something of the man's own unique resonance, a personal darkness, or some quality that attended him as Magister? She had never been close enough to any other Magister to know. After feeling his coin, she hoped she never was close to one again. The sense of it was not right, not . . . not *human.*

The cloth hanging over the doorway of the tent stirred suddenly, as if something other than wind had stroked it. Startled, she looked up, and hurriedly put the handful of coins deep into her pocket. "Yes?"

The voice was male, and as smooth and fine as a deep-hued ale. "Is it beyond the hours of service?"

"Not at all," she said. "Please come in."

She stood, that she might greet her visitor properly, and smoothed her embroidered skirts down about her.

A man drew the flap aside and ducked slightly to clear the low entrance. He was a tall man, handsome in an indefinable way that had as much to do with the quality of his spirit as any trick of the flesh, and he moved with the easy grace of young adulthood. His clothes were plain but the quality of their cut was noteworthy, and though he wore no golden ornaments to proclaim his wealth, her Sight could pick out the shadows of past treasures that had once adorned him.

He piqued her curiosity, enough that she dared a whisper of true magic to know who and what he was . . . and her breath caught in her throat when the answer came.

Her knees folded beneath her, and before she spoke a word she lowered her head to the floor. "Your Highness."

"No need, no need," he told her. "Please, get up."

She did so, and was reassured by the half-smile on his face. It was comforting, even if her Sight could make out unnamed shadows that lay behind it.

"You know who I am?" he asked.

"A prince of the Royal House."

"Andovan. The name is Andovan."

Her heart beating wildly, she nodded. "Prince Andovan. You do me great honor, my lord. How may a humble witch serve Your Highness?"

He looked about the tent's shadowy interior, taking in its trappings. No doubt the brightly embroidered silks and talismanic ornaments which so impressed the usual customers of the marketplace were less impressive in his sight, as he had been raised to silken garments and probably played with precious gemstones like they were a child's marbles. But he did not seem displeased, and when his eyes fixed on her again she felt a shiver that had more to with his maleness than any thought for the difference in her station.

"Rakhel—that's your name, isn't it?" He gestured toward the cushions she had set up for guests. "May I sit?"

"I . . . yes, my lord, of course." She hated herself for being flustered. *Imagine he is nothing more than a customer.* As he lowered himself to the thick cushions she hooded her eyes and tried to shut him out for a moment, to reclaim her professional demeanor. But inside her chest her heart was pounding. First a Magister, now a prince. What were the gods planning for her these days, that they sent her such distinguished visitors?

She could have unraveled that secret, of course, had she truly wanted to. She had the power. But it would be a complex undertaking, and the price would be high. It was easy to part with a second of your life to learn a man's name; it was another thing to offer up years of your existence for a single fragment of knowledge.

Perhaps the Magister would tell me, she thought. *Perhaps if I found him and asked him, he would be willing to use his power to help me.*

But that would make her indebted to him, and if there was anything that witches were taught from the cradle, it was never to owe anything to a Magister.

"You don't mind if I call you by your name, do you?"

She blushed slightly as she lowered herself to a cushioned seat opposite him, with the silk-draped table between them. "No, my lord. Though I'm surprised you know it."

His smile, faint though it was, brought sunshine into the tent. "Your skill is renowned among the city folk. They say your talent is genuine, which few can claim."

His words mirrored those of the Magister but a few days before. "I have the Sight, my lord. Sometimes more than that, if more is required."

"Then you may indeed be able to serve me," he said. The smile faded and an odd, guarded quality entered his tone. "Will you See for me, Rakhel? As witches See?"

"Of course, my lord, but—" Startled, she stumbled over her words. "Do not . . . I mean . . . the Magisters . . ."

"You mean, I have the Magister Royal at my beck and call, and gods know how many black-robed visitors right now so why don't I go to them for help? Is that what you meant to say?"

She bit her lip and nodded slightly.

He looked down for a moment, no doubt musing over what knowledge might be shared with a commoner, witch or no. Finally he said, "The Magister Royal serves my father first and foremost, and tells him what he wants to hear. As for the rest, they are strangers to me, and their masters are rivals to my father." His eyes were blue, misty blue, like the sky just before a rainstorm. "Which of those should I trust, Rakhel? Which of those will give me an honest answer?"

"I see," she whispered.

"You . . ." His blue eyes were fixed on her with mesmeric intensity; she could not have looked away had she tried. "You'll tell me the truth, won't you? Even if it's not what you think I want to hear? I'll pay whatever such service costs, Rakhel. I'll see you never want for anything in your life, if you are true to me in this."

It took her long seconds before she could respond. That long to still the wild beating of her heart, and to be sure she could speak without fear resonating in her voice. "Of course, my lord." Her voice was a whisper. "It is an honor to serve you."

What truth could there be, that such men would hide it from him? What would they do to her if she got involved in Magister business? Her hands trembled in her lap; she hid them quickly in a deep fold of her skirt, hoping he wouldn't notice.

"What is it you want of me?" she whispered.

The blue eyes, misty as a morning sky, studied her for a moment. A woman could lose herself in such eyes, she thought . . . if the woman were not a witch, and the man not a royal prince, and the business between them not likely to be a dark business, rife with razor-edged secrets.

"I have been ill of late," he said quietly. "The Magisters pronounce it a disease beyond their healing, but I know what healing feels like, and none of them have even tried. Ask them why and they scatter like deer before the hunter's horn. I've seen the look in their eyes, Rakhel. They know more than they're telling me. A prince learns to recognize such things."

He leaned forward over the table. "Tell me what afflicts me. Give it a name that I might call it, and I swear to you, though it be that of the Devil's Sleep itself, I will reward you for your honesty."

For a moment she could not answer. Her heart was pounding too loudly. There were too many traps here, too many potential pitfalls; which one would swallow a witch whole?

Then she forced herself to draw a deep breath—to remember to breathe—and told herself, *This is not Danton*. The High King was infamous for taking out his rage upon those who brought him bad news. But this one? She had never heard anything like that about Andovan, or any implication that he was cruel or unjust. Women who talked about him tended to whisper and giggle in the shadows, and men just scowled and pretended not to notice his existence.

She bound a bit of power to read his intentions . . . and yes, he was telling her the truth, he wished only honesty. And hungered for answers so fiercely that she could taste it.

"I am no Magister," she said quietly, "but I will do my best for you."

He nodded.

She reached out her hands. He understood, and placed his own in them. She turned them palm upward and for a moment simply studied the patterns etched across his palms—a callus here, a slender scar there, the marks of an archer and woodsman and hunter who cared little for the perfumed niceties of court.

Then she looked deeper.

As soon as she entered his flesh she could sense the weakness in him. It was an odd kind of weakness, one that seemed to have no source, yet anywhere she looked the signs of it could be found. The flow of his blood was like a stream in midsummer, narrow and hesitant, its course clearly marked for a more powerful current. Yet there was nothing choking off its flow that she could find. The drumbeat of his heart was odd, strangely muted, yet she sensed no malfunction within it. The very muscles themselves seemed to lack in youthful resiliency, but there was no cause for that either: not disease, not parasite, not inborn flaw that she could find, not anywhere.

Then she looked at his soulfire . . . and gasped.

Low, so low! Like a bonfire dying, its last feeble embers shrouded in dust. As soon as she touched it she could feel its terrible *wrongness,* and she knew that here was the heart of his illness, its name if not its cause.

It was said among witches that one should never gaze too closely at the soulfire of a stranger, lest it sear one's soul to ashes. Yet it was impossible not to look. She had heard of conditions where the soulfire would expire before its time, but had never had the chance to study such a thing herself. Could the athra be healed like the body was healed, by correcting the cause of its weakness? If she could probe deeply enough to find out what had caused this, could she make him whole? It was said that witches were better at healing than Magisters, that their nature was better suited to that art; might it be that she could succeed where all the king's ministers had failed?

Trembling, she wrapped her special senses around the dying flame, tasting its essence. Deep inside it she could sense a spark of true heat that might perhaps ignite the whole anew if she prodded it, but the outer boundary was a wispy, shadowy realm that already tasted of Death. It was as if he was already an old man, dying, but without any cause of the flesh to show for it. Yet there must be a cause somewhere, she thought. Men did not die for no reason.

Gathering her will together, drawing on the strength of her own soul for power, she gazed even deeper into the heart of the dying prince. Beyond the outer boundaries of the soulfire where strangers should hesitate, into that central core of the soul's strength, where all living energies were born—

And she sensed something then. Something rooted within the prince's weakened soul, that led . . . elsewhere. In all her years of witchery she had never felt anything quite like it, nor even heard rumors of such a thing. The soulfire was by definition self-contained, and among the morati never extended beyond the bounds of flesh; yet here was something that undeniably led *elsewhere,* outward from his flesh, to . . . what? Where did it go, this tenuous connection, that had no solid conduit to lead it? Fascinated, she drew upon the full strength of her power to taste its true essence, to learn its name—

And the breath was sucked out of her lungs by a crushing force that seemed to come from all directions at once. Instantly she tried to draw back from the prince's soul, but could not; it was as if some invisible power had grabbed hold of her and would not allow her to leave. Even if he had been a master of the athra the prince could not have done it himself; no, there was something else connected to him, some*one* else connected to him, and the witch could feel that alien will wrapping itself about her own essence, tendrils of power like hungry snakes piercing deep into her flesh, seeking the tender soul within.

She screamed. It was a horrifying, empty sound, even in her own ears. Maybe Andovan moved in response, or maybe he just stared at her in amazement. She could no longer control her own senses enough to observe him. Something had gotten hold of her soul and was drawing it out of her body, leaving the flesh behind like an empty carcass. She struggled against it, but to no avail; her soul was as a fish caught in a net, spasming helplessly as it was drawn up into the suffocating air. Black stars danced before her inner vision; she tried to scream again but the breath would not come.

"Rakhel?" She heard the voice as if from a great distance, and could not respond. Was it Andovan talking to her, or her friends from the market? Her screaming must have brought many. "Rakhel, what is it?"

The world was growing dark now, her struggles less intense. The fire within her that would fuel greater efforts was weakening, its substance drawn out of her flesh by that terrible alien power. Hungry it was, terribly hungry, and it tore at her essence the way a starving animal tears at raw meat. She could feel herself bleeding out into the night, into the cold, eternal darkness of Death that beckoned to her.

Desperate with dying, she tried to reach out to the source of the assault. To go forward with strength, instead of struggling to hold back.

And then she saw.

And she knew.

"She's killing you!" she whispered hoarsely. The words echoed strangely, as if from a great distance. Was she speaking them aloud? The picture came to her of a slender young woman with hair like a corona of fire about her pale face. She tried to send the image to Andovan, but her power was weak and she had no way to know if she succeeded.

A roaring filled her ears then as the last of her athra left her, drawn out by that same merciless hunger that was devouring Andovan. She no longer had the strength to resist it, or even to try. Slowly her eyes shut, closing out the last of the worldly light. Slowly her inner senses waned, as the flame of her soul banked low, shivered weakly, and then began to dim.

I'm sorry, she whispered. Soundless words, lost in the dying. *I'm sorry*. As if somehow the act of dying was her fault. As if somehow it should merit apology.

And then the last of her athra was gone, and there was only darkness.

Chapter 8

*S*HE IS *killing him.*" Ramirus said it slowly, then stressed the first word anew. "*SHE.*"

The pronoun hung heavy in the Magister's conference chamber, surrounded by knife-edged silence.

Finally Del spoke. "It could be a witch that's responsible for this, somehow. Maybe that's what the seer meant."

Fadir nodded. "It is not impossible to imagine that some quirk of the power might exist that would allow a mere witch—"

"To what? To draw upon the soulfire of another?" Lazaroth's expression was dark. "If that were the case she would be a Magister, plain and simple. Is that not the very definition of our kind?"

"Perhaps this illness isn't truly a Wasting," Fadir persisted. "Perhaps it's something that appears similar, but stems from another cause."

Ramirus' gaze was narrow and dark. "Andovan suffers from the Wasting. There is no doubting that."

"No." Colivar's tone for once was brooding and thoughtful rather than derisive. "It was the Wasting, without question. I examined him myself."

"So that means there is a Magister involved, yes? And we are back to the same problem."

"Perhaps some woman was the initiating factor . . ."

Severil snorted. "In what sense? Do you suggest someone convinced a Magister to take Andovan as consort? If so she's more adept than any of us, since I myself have never heard of any Magister able to dictate who his consort would be . . . or even to discover its identity after the fact."

"So what are you suggesting—a female Magister?" Lazaroth's tone was harsh and derisive. "I for one find the idea quite insane."

"Agreed!" another responded, and a third muttered, "Impossible!"

Fadir nodded curtly. "If such a thing could exist we'd have learned of it long ago."

"There are many possibilities here," Ramirus said evenly. "Including, of course, that the witch who spoke to Andovan may simply have been wrong. Or perhaps another female intends to do the prince harm, and she picked up traces of that intent instead of the true cause of his illness. An equal threat, having nothing to do with his current . . . condition." He sighed, and for a moment weariness flickered across his white brow. "Of course, even if that were the case, the damage has already been done. Danton knows of the interview, which means that probably half the gossips in the castle do as well, so it will soon get out beyond that. Andovan has the Wasting and a witch caused it . . . that is a bad connection for people to be making, even if the exact details are in error."

"Someone tried to bring a woman through Transition once, didn't they?" Kellam asked. "I seem to remember hearing something about that."

"Someone always tries," Colivar responded. "When they think they find the right candidate, or the right method of training . . . or else they just get bored. It never works." He chuckled coldly, a sound utterly without humor. "Women apparently don't have what it takes to devour human souls."

"What about that one down in the Free Lands?" Seviral asked. "That . . . what do they call her . . . the Witch-Queen?"

"In Sankara," Ramirus supplied. Colivar noticed Ramirus' eyes turn to him, suspicion suddenly dark in their depths. Had he only just realized that Sankara bordered on Auremir, and that in keeping the latter city-state out of Danton's hands, Colivar was effectively protecting Sankara itself? If so, the black-haired Magister observed, the stress of the situation with Andovan was clearly making him sloppy. The old Ramirus would never have missed that.

Colivar shrugged. "She's a witch. Powerful, ambitious, dangerous as all the hells combined . . . but still just a witch."

"You know her." Ramirus' tone was an accusation.

Again he shrugged. "She has a standing invitation to any of our kind who pass through her domain to partake of her hospitality. Have you never been down there yourself, Ramirus?" Colivar shook his head in mock disapproval. "You really should get out more often."

"I've been down there," Kellam said with a dry smile. "She tried to bed me."

"And you said no?"

"I hear that's not so easy to do," Thelas offered. "I hear she has potions that can turn a man's mind to whatever she desires."

"*I* hear she collects the balls of Magisters as keepsakes."

And she likely has taken all of you for lovers, at one time or another, Colivar thought, *though none will admit that fact to all the others.* Of all the Magisters in this part of the world, he suspected that only Ramirus had no concourse with Sankara's ruler. Did the Magister Royal recognize their banter as the misdirection it was, or did he genuinely not know how many of his brothers had ties to Sankara? The latter seemed unlikely. But then, these were unlikely times.

"Brothers." Lazaroth's voice was firm. "We are forgetting the real issue here, are we not?"

"Are we?" Ramirus said softly. His eyes were fixed on Colivar. "I am not so certain of that."

Colivar shrugged again; his face was pointedly devoid of any expression another man might read. "Investigate her if you like. I tell you now I don't see anything she would stand to gain from the illness of Danton's third son . . . he is unlikely to inherit much of anything with Rurick strutting around, but by all means, seek the truth."

"Would you care if I did?" Ramirus said softly. "Would you care if that truth were . . . not favorable to her?"

Colivar's eyes were hard and cold, the gaze behind them as black as a moonless night. "Siderea Aminestas is morati," he said shortly. "Her lifetime is no more than the blink of an eye compared to ours. The shifting of a vagrant breeze that greater winds will swallow. It matters little when that breeze expires, in the face of greater storms. We who mold the storms know that."

"And we don't yet know she is the one responsible for this," Kellam pointed out. "Or have any more evidence than the simple fact she is powerful enough among morati to draw our notice."

"And she is also a suitable target for Danton's ambitions," Fadir reminded them. "Let us not forget that, shall we?" He turned to face Ramirus. "Those of us outside Danton's domain have taken note of his political ambitions. Sankara would be a jewel in any conqueror's crown. I for one would take it poorly to be dragged into an investigation whose true purpose was discrediting a morati rival to your wretched royal house."

The snowy brows drew together in fury. "Do you accuse me of manipulating this brotherhood for morati politics?"

"Please!" Lazaroth raised up a hand sharply between them. "We're not children here, nor are we fools. There's not a Magister on the face of the earth who has not manipulated his fellow Magisters for the sake of some morati prize at one time or another. Let's not waste time pretending it is otherwise."

"Indeed," Severil noted. "If the morati didn't amuse us, if their political games didn't keep us occupied, why then we would have nothing to concern ourselves with but each other . . . and I for one would go stark raving mad."

A dark amusement glittered in Colivar's eyes. "Yes, we are piss-poor company for one another, are we not?"

From a shadowy corner of the room, Suhr-Halim said quietly, "What attempts have been made to seek more information on this mystery woman?"

"You mean using sorcery?"

He nodded.

"Too much danger in that," Kellam said. "If Andovan suffers from the Wasting, as our host claims, any attempt to trace the cause by sorcery would be a fatal enterprise. As it appears to have been for this witch he consulted."

"Witches die," Colivar pointed out. "Usually in the midst of some magical enterprise, since that is ultimately what kills them. Has anyone confirmed exactly why this one expired? Or are we all just making assumptions?"

Silence fell over the table.

"Well then." He leaned back in his chair. "I think that should be the first order of business."

"Are you offering your services?" Ramirus asked him.

The black eyes glittered in the lamplight. "I would not presume to step forward in a matter you are obviously well qualified to handle. Some Magisters might deem that an insult, yes?" He chuckled softly. "Far be it from me to insult anyone."

"There are means that can be applied without undue risk," Suhr-Halim pointed out. His accent was more noticeable than most, with a lilting rhythm that hinted at vast expanses of desert sands beneath golden sunsets. "To examine the prince's fate in a general sense, to seek knowledge of his past associations . . . if this woman is significant to him she could surely be found there. It would not be a dangerous undertaking so long as one did not seek to trace the consort's bond directly."

Lazaroth looked pointedly at their host. "Ramirus, this is your affair, I assume you would be willing to attempt this?"

The challenge hung thickly in the room's still air for a moment. Colivar resisted the urge to either bait Ramirus or come to his rescue. The first would have been excessive at this point and the second simply out of character. Instead he waited, which was a kind of challenge all by itself.

Finally the white-haired mage said quietly, "I will attempt it." His voice was low and even but the look he shot Lazaroth was murderous. Colivar repressed a smile of amusement. Yes, there were ways to seek out such information without running the risk of getting sucked into a consort's bond, but Ramirus had never been the innovative type and it was doubtful he would come up with anything truly creative. Perhaps when enough nights had passed that the Magister Royal became embarrassed over his lack of progress, Colivar might suggest a few. For a price, of course.

My, the game just gets better and better.

"Then it is decided." Lazaroth pushed his chair back, scraping its wooden legs noisily against the stone floor. "With no offense to this company, I see no reason to continue with this discussion until our host has completed his investigation. When he has done so, hopefully we will have some real facts to deal with, not just sorcerous fairy tales about hypothetical creatures." He looked around at the other Magisters, his lips quirking slightly in what could only be distaste. "Frankly, the company here . . . wears thin."

He bowed slightly to Ramirus as he left, a formal gesture not one inch deeper or more sincere than strict protocol required, and left the room. After a moment, with similar leavetaking, Fadir followed. Then Thelas. Then Kellam.

At last there were only Colivar and Ramirus in the room. Colivar was still comfortably ensconced in his chair, and remained in that position as the Magister Royal's cold, steely gaze fixed upon him.

"If I ever find out you were part of this," Ramirus warned, "or that this Witch-Queen of yours was behind it somehow and you knew about it— or even suspected it—so help me gods, Law or no Law, I will have your head. Do you understand me, Colivar?"

"I am as much in the dark as you are," the black-haired Magister responded. "And equally anxious to find out the answers. This matter threatens us all, does it not?"

For a long moment Ramirus just stared at him. Perhaps he was secretly binding power to read Colivar's intentions. If so, Colivar was confident in his own defenses. No man walked into a meeting of Magisters without first making sure that his own mental armor could not be pierced.

He wondered how many of those present had been probing for each others' secrets even while they spoke of other things. What a tapestry of power must have been woven this night, connecting all the Magisters like the sticky strands of some vast spider's web! He almost regretted he had not joined in the game himself, for the sheer entertainment of it. But he much preferred reading men by subtler means—some might say by *morati* means—and he had never cared for working superfluous sorcery in the company of his own kind. Yes, in theory the Magisters were all here under a flag of truce, but he did not wish to wager his life on how well that truce would hold should one of them fall into that defenseless state which accompanied Transition. A thousand spells might be woven about a man in the instant it took him to claim a new consort, and Colivar had no intention of inviting such an assault while he was surrounded by his fiercest rivals.

Imagine what it would be like, he mused, *if we really could control that bond! Imagine what it would would be like if a Magister could cast loose his current consort at a convenient moment, before its athra was completely ex-hausted, and so choose the time and place of his next Transition.*

Would we spare their lives then, if we could? Or simply choose the moment that best suited our own convenience, with no thought for the ones we were de-stroying? If it was no longer necessary to kill a consort to stay alive, would we continue to do so out of habit? Or not even care enough to question it?

The questions were oddly disturbing. But they were also a novelty, and novelty was always welcome in a Magister's life. When one lived as long as Colivar had, divorced from all the normal rhythms of human life, one understood that the greatest danger lay not in the treachery of rivals, or even the possibility of sorcerous mishap—it lay in boredom, and the tricks a human mind might play upon itself when it had no outside matters to occupy its attention.

No fear of that now, Colivar thought dryly.

Chapter 9

AS SOON as Ethanus saw the woodpile, he knew.

It was stacked twice as high as usual, with a neatness rare even for Kamala. The pieces had been fitted together with almost artistic grace, like the interlocking stones of the wall they had built around the house so long ago, and the ends butted up flush against an imaginary plane, each one exactly the same length as the next.

He wondered if she even knew she had done her work differently that day . . . or the reasons for it.

He did.

She was waiting inside. Like the woodpile she was neat and tidy, her normally wild hair tamed to a simulacrum of civilized style, her clothing scrubbed clean of any hint of labor or exertion. Her wide eyes fixed on him as he entered, and he reflected for a moment upon how very beautiful they were, and how much he was going to miss looking at them. Even her fingernails were clean; that was the first thing he had taught her to do, back when he had finally accepted her as a student.

"Master Ethanus—" she began.

But he raised a hand to quiet her. "I'm a bit thirsty, Kamala. Are you? It's a dry day."

He walked by her and went to the fireplace, where a kettle was waiting.

It was far easier to focus on something else now, something that had no feelings attached to it, so he fixed his attention on the kettle. He peered inside to see steam rising from the surface of the water within and nodded his approval. He reached for two ceramic cups from the shelf and set them to one side, then fetched the box of herbal tea he kept by the mantle. He put one pinch in each cup, put the box away, and took up the kettle. He poured hot water over each portion, slowly, watching the dried leaves swirl in the current.

All in silence. Trying not to think. Trying not to feel.

At last, when the ritual was concluded, he brought the cups to where she sat and handed her one. The tiny leaves bled color into the water slowly, gracefully, and the aroma of the herb filled the small house like perfume.

"So it is time for you to leave me," he said quietly. Not a question.

She bit her lip for a moment, staring silently into her teacup, then nodded. "I've learned so much from you, Master Ethanus. And from this place. But there are things I cannot learn here."

He grunted softly and sipped his tea. It was safer not to say anything.

"You could come with me," she offered.

They both knew the answer, so he said nothing, just drank his tea in silence.

Why is this so hard? He wondered. *By the time my other apprentices left me I was practically ready to throw them out of the house. Why is this one so different?*

When she finished her tea she swirled the leaves about in the bottom of the cup and studied their pattern. That was the Seer in her, playing at witchery. From where he sat he could see a simple circle. The wheel of fate. *Time passes, things change, all things have their proper moment.*

"The power burns inside me like fire," she said quietly. "Some nights I think it will consume me if I do not give it an outlet."

"You know the danger in that."

She nodded.

"You must be master of the soulfire, or you will become its slave."

Outside the sun was beginning to set; a random shaft of light flickered in through the window to illuminate her red hair briefly, like a halo, then was gone. Ephemeral beauty. Too wild to be that of an angel, too perfect to be anything less.

"You are a child of the city streets," he said quietly, "of the reeking mob with all its tensions, of casual violence and hot tears and the clamor of multitudes living in despair. You left those places to gain the power that would enable you to survive them. Now you have it and it stands to reason you would want to return. To test yourself."

She nodded.

"I fear I have given you very little to help in that regard." He drank the last few drops of his tea and set his cup aside. His own leaves huddled damply in the bottom, an uninspirational lump. "Perhaps you should have sought out something better than an old hermit for your teacher."

She came to where he sat and knelt before him. Her warm hands took his own in a loving grasp. The long, slender fingers were calloused at the tips, marked by past labors she was too proud to disown. She could have any skin she wanted now.

"You," she whispered, "have given me life, and power, and the hunger to devour all the knowledge the world has to offer. What more could I ask from any teacher?"

"I have not prepared you well for the outside world."

"Ask rather if the world is prepared for me."

Despite himself he smiled. "The Magisters will not welcome you."

Mischevious energies flashed in her eyes. "And I have made myself welcome before, where men did not desire me to be. Yes?"

He sighed, catching her fingers in his own and squeezing them tightly. "Don't underestimate them, Kamala. Men who exist in a private world without women do not take well to its invasion. Not to mention that your very existence puts a lie to much of what they have been taught about the power. And proud men do not like to be corrected."

The proud eyes glittered defiantly. "Are you suggesting I hide from them?"

"You? Never." A faint smile creased the corners of his mouth. "Just . . . be careful. Be discreet. You can be discreet, can't you? Pass as a witch for a while, at least until you get your bearings. Don't let them know something new has come into the world until the announcement can be made on your own terms." He paused, and when she said nothing promised, "Will you promise me that?"

"As much as fate allows me to control such things," she said quietly.

"They will put you to tests once they know. Tests they intend you to fail. Tests that will draw blood from your very soul." His eyes met hers and held them. "They will *want* you to fail. You must understand that. Your very existence upsets the order of the world as they have been taught it. Once they acknowledge you as Magister they may no longer seek your life—that goes against the customs of our kind—but anything else is fair game. And if they can prove to themselves that you are not truly a Magister, but an imposter, a witch with no more than a few fancy tricks and pretensions of grandeur, then they will hunt you in earnest for the sheer sport of it."

The diamond eyes narrowed slightly. Her tone became solemn. "My teacher . . . I was sold on the streets before my adult teeth came fully in, and I survived it. I lost my mother to the Green Plague soon after that, and also my home, and I survived it. I have seen such trials and known such cruelty as I will not speak of, and been tested against the darkest, most base instincts of mankind . . . and survived it all." She stroked his cheek gently with a calloused finger; the corners of her mouth quirked into a smile. "What makes you think I can't handle a passel of Magisters as well? Maybe I, too, would enjoy the sport."

He caught up her hand in his own and squeezed it. For a moment there was something in her eyes too tentative for words that held his own gaze captive. For a moment—just a moment—she was a woman before him, and all the barriers he had placed between them so that they might function properly as student and teacher ceased to exist. He was suddenly very aware of her body—the warmth of her hand within his own, the faint scent of pine wood that clung to her fingertips, the rise and fall of her breath—and of a question in her eyes that was all the more powerful for not being voiced.

No, not a question. An offer.

Remember me, they seemed to say, *for all I have been to you. And more.*

Slowly, carefully, he put her hand down and released it. A faint sheen of moisture remained upon his palm, perfumed with her sweat. He resisted the urge to raise up his hand nearer to his face, to breathe it in. Already it seemed to him that her presence was fading from the house and for a moment he wanted nothing more than to drown himself in it so that he would never forget her.

And then the moment passed, as such fantasies do, and he shook his head ever so slightly, answering them both.

"You were my most gifted—and exasperating—student. And I will always think of you as such."

"That is not Magister tradition," she said softly.

"No," he agreed. "It is not."

He took a ring off his finger. It was a thin silver band given to him many years ago, one of the few adornments he had kept when he left Ulran. He put it into her hands and folded her fingers over it. "With this you can speak to me if you have need, and even come to me, without having need to drain an army of men dry of athra to do it."

"And we are not to be rivals? Antagonists?" Her eyes were teasing but her tone held a note of uncertainty in it; which of the two spoke for her heart? "Is that not Magister custom also?"

"It is," he agreed. "And the morati world would be a lot better off if it weren't." He picked up the two teacups and rose from his seat, swishing them about one last time to see if the leaves within had any final messages to offer. "However, as I am already an exception to the rules by living as I do, and as you are one by your mere existence, I don't think breaking another rule is likely to upset anything." He raised an eyebrow and looked back at her. "Or that you would give a damn if it did."

She grinned at that and the fire blazed in her eyes and the stolen heat of her soul warmed his face like a bonfire.

Yes, he thought, with an ache in his heart, *it is time for you to go. A fire that bright would burn down any house that tried to contain it.*

May the gods help the Magisters if they make an enemy of you.

Chapter 10

MIDNIGHT.

The breeze had stilled long ago and summer's heat lay heavy in the courtyard. The guards spoke little as they exchanged places, new soldiers taking up the pole arms and banners of the old in preparation for their turn at vigil.

Atop the keep, at the uppermost ramparts where only the royal family ever wandered, a figure stirred. The guards might have seen it if they were looking up, but they were not. Their job was to see that no enemies attempted to scale the building to the height where narrow walkways flanked by crenellated walls might facilitate invasion. That was the theory, at least. But as no enemy had ever gotten past the outer walls to attempt such a thing the reality of their service was somewhat more mundane, and the captain of the guard sighed heavily as he anticipated yet another night of prodding would-be lovers out of the nooks and crannies that the royal servants persisted in using for their trysts.

The captain's eyes scanned the shadows below even as the figure above him moved, ghostly smooth, to the edge of the highest rampart. Had the captain looked up he might have seen the flash of blond hair in the light of two gibbous moons, and perhaps his heart might have caught in his chest for a moment as he realized who the figure must be. Only one member of the royal line had hair that color.

But he did not look, and the figure was eerily silent, so the motion went unnoticed.

The figure above was dressed in dark colors, like a man who did not wish to be seen or disturbed. He appeared from nowhere, it seemed, as if drawn from the substance of shadow itself, but the moonlight solidified him as he climbed to the highest point the castle had to offer. It was an archer's nest atop the north tower, one of four narrow structures that marked the cardinal points of the structure.

There he stood for a moment, silent and still, as if contemplating what was to come. Or watching the guards below, perhaps, waiting for a moment when there were no men near the base of the tower.

When the moment came he spread his arms as if to embrace the night, and if anyone had been close enough to see his face, they might have seen fear flicker across it, a fleeting and furtive shadow.

Then he jumped.

It was a long drop to the stone walkway below. The impact was sharp and short and bloody, and brought the guards running with their weapons drawn. The captain was among the first, crying out the alarm as soon as he saw the body. His heart was like ice in his chest, imagining what Danton's response would be if he thought he had failed in his duty—he feared the High King more than he feared any enemy—but years of training made him capable of focusing on the moment at hand in spite of everything. *Sound the alarm. Search the grounds.* The body had clearly fallen from above, which meant from within the castle itself. *Make sure there is no enemy hidden inside, seeking another victim.*

Then one of his men turned the body over, far enough to reveal what was left of the face, and the captain froze. One side of the face had been crushed by the impact, but there was enough left whole to allow for identification.

Andovan.

Those inside the castle were stirring now, responding to the alarm. Lamps flickered to life in the narrow arrow-slit windows as voices shouted orders within. After a moment the great bell in the south tower started to toll, warning all who sheltered within that there was an enemy at large.

Let those who were capable take up their swords, and those who were not lock their doors and wait for word.

The captain stood by the body of his prince, trembling slightly in anticipation of Danton's rage, wondering if perhaps his career as a Royal Guard was about to come to a bloody and unpleasant end.

"Sir?"

He blinked twice, then looked toward the guard who had addressed him and nodded for him to continue.

"He's got something in his hand."

The captain looked down at the body once more. Indeed it did seem there was something clasped in Andovan's hand—crumpled paper with writing on it—a note perhaps?

"Shall I take it up, sir?"

"No." He said it quietly, in the manner of a man who knows the next hour is going to be bad, and what is on one piece of paper will not make it better. "Leave it for His Majesty to deal with." Ramirus would be checking the castle for intruders even as they spoke; it was the kind of thing best done by Magisters. If there was an intruder, Ramirus would find him and deal with him.

If it was one of the foreign Magisters—as it well might be—that could take some time. The captain had never been happy about having so many strangers within the castle, least of all the type that could walk through walls or strangle a man with a thought. What if one of them was responsible?

Only when all that was done would the gates be opened. And the High King Danton—who was called Danton the Fierce, and Danton the Cruel, and sometimes Danton the Unforgiving—would come to see the bloody remnants of his royal seed, and would decide what was to be done.

My Father—

Forgive me.

I know the name of my illness, though none will speak it aloud. I know the manner of death that awaits me, the growing weakness that turns a vital man into an invalid by stages, and I know that none can cure it. I know that at most I have a few years left of life, while my soul's fire flickers and dies within me, leaving me no more than an empty husk of flesh into my last hours.

Forgive me, father, that I choose a swifter death this night. Forgive me that I choose to be remembered by you as a prince in the prime of his life rather than as a dying shell of a man who lacked the strength to leave his bed. Forgive me most of all that I did not seek your counsel in this, for I knew that you would forbid me such an act and cling to hope until time had drained me of the last of my living energy and left me to die that terrible death.

There is no hope. Not for this disease. A thousand generations of men have declared it so, and even these many Magisters you have brought here cannot make it otherwise.

Forgive me, my father. Remember me for what I was before I died, and take comfort in the time we had together, for it was precious while it lasted.

Now the gods have decreed that time is to be ended, and no man may stand against their word.

Andovan

King Danton was not a gentle man at the best of times. Now, with his swarthy countenance distorted by fury, grief, and utter shock, he could have stood among the demons of the nether gates without drawing notice. Indeed, in his current mood they might have been hesitant to stand too close.

No mortal man dared approach him. No man dared speak. Not even the Magisters who flocked about the scene like curious carrion-birds— some of them quite literally, having chosen bird form as the safest means of overseeing the scene in the courtyard.

Even Ramirus was silent. The greatest Magister of the greatest human kingdom knelt by the side of his prince's body, weaving what magics he could to determine the cause of the tragedy. It was a dangerous undertaking, given the risk of connecting with a Magister's consort, even as a corpse. For all he knew the bond between Andovan and his killer had left some anchoring trace in the prince's soul, and if in seeking answers he were to make contact with that conduit, he might well become food for that unnamed Magister himself.

All of which could not be explained to Danton, of course. The only concepts the High King understood were outrage, failure—and blame.

"Who did this?" he demanded. "Who did this to my own flesh and blood? I will have his head!"

The Magister Royal spoke quietly, hoping his tone would help calm the man, knowing in his heart that it wouldn't. "I do not see any signs that force was used on him, Majesty. There are no traces of violence on the body, save his own final act." He looked up at the king. "I can tell you no more from his body. I am sorry. The power we draw on is a thing of life, and once life has left the flesh there is little left to be analyzed."

Danton made a sound low in his throat that might, in a lion, be deemed warning growl. "I don't want your excuses, *Magister*. Only answers."

Ramirus' jaw tightened as he regarded the body again. There was no answer he could give Danton that would satisfy him, he knew that, but failing to provide answers at all was an even greater risk. "Despair clings to his body like a shroud," he said at last. "Not the despair of a single moment; that would have dissipated by now. This is something longer lasting, something of more significance." He stopped at that. No need to state the obvious.

A flicker of pain—or was it anger?—crossed the High King's brow. "My son was a strong man. Not a coward. He would not have let a *disease* defeat his spirit."

He would have if he knew the source of that disease, Ramirus thought. *If he understood that he had been reduced to the status of milk cow in some Magister's herd.* "What is in the note, Majesty?"

The dark eyes fixed on Ramirus with unabashed hatred. For a moment it looked like Danton was about to say something, but finally, with a snort, he simply passed it over.

Ramirus read. He kept his expression steady as a stone as he did so, aware that not only Danton was watching but also Magisters that he might consider enemies.

Then, when he had finished, he drew in a deep breath and read again. Binding a whisper of soulfire to learn the essence of the letter—who had written it and why—tasting the tenor of the words, judging their truth.

It seemed the whole courtyard was frozen while he did so. Even the birds did not stir, waiting for his judgment.

Finally Danton had had enough. "My son did not write these words," he said hoarsely.

"I am sorry, Majesty." Ramirus' voice was a whisper. "He did."

"Then they were forced upon him." The dark eyes narrowed suspiciously. "One of *your* kind took control of him, perhaps. There are enough of them here now, yes? And some hardly friends of my throne. Do you know for a fact it was not one of them? *Can* you know that?"

Ramirus drew in a long, deep breath before responding. The truth of the letter was clear, and it was a truth Danton would never accept.

"There is no sign of coercion about this paper," he said finally. "The words that are written here came from his heart, which no man controlled, and flowed through his willing hand to the paper. Nowhere is there trace of any other motive or cause." He looked up at Danton. "I am sorry, Majesty, but that is the truth."

With a roar the High King snatched the letter out of his hand. "*You!* I bade you cure him. Did you do that? I ordered you to *protect* him! Is this what I receive? Is this the service you promised me when I offered you patronage?"

"Majesty—"

"*SILENCE!*" In a fury he looked about at the birds, his dark eyes piercing through them as if he knew who each and every one of them were and what they were thinking. One of them stepped back a bit as the malevolent gaze fell upon it, a motion more human than avian.

"These!" Danton cried. He pointed at the birds. "I want them out of my kingdom! You understand? These and all those that came with them. Playing at consultation while my son's spirit died within him. Did you laugh about that in the shadows," he demanded of the birds, "while he wasted away? Perhaps some of you helped my son along in his despair? What a crowning glory to take home to your own masters, Danton's own son destroyed!

"And *you*." His eyes were black as he faced Ramirus again, his face red as a demon's. "*You* invited them here. *You* showed my son to them as one would show a freak in a carnival, so that they might report my weakness to their masters, then sat back while he was dying and did nothing. *Nothing!*"

Danton drew in a deep breath; the guards who had gathered were hold-ing theirs. "Hear me now, Ramirus. You are cast out of my presence, now and forever. I will give you such time as it takes a mortal man to walk to the borders of my kingdom, and after that, if you dare set foot in my lands again, may the gods have mercy upon your wretched soul."

He turned his eyes from the kneeling Magister, with a totality that made it clear he was dismissing not only his presence but his very exis-tence. "You!" he said to the captain. "Bring my son's body inside."

As the guard scurried to obey, Danton cast a last malevolent look at the sorcerous birds surrounding him. "You will all be out of this city by dawn," he growled. "And gods help you if you delay."

————

It was later than midnight, but not yet dawn.

The moons were near setting, and their light showed but dimly through the thick woods that surrounded the city. A small hooded lantern set on the ground shed a bit more, still not enough to make out more than shapes and shadows in the meager clearing, mere fragments of description:

A man on a rock. Still, still as the rock itself. Waiting.

A staff in his hand. A horse nearby, tethered in the darkness.

A traveler's pack, canvas and leather, with a roll of woolen blankets af-fixed to the nether end.

After a moment there was a rustling in the trees surrounding him. Most men would not think twice about such a sound, assuming its cause to be the wind, or perhaps some small animal rummaging for food. This man knew the sounds of the forest better than that, sensed its wrongness, and marked its significance. Leaning down, he picked up the lamp beside him while his other hand loosened the hunting knife at his belt, just in case.

A figure stepped into the clearing. He was dressed all in black, and his long hair glistened like a jet waterfall in the lamplight. He gazed into the lamp for a moment, then made a small gesture with one hand; the light changed direction, so that it no longer shone directly in his eyes.

"You are wary tonight," the newcomer said.

"Should I not be?" Andovan put the lantern back down. "You're still an enemy of my father's, Colivar; that much hasn't changed."

"With nothing to gain now from your death, Highness."

"Don't call me that." His voice was grim, determined. "Prince Andovan is dead. Let him rest in peace."

The dark eyes glittered. "As you wish."

Andovan stood, hoisting his travel pack to his shoulder as he did so. "It went as planned?"

"Exactly so."

"Then I shall see the man's family receives the money that was promised before I go."

"It has already been seen to."

Andovan looked at him sharply. "You are thorough, in matters of death."

"I am always thorough," Colivar informed him.

The prince drew in a deep breath and savored it for a long moment, as if sorting out all the tastes of the forest air. "So now I am free to travel, as my father would never have allowed. Free to follow what clues the gods will vouchsafe me, to find this witch of yours. . . ."

"Hardly *mine*, your . . . Andovan."

"My father would have killed them all, you know. Slaughtered every witch within reach, in the dim hope that the right one would die. He is like that."

"There is no guarantee she is in his kingdom at all. You know that."

"He would have done it anyway." Andovan sighed heavily. "I'll be surprised if by dawn he does not find someone to blame for something enough to have his head."

"And thus the great respect that neighboring monarchs have for him."

Andovan's expression darkened. "Take care with your words, Magister. He is still my father."

"Of course. Forgive me."

"He believed the ruse completely?"

"Why should he not? The peasant who took your place looked just like you, thanks to my art. He went to his death willingly, thanks to your bribery. The suicide note was genuine, written by your own hand, expressing your own true thoughts. What flaw was there for even a Magister to find?"

"Yes." He muttered, "Truly, I would rather die by my own hand than waste away a cripple in some royal bed."

"You have chosen a dangerous course, you know that. The sickness will progress. Its worst episodes will come without warning. Toward the end there will be no days of strength left to sustain you."

He said between gritted teeth, *"I will not die in bed."* Then, with a heavy sigh, he asked. "How long do I have?"

The Magister hesitated. "There is no way to know that. I'm sorry. But once the symptoms become this marked . . . not generally long."

"A few years."

Colivar's eyes glittered, black onyx in the moonlight. "At most."

"Very well." Standing up, Andovan hoisted the pack onto his shoulder. He wore simple clothing, not the silken raiments of a prince but the layered, earth-toned wools of a commoner. Dressed thus he appeared to be but a simple traveler, not a prince of the blood who was raised to wealth and privilege.

He just might pull it off, the Magister thought. He had done all he could to support the young man's quest, weaving spells that would draw him toward the one who had claimed him as consort. At least that was the theory behind it. In truth such a thing had never been tried before, and he could not test its efficacy nor strengthen its power without risking that the magical link which bound the two would claim him as well. And of course he could not explain to the young man who he sought, or what she had done; the prince was a homing pigeon, nothing more. A compass point to serve Colivar in his own quest for information.

A woman of power, the Magister mused. *That is worth the experiment, is it not? Worth even a bit of risk to have that answer.*

"Be out of the kingdom by dawn," the prince warned him. "Don't test my father in this, Colivar; he's killed those with the power before."

"I am aware of that, your . . . Andovan." He bowed respectfully. "But I thank you for the warning."

"Not Andovan. Not any longer. I shall have to come up with something else, yes?" The prince paused. "How odd it is, that we let go of our accustomed lives with little more than a night's planning, but abandoning a name, that simple set of sounds, takes longer."

"To change a name is to change a life," Colivar said quietly.

"Yes," the prince whispered. "Just so."

He did not speak again, but set his foot upon the packed earth and began to move westward, his movement silent: a hunter's step.

But you are not the hunter in this quest, Colivar thought. *Merely . . . bait.*

He waited until the dim glow of the prince's lantern could no longer be seen, then drew the power of borrowed soulfire about himself and took on wings. Long wings, black wings, that beat at the forest shadows for strength, to bear him in a direction that was not home. Not yet.

Westward.

Somewhere in the world, unnamed, unseen, his own consort weakened.

The two moons set soon after.

Quickening

Chapter 11

MOTHER?"

The young boy blinked as he regarded the empty street. It was still filled with all the normal smells of life—greasy smoke seeping out of kitchen windows, the reek of emptied chamberpots outside residences, spilled beer and vomit soaking the mud outside the tavern's side door— but other than that the place was empty. Eerie in that emptiness. The young boy stumbled a few steps forward, his mother's name trembling on his lips. "Are you here?" he whispered. A lock of blond hair, crudely trimmed, fell over his left eye; he pushed it back with a grimy hand. "Hello? Is anyone here?"

He had fled the place earlier in the day, with his father's rage bellowing behind him. He'd spent the afternoon playing on the moors, making mud-fortresses with tiny grass soldiers to fight vegetable wars at his bidding. The last one had been to rescue a comely maiden from the grasp of an ogre. The ogre had beaten the woman, not once but often, until her younger brother had run off and raised an army to avenge her. They had defeated the ogre and dragged him off to be stamped to death by all the soldiers. By the time the sun had begun to set a circle of earth had been beaten down flat by their campaign, the grass ogre had been torn to pieces, and the boy felt marginally better.

Only marginally.

By now his father would have left the house or passed out, and his mother would be dressing bruises for all the family. It was safe enough now to risk a return, at least long enough to get some food. There wasn't much in the house—a few scraps of old bread, a few cubes of old cheese— but he was hungry enough now that he'd eat anything. His mother would scold him for running away that morning, but not severely. She understood. She'd run away too, if she could.

"Hello?"

The stillness in the street was eerie. It was more than a question of everyone being indoors, though that was certainly strange enough. Or that they were all so quiet he couldn't hear a single voice through the thin walls and tiny windows. But there was something more to the scene that bothered the boy, on a level he could not have given words to. It was the way that animals are sometimes bothered by unnatural things, that makes them want to tuck their tail between their legs and run. He felt like that.

As he walked down the street, calling out names in a trembling voice, he could feel the hair on the back of his neck rising. He fought to be brave. He had already run away once that day, and now that he was coming home he was ashamed of his former cowardice. Surely mere silence, no matter how mysterious, could not make him run away again.

But someone should have been in the street. Surely!

Skittish as a wild rabbit, the boy made his way slowly down the silent street. Nothing was moving. By now he would have expected a dog to come around sniffing after him, or, or . . . something.

Nothing.

He passed a lump of horse excrement on the street. It wasn't all that old, and had a host of flies gathered around it like greedy peasants at a feast. The sight of it struck such sudden fear in his heart that the young boy almost turned and ran without even knowing why. But he forced himself to stand his ground, telling himself that mere flies and feces could not harm him, and trying to put a name to the fear that was slowly becoming a cold fist around his heart.

"Hello . . . ?"

He passed by the town's small tavern. It wasn't much of one, really, but it served well enough to sell cheap ale to the men who called this place home, and such tidbits of food as the dusty coinage of weathered peasants might buy. In deference to their business the owner dumped his waste in a narrow alley between houses rather than out in the street like most others. The boy caught sight of the refuse pile as he passed by . . . and then stopped, and came closer, and stared at it. Again he was filled with a sense of wrongness so instinctive, so utterly animal in its tenor, that he nearly turned and ran. Again he forced himself to stand his ground and tried to figure out what it could be about a mound of rotting garbage that would make him so afraid.

And then he realized what it was.

There were no rats.

He looked back at the street behind him. None were there either, though the small gray creatures should be slipping out of their hiding places this time of the day, daring a moment or two in the sunset's growing shadows to grab a bit of refuse before all their brothers came out to fight for their share of human filth. Their presence in the town was a normal backdrop to human activity, something that women cursed vehemently but no one had any hope of stopping.

There were no rats now.

Not in the street, not in the shadows, not nosing through the fresh garbage . . . none at all.

He took a few steps back, and inadvertently stepped in a mound of horse droppings. The flies rolled off its surface like tiny black marbles. Dead. They were all dead.

"Mother?"

Panic gripped his small heart. He began to run. Not away from the town, as all his better instincts were screaming for him to do, but down the street, past the main section of the town, to where small houses were scattered along the dirt road, each with its own mound of rat-free, insect-free garbage.

"Mother!"

The birds weren't singing either, he noticed breathlessly as he pulled up before his house. Nor were the insects buzzing. Wrong, wrong, it was all wrong!

He pounded on the front door until it gave way before him. No voice answered his cries. He upset a stool as he staggered inside, tears of fear running hot down his cheeks. No one noticed the stool careen across the floor, or lifted a leg to get out of its way, or cursed at him for knocking it over.

Next to the coarsely hewn table in the middle of the small common room sat his mother. She was slumped on the bench with her head resting on the table's surface beside a dried-up piece of bread. Her expression was almost peaceful, if you could overlook the morning's bruises; had the boy not just made enough noise upon entering to wake the dead, he might have thought her merely sleeping. His little sister had slid off the bench beside her and was huddled on the floor like a broken doll. A small piece of bread had rolled out of her hand, and come to a stop by the hearth. There were a few small black bits nearby that might once have been insects. They weren't moving now.

The air in the small room was stifling. For a moment the boy's chest tightened up and it was hard to breathe, as if the very stillness of the place had a mind of its own and was sucking the life out of him. By sheer force of will he forced himself to move, to look in all the tiny corners of the house where small, frightened children might hide. There he found another body, that of his youngest brother, barely an infant. The body looked peaceful for once, not screaming its hunger and frustration out to all within hearing as it had done most of the time when it was alive. Whatever had taken the people in this house, it had done so with such stealth that no one saw Death coming.

Was that what had happened in the rest of the small town? Was every house like this one, peopled with corpses?

He felt bile rise up in his throat and knew that he was about to vomit, not from sickness but from fear. Out of habit he turned to the door and started toward it, fearing the beating his father would give him if he soiled something in the house. But then he saw a shadow of movement outside, and in his sudden stunned wonderment he forgot about vomiting altogether. Even the sourness in his stomach receded, and the worst of the fear with it.

Motion. There was motion! That meant that something out there was alive, right?

He stumbled to the door, afraid that whatever it was would be gone by the time he got there. But no, it was out there in the street, a flying thing about the size of a bird, and as he came to the door it approached him and hovered right in front of his face, its bright wings beating quick patterns in the dying sunlight.

If he had seen it from a distance he might have called it a dragonfly, for it had the long slender body of one, and its translucent wings fanned out in the same graceful pattern. But it was far too large to be a dragonfly, or any kind of insect, and its head was more like that of a lizard than an insect. Or maybe a snake. The body was supple, a deep blue-black that reflected the sunset in glints of purple, and its flesh seemed to quiver as the matching pairs of slender, gossamer wings beat the air, holding it in position right before his face. What beautiful wings they were! All blues and purples, translucent as stained glass, flashing iridescent in the sunlight. Their motion was rhythmic, hypnotic, and despite his fear the boy felt himself drawn into them, unable to look away. From somewhere in the distance he was aware of two black eyes gazing at him, and perhaps if he had looked directly into those eyes he might have felt a new terror take hold, sensing the nascent intelligence in their depths. But he didn't. His eyes were fixed wholly on the jeweled wings and the play of the dying light upon their moist and glittering membranes.

He had been afraid of something, hadn't he? Something in this town. He struggled to remember what it was, but the memory slid out of his grasp like a wet eel. What a beautiful thing this creature in front of him was. He wondered if it had a name. What if it didn't? What if he was the first person ever to see one? What if he told his mother about it, and she said that no, it had no name . . . could he choose a name for it then? Would people call this strange thing whatever he chose?

His mother . . .

From somewhere in the dark recesses of his mind a memory surfaced. Just for a moment, but it was enough to make him step back.

The creature followed him. Its bright wings glittered as it crossed the threshold into the shadows of the house.

Mother?

He moved back again. The back of his leg hit the bench suddenly and he nearly fell. Reaching out a hand blindly to where the table should be, he hit it with a force that sent the items atop it clattering to the ground. The sound jarred him out of his trance and he looked around just in time to see his mother's corpse collapse onto the floor, like some twisted, broken doll.

"NOOOOO!"

The thing was between him and the door. He didn't care. He covered his head with his arms and just ran in that direction, praying he'd prove stronger than it was. He didn't dare look at it again. As he passed through the space where it had been hovering he braced himself for some kind of attack—did it have fangs like a real snake?—but it made no effort to stop him. A moment later he was out in the street, running faster than he had ever run in his whole life. Now, it seemed, he could sense motion in the shadows—glittering motion, hovering wherever there were dead things— but he didn't stop to look. If he did they would get him too, he knew that now. Like they had gotten his mother. His sister. And everything else in the small town. . . .

Not until he was nearly a mile away did he stop running and then it was only because the pain in his legs was so bad he couldn't go on. It was nearly night by then, and it seemed to him as he collapsed on the ground that the shadows were alive with twilight-colored insects that glittered and bobbed as they surrounded him. He sobbed as he gasped for breath, one arm held before his eyes, trying to remember what prayers you said when you wanted a god to come protect you. But the words wouldn't come. No words would come. It was as if the strange creature had stolen his voice, didn't want him to pray for help.

Slowly, inexorably, night descended.

Chapter 12

GANSANG WAS smaller than Kamala remembered it. Dirtier also, with a scent of decay that she had never noticed as a child. Or maybe it had just never bothered her back then. Now it was a rank smell that seemed to seep into everything: the clothes she wore, the food she ate, even her very skin. She kept binding soulfire to scrub her person clean of it but it kept coming back. Or maybe such a thing was beyond the power even of Magisters, a primal condition of the place that sorcery could not cancel out. If you made the stink of a city go away, would the place itself disappear?

All her years with Ethanus she had dreamed of nothing but Gansang. Coming back to it in triumph, no longer an adolescent whore to be trod underfoot but a sorcerer of the highest order who could weave it a new fate as casually as most men ate their breakfast. But now that she was here—now that she was a Magister in truth—she realized such a task would not be so easy. Like the art of moving clouds, the fate of a city was too complex a thing to be managed casually. Each part of it fit into all the others like a grand puzzle. Move one piece and a thousand other fates would tremble; remove one altogether and something even darker might take its place.

Obliterating the entire place was always an option, of course. And she felt a sudden thrill that radiated from the core of her soul to her fingertips at the knowledge of what she could do if she wanted to. She could bring the whole place crashing down, all its dirty streets and its thieves and its whoremasters with it, until there was nothing left but a vast mound of stinking debris. Many consorts would have to die for her to do that, of course, but then, men would die beneath the rubble too, drowning in the very filth and degradation they had once delighted in. Such a move was measured in death.

There would be justice in such an act.

Night fell early in the narrow streets, tall buildings of aged wood and crumbling plaster blotting out the light of the sun long before it had actually set. In the premature dusk the scavengers of the city stirred to life, rats and humans alike. The beggars who thronged the streets in the sunlit hours had slipped away into alleys and cellars to count their bits of coin, and thieves and whores took their place, taking up stations in the larger streets and outside taverns, waiting like wolves for the weak and the helpless to make themselves known so that they could be separated from the herd and devoured.

I am not one of you any longer, she thought, *nor prey for you, but something else. Something new. Something that stands apart from the world and watches, untouched by human bloodshed or tears.*

She still wore the clothing she had adopted in Ethanus' domain, more like a boy's attire than anything a respectable city woman would wear. The high boots and tight-fitting leather jerkin were black in color, not sorcerous black but dark enough to suggest shadows and secrets. With her flame-red hair tucked up into a cap she could pass for a boy at first glance, though anyone who bothered to look closely might have second thoughts about the matter, which suited her just fine. She hated women's clothing with a passion, and when her mother was alive they had argued often over whether or not she had to wear it. She hated the bondage of skirts about her legs, and hated most of all the way they dragged in the mud and the muck, so that all the city's foulness flapped about her ankles as she walked. Once as a girl she had taken a table knife and cut off her own muddy hem, turning her dress into a sort of ragged tunic. She'd been beaten for that by her mother, soundly beaten, but it had been worth every blow.

Now . . . now she was free to do as she pleased. And if any man took issue with it, let him say so to her face, and he would bear the consequences.

Her mother brought them to Gansang shortly after Kamala's brother had recovered from the Plague, hoping for opportunities that the small town of their birth could not provide. The city had chewed her up and spit her out, but not after forcing her to sell her two children to whatever buyers would have them. Kamala did not hate her mother for what she had done to them, though neither did she forgive her. Her feeling was more of an emptiness, a void of human emotion. She wondered how she would greet her mother if she found her in some alleyway now, if she would acknowledge her as her mother or just pass by in disgust, as she would a stranger. But it was all just empty fantasy. The woman was long since dead, claimed by some disease of the gutters, and Kamala . . . Kamala had chosen a new road, one that hopefully led to better places. Or at least to cleaner ones.

Like a stranger now she walked through the city of her youth, like a ghost, touching nothing, seeing all. The natives gave way to her, and though she thought she saw fleetingly in aging eyes here and there the shadows of people she'd known in her youth, no one spoke to her. They did not know her. Poverty and the reek of failure aged men prematurely, so that she no longer matched the generation she had left behind. The girls who had once stood on a street corner with her, shivering against winter's cold as they sought to bare enough flesh to interest passing travelers, were now as lined and aged in their faces as her mother had been in that time, broken spirits and utter lack of hope etched into their very flesh. Unrecognizable.

And still men paid for them, Kamala thought darkly, because in the end whoring is not about pleasure but about degradation, the pleasure not so much a thing of the flesh as a triumph of power—the certain knowledge that your coin can buy a human being, can render her at your mercy for a few brief minutes. Oh, the fancy lords of the Hill might favor delicately painted ladies, and treasure those courtesans who dallied with them in the shadows of the court while servants played music and burned sweet incense, but here in the poverty-ridden district called the Quarter a man's pleasure had as much to do with the heartlessness and the anonymity of the act as any "higher" calling. Why else would anyone buy a child?

The anger came over her then in a rush, and with it the memory of despair. *It is over now,* she told herself. *No man can ever do that to you again.* For a brief moment she toyed with the idea of using her power to protect those who were still following that road, but the moment passed quickly. There were too many of them in the world for the efforts of one Magister to make a difference, and in a twisted way, it seemed wrong to drain the life of one morati just to save another.

Magister morality is a tangled thing, Ethanus had said. For the first time she understood what he had meant.

As night's humid miasma settled upon the streets she felt the first pangs of hunger. For a moment she fumbled for her purse, out of habit. She still had the few precious coins she had carried with her as a child, back when she had fled the city to seek a better fate. Now . . . now they were little more than adornment, a weight in the purse that hung at her belt to make her look normal. A Magister needed no money.

She passed by a few of the Quarter's taverns, waiting until she found one where the smell of beer and cooking spices was stronger than the reek of human sweat. It took a while. The places were small, usually on the first floor of narrow buildings, but she found one on a corner that had enough air coming in to at least mix up the smells, if not banish the fouler ones entirely.

(The forest had smelled sweet. So sweet. Especially after a rain, when you could hear the insects rustling under newly washed leaves in search of hidden drops to drink.)

There was a beggar at the door but she pushed past him without a second glance. She'd seen enough beggars in this city counting their coin after a good day's take to know what fake wounds and feigned deformities were worth. She had pity for a child tied up in rags to engender sympathy, because usually his cuts and welts were real—parents didn't mind cutting up the young ones, or even gouging out an eye occasionally, if it made their misery more profitable—but grown men made their own choices, and few of the beggars went hungry.

(And for a moment she remembered her brother, the scabs of the Green Plague broken open again and again by her mother until they scarred, because scars

*were worth money, and the rage welled up inside her, and the memories began
to stir from that dark place where they lay hidden, like some deadly serpent coming forth from the shadows . . .)*

"Here for dinner, lad? You've almost missed the serving."

Startled, she looked up. Yes, the words had been addressed to her. In
the shadows of the place the speaker could not see details of her person,
and so had simply accepted the tale that her clothing told.

"Yes, er . . . thank you." She coughed, wondering if they took her for a
young enough "lad" that her voice would pass muster, or if she should disguise it. The sudden thrill of the subterfuge made her toes curl. "I'll take
what you've got." She jingled her purse, to make sure the man understood
she could afford the meal. As if money mattered.

The place was dark and dusty and filled mostly with men ending a day's
labor—or avoiding one. Their hands were stained with grit and their nails
were black and Ethanus would have never received them in that state. A
slight smile quirked her lips at that thought, remembering her own un-
washed condition as a child. Most residents of Gansang believed that
washing too often would do them harm. Given that the Quarter had been
built out over what was once a salt marsh, and was known for the sluggish
channels of brackish water that coursed through it, that might well be an
accurate assessment.

She took a table in the far corner where the shadows gathered and sat
with her back to the wall. A few minutes later a wooden plate and tankard
were brought to her. The latter had something brown in it with froth on
the top. The plate held a greasy meat pie, with far more onions and garlic
than meat. She pulled out a coin from her bag and held it for a moment,
winding the power around it until she was satisfied it felt right, then offered it. She watched, breath held, as he took it up and studied it in the
dim light, then nodded and offered her change. She also watched as he put
it into his own deep pocket, where other coins jingled. Good. By the time
the enchantment wore off and its true denomination was apparent, it
would be mixed in with all the others.

She released a breath she had not realized she was holding and felt
some unnamed tension ease its grip on her heart. She had used the power
since leaving Ethanus, but that had been in private. This was the first time
she'd actually used it to fool someone.

Minds are easier to manipulate than matter is to conjure, he'd taught her. *Learn the art of illusion and you lower the risk of Transition in an unfriendly place.*

She leaned back and sipped her ale. It wasn't terrible. Neither was the meat pie, though it had seen fresher days. From her shadowy corner she watched the men who jostled and argued over the rough plank tables and remembered the days she'd been afraid of such men. Back then, their size and strength meant power. Now the real power was hers.

At whose cost? The words slid into her brain as she drank the warm ale. *What manner of man is fueling my petty thieveries? Giving up his life so that I can eat a warm meal?*

She shook her head, trying to shake lose the tenacious thought. Ethanus had warned her time and time again about such meditations. *A Magister cannot afford to care about his consort,* he taught her. *The moment he does—the moment he doubts his right to claim that life for his own needs— the bond between them will snap and the Magister will become what he rightfully should have been at the instant of his first Transition—a shell of flesh without the spark of life inside. A corpse.*

I do not "care", she thought stubbornly. *I am just . . . curious.*

A sudden rise in the volume of the male voices caught her attention. Apparently two men had had too much to drink, and were now indulging in what men always did when they were drunk—fighting. This argument had something to do with which of them a serving girl preferred, though judging from her frightened eyes and the way she'd just pulled her shift back in place over her chest, she'd be happy if both of them forgot she even existed.

Should I do something to help her? Kamala thought. The fact that she even had such an option was novel in and of itself. Usually she had to sit back and watch while women were abused, with nothing but the angry heat in her veins for comfort. But even if she chose to act, could she do anything that would matter? She could lay these men flat on the table with her power, and ten minutes later a new pair would take their place and be grabbing at the same woman, expecting that their penny's worth of ale had brought them the right to treat anything with breasts like a whore. The cause was not something sorcery could fix in a night; it had to do with poverty and frustration and the fact that when a man's blood rushed to his loins it left his brain empty.

So it was in the First Age of Kings, she thought darkly. *So it will always be.*

At least they were fighting with each other now, and seem to have forgotten the woman. Kamala winced as one of the scuffed wooden tables overturned with a bang—judging from its condition, this was not the first time—and decided that she'd had enough dinner. Others were joining in the fight now, as men often did when they had nothing useful to do with themselves. Bloodshed as entertainment. Kamala pushed her chair back and stood, seeking a safe path out through the fracas. Something small came flying in her direction but she deflected it reflexively, and then skirted the nearest wall to head towards the door. She had to push her way past a few patrons who were too intent on watching the skirmish to notice her trying to get by them. Some of them were even placing bets on the fight . . . not on who would win—that was too simple—but who would come out most bloodied, most bruised, or most humiliated.

She hated them all in that moment. She hated them and the world they came from, the tangle of alleys and slums that had made them the wretched creatures that they were, the reeking foulness of the place of her childhood and all the people who inhabited it. She hated them so much that the power stirred within her like a venomous snake uncoiling, and she had to choke it back with all her strength to keep it from breaking loose and devouring them all.

This is not my world anymore.

The thought was an ache inside her as she made her way out into the warm night air. Not that this putrid city was anything to pine for, and not that she would desire a place among its inhabitants . . . she had become something that was not quite human any more, and had less in common with the thieves and whores of the Quarter than they had with the rats who scoured the filthy streets, but it was disconcerting to suddenly realize that she belonged *nowhere*. Ethanus' woods had been peaceful, but they were not *hers*. This place had become an alien thing. There was a restlessness inside her that she did not even have a name for, something born of power and pain, that was too vast for these simple environments. She hungered . . . for what? What manner of home would satisfy her? What kind of people could she call kin in her new and transformed state?

This was her reverie when the door to the tavern suddenly slammed open behind her and a knot of men stumbled out into the muddy street. A wave of drunken breath spiced with stale sweat preceded them in a powerful gust, and for a moment it was all she could do not to vomit. Had she truly never smelled such things in her youth, or had she simply been so accustomed to the odors of men that she never thought to notice them? She had to bind a bit of athra to keep from being ill as she turned away from the tavern, thinking that what she needed right now was to get as far away from this place as she could—

—but a hand fell on her shoulder and turned her around, yanking her doublet and shirt open as it did so. Precious metal buttons went flying as the garment tore open down her chest, baring the inner curve of one breast.

"See?" The man who had grabbed her gestured toward those watching with an unsteady gesture. He was a burly man whose clothing smelled faintly of urine; a fuller, most likely, who'd be up to his elbows in piss whenever he stopped drinking long enough to work. "I told you it was a girl!"

Kamala felt the snake uncoil a bit more in her gut. Dangerous, very dangerous. These men did not have a clue what manner of fire they were playing with.

Exerting all of her self-control, she put out a hand and called the lost pieces of her costume back to her. The buttons flew up to her hand. A couple of men gasped at the display of power but the majority were too drunk to recognize the move for what it was. A warning. She turned to leave but a meaty paw yanked her back, this time almost hard enough to pull her off her feet.

"What's the matter, witch? Our company not good enough for you?"

One of the younger ones snickered. They were starting to surround her now, some deliberately, some blindly following in a drunken haze.

Apparently one of them still had a bit of gray matter left that had not been saturated by alcohol. "You don't want to fuck with a witch . . ."

"Hell we don't! Haven't you heard where the power comes from?"

"I hear they can fry a man's rod with their nether parts."

"I hear they won't, 'cause it costs them in life force. Isn't that true, witch-girl?" A grimy hand caught her under the chin; she batted it away with a sharp blow. "Witchery's safe enough to do little things, but the big things aren't worth dying for, are they, sweets?" He smiled, a grotesque expression that bared a mouthful of broken teeth. "You don't want to waste all that life force, do you?"

One of the men grabbed her from behind. He pulled her hard, intending to knock her off balance. She knew the move well and instinctively braced herself, even while the serpent within her gut screamed to be set loose.

Control the power. Don't let it control you.

A man at her side grabbed at her arm. She wrenched herself free with the help of the power, but barely in time. Another reached for the neck of her doublet, his grin reeking of rotten teeth and alcohol. Too many, too fast! Too many hands, too many directions to focus! The power only worked as fast as she could give it form, and even as she drove back one attacker another moved forward, all part of a tidal wave of stinking, leering male flesh that threatened to engulf her—

And then, without warning, the power surged up inside her, raging with such force that it left her breathless. It was wildfire that roared through her veins, fear and defiance and hatred searing her flesh as it burst forth from her, enveloping the drunken crowd. Hot magma rage, twenty years in the making. A child's terror. A youth's pain. A woman's outrage. Kamala shook as it poured through her, but it was more powerful than anything she had ever conjured before and she could not control it. The force of it blinded her, turning everything in her field of vision a bright red—blood red—and as the athra burned through her veins she thought she could feel the pulse of the distant heartbeat that was driving it. Laboring now, as the life poured out of her consort like blood from a wound. No man could lose so much athra and not feel it. Was he dying? Was Transition going to take her here in this filthy street, with enemies surrounding her? For the first time since leaving Ethanus' home she felt fear gripping her. How much was too much? What did a man's life translate to when measured in such doses as this?

And then, after what seemed like an eternity of burning, the roaring flames of power quieted and went still. The knot in her chest loosened and she found herself able to breathe again. Blinking, she forced the redness from her vision and struggled to focus on what was around her, not yet sure if the power had actually done anything, or simply been the magical equivalent of a scream of rage.

The street was silent. The men weren't standing around her any longer. She blinked, struggling to see clearly.

There were things on the ground. Man-sized. She must have struck them down with the power, all of them.

Hearing a gasp behind her, she whipped around and saw a young boy staring at her. His eyes were wide in fear—or horror?—and as soon as she looked at him he turned and ran from her, stumbling as he did so.

What . . . ?

Then she turned back, and her eyes focused at last.

She saw.

Bodies. Crushed bodies. Parts of bodies. Bodies like broken dolls that some giant's hand had smashed. One man had been frozen in the act of screaming; his countenance was charred black as if burned by hot cinders, surreal. Another lay twisted in ways no human body should ever be twisted.

You must never let the power rule you, Ethanus had warned.

She ran. Sickness welled up inside her with numbing force as she stumbled away from the carnage, not caring where she went as long as it was somewhere far away from that terrible place. All the fire that had been in her veins was gone now, replaced by an icy terror. *What have I done?* She could hardly think straight. Getting away from those bodies was all that mattered to her. Getting to a place where the walls weren't spattered with blood and the reek of drunken terror didn't hang in the air. Where the serpent of destruction inside her didn't hunger for yet more death, so palpably she could taste it.

At last, exhausted, she stopped running. Her legs were so weak they could barely support her weight any longer and she lowered herself into a trembling half-crouch, gasping for breath as she tried to absorb what had just happened to her. Images of broken bodies crowded about her like ghosts, even when she closed her eyes. What had she done? What *was* she now, that she was capable of doing such a thing? She knew what Ethanus' answer would be, but imagining it spoken in that utterly calm voice of his drove home by contrast the meaning of the words on a level she had never really understood before.

You are a Magister.

Shaken, exhausted, she lowered her face into her hands and did something she had never allowed herself to do before, not in all the years she had lived in this city as a child.

She wept.

Chapter 13

THE DAY was stormy and black, which suited High King Danton's mood perfectly. He had been that way ever since throwing Ramirus and his black-robed vultures out of the domain. In the outer world, of course, sunshine occasionally managed to creep through the clouds and brave the narrow windows of his castle. In his inner world there was no such light.

Right now the sky outside was almost as dark as twilight, and rain pattered on the outer walls in irregular patterns that promised to drive him mad. It was just another irritant in a long list of many. The tithe from Corialanus was days late, which had fostered the usual rumors: insurrection, a sickness of the gut was working the rounds of the castle soldiery, the Inamorand succession had been put in doubt by accusations of infidelity, making the whole western border potentially unstable—the list went on and on.

All of which would have been no more than that, simply annoyances, had he had a Magister to help him deal with them.

He had interviewed five Magisters to replace Ramirus. He had not been happy with any of them, not enough to make them Magister Royal at any rate, though he had accepted three into his service for distant regions. A Magister Royal for a High King must have more than witchery at his fingertips; he must understand the way of politics, he must comprehend the ebb and flow of human aggression and be adept at manipulating men's passions, and above all else he must share the High King's hungers, his dreams, his hopes. Thus far none had proven himself by those standards and Danton was growing more frustrated each day. Who would have thought that the traitor Ramirus would be so damned hard to replace?

It was one thing to throw all one's Magisters out of the palace in theory, but it was another thing to actually have to do without them day after day. He was discovering that the hard way. If he wanted a letter sent to the far border of his kingdom these days he had to send the damn thing by mounted messenger, no matter how important it was, or how much speed mattered. Or he could try to use birds, stupid brainless things that they were, hoping they would deliver their messages to his agents and not to the enemies that surrounded them. So it was with all the other conveniences that Ramirus had offered and which Danton had taken for granted. He was a Dark Age king now in all but name, limited to the reach of his own flesh and the power of his voice, just like it had been in those barbaric days.

Which would have been all fine and good if all his rivals had to suffer the same deprivations, but of course they didn't. The most pitiful domains on his border had their own Magisters Royal, and no matter how incompetent those men were as sorcerers, they were still better than what Danton had right now. He could not move against his enemies or discipline his vassals or even flex his royal fist in warning without knowing he was outpowered by the weakest of his rivals . . . and his subjects knew it, too. It was only a question of time before someone took advantage of that and moved against him.

Curse the gods of the First Age of Kings for this wretched luck, and all the damnable Magisters with them! Had ruling an empire been this complicated back then?

"Your Majesty?"

He looked up, dark brows scowling. "Yes? What is it?"

His servant bowed. "A visitor has arrived. He gives his name as Kostas. He says you will wish to see him."

"Kostas? I don't know the name."

The servant said quietly, "He wears black, Majesty."

"A Magister?"

"So it would appear."

Interesting. Perhaps the storm had swept in something useful after all.

He nodded curtly. "Very well. Send him to my audience chamber. I will meet him there."

He must be from far away, if Danton had never heard of him. The High King prided himself on knowing all the local Magisters and their peculiarities. Or perhaps Kostas was simply a new name taken by some sorcerer who was thinking of leaving his current master for better employ. If so, Danton would allow him the anonymity for the time being. A rival's Magisters were always worth courting.

The audience chamber was a room that Danton maintained especially for such meetings. It was a cold and comfortless chamber walled in rough-hewn stone, whose dark floor and shadowy vaulted ceiling always gave off the impression of being damp, no matter how dry the day was. To mortals and Magisters alike it was a challenge, albeit in different ways. Mere humans were forced to present their petitions in the midst of that cold, unwelcoming space, while the High King peered at them from his throne like a hawk staring down its prey. It was amazing how much could he learned about a man in such a setting. As for Magisters, most of them worked their sorcery upon the space as soon as they entered, subtly or otherwise. One of them had actually dared to conjure himself a chair—a chair!—to mirror the High King's own. In this manner they no doubt thought they would please him, or—in the case of the last—at least make a clear statement about what they perceived the proper relationship between king and Magister to be. Instead of missing the very obvious point about what manner of relationship *he* expected.

He had but a minute to settle onto his reception throne—a heavy wooden piece built at the start of the Second Age, now so heavy with paint and reapplied gilt that he sometimes wondered if any of the original wood still existed—before the wide doors opened and his servants ushered in his black-clothed visitor.

He was a curious-looking man, which sparked Danton's interest immediately. Magisters might reshape their flesh in accordance with any desire, and therefore one could learn much from the body they chose for themselves. Usually it was something dramatic, or at least memorable. Some chose young faces, unmarked by any human hardship; others, aged ones so wrinkled with experience that to gaze into their hooded eyes was to step into ages past. Some chose horrific forms, as a warning to others that access to limitless power had made them something other than human; others sculpted themselves masks of such beauty and perfection that the gods themselves must surely be jealous.

This one . . . this one was remarkably ordinary, Danton thought. And that was an interesting choice.

He was a slender man, whippet-thin, and his black clothes fit close to his body, accentuating that slenderness. His frame was angular and everywhere that flesh showed, bone was plainly visible beneath it: in his face, where harshly angled cheekbones gave him a hungry aspect; in his neck, where lines of tendon and muscle stretched tautly from jawline to collarbone; in his hands, which had the aspect of coarse gloves fitted over a jagged armature. His face was weathered in the way that peasant skin became weathered after a lifetime of fighting the elements, the texture of it coarse and reddened. He reminded Danton of an arctic fisherman he had once seen, whose face had been scored by salt-laden winds and frigid ocean spray every day of his life. There were lines in this man's face also, sharp lines, harsh lines, and it did not seem to Danton that they had been put there for any artistic purpose so much as earned through time, in a purely human manner.

Interesting.

The Magister took a few steps forward and spared a glance to take in the room. His eyes, Danton noted, were the gray of a storm-laden sky, and his hair a shade of brown so unremarkable it must have been natural. It was shoulder length, with ragged edges that said plainly he cared little for fashion. Most interesting of all were the scars that marked his face. That they were old scars was plain, and they had healed as much as scars ever did on their own: a few parallel sharp lines across one cheekbone, perhaps claw marks; a puckering below one side of his jaw. There was a scar right at his hairline from which the hair grew white and coarse, and he had braided it so that it hung down over his shoulder in a sharply defined streak. They all looked like natural scars, Danton noted, which was interesting; why would a man who was capable of healing any wound choose to bear the marks of past injury?

Then the gray eyes fixed upon him and for a moment they held him transfixed; he could sense the raw power behind them, and depths of an existence no single lifetime could contain.

"High King Danton." The Magister bowed. "It has come to my ears that you seek a man of power for your court."

"My last one displeased me," Danton said bluntly. "I banished him."

It was a challenge, plain and simple. Most kings lived in constant fear of displeasing one of the black-robed sorcerers, and spent as much time trying to keep their Magisters Royal content as they did ruling their kingdoms.

Which is why they were the weakling princes they were, Danton thought, and he was . . . something more.

Some of the others candidates he'd interviewed had dared to comment upon his actions. A few had not offered open response, but their eyes made clear their displeasure.

But this Magister nodded his acceptance of the order without hesitation or comment. The gesture was eloquent in its simplicity, and Danton did not fail to catch the message behind it: *This is your kingdom. Not even a Magister may tell you what to do in it.*

A good start.

"I have interviewed many," he said curtly. "None pleased me."

"The world is full of fools," the Magister observed. "Having power does not make them otherwise."

A faint smile quirked the corner of the High King's mouth.

"I am called Kostas," the Magister offered. "Though if it pleases you to call me something else, that can be arranged."

"Humility is unusual in one of your calling."

He shrugged. "Humility is when a man submits to those things which have value to him. Submitting to those things which do not have value is simply . . . expedience."

"And your last royal position was . . . ?"

"Alas, I have not held such a post before." The gray eyes shimmered darkly, like thunderclouds before a storm. "Is that a requirement?"

"No. But it is . . . unusual."

"I have felt no need."

"And you do now?"

He shrugged. Like all things about him it was a sharp gesture, all bones and angles. "My interests change. The politics of this region intrigue me." He smiled slightly; it was a cold and predatory expression. "I am told there is no better seat to observe them from than beside the throne of a great king."

Danton ignored the flattery. "And is that all you wish to do? Observe?"

The stormy eyes glittered. "That is the custom, is it not?"

It was a good answer. The five who had come before him had tried other ones and had been dismissed. Three had attempted to pretend they had no interest in "morati" politics. Two had been honest. Neither had a place in his court.

Of course any Magister who applied for this royal position had an interest in politics. *Of course* he hoped to manipulate the High King, and through him the fate of an empire. To pretend otherwise here, in this chamber, was to accuse Danton of being a fool. And that he was not. He was many things, many hateful things, things that men cursed and women wept over, but he was not a fool.

He was beginning to think this Magister might suit him.

"Tell me of my kingdom," he challenged.

"Strong at its heart, as a lion's heart is strong," the man replied. He cocked his head slightly, like a bird regarding its prey. "But vast, and in its vastness, vulnerable. With a Magister's art such a territory is easily maintained, but you have lacked that for a fortnight now, and the strain is showing."

Danton's dark brows gathered about their center like angry stormclouds. "Tell me about it."

"What need I say that you do not already know, High King? It is no secret that the greater the size of an empire, the harder it is to safeguard its periphery. In times of prosperity it means little if there are mountains between one district and the next, or swampland that would hinder an army's passage. The Magister's art can overcome such obstacles with ease but without the hand of sorcery to ease passage, these are barriers that circumscribe armies. And nations."

For a long, very cold minute Danton just stared at him. It was impossible to read the Magister's expression, and that was a surprise; Danton was adept at reading men.

Finally he rose and strode to a sideboard. That he turned his back on the visitor was quite deliberate: *I do not fear you or your kind.* Beneath the narrow table, on the shelf beneath, handful of heavy scrolls lay waiting. He took one out, removed the ribbon that bound it, and unrolled it across the table.

The scroll unrolled fully and remained flat on the table afterward as if pinned down by weights; Kostas had not missed his cue.

Danton gazed down upon the map of his kingdom in all its vast, terrible glory. It was the single greatest empire since the Second Age of Kings had begun, or so his court historians had assured him. He had long since crossed barriers that his ancestors would have regarded as impassable, at least for armies; that was what the age of Magisters had brought to kings. Nations were unified under Danton Aurelius that had never been unified before, and if it took a strong and sometimes brutal hand to keep them unified, so be it.

There had been witches in the First Age, of course. But a witch only had so much life force to work with, and convincing one to part with all of his supply for a single military campaign was nigh impossible. Geographical features that were impassable in the First Age tended to stay impassable, unless you put knives to the throats of a hundred witches and forced them to serve your cause. Which might work for one project, but tended to leave you short of witches for the next one down the line.

Now things were different.

That was not to say that Magisters always applied their power as liberally as a royal patron might like. Apparently there was some sort of code governing how much they might exert themselves, and when, and more than once Danton had cursed a Magister who had refused to extend himself for a chosen project. They claimed it had something to do with the balance of spiritual forces in the heavens and the inherent stability of the universe . . . but rat piss to all that. He was sure there was something more to it, but apparently no mere morati king could get it out of them.

He watched as the lean Magister moved quietly to the table and gazed down at the map before him. How like a lizard's visage the man's profile was, Danton noted, not with displeasure so much as curiosity. One could almost imagine a forked tongue darting out of that narrow mouth, testing the air for sound as well as smell.

"Defreest stirs," the Magister mused quietly, "and the provinces beyond.

Corialanus to the south, but you know that, I am sure. These . . ." He swept a hand across the small row of provinces that edged the kingdom on the west, some of whom had negotiated semi-independent status long ago. "These are agitated, but it means little. Unless they unify they are no real threat."

"My father put their cities to the torch last time they tried that."

"I am sure they have not forgotten."

Danton looked up at him sharply. "So what would you advise, that you should become my counselor? What would *you* do, if all this was yours?"

There was a double challenge in the words.

They gray eyes narrowed. For a moment the Magister was silent, studying the map. "Prepare an army against Corialanus," he said at last. "It stands between you and the Free Lands and as such will hamper your expansion into that region unless it is securely controlled. They will start testing you soon, to learn your limits—"

"They have already begun," Danton muttered.

Kostas nodded. "Then move against them before they are ready for it, and give them your answer. Without mercy."

"And to the north?"

"Distract them. Give them something to focus their attention on that will not require an army, nor divide your supply lines." The stormy gray eyes met his; their depths were so cold that Danton shivered despite himself. "I can do that for you, High King."

"How?" he demanded.

"Fearsome tricks. Legends of demons, and worse. Things that will have them arming against the shadows themselves, rather than turning their attention south to your border. Humans are easily manipulated through fear, High King . . . and my kind is adept at such games."

"Few of them admit it so openly," he said quietly.

"Yes . . ." A faint, cold smile flickered across his face. "You will find that I am . . . atypical."

"So you favor my expansion?"

"It is the natural condition of a great state to expand, Your Majesty."

Danton snorted. "Not all of my advisers agree with you. Some claim the kingdom has reached its natural limits—whatever that means. They warn me that any power spread too thin will, in time, collapse."

The stormy eyes glittered. "All things collapse, High King . . . in time. The greatest empire of the First Age was no more than dust a millennium later. The greatest empire of the Second will someday be the same. Against such a heartbeat of existence politics are played out, the ebb and flow of human hungers driving them . . . no different than among animals, really, save that we clothe our instincts in prettier raiments, and sometimes use words in the place of teeth and claws. And sometimes . . . not."

The gray eyes fixed on Danton; power stirred visibly in their depths. A lesser man might have quailed, but the High King knew the importance of standing his ground, particularly in such an interview; the statements made this night would establish what Kostas would be to him for as long as they both walked the earth.

He met the eerie gaze without flinching and said, "Go on."

"We are beasts at heart, every one of us, though clad in more fragile flesh than most beasts. We play games of 'civilization' and pride ourselves on having created things like poetry and music, but inside we are as territorial as wolves. The desire of the ruling male to expand his hunting range, to control resources, to spread his seed as far as possible, are drives born of primitive animal hunger . . . whether he expresses it by pissing on trees that were marked by a rival or sending forth a royal army to rape the neighboring domain, the end result is the same.

"That the hunger is strong in you is clear from your history. That you are capable of doing it justice is equally clear. Few men can claim both."

"Few Magisters speak in such terms."

"As I said, I am not typical."

"Those who are I have sent away."

The gray eyes glittered. "Perhaps that was wise."

Danton studied the man again, noting every feature of him, tasting his essence through the inspection. It was his gift to be able to read the hearts of men, even those of seemingly unlimited power. This one was . . . hungry. Just as hungry as the kings he spoke of, or the beasts that howled for blood within men's souls. It was a dangerous hunger, to be sure, and rarely were a Magister's true motives anything that a king might understand. But Danton had figured out Ramirus well enough to control him, and had manipulated his kind adroitly enough to insult two dozen of them and survive it—a feat most monarchs would not even attempt—and now, he thought, he would learn to control this one. For no matter what this Kostas had experienced, no matter what the taste of unlimited power had done to him, no matter what secrets immortality had whispered into his ear, he was, at his core, human. That, Danton had learned, was the secret of the Magisters that they tried to veil with mystery and legends. A tiger, no matter how powerful, could never become something other than a tiger. So it was with men. They might change their bodies at will, and even live forever, but they were still men.

He turned back to the map and regarded his territory once more. Finally he brought down a finger to rest upon the border of Corialanus. The bloodred ruby in his ring glittered darkly as he moved it along the River Kest to the heart of that troublesome state.

"So," he said quietly. "Let me hear what my Magister Royal would advise. . . ."

Chapter 14

SHADOWS, SHADOWS are all around. At first Andovan cannot make out any shapes among them, only random patterns of mottled unclarity, and then they resolve, slowly. He sees trees, outlined darkly against the night sky. A woman, among the trees. She is wrapped in blackness, clothed in blackness, so that nothing of her is visible. Moonlight picks out cool highlights along the jagged evergreen branches, but it cannot reach her.

She is watching him, he knows that. She is always watching him. He can feel her gaze upon him and it tastes of death. He screams his protest with all his might. It is an empty yell, impotent, that leaves his body like smoke. He shuts his mouth but cannot stop the flow. More and more smoke follows, and as it leaves him he grows weaker and weaker. He struggles to turn away and run from her, but he cannot.

The woman waits, silent, eternally patient. There is no sign of emotion in her, but she puts out one pale hand and the smoke comes to her like a tame dog . . . and then she wafts it toward her mouth and begins to breathe it in, absorbing his strength, his life while the evergreen shadows watch all in silence. . . .

―――――――

Andovan awakened suddenly. A cold sweat was upon his brow, and for a moment he just lay there, grateful to be back in the world of real things, freed from the harrowing nightmare.

It was not the first night he had dreamed of the shadow woman. In fact he had done so every night since Colivar first laid the spell upon him, that sorcery which would supposedly draw him toward the source of his illness. Toward his would-be killer.

He saw her every night, but he could not make out her face.

He screamed at her each night, but did not know her name.

The nightmare was worse each time he dreamed it, the pain of his dying more real. Did that mean that Colivar's sorcery was working, and he was getting closer to her? Or was it a warning that the life was draining out of him like sand through an hourglass, and he had very little time left before all searches were ended?

I will find her, he told himself. It was his morning mantra. *I will win my life back, whatever it takes, and make her pay for what she has done to me.*

He tried to move, to get up out of bed, but a sudden blinding pain forced him to fall back, gasping for breath. His limbs felt like lead, and his head felt as if it had been split in two. For a moment he just lay there with his eyes closed, trying to master the pain. Trying to remember what had caused it. But the memory would not come, and when he opened his eyes he saw a ceiling overhead that was unfamiliar to him. He turned his head painfully to one side—the motion took several long minutes, his head throbbing hotly with each new inch gained—and he realized the rest of the room was likewise unfamiliar. Some sort of crude log construct, artlessly patched with mud and straw, that he had never seen before.

Where in the gods' names am I?

Then the throbbing gave way to a sharper pain at the side of his head, and he managed to raise up a hand to feel for the source, though it seemed to him his hand was made of lead. Bandages. There were bandages. Wound around his head. Coarse linen, from the feel of them, one or two layers, tightly wrapped. He pressed his fingers against the fabric, seeking more information. The source of the pain was a spot over his left temple, and fire pierced through his skull when he probed there. Over that spot, soaked into the bandages, was a thick paste. He thought at first it was half-dried blood, but when he drew his fingers away to look at them he saw crumbling bits of herbs in a white, vinegary-smelling paste. Some kind of healing salve, most likely. So . . . someone had taken care of him. But who? And where was he? What had happened to him?

He tried to sit up but his body would not respond.

So instead he tried to remember. That at least allowed him to shut his eyes, which was a small mercy. Even the small bit of light seeping through the small windows was painful to him.

———

There's sour ale in his stomach, food too old for human consumption, peasant fare at its worst refusing to be digested. He walks back toward the woods, thinking he would rather make his bed in the wild tonight than rely upon the hospitality of strangers. One more night in an ill-kept hovel, with the smells of a chamber-pot filling the place and the accumulated reek of a lifetime's sweaty labors closing in about him, and he may well become sick with more than the Wasting. No, the forest is clean and fresh and the ground has provided a bed enough nights during his hunting expeditions that it will seem like home tonight. Perhaps he will even puke up his vile dinner and then can catch himself something fresh to take its place. The sunlight is not completely gone yet, which means the nocturnal animals will be coming out to look for forage or prey . . . if he is lucky he can find some deer . . . hunting would refresh his spirit, he thinks, and his stomach would certainly welcome the change of fare.

How long does he walk, towards that hidden place where he left his horse tethered, before he realizes that footsteps are shadowing his own? He stiffens, not unlike deer when a hunter approaches. Then for a moment he pauses in his walking, reaching for one of the leather straps of his pack as though he would adjust its weight on his shoulder. There are no footsteps when he stops to listen. Of course, for they ceased walking when his own did. But he can sense the people who are behind him by the odors they exude, and he can hear their shallow breathing. The fools probably think they are being silent, Andovan muses. But he is used to stalking game far more stealthy than any human can possibly be, and his nose is as finely tuned as a wolf's. By animal standards they are making enough noise to scare off a deer at thirty paces, and even a wolf with a head-cold could not miss that reek.

He starts walking again, listening now for the false echo of matching footsteps behind him. Yes, there is no mistaking it. Slowly, carefully, he brings his right hand forward, to the hilt of the hunting knife he always wears at his belt. They will wait for him to get to the edge of town, he guesses, where they are unlikely to have witnesses to whatever it is they are planning to do. Such is the way of cowards and thieves. His horse is sheltered in the woods just beyond; he had approached the town on foot. Do they know he has a mount? Will they wait until he reaches it before making their move?

Briefly he wonders if Colivar might have betrayed him, getting him away from the castle so that he might be assassinated without consequence. But no, that makes little sense. Andovan has done nothing to offend the southern Magister, and besides, it would have been just as easy for Colivar to kill him that night at the castle, after they had made arrangements to fake his death, as now. Why wait? And use such crude human tools, when sorcery could do the trick in perfect silence?

Besides, Colivar wants something from him. That much is patently obvious. Ostensibly it has something to do with the woman that is killing Andovan—that much he told the prince—but Andovan is willing to bet there is much more to the story than he is being told. Magisters never confide their true purpose to morati, every prince worth his salt knows that for a fact. And as for anyone else being behind this . . . in theory they all think he is dead now. So no one is going to send out assassins after him. Least of all sloppy, smelly assassins.

He walks slowly down the muddy road, his senses alert for every clue they can pick up. He estimates that his trackers are maybe ten feet behind him, no more. If he turns quickly and steps forward he'll be upon them before they know it. Boars do that sometimes when you hunt them, and they are deadly adversaries for it. One almost gored him when he was younger, teaching him that lesson.

He begins to turn, grasping the bone handle of his knife tightly—

—and suddenly a wave of sickness comes over him. It is like the attacks he has had before but also unlike them. This attack is a hundred times more powerful than those paltry weaknesses, and it turns his legs to jelly beneath him without warning. For a moment the whole world swims before his eyes like a dream gone mad, and it seems he lacks even the strength to breathe. He falls forward onto his hands and knees, dropping the knife in the mud as he does so. Not now, not now! *What is happening? The worst of his attacks have never been like this before.* Not here! *He can hear footsteps coming toward him, swiftly now, and he struggles to reach out for his knife, but his hand is like a dead thing that has neither feeling nor strength and it will not obey him. It is as if all the vital tissue has been sucked out of his flesh, leaving him trapped inside a shell with no sinew inside.* I refuse to give in to this! *Other times he had been sick sheer determination won the day, for his strength of will is no small thing, but*

this time the weakness is so terrible he cannot manage the slightest triumph over it. The arms and legs that are holding him up begin to fold, even as his vision begins to blacken. Figures move in from the surrounding shadows but he can no longer see them. For the first time in many, many years he is truly afraid.

I am going to die, *he despairs.* Not upon the horns of my prey or by the teeth of an angry predator, as it should be, but upon the blades of cowards while I lie sick and helpless before them.

How has he ever offended the gods so terribly, that they would do this to him? He tries to voice a howl of indignation but no sound comes from his throat. He senses something being swung at his head but he cannot dodge it . . . and then the night explodes in a veil of stars and the last of his consciousness pours out of him like hot blood, leaving him at the mercy of the predators. . . .

––––––––––

For a long time after the flow of memories ceased he lay still, trying to absorb it all. Though he was not generally the kind of man who gave way to fear, this was a different manner of beast than a wild boar, or even a maddened lion. This . . . this *disease* did not care if he was brave or not, it was not affected by plans or preparations, and it struck from the shadows when he was least prepared for it. This time he was lucky he was not dead. A well-equipped traveler lying helpless along the roadside was an open invitation to theft and assault, or even slavery if the wrong person came along. He was clearly alive, there were no chains upon him, and someone had tended to his wounds, so the worst had not happened . . . but he might not be so lucky next time.

If the disease had progressed to the point where it would take him thus, without warning, perhaps this journey was indeed more than he could handle.

His mouth tightened at the thought; the bandaged spot on his head throbbed painfully. *No.*

Friends sometimes joked with him that he was not Danton's son in truth. He lacked his father's coloring, his harsh features, his casual brutality, and nearly all the other qualities that were generally considered trademarks of Danton's lineage. He understood the jokes that were made about that and smiled and laughed along with his cohorts. But there was one area in which Andovan was truly his father's son, and that was his stubbornness.

He had gone out into the world with no royal name, no family ties, limited supplies, and no real sense of how his quest was to begin, just the stubborn determination to seek out the person who had caused his weakness, and an unnamed and untested spell that would allegedly help him find his way. He was doing that despite a weakness that sapped his very strength and left him, occasionally, as helpless as a babe. Nothing in that picture had changed now. Any idiot knew that the symptoms of the Wasting grew more and more pronounced as the end drew near. He'd never heard of anyone losing consciousness from it like he did, but it was not beyond imagination's reach. Very well. If that was the newest symptom, then he would deal with it. But he was Danton's son, and he would not abandon his quest simply because of an illness of the flesh. No matter how debilitating that illness was.

"You are awake?"

It was a female voice that spoke, gentle and perhaps a bit hesitant. He tried to raise himself up on his elbows to see its owner, and came near to managing the task. As he looked about he could see the room he was in more clearly. It was a small room lined in split logs, and patched with handfuls of mud and straw, inexpertly applied. He lay on one of many straw pallets near a cold fireplace; four others were currently unoccupied. Through a small window on one side daylight sent teasing streamers that trapped the room's dust in glimmering rays, allowing him to see a few primitive tools hanging on iron hooks, a pile of dingy blankets, old pottery jars by the fireplace that once must have been gaily painted, now relegated to a cruder life. The whole of the place was dismally poor, but it was clean, and the rushes covering the floor smelled fresh. That spoke well for someone.

Then he saw the girl. She was young, not quite a woman yet, but with a prettiness that promised to become more than prettiness as she matured. Her clothes were patched many times over but clean, and her hair had been brushed till it shone. That was rare in any peasant's home.

Blue eyes. She had blue eyes. They reminded him strangely of his mother's. Was there northern blood in her?

"Are you all right?" she asked.

He managed to nod without his head splitting in two, which was a small miracle. Then he managed to smile slightly, an even bigger one. "As opposed to the alternative of being dead, yes, I suppose I feel well."

"My brothers didn't think you would live."

"The gods were merciful, then . . . and perhaps, my nurse skilled."

She blushed, which confirmed his guess.

Little do they know who or what they saved, he mused.

He managed to sit up. She helped him halfway though, so he was not yet sure he could manage it alone, but even that qualified triumph over weakness and pain bolstered his spirits considerably.

"What is your name, lass?"

Maybe it was something in his tone that made her lower her eyes briefly, as if she sensed the rank he had been born to. Or maybe . . . maybe it was maidenly modesty. She was still young enough for that to be the case, though among the poor such a state rarely lasted. Pretty young virgins were worth too much coin on the open market to be kept away from it for long.

"Dea, sir."

"Dea." He smiled, though it hurt his face. "Please don't call me *sir.*" Her deferential manner concerned him. Was it so obvious he was not a townsman? That was something to address when he took to the road again. Maybe it would keep him from getting robbed and nearly killed a second time if he could pass for a peasant more successfully. "My name is—" He hesitated, trying to remember back past the pain to the one he had chosen. "Talesin."

"Talesin." She smiled. My, she would be a beautiful one when she filled out, if the world did not beat her down first, and crush the natural innocence which gave her smile such charm. Which it probably would.

With a sigh he tried to rise to his feet, and to his surprise, managed it. Evidently his body had resigned itself to living and decided to cooperate with him at last. "Where are your brothers? I assume they rescued me?"

"I found you. They brought you here. They said . . ." She hesitated. "They said that you were well-born, by the look of you, and that maybe there would be a reward to be had, if you survived."

There would be if they knew who to tell about it, he thought wryly.

"My hands are calloused," he pointed out, showing her where a lifetime of riding and hunting had left its mark. "Is that well-born?"

"Your fingernails are clean," she pointed out, showing him. "And trimmed to the shape of fine crescent moons, not worn down by labor."

He chuckled. "So they are."

And so I shall have to learn to chew my nails. Though if I had done so before this, I would have been left for dead by my mercenary benefactors. A curious irony, that.

"Tell me of what you know," he said. And, "tell me how long it has been."

"I found you last night, as I left the town. You were lying facedown by the side of the road, where carriage wheels might strike you. Your face was covered in blood and your clothes . . ." She blushed ever so slightly and looked down. "Your clothes were half removed, as though someone had searched through them."

No doubt looking for treasures to steal, he thought. He was lucky his attackers had not needed a new wardrobe. "Go on."

"I went and got Viktor, my brother, who brought the others. They brought you back here, and fetched supplies for nursing. They thought you were going to die, but I . . . I could see the strength in you."

"So it has been only one night?"

She nodded.

He felt about his person, feeling for all the various things which had once been stored on his body. All of it was gone, of course. Anything the thieves did not take his benefactors would have.

"Are you all right?" she asked.

"If I am standing and talking, I am well enough." Actually the *standing* part was a bit hard, but he wasn't going to tell her that. "Whatever trail remains is growing cold."

"Trail?" She blinked. "You mean you are going after them?"

"It seems the thing to do, does it not?"

"But your injuries . . . you need to rest. . . ."

He shook his head. "I can go after them now and take my chances, or take time to heal and lose any hope of finding them. After all," he said, meeting her eyes and smiling, "I can hardly reward you and your brothers if all my coin is gone, can I?"

He reached up to feel the bandages again, and then, with a wince, peeled them from the wound. The flesh beneath was crusted with dried blood, but it felt sound enough. The pain was now reduced to a hot throbbing that blazed behind his left eye. He had survived worse.

He looked about the stark room, searching for tools that might serve his purpose. At last he saw a length of hemp rope coiled in one corner, which he gathered up. Then he went to the fireplace, where he removed the long iron bar from which a stew kettle depended, setting the kettle aside.

"I will need to borrow these, is that all right?"

Eyes wide, she nodded.

"Come then," he said. "Take me to where you found me."

———————

There were no clues at the site. Of course. A muddy road leading to the only inn within miles must be so scarred from wagon wheels, horseshoes, and passing boots he would have been hard pressed to pick out a single human footprint, much less know which one mattered to him. He settled for checking the surrounding brush for any items of his possession that might have been left behind. He had hoped they might have missed his knife, but apparently not.

He sent the girl away, then. He did not want to put her at risk.

A short distance from the road he found his encampment, surrounded by dense enough brush that he had hoped his attackers would not realize it was there. No such luck. His horse was gone, along with his saddle packs and all the supplies they held. Fortunately he always hid his most valuable possessions when leaving a camp unguarded, and a brief foray into the surrounding woods showed him that his hiding place had gone undiscovered. At least he had some coin now, though he would have traded all of it for a good knife. The next time he would have to hide one with his valuables, in case of a repeat of this dismal experience.

Are you sure you want to hunt them? he asked himself. *They are many, you are one. They will be armed, you have only household implements. They will be well-rested and healthy, while you—*

A muscle along his jaw clenched tight. It was an expression eerily like Danton's. He felt like Danton in that moment—stubborn, cold, determined. His father's strength flowed through him . . . and his mother's.

You are a hunter, he told himself. *One whose prey does not expect him to strike. There is power in that.*

It was surprisingly easy to pick up the trail starting from his encampment. They had led his mount away on foot—probably arguing over who would get to ride him—and that had left sharp crescent marks scored in the damp earth, a perfect marker. The hoofprints led away from the small town, which told Andovan that his attackers had not been locals, but rather itinerant scum who preyed upon legitimate travelers and then moved on. Good. He followed their trail moving quickly, quietly, straining his senses to the utmost. Shortly he found a mound of horse droppings that he judged to be at least half a day old, which told him that it had been some time since his attackers had passed this way; but night had been approaching when he was attacked, and with luck they had made camp not far from here and were only just stirring now.

Silently, silently he moved, a ghost among the trees, his passage as soundless as an owl's flight. All those skills that allowed him to sneak up on a hunter's prey were now doubly valued, being turned against men. As it should be. They had the advantage of numbers, weapons, and condition. He must have the advantage of surprise.

It was possible that his head still hurt, but he was too wrapped up in the hunt now to notice it. It had been like that the day a boar had gored his side as well; his mother had raised bloody hell over it, but he hadn't even noticed the blood streaming from his flesh until his quarry was brought down.

Soon he caught the scent of a stale campfire on the wind, and he knew he had found his quarry. He circled wide around the area to where the breeze favored him, and let the scent guide him while he scanned the early morning woods for the sort of terrain that would favor a thieves' encampment. They had left him for dead and probably did not expect pursuit on his behalf; nonetheless they would have taken basic precautions and tried to place their campsite where passing travelers would not notice it. They would probably set someone on watch while they slept as well, and though it was dubious they would keep that up once they were awake, he watched closely for signs of a lookout.

At last he saw the sort of place he himself would have chosen for a blind, a gap in the trees where sunlight had encouraged a thickening of underbrush, which in turn provided a dense screen some ten yards wide, obscuring what lay beyond. He crouched behind a tree trunk and just watched the camp for a while, alert for any sign of human activity. It seemed now that he could hear voices from just beyond it, intermittent, the kind of sounds one made when doing something other than talking. He could pick up the scent of dying smoke, now, and human scents as well. After a moment longer, seeing there was no movement in the blind—guessing that such men would not be disciplined enough to remain perfectly still on watch as soldiers might—he crept forward carefully, placing each foot so that he made no rustling noise, broke no twigs, gave no warning.

At last he found a place where he could see beyond the screen of foliage. They had camped there, all right; four of them, with his horse tethered nearby. There were no other mounts present at the moment, though if they had his gold they'd be able to buy some at the next town along the road; robbing Andovan had improved their fortune immensely. They were as he had guessed they would be, coarse and grimy men dressed in a catch-all medley of stolen bits and pieces of clothing, occasional treasured trinkets glittering from beneath shirt and jerkin, perhaps as trophies.

Two were just beginning to gather their things, while another smothered the fire that must have recently served to heat food or drink for them. He watched them closely and decided they were more brutes than professionals: men who had learned that a pack of four working in unison could take down the strongest prey with no need for complex planning. That was good; such a group was unlikely to be prepared for a stealthy assault.

Andovan's head throbbed hotly for a moment, reminding him of his own weakened condition, but he was too focused upon his prey to let it bother him. With care he lay down the rope he had brought as he had planned, taking care to move quietly, freezing when there was not enough noise in the camp to cover his own movements. But the thieves were not watching for trouble. They were joking now about some woman they'd shared in a distant town, which apparently was the reason they were not anxious to stay in the vicinity. Andovan's jaw clenched tightly as he crouched down in the brush to watch them, waiting for the moment that must surely come, if they had just broken their fast.

And soon it did. Laughing, the tallest of the men made some crude comment about female sexual habits and then moved into the brush surrounding the camp, one hand reaching under his shirt to loosen his clothing. Andovan knew the thief would be but a moment at his business and must be taken swiftly. Fortunately for him the man had eaten well the night before, and had something more substantial than piss to offer to the gods of the woods; Andovan came up behind him like a cat while he crouched, and had his arm around his neck before the man even knew he was there. It was a less effective move than crushing his head with an iron bar would have been, but it was quieter; Andovan's muscular arm choked the man's windpipe before he could utter a sound, bending him upward and backward so that he had no purchase on the ground. He had choked a mountain lion that way once, though the claws had raked him dearly in the process; at least this time he could grab his quarry's wrist and keep him from getting hold of any kind of weapon.

The man was enough of a fighter that he did not struggle wildly, but tried to strike at his attacker. But Andovan's grip was uncompromising, and the kicks and blows that were offered were but weak things, with no power to dislodge him. After a few minutes the struggles ceased. Andovan held on, still, until he felt that special, eerie limpness which meant that life had left the flesh. Then he let the body down, slowly, lowering it to the ground with care so that it made as little noise as possible.

All was quiet, if not utterly silent. He braved a glance back through the brush, parting the leaves until he could catch a glimpse of the clearing. The men were too busy chattering among themselves to have heard him. That meant he had a few moments to prepare himself. He searched the body quickly, cursing under his breath when he saw the man was unarmed. He'd have given much for a knife right now. Hefting the iron bar he'd borrowed, Andovan slipped back to the spot he had prepared nearby, and then waited, listening carefully.

Finally a man's voice called, "Tomas?"

There was a pause, then another came to his ears. ". . . should be back by now."

"Tomas?"

Only silence.

"Damn it all, has he gone off somewhere?"

"Could be an animal got him—"

"Well then we'd have heard it, wouldn't we?"

"Like you ever stop chattering long enough to hear anything."

"Like you ever shut up long enough to listen."

"Tomas!"

Andovan let out a groan then. It was hopefully that kind of groan which any man might utter, devoid of the kind of tone or detail that would identify its owner.

"Ah, damn!"

"Tomas, you hurt?" Andovan said nothing. "Shit, man, I told you to watch where you walked. Probably another damned snake."

"Probably bit him on the prick this time."

Cursing under his breath, one of the men began to head into the brush, near where Andovan was waiting, calling for his lost friend. The fugitive prince could not have asked for better. He fell back behind the bulk of a tree trunk, letting the man pass by him before he swung the iron bar at the back of his head. The sound of the impact cracked through the forest, silencing whatever discussion was going on in the camp. As he had meant it to.

"Fuck a whore!" one of the men swore, then both grabbed their weapons and started to run toward where the sound had come from.

Andovan moved, and this time moved noisily. They heard him first and then they saw him, and quickly turned their steps in his direction. That was fine with him. He dodged an obstacle and then came to an open place where combat would be easy; then he turned and feigned fear as his enemies came running toward him—

And neither of them looked down. Andovan's hemp rope caught the first at the calf and brought him crashing to the ground. The second caught on just in time to dodge the rope, but tripped over the legs of his fallen comrade and went down right on top of him.

It was no fight at all, really. Not with the iron bar giving Andovan the advantage of superior reach, its heft cold and hard enough to steal a man's consciousness in a single blow. It felt good to exert himself, to lose himself in battle, however brief, and feel the blood rushing through his veins at full strength, like it had in the old days. The Wasting might have weakened him, but he was not yet helpless.

When they lay there before him, bloody and still, he raised the iron bar yet again. And hesitated. One good blow to each would put them out of their misery forever, if he had not done that already. Doubtless there were men and women who would thank him for removing such beasts from the realm of human affairs.

But.

Killing a man in cold blood was not the same as killing him in the heat of battle. Cutting the throat of a man was not the same as slicing that of a deer, where the latter might serve for meat and clothing. Andovan had never shied away from killing before, but never before had he had a man's body lying blood splattered and helpless at his feet like this.

They *should* die. They deserved to die. They had hurt enough people that their deaths should be applauded.

He gazed down at the two bodies for a long time.

I am not a judge, he thought at last, lowering the iron bar.

He tied them with strips of cloth torn from their clothing, so that if they did awaken while he was busy with their camp they would make enough noise to warn him. Otherwise he would leave them to the mercy of the woods . . . which meant to the mercy of the gods. Of course, if the deities of these woods were anything like the deities of the northern woods, they would be dead soon enough. Already he thought he could hear small animals stirring in the underbrush, drawn by the smell of fresh blood. Soon other creatures would arrive, bigger and meaner creatures, and the thieves would have bigger things than him to worry about.

He gathered up their supplies, searched out the few treasures they had hidden among their things, broke what weapons he did not care to take with him, and rode his horse back to the road, where soon the muddled track obscured all signs of his passage, making for a trail no man could follow.

———

One of the brothers was at the log cabin when Andovan returned, and the girl as well. Now that the sunlight fell full upon the structure he could see that it had once been well made, but time and inexpert repair had allowed it to fall from grace. This family had neither built it nor purchased it, he guessed, but simply moved in when opportunity afforded. Perhaps they had even killed the family that owned it in order to take possession.

He looked into the eyes of Dea's brother and saw in them that same spark which, under the right circumstances, might have him toasting the rape of women alongside thieves and brigands in the woods. For a moment his hand tightened on the handle of his knife, and the line of muscle along the line of his jaw clenched tight. Then he forced both to relax.

"I am Talesin," he said. "I understand I owe you much."

The others' eyes glittered greedily. Andovan saw him glance at Dea, who turned her face away from him shyly. No, not shyly. Hiding something. Andovan felt a knot tighten in the pit of his gut. Had one of them struck the girl? Perhaps over the items he had borrowed, believing them simply stolen, blaming her for their loss? Was she hiding a fresh bruise from him?

He felt sick inside. And angry. He wanted to kill them all.

"Here." He pulled a heavy purse from his belt: ill-gotten gain from the thieves, a bag of coins and bits of jewelry and even some lady's embroidered fan. It was not enough to make the brothers rich men, but it would keep them comfortable for a long while. "Accept my thanks."

He handed the bag to one of the brothers, who hefted its weight and marked the clinking of small metal bits within, and grinned. "Always pleased to serve your lordship," he said.

Andovan tried to meet the girl's eyes, but she would not oblige him. Still her far cheek was turned so that he could not see it.

You cannot strike a man who just saved your life, he told himself. *No matter how much he deserves it.*

He reached into his jerkin, into the smaller purse that was hidden there, and pulled out a handful of his own coins. It was a goodly fraction of what he had brought with him and its loss would make his journey that much harder, but that could not be helped.

He held up the coins in the sunlight, letting both of them see their golden luster, the finely minted impressions of Danton's own face on one side, Gwynofar's on the other. He wondered if they would notice the resemblance.

"The girl's maidenhead is mine," he announced. "I am paying for it now. I will relinquish my rights if she marries honorably, but if she does not, her virginity is mine to take, or not to take, at my whim." He handed the coins to her brother and thought he saw the man flinch as he did so. Good. He had slipped unconsciously into what his father called an imperial tone, and even if these people did not know his true rank, they could sense his innate authority . . . and his utter conviction backing it. "If you dishonor my rights, if you sell her to another, or allow her to be taken against her will, I will come back and hunt you down. All of you. Like I hunted those men. Like I hunt animals."

He pulled out the iron bar from the straps of his pack and cast it to the ground by the side of the doorway; it stuck upright in the soil like a spear, quivering. The rope followed afterward, its coils marked with spatters of blood.

"Do not forget," he warned.

He would have liked a private moment with the girl, one last minute for a gentle and tender farewell, but he sensed that the brother was not about to leave them alone and let that happen. So he had to settle for one last glance into her blue eyes—filled with such doubt, such wonder, such painful gratitude—and a nod that bade her make the most she could of his gift, for he could not return to help her again.

The world is a harsh place, he thought, *and men are like animals, who will devour their own.*

His heart heavy, his head pounding in pain again, he mounted his horse and turned its nose to the west, and began to ride once more.

Chapter 15

THE HIGH Queen Gwynofar was dressed in black.

It was not the black of the Magisters, pristine and perfect, the stuff of shadows magicked into cloth, but a simpler fabric, like that a commoner would wear. There were many layers of it and each one was torn, as the custom was in the Protectorates, garments ripped each time a mourning cry was uttered until all that was left was a ragged fringe. Her fingers played with the tattered edges as she walked, and she whispered prayers to the gods of her homeland, wondering if they could even hear her in this place. Sometimes the Protectorates and their gods seemed so far off they might have been in a different world entirely . . . or perhaps they were just a dream from which she had not yet awakened, and she would soon discover that her memories had no real substance at all.

She was a delicate woman of northern stock, with skin so fine and white that slender blue veins could be glimpsed coursing beneath it, and gently curling hair of a soft yellow that stirred in the slightest breeze. In her own homeland she had been considered beautiful, in an ethereal sort of way, but it was no secret that Danton Aurelius preferred more substantive stock for his bed, and most of his local bastards reflected the earthy whores that mothered them. Even her own sons, born out of royal duty, looked more like Danton than like her, and she could well imagine his coarse, hook-nosed seed laying down the law in her womb, terrorizing each fledgling infant into accepting his features *or else*. If so, only one son had defied him. Only one child had taken after her instead, defying his father to manifest his mother's pale essence.

And now he was gone.

In Andovan she had seen the windswept snowfields of the far north, the deep fjords and pine-crested mountains of her birthplace, the glimmering Veils of the Gods as they swept across the evening sky, a sight of such terrible beauty that they drove one to one's knees in prayer. Andovan. His eyes were as blue as the northern skies in summer and she had wept to see them, missing her homeland so terribly she could hardly bear it. He was *her* child, the only thing here that had been truly hers, the one thing the ancient gods had given her to make this terrible banishment tolerable.

Now gone.

Her slender white fingers tore at the hem of her gown again, rending another few threads to bits.

All about her the blue pines of her homeland bristled, brought to this place at great expense by a king who was not ungenerous with coin, even if he was tightfisted with his affection. Their close ranks hid the surrounding stone walls from view, so that if she half-shut her eyes she might imagine herself home in truth, wandering free in the mountains as she had done in her youth, and not in some fortified courtyard, a prisoner of royal security.

She had brought in northern craftsmen to train the trees, as was the custom in her father's lands, carving their trunks in the likenesses of her ancestors and then leaving their bark to heal, so that it appeared they had morphed themselves naturally into such images. It was said you might know the favor your family spirits held you in by how the blue pines thrived once they bore such images, but here in the south such trees were foreigners to the land, and the harsh sun and the dense clay soil conspired to make them feel unwelcome. Or so she told herself. It would be a terrible thing indeed if these stunted trees truly reflected how her forbears felt about her, and she refused to consider it.

Danton . . . he gave little more than a passing nod to the ancient gods, which suited a land that had never known the harshness of the northern winter, and a people that had never offered their devotions in thigh-deep

snow before the Spears of the Wrath. Danton's people were not raised believing that if they failed to do their duty for even a night the whole of the
human lands might be swallowed up by a second Dark Ages, and the Second Age of Kings would become what the First Age had . . . a thing men
knew only from the tales in history books centuries later, and by the melo-
dious laments of minstrels. Such men could be careless with their lives and
with their gods, and forget the ancient traditions. She did not have that
freedom.

In the center of the courtyard she had commanded a circle of spires to
be erected, irregular stone monuments carefully carved and smoothed and
polished till they rose like some vast monster's teeth from the ground,
towering well over her head. It was commanded that no drop of water that
fell upon the spires should find purchase, but rather each must run swiftly
down the surface to the bottom without interruption, and so she had ordered them sculpted thus, each in its own twisted, sinuous form. They
were eerie, especially when one stood inside the circle of them. Danton
hated them. But she was the daughter of a Lord Protector, and he knew
the obligations that came with such a heritage. Here in this private place,
in this proxy circle of Spears, she might prick her finger and offer up a
drop of her blood to the Wrath of the gods, promising to maintain her
family's ancient contract with those who had saved mankind from utter
devastation. So did the blood of the First Age of Kings, running in her
veins, guarantee the prosperity of the Second Age. Danton understood
that. He might not believe in the legends behind the custom, but he
understood.

The thin bone pin was but an inch from her fingertip when she heard
a sound behind her. That was unusual, in this place. Guards rarely followed her here, finding the place eerie and discomforting, trusting to the
high walls and the King's land beyond to protect her. Even her own children found the place disquieting, and while they had come here when they
were young to attend her devotions, they rarely did so now, preferring to
wait until she had returned from her worship if they had need to speak
with her. Andovan alone had come here without prompting, as if recog-
nizing that the place was his as much as hers. She had often reflected upon
the fact that he alone truly understood his heritage, and its terrible burden. *You are of the blood of the Protectors,* she had said to him, stroking his

blond hair as he stood beside her in the Circle of the Wrath as a young boy, *and if the time comes when the world must be tested again, then so you shall be called to the task, and you must be ready to serve.*

Now he was gone. And her other sons—her strutting, proud peacock sons—gave no more than a token nod to northern tradition. She had no doubt that if the Wrath failed and the Souleaters returned to feed upon men, they would seal themselves in this keep with their father and send out commoners by the thousands to die in their name rather than risk their own blood in battle. So had the kings of the First Age done in their own time, the legends said, all but a precious few. And they had paid a terrible price for it.

The trees behind her rustled. She turned, the tattered silk of her gown's hem brushing at fallen needles. A man's figure moved from the shadows into the moonlight of the clearing, and as he stepped between the twisted spires and became fully visible she let out a small yelp of surprise and then rushed into his arms.

"Rhys! I had thought you had forgotten me—"

"Shhhhh. Quiet, little sister. You know that is nonsense."

She held him, trembling, and she wept a little. But they were tears of joy rather than pain and he knew them for such, and so he simply held her while they flowed. At last she moved back from him, drying her eyes with a sleeve on one side of her face, allowing him to brush away the tears from the other with his fingers. It was a freedom she would have allowed very few men.

"You came with a retinue?" she whispered.

He nodded. "Father wouldn't have it otherwise. I left them at Danton's table to eat themselves into oblivion."

She rubbed her reddened nose with a dampened sleeve. "How did I not know, then? I should have heard of your coming—"

"Unless Danton agreed to keep it a secret so I might surprise you." His pale brow furrowed as he studied her, seeing the signs of her pain. "You see? He is not so unfeeling. He understands that sometimes you need what he cannot give."

She hugged him again, hugged him long and hard, and perhaps wept a bit more. He just held her quietly and let the tears flow.

He was a tall man, a handsome man, with hair so pale that in the moonlight it seemed it might have been sculpted out of freshly fallen snow. It had been curly in his youth, like hers, but he wore it in the style of the Guardians of the Wrath now, tightly twisted into dozens of slender braids that hung down straight to his shoulders. Moonlight played upon the tokens of rank and fortitude that had been bound to the braids in front, making them glitter like captive snowflakes. His skin was pale, like hers, but his frame was stockier, his broad shoulders hinting at a much more formidable wench for brood-mother than the delicate lady who had borne Gwynofar. In truth Gwynofar knew Rhys' mother was no such thing, rather a mere slip of a girl who had caught the Lord Protector's eye one winter evening and kept him warm till the sun rose. But the gods had visited her with fertility that night and apparently meant to bless her bastard child as well, for he had won favor with the Lord Protector, indulgence from his lady, and friendship with the true-born daughter of their household, the golden-haired Gwynofar.

Now . . . now Rhys was anything but a child. Gwynofar held him at arm's length and studied him. Was it possible he had grown so much since she left, or did she just feel smaller in this foreign place? They were both much older than they had been when they had played in the woods together, making offerings to the wild pines as if the whole northern forest was their personal domain. He wore the uniform of a Guardian now, which spoke of some important promotion, but she didn't know enough about the various ranks and initiations of the secretive order to know how to read his advancement, or to interpret the various charms that glittered about his person. The scar that had been made when he first joined the Guardians was no longer red but a livid white, and it coursed diagonally across his cheek like the war paint of some Dark Ages barbarian, drawing attention to his high cheekbones and cool gray eyes.

You are of the blood of the First Kings, as I am, she thought. *You bear the same burden the Lord Protector does, at least in half. If the Wrath fails us, if the world is put to the test, you will stand on the battlefield beside the Protectors, while Danton and his children will shiver in their beds like frightened pups.*

No, your burden is even greater than ours . . . for my birth was contracted by kings, but yours was decreed by the gods themselves. They have some special purpose in store for you, my half-brother, and I pray for you nightly, for the whims of the northern gods are rarely gentle or pleasant things.

"You came here just to see me?" she asked.

"To see you, bring you news, bring back news of your welfare. Father won't admit it, but he's worried. He knows how you felt about Andovan." He picked at the tattered silk on her shoulder, biting his lip softly as he offered his own silent prayer to her mourning. "So what really happened?" he said at last. "No one is telling us anything of consequence. Least of all the High King's messenger. *We regret to inform you that Prince Andovan of House Aurelius, son of the High Queen Gwynofar, grandson of the Lord Protector Stevan of House Keirdwyn, is dead by his own hand. It is our custom in such cases not to hold a state funeral.* Hardly informative."

She sighed and wrapped her pale arms around herself, trying to make the words come without tears. "He had the Wasting. Danton did not want to admit it, but everyone knew. He even brought Magisters here to study him, to try to discover some other diagnosis." She shrugged stiffly. "But they could not, for there was no other cause. So . . . I have told you of his nature, Rhys. He hated sitting around and waiting for decisions to be made, he always hungered to be active, independent . . . it was eating him alive, to know he would die an invalid. So one night he decided he would not let that happen." She shivered and lowered her eyes; a tear trembled on the pale lashes. "He didn't even tell me," she whispered. "I'd have thought he would have. But maybe he was afraid I would try to talk him out of it."

"Would you have?" he asked softly.

She bit her lip for a moment. "I don't know, Rhys. What hope could I give him? The Wasting has no cure. It's a terrible death, especially for a youth who hated so much to have to sit still for anything. Still I would have . . . I would have thought he would want to talk to me first . . . I would have wanted to say good-bye, at least."

She turned away, toward the Spears. The night was silent.

"You didn't come with the mourners father sent," she whispered. "I'd hoped you would."

"I had duties."

She nodded, accepting that. As much as she would have valued Rhys' company when Andovan died, his standing as a royal bastard might have sent the wrong message had he been included in the formal Deathcall. Danton disdained his own bastards and did not want them having any illusions about royal inheritance, thus he did not encourage them to attend his court, as was done in some other places. If Rhys had come with the Lord Protector's official mourners Danton might have deemed it an insult.

A short time later, however, and by himself, to pay a social call upon his half-sister—that was acceptable. Danton was probably relieved that someone else was taking on the burden of comforting her. Gods knew he was no good at it.

"So tell me news of home," she begged. "Good news, please."

A shadow passed over his face. She felt her own heart skip a beat. "Rhys?"

For a long while he was silent. Finally he said, "The signs are ominous. I would be lying if I told you otherwise. I am sorry."

She straightened her back. She was a Protector's daughter, and must meet such trials with resolute strength. "Father hinted at such," she said quietly. "But he would not give me details." She put a hand on his arm. "I know I can trust you to be honest with me, yes?"

His eyes met hers. How deep they were, how dark in the moonlight, glittering like ice on the surface but shadowed with black secrets behind that. *He is truly a Guardian now,* she thought. She watched him as he struggled with himself over which secrets to keep and which to reveal, weighing his various obligations one against the other. That, more than anything else, told her how terribly wrong things were.

"What would you say," he asked finally, "if I told you I had touched a Spear?"

"I would say that if the Guardians deemed it necessary—"

"I don't mean with the Guardians." He placed his hands on her shoulders. "Alone, Gwyn. No Guardians to flank me, to lend me strength, no Magisters to steady my hand . . . nothing."

She drew in a sharp breath. "That is . . . that is . . . not possible."

"So we are taught," he said quietly.

"When was this?"

"Early this spring. I was near to the edge of the forbidden lands, returning home, trusting to my horse to keep to the proper path. Animals are even more sensitive than we are to the power of the gods; he would not have turned northward without a spear prodding his flanks. Or so I thought. But at one point I looked up, and there in the distance I saw a black spire outlined against the horizon. He had brought me that close to a Spear, that I could see its shape clearly." He paused, his expression grim. "Horses will not do that of their own volition, Gwyn. Not ever. They fear the Wrath even more than demons do, and we often have to leave them behind when we approach the Spears, lest they go mad from terror. But this time, the horse I rode did not even seem to be aware it was there . . . no more than he would be aware of any natural pinnacle of rock.

"That close to a Spear I should have been able to feel its presence, yet I could not. I should have been able to hear the screaming that emanates from the root of it, where the earth lies scarred from its terrible wound . . . I should have instinctively felt the urge to flee at any cost, and had to fight that urge with all my strength even to gaze upon the thing. But it was not so this time. So perhaps, I told myself, my first impression was mistaken. Perhaps this was not a Spear after all, but some natural monument in the same form. That was a simple explanation, and a far preferable one to my mind.

"I turned my horse toward this oddity of nature, determined to examine it. Yet as we came closer I began to feel what I had expected, the touch of the gods upon my spirit . . . only weaker than it usually was. Weaker than it should have been.

"I knew then such fear within my soul as I cannot describe to you. If this was a Spear in truth, why was it so weakened? I tried to urge my horse forward, to test it, but at that point he would go no farther. At last I had to leave him behind. Yet even so he was not so frantic as beasts normally are that close to the edge of the Wrath. It was an ill omen.

"As I came closer to the spire, picking my way across the earth, I could feel the Wrath envelop me at last. Ah, you do not know what it feels like, Gwyn, to be in such a state without sorcery to support you! The nearest I can describe it to you is that it is like standing in a terrible storm, where you must lean into the gale merely to keep your footing. For every step you take forward, the wind might drive you two back. So it was with the Wrath as I approached, for the power of the gods' fury by its very nature drives back all living creatures. Yet despite the terror in my heart I knew I had to go forward, to learn what details I could, that I might report them to my order."

Gwynofar nodded solemnly, captivated by his tale. In her youth she had strayed as close to the ancient spires as a simple maiden might, but the maleficent power of the Wrath had forced her to flee like a frightened deer from their proximity. Later, as daughter of a Lord Protector, she had been given a role to play in the annual sacrifice, and in the company of Magisters had come even closer to the monuments, but even sorcerous rituals were not enough to protect one from the gods' ancient magic entirely, and she remembered shivering to the core of her soul even then, wanting nothing more than to get the ritual finished so that she could go home.

To walk up to one of the ancient monuments by oneself, to *touch* one . . . that was a thing she could not even imagine doing.

Rhys continued. "Against that gale I forced my way to the foot of the spire itself. It was a vast and twisted thing that towered overhead as high as the turrets of father's keep. I kept expecting the gods to crush me like an insect for daring to come so close, but they did not. And at last, may they forgive me . . . I reached out and touched the cold stone surface." His voice dropped to a whisper; his eyes glittering like ice in the moonlight. "I *touched* it, Gwyn. And then suddenly I could hear all the voices that had been silent before: the screams of the earth god whose sacred flesh had been ripped open when the Spear first fell, the howls of all those men and beasts whom the Wrath had possessed down through the centuries, the roar of all the demons that had thrown themselves against that malevolent barrier, failing to break through . . . their screams poured into me like a black whirlwind when I touched the stone, and I fell to my knees, overwhelmed . . . and I think that had my hand not fallen from the spire at that moment, I would have been swallowed whole by that terrible screaming, and never returned to you."

She saw him shudder in the moonlight. It was an uncharacteristic gesture for him, and as such it sent a chill through her heart.

"But Guardians do touch the Spears at other times," she said softly. "Do they not?"

"Aye, when they need repair, when wind and ice have threatened to crack their surface, then we must mortar them freshly, and seal them against winter's ire . . . but the men who do that are of the blood of the Protectors, whom the gods have fortified for just that purpose, and they do not go alone. I am only that on my father's side . . . barely enough to approach it in their company."

He touched a hand to the underside of her chin, gently. "You, sweet queen, possess what this humble bastard lacks. You could face the Wrath directly and not back down, if you needed to."

She shuddered. "Don't even suggest that."

"Why? The time may soon come. If it does, all those who bear the Protectors' gift must play their part in defending the world, else we may witness the Second Age of Kings fall to madness and barbarism, as the First Age did."

"Do you believe that?" Her voice was a whisper. "Do you say these things to frighten me, or do you honestly believe that the Wrath is about to fail us?"

"Gods willing it will stand strong forever," he responded solemnly. "Riders have been sent out to inspect the other Spears and find out what the situation is; it will be months before we have the larger picture. Be grateful the summer is upon us now, at least, so that such travel is possible. In the meantime I am a Guardian, and must be prepared for the worst. As you must, being of the Lord Protector's blood."

Perhaps sensing that the moment had become too intense—perhaps regretting he had brought such thoughts to one in mourning—he glanced back toward the keep. "So tell me of other news. Danton is vile-tempered as usual? Rurick still a strutting ass?"

Despite herself she smiled. "Choose your words carefully. Rurick will be High King someday."

"Aye. Gods help us all." He ran a hand through his braids, which set a few of the tokens bound in it to tinkling. "What of your Magister Royal? I take it someone new has replaced Ramirus? He has not shown his face since I arrived."

Her expression tightened. It was a reflexive reaction, beyond her control, like the instinctive hissing of a cat. "Kostas." She nearly spat the name. "Gods curse the day that vile creature came into our house."

He glanced back at the keep again. "Are you not worried—"

"He never comes here. He disdains these" —she indicated the spires— "and the *northern superstition* they represent. Indeed, sometimes I come here just to escape him. He has left his mark all over the keep like wolf piss. Sometimes I feel like I should bathe just to get out the stink."

Rhys blinked in surprise. "I've never heard you speak like that of a man before. What has he done to earn such venom?"

Her eyes flashed angrily. "Taken all that is worst in my husband and encouraged it to new excess. Ramirus was a temperate man, a fit counselor for a High King. Kostas is a snake. No. Worse than a snake. He is a pestilence, an infection. Ten minutes in his presence and Danton is raging like a bull in season, desperate for some enemy to gore, or else perhaps a rival to mount. Ramirus knew how to calm him. Kostas . . . Kostas does not even try. He seems to take pleasure in Danton's rage."

Quietly Rhys said, "Is that all?"

Startled, she asked, "What do you mean?"

His eyes glittered darkly in the moonlight. "We have known each other a very long time, Gwyn. Granted we do not see each other often these days, your duties and mine being what they are, but I think I know you well enough to know when things are not right. Even the reasons you offer me do not match the hatred I sense in your heart. There is another cause beside these things, clearly." When she did not answer him he prompted gently, "Is there not?"

With a sigh she turned away from him; her pale hand reached out to rest upon the surface of the nearest spire, as if she might draw strength from the gods through such contact. "I do not know," she said at last. "With any other man I could capture his essence in words and be content. But Kostas—my feelings about him defy the bounds of language, my brother. It is . . . it is a sensation almost animal in tenor, that comes upon me when I am in his presence. Like the deer mouse must feel when the shadow of a hawk passes over it. I want to run, or I want to strike at him, to see his blood flow . . . I want to do *something* other than pass courtly pleasantries and pretend nothing is wrong when everything in my soul cries out to drive him from my castle, away from my home and my family, at any cost . . ."

She stared off into the darkness for a moment. "Sometimes I have dreams," she whispered, "in which I come to him while he sleeps and slit his throat. Or I stab him in the heart, so that his blood spurts out across my hands . . . and it is ecstacy. In those dreams he is not a Magister at all, but something . . . something else, that I cannot give a name to. Something that I know must be destroyed at any cost.

"When I awaken from those dreams that feeling remains with me for a time. I must struggle to hide it from him, and yet . . . yet . . . he *is* a Magister, beyond question. He serves my husband as dutifully as Ramirus ever did. And if he is cruel at times, if he manipulates Danton's darker instincts for some private purpose, or even just for his own amusement . . . that is what men become when they live centuries beyond their natural lifespan. I have met enough Magisters in my days as queen to know that. And I accept it, as must all royals who rely upon their sorcery." She wrapped her arms around herself and shivered. "Why is this one different, Rhys? Why can I not accept him as I did all the others?"

Gently he came up behind her and put his hands on her shoulders. When he saw she did not pull away he drew her gently to him, until she rested her head against his chest. "You bear the blood of the Protectors in your veins," he said softly. "There is a magic in that we do not understand, save that we know it was given to us by the gods to protect us. Trust in it to guide you."

"They think we are ignorant savages, you know." Her voice was fierce with bitterness. "They will never say it to my face, not even Danton, but I can hear it in their silence. Superstitious savages with strange blood rites who worship rocks and talk to trees, like the men of the Dark Ages did. Danton would never have asked for my hand if had he not feared that the Lord Protectors would look askance at his northern ambitions . . . this marriage bought him a border treaty that lets him swallow up other nations at his whim, provided he leaves the Protectorates alone." She sniffed. "Apparently he did not mind wedding a *barbarian* for that."

"It is the fate of royalty to be bartered for treaties," he said quietly. "Especially the daughters of royalty. You know that."

She shivered against him as if she were cold; he wrapped his arms around her. "I know," she replied.

He kissed her gently on the top of her head and sighed. "Ah, Gwyn. I wish I could stay with you longer than a few days. You need to be with your own people for a time . . . more than even I guessed. But I cannot."

Silently she nodded. "I understand. I have my duty as Protector to be sold into foreign lands, to safeguard my father's domain . . . you have a duty to see that the Wrath never wavers." She sighed. "Had you not told me that tale before I might beg you to reconsider . . . but with that in mind I cannot."

"We are both creatures of duty, yes?" Gently he released her. "Not a thing I expect a 'civilized' king to understand."

Despite herself she smiled faintly, sadly.

"I will ask Father if he can send you more servants from home," he told her. "You need the comfort of your own language, and to be surrounded by those who do not need to be taught your customs. Servants whose silence is only silence."

"I would not ask that of him, Rhys."

"I know, little sister. You are far too proud . . . and far too stubborn. That is why I will ask him for you."

He knelt down in the moist bed of pine needles that covered the ground and picked out a slender white object from among them, where she had dropped it. It was made of bone and carved with figures in an ancient style, of creatures whose names had long ago been forgotten. "You were going to make offering."

"Yes."

He handed the pin back to her. "So tell me then. Will the gods accept the sacrifice of a halfbreed?"

She put her hand over his and gazed into his eyes. They no longer seemed dark but comforting, familiar. "The gods will welcome the offering of a Guardian," she told him gently. "And I that of a brother."

In the light of two moons, in the circle of House Kierdwyn's ancestors, they offered up a drop of blood to each of the stone spires in turn, and prayed that the world would not be destroyed a second time.

Chapter 16

"YOU ARE the witch from the tavern?"

Startled, Kamala turned around. She half expected it to be some sort of local authority addressing her, backed by members of the guard perhaps, and as she turned she braced herself to let loose such power as was necessary to keep them at bay, but it was only a single man, and one not even carrying weapons. She blinked, surprised, but no guards appeared. Nor was there anywhere nearby for them to stage an effective ambush.

"Who are you?" she demanded. "And why do you ask me this?"

Truth be told, he looked less than happy about being there, in one of the worst neighborhoods of the Quarter, and he glanced back over his shoulder repeatedly as he spoke to her, as if expecting an army of thieves and whores might descend upon him at any moment. When his woolen cloak parted once Kamala could see flashes of fine silk clothing, but he quickly grabbed the edges of the cloak and wrapped it tightly about himself, denying her any more insight. No doubt that was the reason there were beads of sweat running down his face; it was a warm day to be wearing such a wintry wrap.

"My master sent me to search you out. He said . . ." He hesitated. "He said, 'look for a tall girl dressed like a boy, with hair as red as the Hunter's Moon, for that is how they have described her, who were at the place.'"

"Who is your master?" she demanded. "And what makes him think this is a witch he describes?"

He pulled at the neck of his woolen cloak, allowing the sweat to trickle down inside the collar, and glanced back down the narrow street once again. "It is said by those who were there at the time that this woman stood single-handed against a gang of ruffians and killed them all, and must either therefore have witchery of her own, or have as a patron someone of power."

Kamala cursed inwardly. She had hoped no one would put two and two together after her little adventure, but that was apparently too much to ask. It was her own fault. She should have stayed behind to watch the aftermath of her battle, to take what steps were necessary to guard her anonymity, but all she had wanted then was to put as much distance between her and the slaughter as possible. Now she was paying the price for that choice.

This meant she would have to leave the city soon. Not because she feared what the local elite would do if they found her—they rarely gave a damn what happened in the Quarter or muddied their silk shoes trying to fix things—but simply because this was not the way she had wanted to begin her new life.

Of course, she thought to herself, *you could just wear women's clothing for a while. No one would recognize you then.*

He was still there, silently waiting. The servant of a nobleman, waiting on her. The thought was oddly pleasing.

"You did not answer my first question," she pointed out.

"Of course." He glanced back over his shoulder once more—there was still no one closing in on him from behind—then bowed to her. How odd it felt, to receive such a gesture as if she were some highborn lady! "My master is Pahdman Ravi. No doubt you have heard his name." He waited for an answer. She blinked and said nothing. "He wishes me to extend his hand in greeting to the lady of power, who has helped clean the streets of his city of some of its more bothersome vermin, and to suggest to her that he may have business that would be of interest to her, if she would do him the honor of attending upon him to hear it."

She had never heard the name of Ravi, but she could guess what it was associated with. Likely it was one of the many ambitious merchant houses that swarmed about the political heart of the city like flies on fresh dung. Many such houses owned property in the Quarter, and periodically a name would arise suddenly like foul gas from a swamp when some brothel collapsed beneath its own weight, or when a building project ill-suited to time and tide blocked the waters that drained the city of refuse, turning the summer air into a thick soup of rotting garbage.

She bound enough soulfire to determine that there was no malicious intent inherent in the invitation. That *this* man knew about, anyway. His master was another matter.

"What does he want with me?" she demanded.

He bowed slightly. "I am not privy to that, my lady." There was ever so slight a hesitation before he spoke the title, as if the word was sour on his tongue; it pleased her in a darkly perverse way that a creature more accustomed to stone-paved roads and silk hangings had been ordered to address her thus. "Perhaps if you will accept my master's invitation, he will explain it to you himself."

She bit her lip and considered. All her childhood instincts warned her against trusting such an invitation. Ravi might be impressed by her power but he still regarded her as vermin. Class distinctions did not disappear just because one had power, though a subtle man might dance around them carefully if it suited his purpose.

Then the truth struck her.

He does not know what you truly are. He has no clue as to your origins. You are a clean slate, a cipher, and he will know of you only what you allow him to know.

She glanced down instinctively at her hands and noticed how clean they were. It had been a long time since the ingrained dirt of the Quarter had stained her pores and marked every crease in her flesh; Ethanus had seen to that. How many other signs of peasant birth and harsh use were no longer apparent? What would a wellborn man who had no more information than the ambiguous *she killed some men in the Quarter* think of her?

It was a heady thought.

She remembered the moments right before her fight. The frightening discovery that though soulfire was nearly unlimited in its potential, it still took time and concentration to use, and that that could mean vulnerability. She also remembered the warnings Ethanus had given her, especially about Transition: *When your current consort dies you will be helpless, as you must concentrate upon seeking another. That state lasts only a moment, but if you are in the presence of enemies at the time, a moment can be enough.* Being a Magister might help keep her safe, but it was not proof against all possible threats.

But.

She also remembered the feel of the power coursing through her, so awesome in its rage that no man could bridle it. Like some vast creature bellowing its fury from inside her soul, so magnificent and powerful that it made her giddy. It made her hungry. It made her want to test herself against the world.

What have you to fear from this Ravi? He does not know what you truly are, so he can hardly set a trap for you.

The servant was waiting. He would wait all afternoon if she so decided. So had he been ordered, clearly.

That was what decided her.

"Lead the way," she told him, in her most imperious voice. "I will meet your master."

———

She had never been to the Hill before, save for one brief journey by her mother's side, when the woman had sought a better price for her daughter's virginity than the small town of their birth could afford. Even at that young age Kamala had been acutely aware of how out of place they were there, how vast and impenetrable the cultural barrier was that divided peasant from gentry, and how clear it was to everyone on the other side of that divide that she and her mother had not crossed it. She could see the scorn in men's faces as they passed by, the disgust with which they acknowledged her mother's offer of peasant flesh to serve their pleasure, as if she was serving them food at a feast and had offered them a plate of rotten meat.

She remembered trembling all that day, in fear and shame, until her mother had declared the day a failure and brought her back to their ramshackle home in the Quarter. At which point Kamala had fled to a secret place beneath one of the wooden walkways, a dank cubbyhole suspended above the brackish tide where only a child might fit, and stayed there until hunger finally forced her to return to the world at large.

Later her most precious commodity had been sold to a dark-skinned tourist from the southern kingdoms whose skin was redolent of musk and sweat and who considered every natural orifice of a young girl fair game for his pleasure. It could have been worse. She knew of young girls so debased in their breaking that they drowned themselves rather than live with the shame of it. Though she sometimes wondered if their experiences had really been so much worse than hers, or if the girls were simply not as strong as she had been, did not cling to life with the same fiery passion, willing to do whatever it took to stay alive, knowing that *tomorrow* could not be better if one failed to survive *today*.

No man would ever touch her like that again.

No man or woman would ever profit again from the sale of her dignity.

May hell claim anyone who thought otherwise.

The streets of the Hill were paved in stone, not out of necessity—unlike the rest of Gansang it stood high above the water table—but to distinguish it from the muddy roads and mildewed wooden walkways of the poorer districts. The very air Kamala breathed seemed to be cleaner here. Drier. Overhead she saw towers soaring into the sky, expanding upward rather than outward, making the most of that small bit of prized real estate. Slender bridges joined them one to another so that a nobleman might visit neighbors without ever setting foot upon the earth; silken curtains fluttered in hundreds of windows like brightly colored birds. The lowest levels of the towers had been given over to merchants, and their wares filled shop after shop with jewelry, fine leather tack, polished knives, and bolts of silk as sheer as a spider's web. Kamala wanted more than anything to stop and look at everything, to run her fingers over the treasures of the rich and powerful, to drink them in with all her senses, but the servant would not pause for such indulgences. To him this display was commonplace, merely one more thing to hurry past on his way to more important affairs, and if she paid it more than a passing bit of attention she would be revealing more than she should about her origins.

You can have any of this that you want, for a bit of power. Pay for it with false coin or simply take it, as you please. Later, at your leisure.

He brought her to a gray stone tower with a crest engraved on the heavy

oaken door. Servants opened it from the inside before her guide even
knocked. They seemed to know who Kamala was—or at least they knew
that some sort of important guest was due—for they ushered her past with
lowered eyes, in which she almost did not see the passing glance of disapproval for her weathered attire.

It was clean inside. Very clean. You could not keep a house this clean in
the Quarter no matter how hard you tried; the mildew alone would defeat
you. The stone walls had been painted an unblemished white and the windows along the stairwell were large, inviting in the sunlight. Noting the
lack of dust anywhere, hearing the flurry of servants behind her as they
rushed to sweep up the dirt she had left on their stairs before their master
noticed it, she guessed he was likely a cruel man whose servants lived in
fear that the slightest speck of dirt would displease him. Or perhaps he
was the sort of man so unnerved by disorder that he must exert total control over every aspect of his environment. Or perhaps both.

He was waiting for her in a room that was bigger than the entire house
she had been born in. Most of the space was empty, wasted, with a single
ornate table with finely carved chairs set by the fireplace at the far end. He
nodded as she entered, acknowledging her presence with requisite politeness but no particular humility. Overhead . . . overhead there were murals
of the most extraordinary design, covering the top third of every wall. In
each was depicted some scene out of mythic history—the birth of the
Huntress in one, the destruction of the Souleaters in another, the found-
ing of Gansang in a third—with eerily lifelike figures the size of living
men. Yet it was not that which made the display so remarkable. It was the
man who stood before her, who was depicted in each and every mural, not
as a participant in the scene but rather as a tourist passing through it. His
painted image seemed to show little interest in the events depicted, but
rather looked outward toward the viewer in the manner of formal portrai-
ture, turning the most dramatic events of human history into no more
than a backdrop for his presence. Goddesses were born, Souleaters lived
and died, but the eye was drawn to him.

It was the most astonishing—and expensive—display of human ego she
had ever seen.

So this is what men do with money when they are not wasting it on whores.
The man whose face was so meticulously reproduced above them was

perhaps thirty years of age, and his clothing betrayed the same meticulous attention to detail that she had noted in the maintenance of his abode. The layers of heavy silks that he wore and the gold rings which adorned both hands made it clear he had money and wanted others to know it. His long robe was embroidered with some sort of heraldic motif—likely a family device, she thought—and was clasped loosely below his waist with a belt of figured gold and rubies. He was not a bad-looking man, overall, though the long curls of his black hair looked like they came from a hot iron rather than nature and his carefully plucked eyebrows were a tad effeminate for her taste. But she was hardly one to criticize such things, with her own close-cropped locks and boy's attire.

They took each other's measure for a long silent moment, and she could see one plucked brow arch a bit as he took note of the dust that clung to her boots. No doubt he was concerned that she might spread some of it about his whitewashed home if she moved. *Well,* she thought dryly, *that is what happens when you summon someone fresh from a brawl in the Quarter. Take it or leave it.* With a long stride she crossed the room toward him, not a little amused that as she did so she probably left a wake of dust stirring behind her. Serendipity.

"I am Pahdman Ravi," he said. This close to him she could smell his perfume, a faintly cloying sweetness, like that of sugared fruits. "Welcome to my house."

She met his gaze with brazen frankness. "You don't even know my name, do you?"

One corner of his mouth twitched slightly. It might have been a smile. "You did not give it when you arrived. Not that my men could discover." He reached back behind him and pulled a braided cord that hung upon the wall; its upper end disappeared into a hole leading somewhere else.

"You can call me Sidra." She said it in a tone that implied there was more to her name than that, but she wasn't yet ready to share it all. It seemed appropriately pretentious.

"Very well." A servant appeared, replete with a tray holding two silver goblets and a decanter to match. He brought it to them and set it on the table, then backed, bowing, from the room. Ravi did not acknowledge his presence in any way, but when the servant was gone he uncapped the decanter, poured an inch of something thick and syrupy into each goblet, and gestured again for her to take a seat at the table. "From the vineyards of Seraat. Sidra." He raised his cup to her. "To your . . . power."

Her eyes fixed upon him, she sipped the offering. It tasted as syrupy as it looked and coated the tongue like the aftermath of a hangover. With a whisper of effort she applied enough soulfire to change it into something more palatable. Her eyes never left his. Her faint smile never left her lips.

You had the test all wrong, Ethanus. It is when you can steal someone's life merely to improve a cup of wine that you know you are truly a Magister.

"Your servant said you wished to speak to me."

"Yes. Please, make yourself comfortable." He gestured toward the chairs again; after a moment she lowered herself onto one of them. He sat opposite her, set his goblet on the table, then steepled his fingers thoughtfully, as if musing over exactly what to say. It was a bit too studied a move to read true; she guessed that he had rehearsed these words in private many, many times.

"I heard of your fight in the Quarter," he said finally. "Impressive use of power, that."

She shrugged, but said nothing.

"Witches rarely indulge their power thus."

"Witches don't like to be raped," she said curtly.

Ravi chuckled his amusement at the image. Kamala felt a knot of distaste rising in the back of her throat, and fought it down with effort. *Don't underestimate this man*, she warned herself. *The fact that he looks and acts like a strutting peacock may simply mask the heart of a wolf . . .*

. . . or more likely a vulture.

"And yet," he said, "there are many witches who would submit to such an assault rather than waste a precious portion of their life essence. Am I wrong?"

An easy denial rose to her lips . . . and died there. Was he right? Did the most powerful women in the world lie down in the mud and permit themselves to be used like whores because by defending themselves they would hasten their own deaths? The thought was sickening. And yet probably true. She knew that in the core of her soul even as Ravi spoke the words.

I would rather die than live like that, she thought. And she looked up at Ravi and for a brief moment saw the intelligence that glimmered behind his painted eyes. *He knows that.*

"Go on," she said quietly.

He leaned forward on the table. "You have so much power, so much potential, you can do things most men do not even dream of . . . yet you are shackled by necessity, unable to shape the world like the Magisters do because of the cost, unable to alter your own fate except in tiny fragments. It's never enough for you, I am guessing. Never as much as you would like." He leaned back again, his hands folding before him; his sharp eyes never left hers. "Am I wrong?"

"You do not know who I am." She said it quietly. "Or what I truly want."

"Perhaps." He did not seem disturbed by her chill response, but took up his goblet and sipped from its contents as casually as if he were sharing an amiable dinner drink with an old friend. This was also a well-rehearsed move, she sensed. "Let me tell you then what I would offer to another woman who had your power, but perhaps wanted . . . different things. I would say to her, come into my service, and I shall give you all the things you dare not conjure for yourself. I will clothe you in silks and adorn you in jewels, and set before you all manner of delicacy in food, wine . . . even bring you men, women, boys, as you please, to serve your pleasure. Speak of a desire and my house shall do its best to provide it. Whisper a need and all my staff shall come running to attend upon you."

She raised an eyebrow. "And in return?"

"In return?" He shrugged. "Only such small services as might be needed now and then by a businessman such as myself. The turning of a mind. The easing of a contract. The cultivating of favor where mere diplomacy could not manage it . . . or perhaps an occasional error in a rival camp, if that is required."

She drew in a breath very slowly, very carefully. Words and emotions were a wild storm within her; she had to pick her way through them carefully to find the proper path. "You understand the power that fuels witchery is one's own life."

"I understand that spells have a cost, yes. I would not offer to pay you so well for them if it were otherwise." He leaned back across the table again, intending the motion to seem relaxed, but the hunger in his eyes was undisguised. "Give me those few minutes' worth of service, and I will make of all the rest of your life a thing other women will envy. Or if that does not tempt you, then state your price. I will meet it, and more."

He was offering her a Magister's contract, but he could not possibly know she was a Magister. All he knew was that as a witch she was free with her power, seemingly unconcerned with the ultimate cost of wielding that magic. Willing to die young if that meant she might indulge herself now.

It was an assessment so opposed to what Kamala truly was, so totally and absolutely wrong, that for a moment it left her speechless.

"You are so sure I have a price," she said at last.

The answer was in his eyes; he did not have to voice it. A merchant's answer: *Every man has a price.*

Wordlessly she rose and turned away from the table. She did not want him to see her expression right now. The indignation, the disgust, burned too hotly in her to be disguised . . . but would he even recognize those emotions if he saw them? Would he understand the cause? In his mind he had done nothing wrong. He was just playing the same game that the rich and powerful had always played with the lower classes. Money could buy anything, including human life. Why not apply it in this case?

"You would make me your whore," she muttered.

There was a moment's silence. Perhaps he heard the razor-sharp edge in her voice and took warning from it. That was a good thing. It would take but a moment's effort for her to release all that anger inside her in a blazing firestorm of sorcery, and she was sorely tempted to do so. Yes, he was only one fool among many—there were a million others like him in the world—but oh, how sweet it would be to give this one painted peacock the fate he deserved! She would let him know in his final moments just who and what he had insulted, and see the horror of it in his eyes as he struggled for his last breath.

With effort she shut her eyes, took a deep breath, and forced the impulse to subside. *You did not tell me, Ethanus, that the hardest part of my struggle to control the power would be learning to control myself.*

As insulting as Ravi's offer was, it was also tempting. That was the distasteful truth of it. Not for the reasons the merchant had given her, or any reason he would understand. But she had realized after the fight in the Quarter that she was not yet ready to wander the world on her own. Her power was too wild and untested, and her soul . . . her soul did not yet know what it wanted. And now, in Ravi's presence, she was acutely aware of the great divide between his class and hers, and the fact that it would take more than sorcery to cross it. She needed practice. She needed cover. This peacock could provide her with both.

And then there were the Magisters. Some would be in Gansang, serving the powerful nobles of this prosperous city as they served princes and kings in other places. Ravi was clearly no more than a petty merchant in their eyes, not rich enough or important enough to merit a sorcerous attendant—else why would he be courting witches?—but he was an ambitious man, and that meant he would be moving in the circles where the black-robed sorcerers held sway. A cold fluttering filled her heart at the thought of them. As one of Ravi's people she could meet other Magisters without having to reveal what she was. She could take their measure first, learn their ways, plan out the moment of revelation . . . what other arrangement could offer her that?

Slowly she turned back to face Ravi. Her expression was cold, offering no hint of the emotions roiling inside her. She would never let him have any true insight into her, or anything else he might use as a tool for manipulation.

"You will give me whatever I ask for," she said, "without question, and without limit. You will introduce me into your society as you would one of your own blood. Your servants will attend me accordingly, and teach me anything I need to know. Yet none shall know what I am to you, save that I am a lady honored by your favor." Her green eyes glittered. "Women shall envy me your generosity, men shall wonder at it, but none shall know its cause."

"And in return?" he asked. The hunger in his voice was undisguised now.

"In return . . ." She smiled coldly. "You may request of me whatever service you like. I will measure your need against the cost, and decide if I wish to assist you. If so, you shall have what you ask for. If not . . ." She shrugged. "You are free to end our contract whenever you wish."

You would make me a whore, she thought, *but you do not understand what a whore really is. There is power in having something a man wants and making him pay for it. There is power in knowing you can cast his coin in the dirt if it pleases you, that coin which he thought could buy him anything.*

He stared at her for a long moment in silence. She could have used her power to learn what his thoughts were, but there was no reason to drain her consort just for that. She could guess well enough.

I am the only one who can give you what you want. You will pay my price or go hungry.

"Very well," he said at last. His tone made it clear that he was not pleased by her conditions, but he nodded. "It will be as you describe."

And he pulled the tasseled rope again, that his servants might come and be introduced to their new mistress.

Chapter 17

HIS BROTHERS could not have survived this journey, Andovan thought.

Rurick, of course, would never have set foot outside the palace without a host of retainers to attend him. Part of that was the rightful caution of any royal heir—enemies would have much to gain by taking Danton's firstborn prisoner—but really, it had more had to do with Rurick's perpetual need to be admired. While Andovan hated being fussed over by servants (he insisted anew each morning that he really could dress himself), Rurick would not so much as roll up his hose without a cadre of servants to prepare for the act, assist with its execution, and then comment upon its excellence. Left alone in the woods, as Andovan was now, he would probably drive himself mad trying to get the squirrels to sing his praises.

Salvator was a different story. The High King's second son was already mad, some claimed, and one could tell by the way the court doted upon Rurick that they desperately hoped he would inherit Danton's empire, not because he was worthy of it but because the alternative was much more unsettling. Salvator claimed he could hear the voices of the gods speaking to him, and some years ago had entered a monastery to discover how to hear them better. Danton wasn't happy about that, but didn't go so far as to forbid it. There really was no precedent for refusing a royal prince the right to worship whatever god he chose, and even though Salvator had chosen some obscure deity that was focused upon the sins and failings of mankind rather than its passions or conquests, that really didn't matter. Rurick was hale and hearty and already had a son on the way; it was unlikely Andovan's priestly brother would ever be called to the throne.

Salvator would not do well in the wilderness either, being accustomed to food appearing on his plate at the monastary table rather than having to hunt it down himself. But at least he was practiced in fasting. And he would not be so alone here as Rurick was; after all, he had his strange gods to talk to. No doubt they would have an excellent discourse upon how Salvator's own failings had brought him to such a pass. Andovan shook his head in amazement. He was used to his mother's gods, as cold as the land they inhabited, whose eyes were fixed upon battles and bloodshed and whose conflicts affected the fate of the mortal world. He found it very hard to respect a god who spent his time tallying up the personal faults of each worshipper. It seemed somehow petty.

Valemar would not be completely helpless out here, Andovan thought. The youngest of Danton's sons had even gone hunting with him a few times, though he nearly suffered a stroke when Andovan suggested they leave the retainers behind and go off on their own. He was something of a ladies' man, which had more to do with his skill at seduction and his charisma than any physical advantage; like all of Andovan's brothers he took after their father in appearance, and his harsh, eaglelike features were ill designed for seducing fair maidens. But power and station were equally seductive to women as looks, and Valemar was a master at playing those qualities to his advantage.

Valemar was continually surrounded by retainers not simply out of royal custom, but out of Danton's belief that someday he would wind up in the wrong bed and disaster would come of it. Thus it was that even in his most secretive trysts there were servants somewhere in attendance . . . though not always where the subject of his attentions would notice them. If left alone in the woods tomorrow, with neither maiden to court nor watchdogs to attend him, he would probably be so disconcerted he would not know which foot to put forward first.

Not so with Andovan. He had always preferred solitude, and the woods were his favorite venue. To ride through the shadows of an ancient forest and suddenly come upon a deer feeding that had never learned the fear of man . . . that was a pleasure to him as great as any which Danton's court had to offer. Once Rurick's wife had announced her pregnancy and Ramirus had confirmed that the child-to-be was male, the High King had finally, reluctantly, accepted Andovan's antisocial proclivities and allowed him to venture out into the royal grounds without a flock of retainers guarding his every step. But only into those bounded woods where commoners would not venture. He would never have allowed Andovan the freedom he had now, to do anything, to wander anywhere, without a phalanx of servants to guard him . . . a freedom that was as intoxicating as it was unfamiliar.

If only he were not dying, he might have enjoyed it.

He had left the crowded cities and shadowy woodlands of the eastern kingdoms behind and headed, for the rolling green farmlands and open plains of the Great Plateau. Here, where trees were scarce, villages were few and far apart and were generally constructed from the earth itself, like some organic being. The people were generally hospitable—unlike the eastern farmers, who tended to attack strangers first and ask questions later—and he spent more than one night trading gossip for a night's bed, or offering his advice on how best to break the wild horses of the region to a bridle.

At night a jeweled sky stretched out from horizon to horizon above the grasslands, and one could almost believe that it went on forever, rather than ending, as the scholars taught, in the Sphere of the Heavens. The sight of it was strangely humbling. Andovan knew that his mother's people had come of age in a similar—though far colder—landscape and worshipped their strange, violent gods beneath the same glittering skies. Indeed, in a place such as this the northern gods were said to have blessed her bloodline—Andovan's bloodline—above all others, granting them secret powers for the day when their efforts would be necessary to save the world.

But it was hard to feel like a savior of worlds with the Wasting sapping his strength. Hard to focus upon any earthly pleasure when he could feel Death breathing down his neck. And so he pressed on, westward, following in the wake of the murky dreams that seemed to be guiding him.

What was the spell that Colivar had placed on him? How was it supposed to work? The Magister had not given him details, merely said it would "sensitize" him to his killer. What did that mean? How was the woman connected to him in the first place? Would he even know her when he saw her? These questions and others plagued him during the long hours when he was alone. He wished Colivar were there to advise him, and at the same time, knew he should not trust the southern Magister. The man was his father's enemy, after all, and Andovan would never have turned to him for help in the first place had he not believed that any other Magister would have told Danton what he intended. Only Colivar could be trusted to keep his silence.

Yet he had seen the hungry spark in the Magister's eyes when he had broached his plans, and he knew with certain instinct—the sixth sense of royalty—that Colivar wanted to know who this woman was as much as he did. Which meant that, for his own selfish reasons, Colivar would serve him faithfully in this. That was how Magisters worked.

Or so Danton had taught him.

At night he dreamed dark dreams, sometimes terrifying dreams, filled with demons who tore the living flesh from his body to feast upon, succubi who drained all the strength of his manhood, and worse. He awoke from those nightmares in a cold sweat, trembling. Part of him wished the dreams would stop, but another part of him, desperate for answers, clung to them even after waking, turning every detail over in his mind like a child turning over stones at the beach, looking for tiny creatures scuttling beneath. Yet there was no meaning he could find in them, beyond a simple expression of his fears. Certainly no clues that would help him find the source of his illness, if such a person existed.

Open grasslands gave way to badlands, whose maze of twisting ravines marked the westernmost border of Danton's territory. He had to hire a guide to get him through, a local who knew which routes would not circle back on themselves or terminate in a dead end at the brink of some serpentine canyon. The traveling was hard and his horse was tired and it was not until they reached the other side and his guide left him, that Andovan realized exactly where he was.

Mountains reared skyward to the west of him, glowing an eerie red in the late afternoon sunlight. This was the Blood Ridge, supposedly named for the red maples that covered its lower flanks, lending the whole range a crimson cast. At least that was what Andovan had been taught back home. But out here the locals assured him the name came from something else entirely, and commemorated the brutality of Danton's troops when they first entered the region. It was a border marked in blood, they said, and the gods had turned the trees themselves red so that the children of those the High King murdered would never forget.

If they had realized that Andovan was of Danton's line they would probably have added his blood to the mix.

Now, standing in the shade of a vast maple whose leaves were like dark red hands grasping at the sunlight, he felt a sense of mixed exhaustion and awe. This was the end of his father's territory, the gateway to lands beyond. Which meant that the woman he sought was in a place where the Aurelius line had no authority. Was she perhaps some distant enemy of his father's House, working ill upon Danton's line? He could think of no other reason for a person so far away to have given him this disease. If that was indeed what had happened.

If my dreams are true, she is out there. I will find her.

A large hawk circled overhead as he made his camp, its brown wings gleaming in the dying sunlight. By the time Andovan had seen to his horse's needs and his own and then settled down to sleep, it had flown away.

That night he dreamed of his quarry.

Dark, the streets are so dark; the narrow towers press close, crowding out the sunlight. On the streets below them a beggar boy crouches, his pale skin crusted over with half-healed scars from some past plague, his eyes bloodshot and hungry. Beside him a woman stands, gaunt and desperate, begging the nobles who pass by for the spare change in their purses, crying out that she has a virgin daughter of pleasing aspect, if lust moves them more than pity. Then the image fades and the street is clean and the woman was never there at all, save perhaps in his dreams.

Overhead a single tower looms, a surreal structure devoid of any doors or windows, save at the topmost level. Near to it a dozen lesser towers stretch their necks upward like ducklings attending their mother, curtains fluttering like ag-

itated wings. The breeze coming from the west is a foul thing, redolent of rotting fish and algae, the noxious vapors of a stagnant swamp. It seems out of place in the dry and pristine streets.

Amid the towers a woman walks, and he knows it is his quarry as soon as she appears. He tries to cry out, to get her to turn toward him, so he can see her face and learn her name, but the weakness within him is suddenly too great, the words die in his throat, and he falls gasping to the cobblestoned street.

Now, now, she is turning toward him at last, and he looks up at her. Why? *he demands of her silently, unable to draw in enough breath to form the words. But his vision is fading, the Wasting is claiming him, and everything goes black just before he can see her face . . .*

———

He awoke shivering, his body drenched with cold sweat. For a moment he felt as weak as he had been in his dream, and panic overcame him. He struggled to his feet, needing to prove to himself that the dream had not truly sapped the last of his strength. When he managed to get himself upright with no greater difficulty than the night before the wild beating of his heart began to slow a bit, and he managed a few long, measured breaths, trying to steady his spirit.

It was a dream, Andovan. Worse than some others, but likely not the last nightmare you will have on this journey. Are you so weak of heart that mere dreams can unman you now?

Did she know he was searching for her? The dream would imply so, but he was reluctant to read that much meaning into it. Nightmares were more often the simple product of a sleeper's own fears than any prophetic vision, and this one was certainly cast in that mold.

But the towers . . . how strange they were, all clustered together . . . surely they had some meaning. What was the significance of the tower without doors? Why was the smell of a swamp so pervasive? And who was the beggar woman who so clearly did not belong in that place, that disappeared when he looked at her?

He wracked his brain and came up with nothing, and finally, with a sigh, broke off a piece of cheese from his supply and ate it, letting the sharp flavor drive the remembered taste of swamp muck from his mouth.

And then he remembered.

Gansang.

It was built in the marshes of the western delta, on walkways and stilts set over what had once been thriving wetlands. Shoreside it was said there was one section where the bedrock was solid, and it rose in a crest above sea level just far enough to escape the flood plain. The nobles lived there, of course. Andovan had been taught about Gansang as a child. Taught that a city is a living thing, and as with any living thing, if its growth is frustrated in one direction, it will expand in another. The nobles of Gansang could not expand outward without moving into the marshes themselves, and so they had expanded upward instead, building towers that were taller and finer than any others on earth—or so they claimed. Andovan had been told the story by his tutor when he was a young boy. It had seemed unreal to him then. But now . . . Gansang was due west of him, if he remembered it right. Which meant that he had been heading in that direction all along. Could that be where Colivar's sorcery had been driving him? Was his would-be killer there at this very moment, might he surprise her there if he moved quickly enough?

Gansang was on the other side of the Blood Ridge, he recalled. Not a day's ride past the western foothills.

Feeling more confident than he had in a long time, Andovan pulled his tightly rolled maps out of the saddlebag, and by the light of a single moon began to plot the journey to Gansang.

Chapter 18

"COME IN, my dear."

The tattered edges of Gwynofar's silk gown fluttered like the wings of a black angel as she entered the chamber. Her clear eyes took in everything at a glance: her hawk-browed husband in a carved wooden chair, black eyes squinting in what he doubtless believed was an expression of affection; the Magister Kostas in tight-fitting ebony robes sitting upright in a cushioned chair opposite him, tracking her every movement like a hungry bird; the fireplace behind them, cold due to the summer's heat, with its polished silver mirror over the mantle. In it she could see herself, pale of face and dusty of hem, a mere ghost of a presence compared to the aggressive and powerful men who had called her to audience.

There was no chair set out for her, she noticed. Doubtless Kostas' idea. As always his presence made the bile rise in her throat, and she had to swallow hard to smile with requisite royal politeness as she curtseyed to them both. Then, disdaining to meet Kostas' eyes, she fetched a chair for herself and sat, daring her husband's disapproval to do so. But a small smile played on Danton's lips, which told her she had guessed correctly. He liked it when she had spirit, providing it was not him she was defying. Other subjects would die for the same gesture.

"You summoned me, Sire?"

"So I did." He reached for the flagon of wine by his side and poured out a third goblet full, then offered it to her. She accepted it gratefully, using it to wash down the lump in her throat that Kostas' presence had conjured. The Magister Royal watched the exchange impassively, utterly still but for his eyes. Like a spider's, she thought. She half expected a spider's quick movements out of him the moment she touched the wrong string of his web. "Kostas expressed an interest in the religious beliefs of your homeland. I thought it better coming from your lips than mine."

Gwynofar nodded politely, as if conversing with Kostas was not an unpleasant task at all. She knew what Danton thought of her religion—"rock worship," he called it—and he had probably meant this audience as a courtesy to let her explain things herself. He knew she disliked Kostas—she had never lied to her husband about that—but he had no idea how deep within her soul the revulsion was rooted, how hard it was to be in his presence long enough even to exchange niceties.

Nonetheless, she was queen, and that meant learning to hide her true feelings, no matter what the cost.

She forced herself to turn to the Magister and meet his eyes without flinching. He must never suspect how much she hated him, she knew that, or how much she feared him. You must never let a Magister sense your fear. So she forced her voice to be steady and soft, even casual, as she asked him, "So what do you wish to know?"

His voice was a low hiss, the kind of sound you would expect out of a lizard or a snake, not a man. "Tell me of the Lord Protectors."

She glanced at Danton, who nodded. "They are the leaders of bloodlines founded to maintain the Spears of the Wrath, to guard against its weakening, and to stand in the front lines of battle should those protections fail us."

"Gods save us from a woman's recitation," Danton interrupted. "You start at the end of the story when he does not even know the beginning yet. Tell him of the war itself . . . yes, Kostas?" He glanced at Kostas, who said nothing; his eyes were fixed upon the High Queen with an intensity that made her skin crawl. "That would be best, I think. The end of the war, the coming of the Wrath . . . that is what he wants."

She nodded. "As you wish, Sire."

She drew in a deep breath and tried to ignore Kostas' stare. "Long ago, in the Dark Ages, when demons roamed the earth freely, feasting upon human souls, there gathered a band of the witching folk. These alone had resisted the power of the demons enough to remember the First Age of Kings, and they believed that man could be restored to his rightful inheritance if the vile creatures were destroyed.

"It was decided that they would seek out those last few warriors who still had the spirit to fight—for you must understand that the demons' magic robbed men of all aggressive instinct, so this was no small thing— and they would launch a final campaign against the enemy. Not to kill the demons in the lands they had invaded, the ruins of the First Kingdoms, for all efforts to do that before had failed. Rather they would attempt to drive them to the far north, to the lands of ice and snow, where the kingdoms of man had never taken root. For it was believed that the deep cold weakened them, and perhaps in such a place they would become feeble enough that men might destroy them at last."

"Tell me of these demons," Kostas said quietly. His eyes upon hers were like a lizard's, cold and unblinking; she dared not look at them directly, lest her revulsion show.

"It is said they were born of the souls of corrupted men who feared entering the lands of Death, yet who might remain in the world of the living only by feeding upon the souls of others. They took on the forms of great flying creatures with wings so vast and black they cast shadows upon the earth beneath them as they flew. It is said that their gaze could turn a man to stone, so that no warrior could stand before them. Many armies tried when they first appeared, and many stone monuments remain to bear witness to their failure."

"But this time would be different," the Magister offered.

"Yes." She glanced at Danton. He believed in some of this, she knew that, though he did so in the manner of his own people, preferring to believe the demons were merely fearsome beasts and the tales of their supernatural powers no more than legends. Yet *something* had ended the First Age of Kings and plunged mankind into spiritual and intellectual darkness for the span of ten centuries, she thought stubbornly. No man doubted that. And *something* had then killed all the invaders, so that the Second Age of Kings could begin. No man doubted that either. Why was the tale of a sorcerous war less credible than believing mere beasts had been the cause?

"There are many tales told in the north of the witches' quest to find the few remaining heroes among men. If the Lord Magister has interest in that . . ." Kostas gestured with a short wave of one bony hand that he did not. "Some believe the gods aided the witches in their search, for otherwise it would surely have been impossible. At last they succeeded in finding a handful of warriors whose spirits were resistant to the demons' power, seven men in all, to whose banners others would flock in order for an army to be mustered."

She was remembering the epic tales of her childhood now, offered up by minstrels before a roaring fire in the darkness of the northern winter. It was hard not to fall into their cadence, or offer up half-remembered fragments of their songs, as she tried to distill centuries of speculation and myth into a few simple sentences for Kostas' consumption. In truth as a girl she had been more interested in the tales of the exciting search for the Seven Heroes and of the magical exploits that were said to attend them, but that was clearly not what Kostas wanted to hear, and so she skipped over it.

"All the witching folk who existed in that day came to fight by their side, for the gods had revealed to them in dreams the importance of this battle, and they knew that mankind would rise or fall based upon their efforts. Terrible war was waged across the whole of the earth then, not merely with weapons, but with sorcery as well. In all the places where great kingdoms had once stood, the bodies of fallen soldiers were now strewn, some torn to bits by the claws of their enemies, some whole in body but with their souls rent by the demons, their ghosts howling in agony. The bodies of countless witches lay beside them, empty shells from which the life had been drained as fuel for magic. The whole of the earth had become a place of blood and death, and those who could not or would not fight fled and hid trembling in holes like rats, lest the enemy find them and devour them for strength.

"In time the seven great warriors and their armies drove the demons to the far north. Ice froze upon their wings then, and it robbed them of strength, just as the Seers had foretold. Yet even such an advantage could not turn the tide of battle completely. The blood of countless men was spilled in that great battle, rivers of it churned to scarlet mud beneath the soldiers' boots. Long summer days began to give way to the darkness of winter as the fighting went on, and the armies of men knew then that they were not strong enough to carry the battle to conclusion by themselves, not before the Great Night enshrouded all the northlands in darkness."

In the springtime, maidens of the Protectorates would make themselves garlands out of the crimson daisies that grew in the northern plains, which the legends said had once been white but were stained with the blood of heroes. She still remembered the look on Danton's face when he first caught sight of her in her wedding dress of that same arterial color. Why? she had wondered. Was not the color of courage and sacrifice suitable for weddings?

"So the witches offered up their lives in final sacrifice," she whispered, "if the gods would free mankind from the Souleaters and let the battle be won. And the gods heard them, and accepted their offer."

Kostas stiffened slightly. He seemed to be listening to her more intently than before. With his long thin limbs, staring eyes, and bony edges he reminded her of nothing so much as a praying mantis about to strike.

"The gods forged spears out of lightning and cast them down into the earth one after the other, in the midst of the battle, between the demons and the men. They struck in a line that stretched across the snow as far as the eye could see. The blood of the earth gushed upward where they pierced, and was frozen into fearsome spires many times the height of a man as it struck the air. The Wrath blazed forth from each earthwound, so terrible in its power that no living thing would go near it, nor could any living creature pass between the spires without going mad.

"The demons to the north fell back shrieking in fury, for they knew themselves bested. It is said the whole of the night sky blazed with fire, then, and veils as red as blood flickered from horizon to horizon. The soldiers killed those few demons that had been caught on the southern side of the barrier, and then an army of witches—the last ones living—crossed the Wrath to hunt down the last of the creatures. Trapped in the winds of the icy north the demons were truly helpless, they believed, and might be destroyed at last."

How could any outsider understand what it was to be born in a land that still echoed with the cries of that great war? The demons were still out there, or so the priests taught. If the Wrath ever faltered and the battle resumed, her kin would be in the front ranks. Even the women. That was their duty.

She thought of Rhys and the other Guardians, traveling from spire to spire along the edge of the Wrath, braving its terrible power to inspect the frozen founts of earth's blood, to repair them if necessary, and to lend the strength of their prayers and their offerings to the gods who maintained them. For if and when the demons did return, the Wrath was the only thing standing between them and the fertile, civilized southlands, and not Danton and all the High King's armies could muster a defense against them if it faltered.

"This is why," she concluded, "when the Second Age of Kings began, there was no sorcery. All those who could work the soulfire had been sacrificed."

"Tell me of the Protectors' bloodlines," Kostas said quietly. "Their . . . special powers." His tone had not changed, nor was their any change in his demeanor . . . yet the question cut into her soul like a knife. She had felt such things before with Ramirus, when he used his power to read the truth behind her words. It was chilling to think this hollow-faced Magister was weaving his power about her now, but she kept any sign of the knowledge from showing on her face as she responded while hating him silently for daring to touch her with his sorcery, an invasion so unclean and intimate it felt like rape.

Yet even while she hated him she wondered why it was so, and she remembered Rhys' words in the courtyard: *The reasons you offer me do not match the hatred in your heart.*

The King's hounds do not like the new Magister either, she told herself. *They do not have to know why.*

"They are descended from the surviving leaders of the great battle. The priests decreed that those bloodlines should serve as kings in the north, and so they have, ever since." She paused, watching him closely. "What more do you wish to know?"

"It is said the gods gave them gifts, is it not? Special powers that would help them protect the world against the demons, should they come again. At least that is the rumor."

Like a deer catching scent of a hunter, she stiffened. *This is the question he wished to ask all along,* she thought. *This is why he called me here, rather than letting Danton tell him tales of my people.*

It made her wary. It made her want to hide the truth. "There are many rumors, my lord."

"Superstition," Danton snorted.

She blushed and looked down in what she hoped would seem to be feminine embarrassment; sometimes with men that could deflect suspicion. "Perhaps, Sire."

"You have not answered my question," Kostas pressed.

She shrugged, attempting to make it seem like the matter was of little import to her. "It is the duty of the Protectors to guard the Spears, hence it is said that the gods granted them the ability to approach them more closely than the common man is able to. I do not know if you would call that a 'gift,' Lord Magister. They are fearsome things, and only those bound by duty would ever wish to be near them."

"Perhaps," he said quietly. "But it is said the blood of the witches runs in your veins."

She felt her heart skip a beat, and drew in a slow, measured breath to keep her outer aspect calm. If his power was focused upon her now she could not lie to him, but neither did she wish to give him the whole truth. "I do not know what legends you have heard," she told him. "Some claim that seven witches survived to become the wives of the great generals, to bear them their firstborn sons. Some claim that the power of all the witches who died was absorbed into the land itself, and that the first Protectors were bequeathed luck in their name. But the first generations are long dead now, Lord Magister, and witchery is not a thing inherited along with a father's name, nor transferred by the telling of tales."

"She is not a witch herself," Danton said. "If that's what you are asking after. Ramirus made sure of that before we were wed."

Now Gwynofar flushed with genuine embarrassment. "Magister Ramirus—?"

"I ordered it," Danton told her. He cut any protest short with a wave of his hand. "What did you expect? I was not about to take a wife from a family of some enchanted race. And you are rumored to be that, you know it." He looked to Kostas. "Apparently the gods promised the Protectors something like, *if and when you need the power you will have it.* Whatever that means." He chuckled softy. "Gods are nothing if not obscure, yes?"

"So it seems," the Magister said quietly.

"Well the Lord Protectors have built an empire based upon such legends, and I respect that. But you'd best look elsewhere for your enchanted races, Kostas. My wife is as pure blooded as Protectors come, and Ramirus assured me she had no more witchery about her than any other noblewoman." He looked at Gwynofar. "I'm sorry, my dear, but you know that's the truth."

Acknowledging the point with a nod did not require her to answer. Without an answer, Kostas' truth-sensing magic had no hold on her.

She nodded. "Is the Lord Magister satisfied, then? Or does he need anything more from me?"

It was impossible to ask the question without meeting Kostas' eyes. A shudder ran through her as she did so. Their pale gray substance, not dissimilar from Rhys' in color, seemed utterly unlike anything human in their essence, and for a moment she imagined she could see dark things slithering in their depths, hungry things, ready to swim down the conduit of his gaze to feast upon her soul the moment she gave him an opening. Or else ready to celebrate her weakness if she looked away. So though it took every bit of fortitude she had, she did not look away. His unblinking eyes held her for a moment, then two, then a small eternity, testing her mettle. Finally he said, "No. You have given me enough," and looked back to Danton. She did not even hear what he said then, but breathed a secret sigh of relief that the contest had not lasted longer. She was a strong woman, despite her fragile seeming, and doubly strong in the kind of moral certainty that came of being a Protector, but staring down a Magister, even of the ordinary kind, was a contest few people ever won.

Danton drank again, this time draining the goblet. Had he filled it yet again? If so he was drinking more than usual today; that was not a good sign. "I told the Magister there was little substance to your myths. But he insisted upon hearing them. Now then Kostas, you have heard the fairy tales, yes? For what they are worth." He nodded toward the door, waving absently in Gwynofar's direction. "You may go, my dear." Even as she rose obediently and curtseyed, it was clear that his attention was already elsewhere, and she dared to breathe a sigh of relief to be officially released from the interview.

Not until she was safely on the other side of the heavy oaken doors did she pause to lean weakly against them, to draw in one long, shivering breath, and to wonder, *What was the purpose of that?* For the one thing that Ramirus had taught her was that all things had purpose to a Magister, and rarely were their intentions of the sort that a mere mortal might guess at.

But try as she might she could not untangle the twisted knots of it all, and at last with a sigh she returned to her rooms, where at least she could put thick doors between herself and the new Magister Royal, and try to forget the unclean touch of his sorcerous scrutiny.

Danton grunted and poured himself more wine. "Well? Did you get the information you wanted?"

Kostas nodded slowly.

"If you ask me it's all patent nonsense. Myths written by men who wanted to assure their place in history. All dynasties inherit such tales, or else must create them later."

"*You* rule without the need for such legends."

Danton laughed heartily. "I daresay there are places on this earth where my name is granted religious significance, though I doubt it's of the benevolent sort. That is good, though. I encourage it. Fear keeps men in line." He took another deep drink of wine. "Meek rulers ask gods for permission before they take a piss."

A faint smile quirked the Magister's lips. "And you do not?"

"I piss on such men. And their gods."

"Your wife feigns a meek demeanor," Kostas observed, "but the spirit within is defiant."

"And so?" Danton reached over and splashed more wine into Kostas's own cup. "A mare with no spirit breeds poor stallions, Magister."

"Yes, and she has bred well, has she not?" He leaned back in his chair and added quietly, "Though not without aid."

A thick, dark eyebrow arched upward in curiosity. "Eh?"

"Ramirus' hand is upon your line, is it not?"

Danton's expression darkened. "What makes you say that?"

"Come, my king—four male heirs in rapid succession, perfectly healthy, births evenly spaced, followed by two comely daughters appropriate for marital barter, at the same interval. Do you honestly expect a record like that with no assistance? Fate is rarely so kind to women. Or to kings."

"I never asked for Ramirus' help."

"I never said you did." Kostas sipped his wine slowly, letting the faint emphasis on *you* hang in the air for a moment.

Danton scowled. "The House of Aurelius has never required the aid of sorcerers to beget its young."

"I am sure it does not."

"So what, you think that my wife—?"

Kostas' eyes glittered. "How would I know? It was before my time. I merely note that such aid means different things to a man and to a woman, for it is her life that is risked when an infant is brought into the world, not his."

"She knows I would never approve of such a thing."

Kostas inclined his head. "Then I am sure she would not think of displeasing you." He sipped from his wine. "She is merely . . . lucky. Some women are like that."

Danton rose from his chair and stood before the fireplace. He liked the drama of a crackling fire, for it reminded him of an enemy city put to the torch when siege was broken. Summer's heat robbed a man of such simple pleasures. "Ramirus would never have done such a thing without being asked."

"You know him better than I, Majesty."

"He was my servant. As are you."

He waited a moment to see if Kostas would protest the designation, but he did not. Finally he returned to his chair and poured himself another helping of wine. He drank from it in the manner of a man who is trying to wash a bad taste out of his mouth.

"I admit," Kostas said, "I am curious about one thing."

Danton looked up at him. "What?"

"Six children—one each year—the perfect royal family, and then no more? It seems . . . odd."

Danton snorted. "No mystery to that one. She asked me after Tiresia's birth if she might be spared further duty of that sort. It was a reasonable request, given that she had stocked my household well, and I granted it."

"Ah, so she has . . . turned you from her bed?"

Danton's glare was fierce. "Watch your words, Magister. Some kings might find them offensive."

"I am simply concerned for your welfare. And for the loyalty of those surrounding you."

"The queen's loyalty is not in question."

"Nonetheless, it remains my duty."

Danton drank deeply, wiped a stray drop of wine from his face with the back of his hand, and settled into the heavily carved chair with a noisy exhalation. "There's very little flesh on her. No comfort to a man. I married her for her family crest, not for warming my bed, and she knows it. She gave me four sons any king would be proud of. Our daughters bought me valuable alliances. As far as I know she has no lovers, which is the only offense I would never forgive. When she sits beside me at dinner, visiting princes smile more and conspire less. I have no issue—*none*—with her queenly performance. Do not raise the topic again."

"As you wish, Majesty." The hollow eyes lowered briefly, respectfully.

"Outside of that nonsense with the rocks, of course." The High King snorted softly. "But she keeps that to her own courtyard. So long as she does not offer up anyone's blood but her own I have no issue with it." He stared into his wine for a moment. "What do you make of all that? The truth, now."

Kostas steepled his fingers thoughtfully as he considered the question. "I have been to the north, and seen these 'spears' myself. They are rocks, nothing more, which the locals mortar and carve into fearsome shapes to keep the populace cowed and reverent. As for the so-called Wrath, there is without doubt some odd power present in that area—I have felt it myself—but not on the scale the High Queen describes. Say rather an ominous sensation that increases as one approaches the stones. Since the Protectors are rumored to have witches among their blood, I suspect that the effect is nothing more than simple witchery. That is why I asked after the High Queen's bloodline. I myself believe the blood rituals they practice are in fact what raises the power, whose purpose is simply to establish awe in the hearts of worshippers. It is not strong enough to do anything else, I assure you."

"There are Magisters up there, aren't there? I am sure they would know more about it."

Kostas's lips twitched briefly. "And they are as unlikely to give away the secrets that sustain their domains as I am to betray yours, my king." He bowed his head respectfully. "Besides, is it not a fair sport for Magisters to try to discover things from one another? We must have something to amuse ourselves with while our royal masters plot out their campaigns of conquest."

Danton snorted. He was a proud man, and Kostas' suggestion about his family was like a thorn digging into his side; it was hard to think past it. "Is there any way to know for certain?" he asked at last.

"What, Sire?"

"About the children. Gwynofar. Any way to know if my sons' births were something other than natural."

"Ah. Well, a woman would tell you that birth is never *natural*, but theirs is a different perspective."

"You know what I mean."

The Magister put his goblet aside. "If you are serious in that question, I could undertake to discern the truth. The mark of Ramirus' sorcery might still be on her, or on the children. But such things are faint after so many years, and failing to find it would be no guarantee of anything save that sorcery is an uncertain art."

Danton grunted and stared into his wine. Clearly the answer did not please him.

"You say she is loyal, Majesty. You say she would not seek Ramirus' aid against your will. You say you are sure of these things, and of her. Is that not enough for you, then?"

"Aye." The wine was a blood-colored mirror that reflected Danton's scowl back at him. "It should be, should it not?"

"Men were not meant to know all the secrets of childbearing," Kostas said quietly. "The gods gave that gift to women, and also exacted a price for it, that she should bear her knowledge in pain. Or so the priests say." He shrugged. "Frankly I think the southern tribesmen have the right idea—lock the women away from men and Magisters both, until such time as they can no longer bear children. That way no man can interfere with what should be a *natural* inheritance, yes, Majesty?" He paused. "Of course, I do not imagine they make such bargains with their women as you have struck with Her Majesty, but we are a far more civilized land and must respect such things, yes?"

Danton said nothing.

A cloud crossed in front of the sun outside. It shadowed the light coming into the room briefly, but could not abate the heavy humidity that clung to the chamber, dampening a man's skin. It was an unpleasant afternoon, by Danton's reckoning. That did not improve his mood.

"It is not your affair," the High King said finally. "You will not raise the issue again."

"Of course, Your Majesty." The Magister Royal inclined his head respectfully. With his thin neck and sharp features, the gesture seemed more appropriate to a vulture pecking at carrion than to a man.

But Danton did not notice. His mind was on other things. And finally, when it seemed that his private thoughts had reached some turning point, he set his goblet aside on the heavily carved table and left the room without further word or backward glance.

On a more human face, the Magister's twisted expression might have been deemed a smile.

Chapter 19

It is with great pleasure that Lord Entares Savresi and Lady Tandra invite you to a fete to celebrate the naming of their son, to be held upon the Night of the Twin Moons, in the Tower Savresi, Gansang. Festivities will begin at six in the evening.

THEY MADE Kamala wear a formal gown. It was a heavy silk creation embroidered in gold, worth more than all the money she had earned in her lifetime and then some. The style had some fancy name she could not pronounce which made it even more valuable (or so she was assured), and it had been made by a dressmaker who normally worked only for royalty (so she was told), and it was actually a very beautiful shade of forest green that brought out the color in her eyes . . . but still. It was a *formal* gown, which meant it embodied everything she hated most about women's clothing.

She had fussed and sputtered and complained for the better part of a day, but the servants had insisted that nothing else would be acceptable if she was to attend an event as Ravi's companion, and so in the end she was forced to acquiesce and allow them to fit her in it. It had a train, which she had tripped over several times, and the sleeves had long hanging ends that kept getting caught on things as she moved, but the maidservants insisted she looked absolutely wonderful, and one young girl who had run up from the kitchen just to see the fitting declared she hoped she would be as beautiful as Kamala some day. So it seemed in poor taste to keep complaining.

The day of the fete Ravi sent her a hairdresser, who spent the better part of two hours fretting over Kamala's short hair, finally dressing it back in waves over the front of an opulent wig made up of coiling, pearl-studded braids. The wig was made of real human hair, the hairdresser told her proudly, not the combed wool or horsetail which might be used in poorer places. Kamala felt a knotting in her gut when she heard that, and for a moment the look in her eyes was so dark and terrible that the woman instinctively stepped back from her. What could Kamala say? That she had once lived among the kind of people so desperate for money that they might sell their own body parts for a few bits of copper? That the long red locks which so perfectly matched her own had probably once been the pride of a young peasant girl, now shorn like a sheep for Kamala's pleasure? She had left that world behind now and become another kind of creature, the kind who wore the hair of other human beings as casually as Kamala the whore had once worn sheep's wool.

When Ravi came for her he assured her that she was beautiful. He seemed to mean it, too, though she suspected he'd have said the same words if she looked like a warthog with a mustache. It was a first time a man had ever complimented her in such a tone, and even though she really did not give a damn what this plucked and powdered fool thought of her, still, it was oddly pleasing to hear the words.

There would be Magisters at the fete. So Ravi had said. They were not social creatures, he had warned, and she would do best keeping her distance from them. She had the distinct impression that he was afraid that if she talked to a Magister she would be convinced to break her contract with him. *Little chance of that*, she thought darkly. Ethanus had made it clear that most Magisters regarded their mortal cousins with utter disdain, and were more likely to be amused by the pathetic self-destructiveness of such a contract than exert any effort to talk her out of it.

They manipulate morati because it passes the centuries, he had told her, *and are not above driving lesser beings to their deaths if that serves the moment's amusement.*

Would she become like that in time, she wondered. Not only willing to kill, but thriving upon death, encouraging the suffering of others simply to ward off boredom? Ethanus had said it was likely, and a sadness had entered his eyes then, as though he would mourn the change in her. For the first time she had wondered if that was not what had truly driven him to his hermitage in the woods, the desire to safeguard his fading humanity. It was something she could never ask him aloud. But she remembered what he had told her once, about judging her own condition: *Look in the mirror and ask yourself, do you like what you see? If the answer is no, it is time to reassess your choices.* Had he fled to the woods because the face that looked back at him in Ulran was too distasteful to bear?

The day of the fete was cool and crisp and the wind was westerly, which blew the foul air of the Quarter out to sea; all in all, a pleasant day. Ravi and his entourage began traveling in the morning, making their way through the network of towers and bridges that enveloped the Hill according to some complex and—to Kamala—indecipherable pattern. At each new tower they stopped to pay their respects to the owner, exchange gifts and gossip, and then Ravi added his entourage to those that had already assembled. By midafternoon they were thirty strong, bobbing along the slender bridges in their jeweled silks like a pride of peacocks, with the richest and most important nobles of the city at the head of the line. Kamala walked by Ravi's side, as he had promised. It gave her a secret thrill to know that the nobles surrounding her thought her their equal, but it also inflamed a silent anger to be forced to such subterfuge. If she were a man she could simply don the traditional color of the Magisters and all the world would give her the respect she deserved. Only because she was a woman was she forced to continually pretend she was something else and to receive her respect secondhand.

You could always make yourself look like a man, she reminded herself. Sorcery could sculpt her flesh into any shape she liked. All she had to do was put on a man's face, add a little height and breadth of shoulder, and drape herself in the occult black of a Magister's traditional dress; she wouldn't even have to transform the parts that mattered, if the gown were long enough. Who would think to question her then?

But that was a kind of defeat, and one that she was not willing to accept. She had not slaved for long years in training and then risked her life in her first Transition only to have her status determined by some puerile masquerade. *The Magisters will accept me as I am,* she thought stubbornly, *or I will go without their approval.*

Ravi's party arrived late, which was apparently deliberate, a choice determined by the illustrious rank of those in his procession. Guests were announced as they entered the great hall, and Gansang's ruling elite preferred there to be enough people present when they arrived that they might be properly admired. Ravi himself was one of the last of the group to enter—apparently a sign of his station—and Kamala entered on his arm, heralded as "the Lady Sidra" by a youth wearing the gold-and-black livery of House Savresi. Heads turned as she descended the marble stairs by Ravi's side, and she could hear a thousand curious whispers surrounding her, details inaudible, like the humming of locusts.

The great hall of Tower Savresi turned out to be immense, and crowded to its last inch with the most illustrious peacocks of the realm. It took up the entire ground floor of the building, and had a vaulted ceiling that faded into shadows high overhead. There were stained-glass windows set high up in the walls that must have been magnificent in the daylight, but in the evening the only light coming through them was torchlight from the bridges and streets beyond, a flickering, eerie illumination that caused colors to shimmer across the floor as breezes fanned the flames. One end of the great hall had vast tables piled with expensive foodstuffs, including sweets carved into the shapes of merchant ships, castles, and even exotic animals; the other was occupied by a raised stage upon which musicians played, a southern melody that suggested perfumed gardens filled with dancing girls. It was almost too much for Kamala to absorb; she looked about half-dazed by it all, trying to get her bearings, even as Ravi led her through a gauntlet of mandatory introductions.

She had been taught how to greet the peacocks of Gansang properly, which was a good thing, because for the better part of an hour that was all she was able to do. It seemed that every man in the room must come to pay his respects to Ravi, and every woman must find some excuse to come inspect her more closely. She did not need sorcery to see the desire in the men who kissed her hand, nor the cold envy in the faces of the women who greeted her. Did her body entice the men, long and lean and gleaming in its carapace of jeweled silk, or was it simply that she was something new, a mystery, a prize that had been claimed by Ravi before anyone else had a chance to despoil it? She had seen enough of the dark underbelly of male desire to have no illusions about its source. Nothing inspired a man's lust more than the presence of a woman he could not possess.

Through all of this she did not catch a single glimpse of the Magisters. She found it hard to concentrate on anyone else with them on her mind, not even the entertainment, which ran the gamut from jugglers to fire eaters to a sextet of half-naked dancers from some exotic island. At another time she would have been fascinated to see it all—and thrilled to be watching them from a position of honor, rather than stealing a peek at them from some hiding place in the shadows—but tonight there was only one thing on her mind.

And then she saw one. Or *felt* one, rather, for his sorcery was a cold thing that whispered across the back of her neck, and no Magister could miss its meaning. She looked up, high into the shadows of the upper hall, seeking the source of the spell. There were balconies and galleries perched all about the circular walls at a variety of heights, linked together by a network of staircases. The uppermost perches were small and dark and offered a modicum of privacy; she could make out pairs of lovers nestling together in their chosen roosts, merchants whispering bargains out of earshot of the crowd below, nobles politicking, and of course a few antisocial creatures who simply preferred the height as a vantage point, from which they might watch the festivities on the main floor without the need to smile at anyone.

It was there she found one of the Magisters, standing as still as the stone itself, and as dark as the shadows surrounding him. As soon as she looked in his direction she knew with utter certainty that his eyes were fixed upon her, and she felt the chill touch of his power inspecting her, seeking information on her history, her identity, her purpose. It took little effort to turn it aside; it was one of the first tricks Ethanus had taught her. She was only sorry she could not see the Magister's face more clearly as his spell failed, could not judge his reaction. Had he heard she was a witch, or was this the first hint he'd had that she possessed power of her own?

She began to ascend one of the staircases, not heading toward the gargoyle-like Magister—it was clear from his aspect he would accept no invasion of his space—but seeking a higher vantage point from which to look for others of his kind. Holding her clinging skirts up perhaps a bit higher than a lady should, she ascended to a narrow balcony, where a group of young men who were clearly in their cups invited her to join them in making ribald comments about the crowd below. She smiled as politely as she could and kept climbing. A deep-set gallery lined with armorial displays finally offered her what she was looking for—a comfortable perch from which she might observe the whole of the great hall, balconies included; she pulled up a bench to the railing and knelt upon it, tucking her train underneath so that passersby would not trip over it.

Now that she knew what she was looking for, she was able to locate them all. They all stood at the periphery of the gathering, watching over the morati like hawks. The unnatural black that they wore made them almost invisible in the shadows, but their power blazed forth like beacons to her sorcerous senses. Now and then one of the highborn guests would approach one, and they did so with such obvious humility as made her toes curl. Princes might drape themselves in jewels and silks, build great towers, and even send out armies to conquer nations but in the end, the real power lay in the hands of the Magisters, and the course of mortal empires was determined by whom they favored, and whom they did not.

There were four of them in all. One kept to the shadows, drawing power about him so that only with the greatest effort could she make him out at all, and she could see no details of his person. Another looked almost youthful, and eventually he made his way down to the main floor and spoke to a few of the guests—though most stayed well clear of his path—but his presence was without warmth, and he allowed no one to touch him. Another had taken up station on a balcony opposite Kamala's, and at one point she looked up to find him staring at her with an intensity that left her shaken. He had a deep scar running down one cheek that had healed badly, twisting the surrounding flesh like some grotesque sculpture, and when at last he moved she could see his long robes rippling as if stirred by a breeze though no breeze was present. *You may know a Magister by the flesh he chooses to wear,* Ethanus had told her. What kind of man could adopt any appearance he liked, yet preferred such a twisted, damaged countenance?

The fourth Magister appeared so old and fragile it was hard to believe he was a living creature; that was a show of power all its own, she realized, intended to make the morati aware of just how ancient a sorcerer he might be. Like his youthful counterpart he eventually descended to the main floor of the great hall to greet several of the morati; like the other he offered his hand and cheek to no one, encouraged no false intimacy, tolerated no foolishness for the sake of polite society. These men were soulmates to her spirit, she thought, playing by their own rules, and she hungered to meet them, to begin the process that would win her acceptance as one of their kind. But she did not know how to begin. She'd been spoiled by Ethanus, and had perhaps assumed that the others of his kind would be equally approachable . . . equally human. But these black-robed creatures seemed like a different species altogether, and she was beginning to realize just how difficult it would be to strike the right note when she finally presented herself to them . . . and how badly things might go if she failed.

Take your time, she told herself. *You have as many lifetimes as you need to work this out.* But the words echoed emptily in her soul, where the fire of restlessness blazed with mortal heat.

Your lack of patience, Ethanus had warned her, *will be a greater danger to you than any enemy.*

A party of revelers was making its way up toward where she knelt; drunken voices promised a more aggressive invasion of her space than she was in the mood to deal with. Looking about for some convenient path of exit, she spied a small door leading outward from the next balcony over. The sudden thought of fresh air and a moment alone to gather her thoughts was appealing, and she hurried along the staircase that led from her current perch to that exit.

It was a small door, and a mere whisper of power was sufficient to unlock it; she opened it and peered out into the twilight. There was a bridge beyond, a narrow thing, clearly not intended for grand processions but for more private use. It probably led to a subsidiary tower owned by the Savresi, permitting them to come and go without drawing attention to themselves. Whatever its intended purpose, its position out of sight of the crowded walkways near the main entrance of the tower promised a few moments of peace and solitude, a welcome respite.

She stepped through and let the door close behind her, moving out onto the bridge, into the fresh night air. There were torches burning at both ends of the bridge but none along its length, and azure shadows danced before and after her as she walked to the middle of the bridge, sighed, and leaned against the rail.

Her spirit was tired, she realized. Tired of letting strange men kiss her hand, strange women kiss her cheek, the things that were expected of her here. She had once sworn she would never let a stranger touch her, and now she had let dozens of strangers do so. She smiled at jokes she did not think were funny, admired jewelry she did not think was beautiful, and endured the suggestive comments of men whose brains were clearly in their codpieces. And all the while the Magisters watched, disdaining such social games, aloof and independent. She hungered to be one of them. No . . . she *was* one of them. She hungered for them to know it.

Choose your time carefully, Ethanus had warned her. *They are creatures of habit, more wary of change than any morati, and they will not accept a woman as one of them without considerable resistance. Do not let any of them know what you are until you are sure of what your reception will be. Remember that if they deny you are truly a Magister, their Law will not protect you.*

But how can I ever be sure? she despaired. For one brief, mad moment she wished herself back in Ethanus' forest. There at least she had understood the rules.

"Ravi's witch." The sudden voice startled her; she had not heard the tower door open. "Tell me, does he pay you in coin for the life force you sacrifice? Or is it love that buys death, these days?"

A sharp retort came to her lips and she turned around to let it loose . . . and then stopped, the words frozen, and felt her heart skip a beat.

It was the Magister with the scar.

He walked out onto the bridge. She could see his black robes ripple about his feet as he moved, a strangely sensual movement, unnatural. Each movement of cloth cost some morati a moment of his life, she thought. Would she too someday reach the point when she would be willing to drain a consort of life for such a pointless affectation?

The torchlight played upon the scar on his face, making the wound look livid, fresh. "You have not answered me, child."

A flush of indignation rose to her cheeks, but she managed to keep the worst of her temper bridled. "You assume you know what I am. Assume whatever answer pleases you."

Anger flickered in the backs of his eyes; clearly he was not accustomed to having mere witches talk back to him. "Your manners were better inside."

"Men were more polite to me inside."

"Morati men fawn upon you. Magisters watch in silence. Whose judgment is more meaningful?"

A faint smile flickered across her lips. "Perhaps I did not come here to be judged."

His voice was knife-edged. "Perhaps it is not your choice."

He stepped closer to her and reached out a hand toward her face. Her smile vanished and she stepped back out of reach, hackles rising. *I have not given you the right to touch me.*

The Magister's expression darkened. "Afraid?"

She said it simply, with an equally cold expression. "No."

He reached out for her again. This time when she tried to move away his power wrapped itself around her and held her in place. For one brief moment his hand fell upon her cheek, a mocking caress . . . then she gathered her own power and broke through the sorcerous bond, stumbling over her train as she backed away yet again. Her heart was pounding so loudly she could hear it. Could he?

"Don't," she breathed.

"Do what?" His black eyes glittered in the torchlight. "Touch you as a man might—as Ravi no doubt does? But you are used to that, aren't you? Whoring and witchery are the same art, after all. One barters one's soul instead of one's flesh, but the act itself is no different."

Her first instinct was to respond indignantly to his words. Her second, more intelligent one, was to say nothing, to keep her expression calm. *Ravi did not know I was a whore,* she told herself, *and the Magisters at the fete who tried to read my past failed to do so. He is but casting out random insults to see which will make me lose control. He knows nothing of my past.*

"So . . ." There was amusement in his eyes, but it was a cold, reptilian thing, wholly divorced from any mortal concept of humor. "Will you best all my sorcery with your witch's art, if I persist? Or simply run away?"

I know your kind, she thought. *When you were young you beat up anyone who crossed you, and probably assaulted any maiden that took your fancy. Your peers feared you and your parents feared you and probably the authorities as well, and now that you have the ultimate power you expect the whole world to do the same. Only I won't. I am your rival in power, your equal in fierceness, perhaps even your better . . . you just do not know it yet.*

"I do not run," she said quietly.

The hem of his gown suddenly stopped its obscene fluttering. He was drawing the power to him, she realized, readying it for some more significant purpose. A cold chill ran down her spine. Did he think he could toy with her like he would a morati? If so he was in for an unpleasant surprise.

. . . and a voice whispered in the back of her mind that this was the not way she should be dealing with Magisters . . .

But great waves of rage were roiling to the surface, the frustration of too many hours spent pretending to be something that she was not. She had not come this far in life, at so great a cost, only to have this snake of a Magister treat her like a common whore. Very well, if he wanted to spar with her, let him try. He was in for a bigger surprise than he could imagine.

He struck.

His power was a whirlwind that sucked the breath from her lungs, leaving her stunned and gasping. She grabbed the railing beside her as she tried to defend herself, but the raw power of the assault was like nothing she had ever felt before, and it broke through each spell of defense she invoked. She could feel tendrils of his sorcery winding themselves around her legs, sucking the strength from her muscles, forcing her limbs to fold, and she realized with a rush of fury that he meant to make her kneel to him. Not with some sophisticated spell, like the kind Ethanus had taught her to counter, but with a battering-ram assault, primitive in form, brutal in purpose.

NO!!!

Reaching deep into her own soul—and through it to the consort who fueled her sorcery—she called up all the power within her own reach. Stolen life raged through her veins in a flood tide and she forced it to take the form she desired, she fed it on her fury, she armored it with her determination . . . and then she let it loose. It was a wild and terrible thing, better suited to her own fiery spirit than the studious habits of her mentor. It burst forth from her in a blaze of sorcerous light that would surely have blinded any morati spectator. Even so it could not could not drive back his sorcery entirely, though it was enough to break the stranglehold he had upon her flesh. Her legs straightened, her muscles regained their accustomed strength, and just in case the meaning of those things was not clear to him, she stiffened her back and raised up her head and met his gaze squarely with her own.

"I also do not kneel," she said quietly.

He did not seem angered, but rather amused. For a moment she was startled by that and then, with a cold shudder, she realized the truth. The man believed she was a witch. That meant that, as far as he knew, every time she used her power to defend herself from him, she must sacrifice precious moments of her life to do so. That was what this was all about, she realized. He was daring her to waste the essence of her life in self-defense and laughing inwardly, no doubt, as she took the bait and hastened her own death. *You are not my equal,* his actions pronounced, *and if you persist in pretending that you are, your pride will cost you your life.*

It was the ultimate violation of her person. The fact that she was not truly a witch only made it worse. How long would he play with her like this—toying with her as a cat does with a mouse—forcing her to use up more and more of her life essence, seeking that moment in which her prideful soul would expire of exhaustion at his feet? The fact that such moment would never come, and he did not know it yet, only made the game more repulsive in her eyes.

I am no mouse, she thought. *It ends now.*

Rage was a conflagration within her, and she loosed it in all its heat. Not as she had in the Quarter, blindly and desperately, fearing her own power. This blow was focused and deliberate, and targeted to the seat of his male pride. He wanted to play dominance games with her? Very well, let him learn what *violation* felt like.

Perhaps he did not expect her to strike at him, or else the time between impulse and action was simply so short he had no time to respond. The battering ram of her power broke through his defenses—if there were any—and slammed straight into his gonads. The force of it drove him backward against the far railing, and for a moment he acted like any man would, gasping for breath as he tried to master the pain and do something other than vomit. *You chose the wrong whore to play with,* she thought, as she made the rail shatter behind him. A cascade of stone fragments rained down upon the street below as he struggled for balance, but his weight had been too far committed to the railing for him to save himself now, and—

He fell.

She stepped quickly over to his side of the bridge to watch the fall. Any sorcerer could save himself, of course, but how would he do so? Would he turn himself into a bird, perhaps, or some great cat that could land safely on its feet? Or simply slow his own fall so that he landed safely, still in human flesh? In the end it was all about power, of course, and whether one wished to make modest demands upon one's consort, or suck a stranger dry for the sake of some dramatic flourish. She had little doubt about what choice this kind of man would make. But would he save himself first and then strike back at her somehow, or combine the two intentions into one smooth action in the hopes that she would not see his attack coming? That was an answer that mattered.

She watched as he fell, and she made ready to defend herself yet again.

And then he struck the ground. The sound of the impact echoed between the towers. It was not unlike the sound a man's head might make when struck with an iron bar, but ten times louder, and a hundred times more final. It passed through her flesh like a shockwave and left a cold knot of dread lodged in her gut.

He did not move.

She waited.

He still did not move.

There were voices coming now, approaching from below. Seeking the source of that terrible sound.

Get up, she thought desperately. *Strike back!*

He did neither of those things.

She leaned over the edge of the railing and expended enough power to magnify her senses in order to study him more closely. It was hard to see him in the shadows of the towers, but she thought that his robes no longer seemed to be that sorcerous black, but rather something more normal. There was no rise and fall of his chest, nor any heartbeat she could detect. And the angle of his neck was wrong, all wrong. Living men did not lie in that position.

Cold, afraid, she backed along the bridge to the nearest wall and leaned against it, trembling. The fall shouldn't have killed him. No fall could kill a Magister. The only death a Magister need fear was one that came too swiftly for him to react to, and a fall was not that kind. A fall was a long, leisurely end, full of opportunity to reach out with sorcery and save oneself—

Unless his power failed him, she thought.

Unless he went into Transition.

Unless he could not claim a new consort in time.

There were men down by the body now, shouting things. She heard them as if from a great distance, without understanding, as if they spoke a language she had never learned.

She had killed a Magister.

There is but one Law, Ethanus had told her, *paramount above all others: no Magister shall ever kill another.*

Someone came out of Tower Savresi, to see what the ruckus was about. She wrapped the shadows of twilight about her closely, that none might see her. Her legs were weak, and without the strength of the wall behind her she might have fallen.

I have broken the Law.

Any minute now, one of the visiting Magisters would come out and see the twisted body. She did not know what would happen if they looked her way. Probably they would see right through her trembling sorcery to the pale, frightened woman within. She could certainly not return to the fete and try to pretend that nothing was wrong; any sorcerer who looked at her would be able to sense the deception.

I cannot stay here.

The thought was horror and despair and failure and fury all in bound up together, emotions too hot and terrible for one living soul to contain. It burst forth from her and she screamed, screamed to the skies above and to all the hells below, screamed till her throat was raw and her voice began to fail. Though she bound enough power to keep any other living creature from hearing her, still she could hear herself, and she trembled to have such a bestial and terrible sound issue forth from her own throat.

There were more figures coming from the tower now, and some of them were wearing black. With a final sob she drew enough power from her consort to saturate her flesh with power, preparing it to transform. It was a high order spell, and almost more than her trembling spirit could handle. But she had only seconds to see it to completion before someone would look upward, surely, and that added fear gave her strength.

One of the men did look upward a moment later, seeking the place the Magister had fallen from.

One of the black-robed sorcerers followed his gaze, seeking the kind of clues that morati eyes might miss.

There was nothing for either of them to see. Only a single broad-winged owl circling overhead, that dipped low once as it passed, and then turned its course southward, and soon passed out of sight.

Chapter 20

A T SUNSET Andovan thought he could see the towers.

He was high on a hill at the time, with a clear view to the west, and the orange light of the setting sun blazed fiercely along the horizon, as if the earth itself were burning. Against that light, if he peered closely enough, he thought he could see Gansang. Or at least its towers: high enough and clustered together closely enough that the light of the setting sun could not break through their mass; a black spot upon the orange horizon where the sunset fires did not burn, beneath a sky of swollen purple clouds with salmon underbellies.

It was Gansang. It had to be.

There was no telling how far away it was—the landscape was the sort that distorted one's sense of distance. But surely it could be no more than a day's ride, or two at the most, from where he stood.

He drew in a deep breath, trembling despite himself. Each night the dreams had been stronger, clearer, the image of the towers etching itself into his brain. Each morning he was more and more certain it was Gansang he had dreamed of. Now he was almost there; it made him dizzy to contemplate it.

And dizzy for other reasons as well.

The Wasting had progressed, just as all the doctors and Magisters had warned him it would. Slowly, inexorably, as if some unseen serpent were slowly squeezing all the life out of him. Sometimes he had to stop at midday and dismount, no longer able to bear a whole day in the saddle as he had once done so easily. In the morning, when the dreams faded, it was harder and harder for him to force himself to rise and dress and begin the rituals of morning. When he made his final camp at night it took everything he had to see to his horse's needs before he retired, rather than simply collapsing upon the ground in a faint.

Only sheer willpower kept him going. That and the distant siren's song of hope, that if he found the woman responsible for his illness, if he could figure out how and why she had done this to him, surely he could find a way to save himself. Even if that meant killing her.

Tonight, the sight of the towers energized him. The moons were high and the light was good and his mount did not seem overly tired. He decided after a break for dinner to go on a bit farther, and see if he could cut down the distance before him to a single day's ride. He rarely had good days anymore, and wanted to take advantage of this new rush of energy before it expired.

Sunset gave way to twilight, the sky a brilliant blue. He could no longer see Gansang ahead of him but it seemed to him he could *feel* it there, waiting for him. Was it an illusion that he could sense *her*, as well? Was Colivar's spell that strong? Would he, when he arrived—

—black fury engulfing him, turning to fire, molten hatred —

He gasped, clinging to the saddle with both hands lest he fall—

—black hatred, fury, I WILL NOT KNEEL! stone shatters, twilight screams—

He could not breathe. A wave of dizziness overcame him and despite the best of his efforts he could feel himself losing his grip. And then his horse reared up in fear, sensing the wrongness of the moment, and he was falling, falling—

—plummeting into blackness, blood-filled, shards of stone and screaming, screaming—

He managed to fall free and roll, far enough that his mount did not trample him, but it was all that he could do, and pain shot through his shoulder—

—and hits the bottom and does not move, broken black-robed doll, FIGHT ME FIGHT ME FIGHT ME!

Gasping, he struggled to remain conscious. This was by far the worst attack he'd had yet, and he was terrified that if he gave into it he would never wake up again. But it was not only weakness that assailed him this time, but a fearsome storm of images and emotions pouring into his brain with a hurricane's force. Was all this really happening somewhere, these images he was seeing, or had the nightmares taken hold of his waking mind as well? Was his illness driving him mad?

The towers of Gansang fell. He saw them fall. Slowly at first, their upper stories shattering one after the other, balconies and balustrades crumbling, silken curtains catching fire as they fluttered to the ground like dying birds . . . then a rumbling shook the earth and the broad, solid bases of the towers split, fire licking outward between their stones. It was as if he were there on the street himself, watching the destruction, too fascinated—too horrified—to run. Chunks of granite and marble and concrete and wood rained down like hailstones, but there was nowhere to take shelter. Nowhere to hide. The ground buckled beneath him as the towers fell, one after the other—all save the surreal tower in their center, without doors or windows, that stood strong and tall, a sentinel overlooking their destruction.

And he knew with sudden despairing clarity why he was seeing this vision, what it must surely mean. If he had been stronger he would have cried out in rage at the heavens, cursing the gods for their cruelty, but as it was he was too weak to do anything more than whimper his anguish as the visions slowly faded from his sight, giving way to utter exhaustion and a weakness so terrible he wondered if he would ever be able to move again.

She was gone. No longer in Gansang. He had lost her . . .

And then the final tower faded, and there was only darkness.

Chapter 21

THERE WAS a bath waiting for Gwynofar when she returned to her bedchamber after her meeting with Danton and Kostas. Apparently her maidservant Merian had grown accustomed to the fact that she liked to bathe after meeting with the Magister and had anticipated the request. On another day that might have bothered Gwynofar—it meant she had been less than perfect in hiding her true feelings about the man—but the truth was that right now she was too tired to care. Her body and soul felt as if hordes of roaches had been scuttling across them, and experience had taught her that soap and water would at least make the physical sensation go away. The rest—the rest just took time. Kostas' foul presence was something she had to digest and then purge before she could be free of it.

She smiled gratefully over the bath, glad for once not to have to be giving orders. She knew that if the older woman ever did guess just how much Kostas disturbed her she would never speak of it to another soul. Such loyalty was rare among the High King's staff, but Merian was of northern blood, Protectorate born and raised, and had come to this land in Gwynofar's own retinue. Her first loyalty was to the Lord Protector's bloodline and to the gods that were their patrons, not to this castle full of iconoclastic foreigners, no matter how fierce and feared its royal master might be.

Gwynofar let Merian help her off with her black gown and the thin chemise she wore beneath it, then lowered herself gratefully into the iron-bound tub, letting the late summer heat seep out of her flesh into the cool fresh water. Sprigs of rosemary and summer mint had been sprinkled into the water, and the smell helped open her pores and relax her mind. The soap was likewise perfumed, and after holding it to her nose for a moment she began to rub it languidly along her skin. The smells reminded her of the world she had grown up in, always filled with the scent of fresh bread baking in the great ovens and the sound of children's laughter. So different from this dank place. No one ever seemed to laugh here except her husband, and his laughter was deemed by many a thing to be feared. With a sigh she sank down deep into the perfumed bath, letting images of the past comfort her as the knotted tension in her body began to give way.

It made no sense, really, this need she had to scrub herself clean after leaving Kostas' presence. But whatever the foulness it was that she sensed within him, it seemed to cling to her skin like a skunk's smell afterward, and she never felt right until she had washed it away. Ah, would that mere soap could cleanse the spirit as easily as it cleaned the flesh! She leaned forward and let Merian attend to her back, ordering her to rub harder when her first gentle strokes failed to banish the Magister's perceived stink. Yes, she knew in her heart that it was all nonsense, this fantasy of hers, but it gave her some small comfort to indulge it. She could not make the Magister leave her life in fact, but in the privacy of her bath she could banish him from her presence. Soap had that power at least.

Why do you hate him so much? Rhys' voice whispered in her mind. *Why does he make you feel so unclean?*

I don't know, my brother. I wish I did.

"Shall I wash your hair?" her maidservant asked.

She nodded, and shut her eyes as Merian began to remove the ivory pins that held the twisted blonde coils tightly against her head. There was some noise in the hallway beyond the chamber's door, but Gwynofar put it out of her mind. Her other servants knew enough not to bother her when she was bathing, and they would doubtless waylay anyone who would seek to do so.

A long coil of blond hair slipped down onto her shoulder and she began to stroke it with a soapy hand, drawing it into the perfumed water, separating the strands—

—and the door swung roughly open then, and Merian's gasp made Gwynofar look up.

High King Danton stood framed in the doorway.

"My . . . my lord?"

He strode into the room as if it were his own, this sanctuary which was hers, this private room which he had never invaded. He nodded sharply to the maidservant to leave them and for a moment Merian just stood there frozen, like a deer staring down the shaft of a hunter's arrow. Then, with trembling hands but great dignity, pointedly *not* leaving, she lifted Gwynofar's robe from off the bed and held it out to her.

There was no point in ordering the woman away, even though her disobedience put her at great risk; she would not leave her mistress in this state. Gwynofar stood up silently in the bath, determined to be dignified even in nakedness, and let Merian wrap the thin linen robe around her, its lower end trailing into the soapy water. Then she looked at her and said softly, "Go." She could see the doubt in the woman's eyes but her own queenly gaze did not waver, and after a moment Merian lowered her eyes, curtseyed low, and scurried from the room. Danton did not blink as she passed, nor avert his eyes from his wife, which was probably a good sign for Merian, though an ominous one for Gwynofar.

The High Queen felt herself tremble inside as she stepped out of the tub, but she steeled her flesh so that Danton would not see it. The king had never made any formal promise he would not visit her bedchamber. It was just that in the years after their daughters were born, he simply had not done so. Very well. Now he was here. She was his queen, and would receive him appropriately. Never, ever would she let him see that she feared him, that she feared his temper, that she feared most of all what he was like in the moments when he had just left his Magister, when Kostas' black sorcery seemed to swirl palpably about his soul and bring out all that was worst in his nature.

"You wish to speak to me, my husband?"

He huffed and looked about the room, taking it all in in a glance. His eyes lighted briefly upon the bedside altar, strewn with talismans of northern manufacture and set with half a dozen blood-colored candles. He knew that when he wasn't around she would prepare for sleep with a litany of prayers to the ancient gods and their mystical rocks, which had as much meaning to him as if she skipped around the bed chanting children's rhymes. But the practice seemed to comfort her and so he had never forbidden it, just asked that it not be performed in his presence.

Today however he scowled at the altar directly and she felt her heart grow cold, wondering what had brought him here so soon after the meeting with Kostas, and dreading the answer.

The Magister must know how much I hate him. One cannot keep secrets from his kind.

"A strange hour to be bathing," he said quietly.

The knot that was forming in her stomach tightened a bit more. Danton was a direct man—some said brutally direct—and the fact that he was commenting upon something so innocuous as her bath hour did not bode well for his purpose here.

"I was not aware there was some specific custom here regarding bath time," she replied evenly. "Of course if there is, I shall be glad to accommodate His Majesty."

He huffed again. His eyes flicked back and forth restlessly, as they did when he was angry about something—*about what?*—but as always her steady, soft tone seemed to disarm him. She had been his wife for two decades now and had weathered more than one storm by the strength of her serenity.

But that was before Kostas came, she thought. The knot of fear grew at the thought of him but she kept her expression calm, steady, radiant.

The High King's roving gaze took in the altar, the ironwood bed with its northern carvings, the hanging tapestries with their scenes of snow-covered mountains, winter hunts, and the Veil of the Gods. "This is more a foreign place than when I last was here."

"You had less interest in the furnishings when you last were here," she reminded him.

It should have brought a smile to his face, but it did not.

He came to where she stood, the fine linen of her gown now wet enough to cling to her body, revealing its contours. She bore herself as though she wore a fine gown with all its trappings. He fingered the edge of the robe, which she had scored with small cut marks in deference to her mourning. His fingers brushed the line of her neck, the damp curve of her breast. This close to her it seemed she could smell the stink of Kostas on him, and it took everything she had not to pull away in revulsion.

" 'Tis a hard thing, losing a son."

Her voice caught in her throat. "So it is, my husband."

"Hard for the kingdom as well, losing an heir."

She simply nodded. Andovan would rather have been eaten alive by jackals than take upon himself the stifling responsibilities of the High King's throne, but she was not about to tell Danton that. She and her son had whispered of it in the garden, in *her* garden, where only the gods were listening, and she would not betray that confidence even after his death.

"You served me well. Four sons in four years. Though some say there must be magic to such a family line, to have been managed so perfectly."

Though his tone had grown colder by merely a single degree, she did not miss its sudden edge. "Sire?"

His finger caught her under the chin; his dark eyes narrowed. "Few women have managed such perfect fertility. Even those whose lives depended upon their success." He let the words hang in the air for a moment, allowing her time to remember his father and his habit of executing wives who failed to provide heirs in a timely manner. "I am grateful the gods have given me a wife so *skilled* in the womanly arts."

She lowered her eyes humbly, hoping he could not hear her heart pounding, nor sense its rapid pace through his finger on her skin. "It is simply a gift of the gods, Sire, for which I am humbly grateful."

"*Is* it that?" She could sense the barely tethered rage in him, held just beneath his surface. What had caused this? Was there some news about Andovan she did not know about, or had one of her other children committed some act that angered their father? Or was it simply that Kostas was interfering in her personal life, for gods alone knew what reason?

He hates me as much as I hate him, she thought.

"Only the gods?" he demanded.

"Sire?"

He grabbed her by the shoulders and pulled her toward him. His grip was harsh and painful, his fingers digging bruises into her pale flesh. "What other man has had input into my line?" he demanded.

The question was so unexpected that for a moment she just stared at him. Then, in a trembling voice, she managed, "You think I was untrue to you?"

With a cry of rage he threw her across the room and onto the bed. In that moment she could smell the unwholesome reek of Kostas all about her, and for a moment—just a moment—it seemed she could hear his laughter.

Is he behind this? she thought desperately. *Does he mean to have Danton kill me?*

"What, to make me a cuckold? That I could deal with. That is a *human* thing." He came over to where she lay and caught her slender neck in one brute hand. "That requires only the death of the offender—the public execution of the wife—preferably in some dramatically unpleasant manner, to warn others who might follow in her footsteps . . . business as usual for a king, my dear, yes?" His dark eyes blazed. "My father did it often enough."

Before she could answer him he reached up with his other hand, grabbed the neck of her robe and pulled. The seams of the garment gave way with a sharp ripping sound, leaving her torso stripped bare, the sleeves still tangled damply about her arms.

"Your crime is not nearly so simple, is it?" His voice was a low growl, black with fury. "Only to foul my line with sorcery, as a woman might do with a weakling king that could not beget his own."

Speechless, she stared at him. And it seemed for a moment she could see Kostas' power surrounding Danton, not as an illusion of foreboding but a more palpable power that blazed about him like a black corona and streaked his skin like veins of jet. Whatever response she might have offered was choked off by the horror of the vision. What enchantment had the vile Magister worked upon her husband that was revealed to her senses in this way?

Danton took her silence for an admission of guilt and with a growl low in his throat pinned her back against the bed with one hand, reaching to his own clothes with the other. With a sudden understanding that was almost surreal she knew he was about to rape her, knew as well that the act was not wholly his, that some vile magic was lodged in his brain like a parasite, driving him to this bestial rage. She watched in horror as he bared himself for the act, revealing an organ that was not only swollen red with rage, but with corruption. For her vision was bolstered by the gift of the northern gods, and she could see a webwork of black, swollen veins wrapped around his flesh, the conduits of some unnamed sorcery. Whatever that power was, whether it came from Kostas or some other source, she could not let it into her body! She struggled against him in fear, trying to deny him entrance, but his rage lent him unnatural strength and she was but a small woman, lacking either the strength or the skill to dislodge him. His knee forced her legs apart with a force that made her cry out in pain and in terror, and then—and then he was inside her, thrusting his rage deep into her body, and with it that foreign sorcery. Where did it come from? What did it want? What was it using Danton for, riding the heat of his rage like a hunter might ride a mount, forcing the High King to do its bidding? She knew the answers mattered but she could not focus on them, she was lost in the pounding rhythm of her husband's rage and the desperate need to deny that her husband would treat her thus.

It is not him. It is someone else, causing this. Danton would not do this to me.

And then it was over. She turned on her side, curling up around her pain and her shame, and wept. Her insides felt bruised and raw, and her soul throbbed with a pain that was almost beyond bearing. *Would that I were really a witch, that I might heal such things!* She was aware of Danton watching over her for a moment, aware also that he had never seen her weep like this before; she did not look up at him, but curled herself even more tightly into a ball on the bed, feeling a thin trickle of blood run down her thighs; her flesh stung in a dozen places where he had bruised her, angry purple blood already rising to the surface in witness to his violence.

Then, with a final snort of disgust, he left her alone. She listened to his footsteps moving across the room, heard the door open, heard it fall shut of its own weight behind him.

A short while later Merian returned, and the servant held her mistress in her arms for a while as the tears flowed, murmuring curses against the High King that would have gotten her executed on the spot, had they been witnessed. Gwynofar felt too weak to silence her. At last Merian helped her back into the tub, where she scrubbed her down with soap and gentle caresses, as one would an infant. But soap could not cleanse her spirit of the pollution that had taken root inside her, and several times Gwynofar almost vomited, remembering the sight of her husband's body streaked black with that foreign sorcery. Was that inside her now, riding Danton's seed like some ghastly stallion, into the secret recesses of her body? If not, why had she seen it? What was its purpose?

And then, late in the night, when moonlit shadows shivered across the bed, creeping along the body of the battered queen, the gods of the Protectors whispered the truth in her ear. Just as they always did with the daughters of their most favored race, a gift they had granted to the women of the Protectors' bloodlines many, many centuries ago.

There will be another child, the gods whispered to her, in that moment when sleep fell upon her. *Already he makes ready to draw strength from your flesh in order to grow. Can you feel him inside you yet? Does he stir your maternal loyalty?*

"Is it a true child?" she whispered into the darkness. "Or something else? Please tell me!"

But the gods, as always, choose what questions they wish to answer . . . and this time there was only silence.

Chapter 22

THE SKY was pitch black, with a pair of crescent moons facing in opposite directions. They were the color of freshly spilled blood, and the sky that backed them had no stars or other natural features, but was lightless and empty for as far as the eye could see. The dark pines beneath them glittered as if with dew, but it was not the time for dew, and teardrops of ice hung suspended from every needle, as if the trees themselves had frozen in the act of weeping.

It was an impossible landscape from start to finish and therefore, Ethanus reasoned, a dream.

There was only one person walking the earth these days that would send him a dream. He was pleased that she had taken his lessons to heart so well, and designed a setting that would alert him to its nature, but he was disturbed by the tenor of her creation. The moons in particular looked more like wounds in the sky than natural spheres. It was a small detail, but it worried him. Dreams were a strangely insightful medium, that reflected in shadows and hints the condition of the soul that created them. These signs, if they truly reflected the state of Kamala's soul, were anything but reassuring.

After a moment the shadows parted and a figure approached him. It was draped in a long black cloak, the hood drawn forward so its face could not be seen. For a brief moment Ethanus wondered if his assumption about the dreamcaster's identity had been incorrect but the figure reached up and pushed back the hood, and Kamala was revealed to him. She was pale and drawn and had deep circles under her eyes, such as might come of exhaustion or grief. Her clothing was streaked with black and in tatters, yet another reflection of the torment within. Bad signs all around.

"Kamala?"

Her voice was a whisper, hoarse as if from crying. Surely his fiery pupil could not have been crying! "Forgive me, my master." She lowered her eyes in a rare gesture of submission; wrong, all wrong. "I know it is not the custom for students to seek council after they have left their mentor—"

"If I did not expect you to break that rule I would not have given you my ring." He wished he could use his sorcerous senses to gain more insight, but in a dream all he would see was what she wished to show him . . . and that was probably already visible. "What has happened?"

Her gaze was a terrible, haunted thing. Her bloodshot eyes fixed on him for a moment as if she was deciding what she dared say, and finally, in a voice no louder than a breath, she whispered, "I have broken the Law."

A cold chill ran up his spine. "How so?"

"I killed a Magister."

He shut his eyes for a moment, and whispered a short prayer under his breath. When he was sure he could keep his voice steady he looked at her again and asked quietly, "How so?"

"It was an accident. He accosted me, and I defended myself, and he . . . fell." She shook her head. "It was a long fall. He had time to save himself." She bit her lip, hard enough to draw a drop of blood. "He did nothing. Just . . . fell."

Ethanus drew in a sharp breath. "Transition?"

"I don't know. He looked like . . . like a morati. Just helpless."

"Do the others know?

She winced. "Magisters?"

He nodded.

"Probably. There were at least three others nearby."

He had to ask it. "Do they know what you really are?"

"I don't think so."

Exhaling noisily, he turned away from her and tried to think. By all rights and Magister custom he should cast her out of his territory, now and forever. Then again, by all rights and Magister custom they should not even be talking. She should not have his ring. She should not have been made a Magister in the first place. There were so many other rules that he had broken for this one that had once been sacrosanct. . . .

He turned back to her, and saw with a start there were tears on her face. He had never imagined that anything could shake her badly enough to make her shed tears in front of him. He swallowed the knot that rose in his throat at the sight and made his voice as steady as it could possibly be. "You must retrieve your things," he told her. "Everything that they could possibly use to track you down. Not only clothing and possessions—the obvious relics—but every hair, every fingernail clipping, every flake of skin you might have left behind. Your scent upon the sheets, the oil of your skin on a doorknob, your finger's smudge on a bedpost—all of it."

She nodded.

"They may catch you doing that—there is that danger—but if they do not know you are a Magister, I doubt they will be alert for sorcery." He rubbed the bridge of his nose between two fingers, trying to think. "They know your name? What you look like?"

She whispered, "No. I don't think so."

"You can change your flesh now, if you are not certain of it."

She nodded, "I know."

Often before he had suggested she change her flesh, for one reason or another, and she had always responded with indignation, declaring that she would not be forced out of the body she was born into for any other man's convenience. The fact that she did not protest the suggestion now told him just how much this affair had shaken her.

"Will they hunt me?" She asked it softly.

"Do the morati know that a Magister was killed?"

She shut her eyes, remembering. "Yes." The ice-laden pine trees sighed in the wind. "They were gathering around the body as I fled."

He exhaled sharply. "Then, yes. I am sorry. There might be more options if the death were a secret, but if the morati know the Magisters will need to hunt down the killer and execute judgment as quickly as possible, lest the common folk learn that they can kill one of us and get away with it." He shook his head grimly. "It is bad enough when they learn that we can die."

She nodded. Her shoulders trembled slightly. "Master Ethanus, you must believe me . . . I did not intend this to happen—"

He raised up a hand to silence her. "I know, Kamala. I am the one who taught you the Law, remember? You would never seek the life of a Magister. If only because you knew what the cost would be."

What it must be now, he thought.

Ah, my beautiful but wild-hearted apprentice, could you not have waited a while before offending against our entire brotherhood? Maybe all of one peaceful year before you shook our world to its very roots?

"I will do what you say," she whispered.

"Get far away from them, quickly, and stay away. Do not play at laying down false trails for them to follow, or any other fugitive trick. They have centuries' experience more than you do at that kind of thing; you may wind up giving them more information than you intended."

Her eyes flared defiantly for a moment, diamond-bright in the darkness. Even in the midst of her troubles, the suggestion that she could not best another Magister was unacceptable to her.

Ah, Kamala, that same spirit which is your strength is also your greatest weakness. May the gods watch over you for its sake.

"I do not ask you to help me," she said. "Or protect me."

"No." He nodded. "You do not."

"Nor will I come back here and bring trouble to you. Do not fear on that account."

There was a brief tightness in his heart. "No," he said quietly. "You cannot return to me."

You stand outside the Law now. That fate cannot be shared with another.

She bowed her head respectfully. The gesture reminded him of when she had first come to him, a fiery and determined child ready to take on the world. *And now you have done so,* he thought. *Was it worth it? Do you, when the shadows of doubt draw too close, regret the course you have chosen?*

It was more of a rhetorical question than a real one. If ever she truly regretted becoming a Magister her soul would lose the strength it needed to fight for continued life, her consort would break free of his bond, and she would die. The fact that she still walked the earth bore witness to her continued commitment.

"I am sorry to come to you now," she whispered. "I know you must break the Law even to talk to me—"

"No, I have broken no Law."

He met her bright eyes with his own, willing all the strength he could into his voice, that she might partake of it and refresh her own spirit. "I had a dream, nothing more. It is hard to tell dreams from reality, sometimes." He paused. "This was an odd dream, for I imagined that an old student of mine returned to me and revealed that she had broken our Law, and then asked for my counsel. Of course she would not do that, for she knows our ways. And I would not give my counsel to one who had killed a Magister."

She nodded. Her eyes glistened. There were no tears this time. That was good.

"Besides," he said softly, "The moons were at odds with one another. So how could it have been real?"

"How indeed?" she whispered.

For a moment she just stood there. The trees groaned softly in the breeze; a single frozen teardrop fell to the ground and shattered there. He had the sudden desire to take her in his arms, to kiss her gently on the forehead, as one might with a child. To give her comfort. But it was not his way . . . nor was it hers.

"Thank you," she whispered. No louder than a breath. Then she drew the cloak's hood forward over her head once more, and with it the shadows of the night, until she became one with them, and slowly faded from his sight. He stood there until she was wholly gone, silent and unmoving, savoring the last moments of her presence, wondering if he would ever see her again except in a dream. While overhead the bloodred moons grew pale and silver even as she vanished, and the pines beneath them shed their frozen coats and the world became normal once more.

Except for the ache in his heart, more terrible than any earthly wound could ever be.

Go with the gods, he thought.

Chapter 23

THE PALACE of the Witch-Queen glowed like a beacon in the sunlight, its outer colonnade almost too bright to gaze upon directly. One could see it from miles away, perched on a hilltop overlooking the port city of Sankara, an elegant monument set against a backdrop of soft clouds and the rich turquoise of a late summer sky. Peaceful, Colivar thought. It always looked so peaceful.

The wind had been quiet for three days when he arrived, so the harbor below was filled with ships of all kinds, awaiting passage through the Narrows to the eastern seas. From the cliff-top gardens they looked like a flock of white birds perched upon the water, bobbing gently with the rhythm of the waves. Doubtless a few of the captains had access to a witch or Magister who could make the wind blow, but either those efforts had been stalemated by other sorcerers who wished it to remain calm, or all were simply content to wait. And why not? It was a beautiful city that had been catering to travelers for centuries, a regularly scheduled stop for merchant ships before they committed themselves to the waters of the east. Some considered themselves lucky if the wind died while they were there.

Most Magisters who visited the palace traveled in one winged form or another, but Colivar preferred to make the trip as the morati did, riding up past terraced gardens on horseback until at last he reached the uppermost levels. There were always servants waiting to see to the welfare of guests, and one took his reins as soon as he dismounted while another went running to the palace to announce his arrival. It was of course no problem that he had arrived without warning; the woman they called the Witch-Queen was always ready to receive Magisters, announced or otherwise, and their arrival took precedence over all other business.

Soon a young girl appeared to lead Colivar to her mistress. She was a slender little thing dressed in layers of silk that fluttered like butterfly wings as she moved, and she wore a veil of translucent gauze that did more to draw attention to her features than to hide them. Probably from the desert lands, Colivar thought. Siderea's servants came from all over the world and she let them dress as they preferred, which made for a remarkable court. Doubtless she had sent this child to Colivar because she associated him with the tribes of Anshasa and thought it would please him, though if she knew him better she might have sent a hardy blonde in northern furs instead.

Siderea Aminestas was waiting for him in an audience chamber fashioned in the southern style, with low couches laden with silken coverlets and thick, plush cushions scattered about the room. She was a striking woman, not beautiful in the traditional sense, but possessed of a presence that permeated whatever space she was in. Her coffee-colored skin glowed with the warm highlights of the Sankaran sun, and her long black hair was braided with jewels that glittered as she moved. A thin line of gold paint bordered her eyes, giving her the aspect of a great cat, and as she stretched forth a hand to greet Colivar it was almost as if some feline spirit had entered her flesh, along with all the languid sensuality of its species.

"Colivar." She smiled. "I was just thinking of you."

He kissed the hand she offered and smiled in turn. "You say that to all the sorcerers."

"Posh on that. Only to the pretty ones." She rose to a more upright position on the couch, making room for him beside her. "Why do they come to me in such awful bodies? You would think if a man had the power to look like anything he wanted he would choose something more appealing. Like this." Her slender hand caught up a lock of his hair, twisting it playfully around her index finger. "I have always liked this one."

He chuckled. "It has served me well."

As he settled himself on the couch beside her another servant entered and stood by the door, awaiting her word. "You will take refreshment?" she asked. "I have a fine pomegranate cordial I think you would like. Sent to me by an admirer in Eskadora. Will you try it?"

"You know I cannot refuse you, lady."

She nodded to the girl, who backed out silently to fetch the drink. "You are my greatest flatterer, you know that, Colivar? Some days I think that Magisters are above mere social pleasantries and then you show up at my door, as silk-tongued as the finest courtier, and prove me wrong. In truth, you make the others seem like barbarians by contrast."

He raised her hand to his lips and kissed it softly again. "And you, my lady, are known to flatter whichever sorcerer is by your side in terms so pleasing we do not care if there are others waiting in the shadows."

She laughed softly. "Ah, but you would not wish to have me all to yourself, would you? For then I should become demanding, and perhaps expect loyalty in turn."

"And we cannot have that," he agreed.

The young girl returned, and the two of them fell silent. Colivar noted that she kept her eyes low as she set a silver tray on the table before them, as if she was not worthy of looking directly at her superiors. That too was a desert custom. He wondered if it was a habit natural to the girl, or something Siderea had asked her to do while Colivar was present.

When she was gone the Magister leaned back on the couch, watching as Siderea poured him a portion of the bloodred cordial. "So what do the barbarians gossip about, these days?"

"That the High King Danton is mad, and threw all the Magisters out of his domain."

He chuckled as she handed him a glass. "All too true on the latter count, I am afraid. It was quite a scene. The madness . . . that is not news."

"They say that another Magister has come to serve him now, one called Kostas, and he is a mystery to all of you."

Colivar shrugged. "No Magister seems to have heard the name before, or recognizes the body he wears. Which in itself does not mean very much. We can change such things as easily as other men change their clothes."

"But most do not do so, yes?" She sipped from her own glass and then reclined on the couch beside him. The layers of her gown parted over one leg, baring sleek copper skin. "Magisters seem to enjoy their reputations."

"Aye, most do," he agreed. He sipped the cordial, and nodded his approval as it slid warmly down his throat. "He is welcome to Danton as far as I am concerned. The man has been mad from the cradle."

"But his madness has made him powerful, and men are drawn to power."

He smiled slightly, running his glass along the line of her thigh. "And women are not?"

She sniffed. "I would rather bed an iguana."

"Interestingly," he noted, "that is how I have heard this Kostas described. Perhaps you should add him to your collection."

"You do not think he is dangerous, then?"

"All Magisters are dangerous, my lady."

"I meant Danton."

"Ah." He stared into the deep red depths of his glass, considering an answer. "Danton has always been dangerous," he said at last, "especially to princes who are in the way of his expansion. But I think perhaps his glory days are coming to an end. For years he had Ramirus to guide him, and to rein in his temper. The High King has yet to prove that he can manage the same feats without such a mentor." He shook his head. "I never understood what that bearded old fool saw in him. Maybe just a challenging project."

"Corialanus is worried."

"Corialanus should be worried. As should all of Danton's immediate neighbors. When madmen fall they tend to take other people down with them." He looked at her. "Sankara will be spared, I am sure. You have enough Magisters wrapped about your lovely little finger to see to that."

She pouted sweetly. "I am not sure if that is a compliment or a challenge."

"Perhaps both," he said with an enigmatic smile.

You will be safe, he thought, *because in all the world there is no other person who can offer the Magisters what you do. To serve as a repository for news of our kind, so that those who visit you may be thoroughly updated. To give us a way to ally our common interests, without needing to admit that we value alliance. Where else has such a thing ever existed, in our world? Who would take your place if Sankara fell?*

He drained the last drops of cordial from his glass and set it aside. "What other news, besides madmen and iguanas?"

"There was a death in Gansang. A Magister. So my contacts say."

He stiffened. "A Magister? Are you sure?"

"How can one be sure of things half a world away? I give you what I have heard. You have better means than I to discover the truth."

He nodded. "Fair enough, then. Tell me more."

"They say he fell from a high bridge, or else some sort of tower, my sources were not sure which. They say he hit the ground without aid of sorcery and died as mortal men die, crushed by the impact."

"But that is . . ." He could not find an appropriate word. Yes, an accident might claim the life of a Magister, but it usually was an end that struck swiftly, so that the victim had no time to muster his power in self-defense. A falling man would have time enough to conjure up any of a dozen spells to save himself on his way to the ground. If this one was dead, then there was some reason he had not done so. Perhaps he was even dead before he had begun his fatal descent. Why? "How did he come to fall? Do you know?"

She shook her head. "Apparently he was following some woman at the time. None saw them meet. The next thing anyone knew was that passersby saw him plummet to the ground, and by the time anyone thought to look up to the place he had fallen from there was no one there. The woman is gone, apparently. Though they are searching." She sighed. "I do not blame her—even if she is innocent of wrongdoing, they will want someone to blame, and women are always easy targets for that."

"You know the names? The one who died? This woman they think he was following?"

With a smile she reached into her bodice and brought forth a folded slip of paper. "I thought you might ask for that. Here it is, all of it. And the names of three other Magisters said to be present. The woman was new to the city, I have only her name—for now."

He took the paper from her. "You are a treasure as always, my jewel."

He looked over the list of names. The Magister who had died was unknown to him; the others were vaguely familiar from ages past, men of minor power and little renown. Would any of them have breached the Law to bring down one of their own kind? It was a dark thought indeed, but not one he found likely. The Law was the Law because all Magisters understood that staying alive required such rules to be absolute. Magisters did not kill Magisters; never had, never would.

But there must be sorcery involved in this somehow, he thought. *He would not have died otherwise.*

"Tell me about this woman," he said quietly.

"No one seems to know very much about her. Some witch that one of the local merchants had brought with him. They said she was very beautiful, but very cold. Do you think that is why he followed her?" Her lips curled into a smile. "Maybe the Magisters of the west are starved for beauty."

"No doubt that is it," he said distantly.

Andovan's little fortune-teller had told him that a woman was killing him. Now there was a woman involved in a Magister's death. Was there any connection between the two? Women of power were rare enough in the world that it was a reasonable thing to consider.

And then there was the Witch-Queen herself. He had defended her in the company of the other Magisters, insisting she had nothing to do with Andovan's illness, but that was more to put others off her trail than because he was sure of her innocence. If a woman of power was somehow connected to the prince, draining him of strength . . . well, there were not all that many in the world who might be capable of such a thing, and Siderea Aminestas was one of them.

If she ever claimed her immortality, became a Magister in truth, would she even tell us? Or would she continue to play the same game she always has, delighting in our ignorance?

"Tell me," he said softly. He leaned close and whispered the words into her hair, in lover's tones. "What do you know of Prince Andovan, of the Aurelius line?"

"Danton's get?" She drew back far enough to look up at him. "Isn't he the one that killed himself?"

"Yes."

She nodded. "There was quite a flurry after that one. I had more guests than I knew what to do with. Seating that many Magisters at the same dinner table is not unlike putting rival wolves in the same pit."

He smiled faintly. "Doubtless those who were visiting from halfway across the world did not wish to return home without witnessing your legendary charms first, my lady."

"They said he was a skilled hunter, strong in health until the illness took him. That Aurelius had called many Magisters together to find a cure, and they had failed him, and he had cast them all out in fury, including his own Magister Royal. Whom I have not yet met, by the way."

"Ramirus?" Colivar chuckled. "He is not your type."

"Ah, do I have a 'type?' I did not know."

A Magister who can kiss a morati without feeling as if he is kissing dead flesh. That is no small thing, my queen.

"Perhaps not," he said. "Tell me more of Andovan."

She knew the invitation for what it was, and though she raised a finely plucked eyebrow in curiosity, did not ask why he required it. She had dealt with Magisters long enough and intimately enough to know that some secrets would not be shared. So she told him of Andovan, passing along such court gossip as had reached Sankara, while Colivar used his power to measure what was hidden deep within the depths of her soul.

She did not know him, he determined at last, *or have any reason to harm him. She had nothing to do with his illness.*

A wave of relief passed over him; a burden he had not even realized he was carrying was lifted suddenly from his shoulders. She must have sensed the change in him for she asked softly, "Are you satisfied?"

He nodded.

There were too many puzzle pieces to sort out in all this. Too little sense of the overall pattern. Not for the first time, he wished Siderea were someone he could truly confide in so that she could help him ferret out the answers. But she was morati, and no matter how many Magisters might trade gossip with her in her gardens, no matter how much useful information she might give him, that meant there was a barrier between them that could never be breached.

Another servant entered, this one a young boy with the fair skin of the northlands and a costume to match. He carried in his hands a finely carved ebony box with golden hinges, which he handled as if it were a priceless treasure. He came to where the two of them sat and knelt before them, offering the box to Siderea with his head bowed, as if he would not deem himself worthy to view its contents. She drew a small golden key on a chain from out of her bosom and unlocked it, fingered the few dozen papers inside, and at last drew one forth. "I believe this is for you." She relocked the box, slid the key back into the neck of her gown, and nodded for the servant to leave them. "Left by a Magister named Sulah. A student of yours, I gather?"

"Long ago. I did not know he had made your acquaintance."

"All Magisters do, in time." She smiled. "Or so they tell me."

The paper was a simple note, unsealed. He unfolded it and recognized Sulah's neat handwriting within. *Contact me soon,* it said, with the single initial *S* scribed below. Colivar ran his fingers over the words and felt the whisper of power adhering to them. Enough to enable him to establish a link with Sulah one time before it faded. Good enough.

He tucked the note away.

"I have served you well tonight, my sorcerer?" she murmured.

He reached up to her face and stroked her cheek softly, a lover's touch. "Always. Now how may I serve you in turn?"

"That is not necessary. It is a humble woman's honor to serve the Magisters."

"And my pleasure to thank the humble woman for that service."

"Ah. Well then. I would not deny you *pleasure.*"

"Speak, then." He leaned back on the couch again. "The power is restless within me. Tell me where I may give it outlet."

She lay down beside him, playing with a lock of his hair. Her skin smelled like sweet almonds, warm and inviting. "I hear the western fields of Corialanus are wanting rain. The summer has been long and dry there, the crops are suffering. Perhaps you would like to help?"

He chuckled softly. "You promised rain to Corialanus?"

"Lord Hadrian knows I am a witch. He asked me to help his people. How can I refuse?"

"I am surprised he does not ask his own king for aid. There are sorcerers enough in that court."

"I gather he does not wish to become indebted to his king more than he must." Her dark eyes glittered. "It is . . . interesting, yes?"

He chuckled softly. "He will pay you well enough to compensate for true witchery?"

"He will, when I require it. For now, let us say he will owe me a great debt."

"Very great, when he asks that a portion of your life be expended for his sake."

She laughed merrily. "Yet the people see that the years pass and I do not die, and they wonder why, Colivar. Do you know what they say now? They whisper that I am a Magister."

"Yes. I have heard those whispers."

"When the truth is merely that I please the Magisters." She leaned close and brushed his lips with her own. It was a tantalizing half-kiss that stirred Colivar's flesh more than he expected. Normally Magisters were immune to such temptation, not because they were incapable of physical indulgence, but simply because when a man could have any woman that he desired, or create a simulacra of any woman for an evening's pleasure, the game simply lost its edge.

Except in this place.

Truly, Colivar thought, if there was any woman fit to be a Magister it was this one. She was already closer to their brotherhood than any woman had ever been; what a small step it would be to manage that final transformation! Though, if she claimed that kind of power and still kept her alliances she would be the most dangerous Magister alive, and in time those who did not share her bed would probably unite to bring her down. Maybe even those who did. The black-robed sorcerers were loyal to allies only for as long as they needed them—or until they decided someone was a threat to them.

Thank the fates there are no women among us, Colivar thought. *Our society would be torn to pieces if there were.*

And then the hand that stroked his cheek moved on to other places, and he let himself surrender to the moment, and to such pleasures as a morati woman might inspire.

————

The night breeze swept in from the Sea of Gods, rich with the scent of salt tides and seaweed. It stirred the gauze curtains as it entered the bedchamber, and set to shivering the fine silk hangings that were draped from a frame above the wide bed, thwarting the approach of insects.

Colivar lay awake for a long while, tasting the breeze, reading its message. In another day the wind would blow strongly enough for ships to sail through the Narrows. The harbor would empty then, and Sankara would prepare for its next round of visitors while its ruler prepared her house for the visit of still more Magisters, who would come to share gossip, leave messages for one another, and perhaps seek a brief respite from the machinations of less personable monarchs.

The world will be a darker place when this morati dies, he thought.

He wondered just when that would be. Already she had ruled Sankara for four decades, but no one was sure of how old she'd been when she arrived. He did not think that any Magister knew her true age, and she certainly never spoke of it, preferring to surround herself with mystery.

She was young. That was all that other morati saw. Eternally, supernaturally young. In the beginning it would not have seemed so remarkable—any witch willing to pay the price could alter her flesh to look youthful—but as the years went by and she did not die the premature death of a witch, as her lifespan equaled and then exceeded that of the healthiest of mortals and still she showed no sign of weakening, it must have become clear to all that something other than witchery was involved.

He wondered if any of her household had guessed the truth: that each visiting Magister in his turn repaired her aging flesh, taking on that duty just as they voluntarily took on other projects for her. That the power the "Witch-Queen" wielded was not her own power at all, and therefore did not cost her a fraction of her own life. How far back in her history did that arrangement go? Had she lived a witch's life before her first affair with a Magister, or waited until a sorcerous patron was located before even thinking of using the power? Without knowing her true age, he could not hazard a guess.

Yet you are morati, my queen, and so there will come a point when even all our sorcery cannot save you.

Gently he placed a hand upon her brow, binding stolen soulfire to his fingertips, and caressed those places where the first lines of age were beginning to show. Delicate crow's feet vanished at his touch, and the fine lines at the corners of her mouth grew faint and disappeared. She sighed in her sleep and turned her head slightly but did not awaken. From his distant consort Colivar drew yet more power, and he bathed her in it, letting her skin draw nourishment and youth from the immersion. The irony of killing one morati to benefit another was not lost on him. Did she sense his efforts in her sleep, perhaps suffering shadowy nightmares that hinted at the cost of her beauty? He would never ask, but he always wondered.

When he had done all he could to preserve her youthful appearance, he gathered his power and looked deep within her flesh, seeking less visible hallmarks of age. Where her muscles had weakened, he strengthened them. Where blood flowed too sluggishly, he cleared its path. There was a place in her heart where the beat was not certain, and he repaired its rhythm. There was a place in her female parts where the flesh had grown awry, and he dissolved the growth and encouraged her body to reabsorb it, not resting until he saw that safely done.

He had done such things for her many times, as had the others. But one other thing he did regularly as well, one that he had never told her about. Deep, deep within her soul he looked now, following the currents of athra to their source, seeking that inner flame from which both life and sorcery drew their strength. That one thing alone which no Magister could bolster or repair, and which in time would falter and expire, as it did in all living creatures.

When he found it at last, he felt a cold chill run down his spine. No longer was the fire of her soul a blazing furnace as he remembered it, but a quieter thing, measurably dimmer. There was no question what that meant; not even a witchling could mistake it.

Her life was nearing its end.

How long would it be before she realized that something was amiss, and searched within herself for the cause? She still had a few years left to her—maybe as long as a decade if they kept her in perfect health—but in the end, the simple law that governed all living things could not be denied. Soon her vital energies would begin to sputter and fade, and not all the healing tricks of the Magisters could save her then.

What will you do when you realize you are dying? Surrender to the inevitable as the morati do, as all true witches must, and die with grace? Rage against the gods who made you a woman, and thus put salvation out of reach? Or perhaps curse the Magisters whose sorcery failed to save you?

Either way it would be the end of an era, he thought soberly, and he would mourn its passing.

He lay back down by her side, his cheek against a tangle of fine braids, and tried to quiet his thoughts enough to let the sea breeze carry him back to sleep.

Chapter 24

KAMALA STOLE some clothing.

She didn't have to. She could have just conjured something into existence and it would have covered her up just as well as the coarse woolen tunic she found hanging on a clothesline. But she didn't.

The role of thief was a comfortable one, familiar to her, and right now the role of sorcerer was not. The death of the scar-faced Magister still haunted her. In real life she had not seen his eyes as he fell but in her dreams she did, over and over again, and they were black with terror as he felt the power slipping from his fingers at the moment he needed it most, his desperation a thing so palpable that she could taste it on her lips as Transition rendered him suddenly helpless—

And he hit the ground.

Again.

And she awoke, shuddering.

Thievery did not have such a cost. Not if you were careful. She was a bit out of practice from all her years of living with Ethanus, of course, but they said that stealing a horse came back to you as easily as riding one did. Certainly sneaking around clotheslines under cover of night was an effortless task that quickly netted her the essentials of a peasant's costume. A boy peasant, of course. She wanted no more of the trouble that came from being a lone woman on the open road. Or anywhere else, for that matter.

Now, with a shirt torn into bands that she wrapped around her chest before dressing, flattening her breasts, and her wild red hair tucked into a cap, she appeared to be nothing more than a nondescript youth a bit down on his luck, dressed in patched and mended hand-me-downs. She even found a knife embedded in a tree stump where someone had left it for the next day's work, and liberated a loaf of bread from a windowsill where it was cooling. The bread was strangely satisfying, moreso than all the elite delicacies served by Tower Savresi. This simple fare was honestly made, honestly baked . . . honestly stolen.

She did not use sorcery. At all. It made a chill run up her spine just to contemplate doing so, knowing that any spell could plunge her into the darkness again so that she must find another consort or die. Ethanus had assured her that once First Transition was past there was really no doubt about the process succeeding—any Magister without the strength of will to claim a consort would not have survived that trial in the first place— but deep inside her soul, in that place where doubts and fears scurried about like beetles, Kamala was not so sure of herself. Transition was a quick process, Ethanus had taught her, nigh on painless after the first one. But had not he himself fled a royal appointment because of a bad experience with it? Had he not taken pains to teach her that she must try not to fall to Transition while surrounded by enemies, while also teaching her that there was no real way to control the experience?

Now it seemed she understood the true danger of it at last, as no mere words could have taught her. By its very nature, Transition was likely to weaken a Magister at the moment he needed his power the most. The greater his need, the greater his expenditure of athra, the more likely it was that his efforts would drain his current consort dry and suddenly leave him stranded, without power or consciousness.

She shuddered, remembering the terror in the fallen Magister's eyes.

No wonder some sorcerers were miserly with their power. No wonder so many chose to attach themselves to morati patrons, so that their daily needs might be met by mundane means in exchange for a handful of spells to suit their patron's less ambitious whims. There was far less effort involved in fixing a love potion for a morati prince and then letting him build a castle for you than there was in conjuring the same castle out of stolen athra . . . and therefore less risk. Little wonder that even such a bargain was not enough for some Magisters, who chose to leave the kingdoms of man entirely, as Ethanus had done, so long ago. Trading power for peace and draining their consorts slowly, gently, not because they cared if their victims lived or died, but because the time and place of that dying mattered.

It was all too much to think about. Too much to absorb right now. Easier for a while to just avoid using the power, and thus dodge the issue altogether.

When she had her new clothes on just right, and her reflection in a pool of water assured her that she looked passably like a boy, she caught a ride on a wagon loaded with bales of wool whose driver was too drunk to notice her clamber aboard. The bales smelled of sheep but they made for a soft perch, and she nibbled the last of her stolen bread as the wagon lurched onward, as comfortable in her wooly nest as the richest southern pasha reclining on silken cushions.

Which you could be, she reminded herself. *You might be anything you wanted, if you did not fear using the power.*

But that thought raised questions she was not willing to face just yet, and so she pushed the thought out of her mind and settled back into her nest of pungent bales, trying to find some state between waking and sleep that would allow her to rest without dreaming.

"They call it the Wasting."

The voice cut through all other sounds in the market, heading straight for Kamala's ears. She stiffened, seeking the source.

The wagon had brought her to a small but crowded plaza—probably a common market for several towns surrounding— but where exactly that was, she didn't know. Despite her best intentions she had dozed off during the journey; upon awakening she did not have a clue how far they had gone, or what turns they might have taken getting there. She had only just managed to slip free of her perch before the wagon had stopped to unload its goods, in time to avoid detection. There was no way to get her bearings in any larger sense.

The power can tell you where you are, an inner voice had chided her. She ignored it.

Now something more important had her attention: a phrase carried to her on the warm currents of the crowded market, as surely as if it had been intended for her hearing. She looked around, trying to locate the speaker. Finally her gaze fell upon a couple of women in coarse but serviceable woolen garments, standing by the cart of a fruit vendor. The voice of one seemed to match what she had heard in tone and cadence, even though she could not make out most of her words now. Carefully Kamala made her way nearer to them, trying to remain inconspicuous. *The power can keep you from being seen,* the inner voice chided. *Use it!* As she came closer she strained to catch their words, trying to sort them out from all the other sounds of the busy market.

"No doctor can help her," the woman was saying. Her face was pale and drawn, sharp lines of grief etched into her flesh. "Though they charge well enough for the show of trying."

"Like as spit the potions out of their own asses," the other muttered, "for all the good it does."

"Aye, the last round made her sicker than she was to start with."

"Have you asked after witches?"

The heavy sigh was loud enough to be audible even from where Kamala stood. "No one will serve without more coin than we have. Life costs money, they say. Besides, if it is the Wasting, what can they do?"

Kamala's heart was pounding. If it was the Wasting, that meant the person they were discussing was some Magister's consort. Was it possible it was *her* consort? Common sense cautioned her that the odds were against it, and yet there were only so many Magisters in the world. It was not impossible.

What would it be like, to gaze into the eyes of the one whose athra she was stealing, to connect a name and a face to that exchange? The thought was strangely thrilling. Ethanus had warned her against ever trying to do such a thing, but then, he had given her many warnings which had more to do with his own weakness than hers. And besides, if the consort was not her own, then she was the key to the power of some other Magister. That was surely a possibility worth exploring.

So she drew in a deep breath and stepped forward to where the women stood, waiting until they took notice of her before speaking. She tried to pitch her voice in a voice she thought a boy would use as she said, "Forgive me for overhearing your words . . . you speak of a sick one? Perhaps I can help."

The two women looked her up and down with obvious misgivings. From the dusty cap that covered her hair to her patched and mended shirt, she seemed the very embodiment of a youth down on his luck. What possible help could such a person offer them?

"You barter in medicines, boy?" one of them at last said.

"No."

The brow of the other woman furrowed. "What then? Witchery?" It was clear from her expression she would find that claim doubtful; anyone possessed of true power could surely manage a more prosperous lifestyle.

"I have the Sight," Kamala said. "I can see disease, and perhaps put a name to it." That much was true, anyway. Even before she had met Ethanus she had possessed that simple gift. "Sometimes that is enough to help. Sometimes I can manage other things, as well."

The women looked at each other. Kamala did not need sorcery to read their thoughts. From one: *What insanity is this? Who is this boy? Do you know him?* From the other: *All else has failed. What do we have to lose?*

"And for payment?" The edge in the woman's voice was undisguised.

Kamala tried to shrug like she thought a young man might do. Inside her shirt her breast bindings slipped a bit, almost coming loose. "Food for a traveler, if you have that to spare. A bed for the night, perhaps. My Sight is a gift from the gods, I do not charge men for its use." She tried to make her words sound casual, as if she hardly cared whether they accepted her offer or not, though inside her chest her heart was beating wildly. Surely they would not trust any stranger who seemed too intent upon visiting this invalid.

Again the two women exchanged glances. The doubt in the eyes of one was undiminished, but in her grieving companion there was another emotion evident, even stronger: desperation. *What is there to lose?* her expression seemed to say. *He cannot make things worse.*

Finally she turned to Kamala. "What is your name, boy?"

"Kovan." It had been her brother's name once, and was the first thing that came to mind. It stuck in her throat for a moment as she spoke.

"Well then, Kovan. I am called Erda, this is Sigurra." The woman nodded stiffly toward her companion. "You can try your Sight, for what good it will do. I won't turn hope, however slight it might be." She sighed heavily. "Perhaps the gods will favor your efforts as they have not favored others."

———

The dwelling that Erda brought her to was a good mile from town, a long hike on a humid day. Kamala shouldered the heaviest burdens from the day's shopping, as she thought a young boy would offer to do. Her back was sore from the effort (how easily sorcery might have lightened the load!) but she hardly felt the pain for the excitement of what was to come. Was it possible she was about to meet the source of all her power? Or if not hers, then that of some other Magister?

The cabin was a small one, crudely built out of logs from the surrounding forest, with a pen for livestock flanking it on the near side and some kind of cultivated garden at the far end. Erda ushered Kamala inside, into a single living chamber with a stone fireplace dominating its center. The windows were small, better suited to keeping out the winter's cold than admitting a cool breeze in summer, and the smell of sweat and sickness hung heavy in the still air. It took no sorcery to locate the source. There were several narrow rope beds set into alcoves flanking the room, and on one of them a small figure lay still, swathed in blankets better suited to winter than this humid season.

When in doubt, sweat the sickness out, her mother had once said. It hadn't worked for Kamala's brother; she doubted it would work for this patient either.

"That's her, over there." Erda put down her basket on a rough-planked table and made some manner of religious sign over her heart, as she indicated a small bed in the farthest alcove. "May the gods ease her suffering."

Kamala lowered her own bundles to the floor. "How long has she been sick?"

The woman hesitated. "It began in late winter, we think, though the first signs were subtle, so we may mistime it. We thought it a lesser illness, at first. Been a short month now since she took to bed for most of the day, and she's too weak these days even to rise to use the pot." Her eyes met Kamala's and for the first time were not filled with suspicion or even despair, simply with exhaustion. "Please do what you can," she begged. "I've tried all else."

Kamala nodded and moved toward the bed. She could not see the figure within it until she drew close, and when she did at last, she exhaled sharply in surprise.

It was a child.

She was a tiny girl—so very small!—with hair of that pale shade that never lasts to adulthood, now plastered by the sweat of sickness to her brow. A frail wisp of a girl, ghostlike. Her eyes were a beautiful shade of blue but they stared vacantly into space, lifeless, and she did not acknowledge the presence of others around her by either sound or motion. A tiny doll of a child, porcelain-pale, whose hollow cheeks and deep-shadowed eyes bore witness to some sort of wasting disease.

"Can you help her?" her mother asked, wringing a corner of her apron in her hands.

With effort, Kamala quieted the queasy feeling in her stomach. Was this really someone's consort? What if it was *her* consort? The thought that she might have been killing a child for her sorcery should not have bothered her, but it did.

All life is the same, she told herself stubbornly. *Young or old, male or female, it should not matter.*

For a small eternity she stood by the side of the bed, staring down at the girl. Then she reached out to touch her small face, gently. A shudder ran through her as her finger stroked the colorless cheek. Should she feel a flow of power, if she touched her own consort thus? Or was the passage of athra a secret thing that flesh could not detect? If she summoned her power to gaze into this girl's soul, would that be enough of a spell to claim the child's last vital energy? What did it feel like to watch your consort's soulfire expire, to hold a tiny body like this in your hands as the last living warmth bled out of it, until her flesh was no more than an empty husk?

. . . The young/old woman holds Kamala's brother, cradling him in her withered arms, singing to him softly. Snatches of lullabies laden with witchery. Kovan cries out in pain as the fever in his blood flares up hotly, green pustules on his face throbbing. The old woman looks up at Kamala, just for a moment. Her eyes are deep-set and gray and filled with unfathomable sadness. Resignation. "For this young one I will die," they seem to say . . .

"Can you help her?"

Erda's voice brought Kamala back to herself. Gods above, how many years had it been since she had last thought of that visit? There was a time when the old witch's eyes had haunted her dreams, even as the scar-faced Magister's did now. Truly, she thought, there must be nothing more terrible than knowing you were about to die and not being able to summon the power to save yourself. The witch had spent her life helping others, the Magister had lived for centuries of unparalleled selfishness, but in their last moments, did that make any difference? Did Death care a whit how they had lived, when he came for them at last?

This girl was young. So very young. Kamala's brother had been about that age when the Green Plague had sickened him. Kamala remembered sitting vigil by his bedside, listening to her mother offer up desperate prayers to any god that might intervene. Probably the same kind of prayers that this child's mother had voiced, night after night. The gods were notoriously callous when it came to such things; they had not helped Kovan then, and Kamala doubted they would help this girl now. Especially if the cause of her dying was not some natural sickness, but the predatory power of a Magister.

Drawing in a deep breath—trying to banish the image of her dead brother from her mind—Kamala focused her Sight upon the tiny figure in the bed. It took little effort to see the shadows of death that hung over her, or the chill fog that accompanied each breath, like the mists of winter. But though the Sight could confirm that the girl was dying, it could not tell Kamala what was wrong with her. Only sorcery could do that.

You know what you came here to do. Why do you hesitate?

Slowly, carefully, she loosened the stranglehold she had imposed upon her power. As she did so the child moaned softly, twisting in her bed. Kamala's heart lurched in her chest. If this *was* her consort, would she feel the life being drawn out of her? Would she suffer the kind of instinctive terror that animals did when the shadow of a predator fell over them? A sudden wave of sickness welled up inside Kamala. She had come to accept that she must kill strangers to remain alive, but that was a far cry from torturing a child.

A cold wind blew across her soul at the thought, and her vision began to go black; bands of ice suddenly wrapped themselves around her chest, choking off her breath. For one brief and terrifying moment she could sense the abyss that yawned at her feet, could feel the touch of that great nothingness which would swallow her whole the minute the link to her consort was severed. Too late, she realized her error. *It does not matter if your consort is a child,* she told herself desperately, *or an infant, or a cripple, or any other manner of pitiful thing. The gods choose who is to die for you, and you must accept their choice.* But words were clearly no longer enough. Her lungs were frozen and would not fill with air; she fell to her knees at the child's bedside, the room spinning about her. Inside her she could feel the precious link that bound her to her consort beginning to fray, like a rotting cord, and the more she focused upon it, the more rapidly it seemed to disintegrate.

NO! She screamed the word inside her head, but could not draw in enough air to make the sound real. Black spots were spreading across her field of vision, bleeding into one another like puddles of ink. *I WILL NOT DIE FOR YOU!* Summoning up the last of her energy, she envisioned herself with a child in her arms, envisioned herself taking its head and tearing it off until blood gushed from its neck in a scarlet fountain, and she held the tiny body over her head and let its blood rain down upon her, holding its head aloft in her other hand like a talisman. *I WILL NOT DIE FOR ANY CREATURE!* As the child's blood soaked her hair and her clothing it seemed to her that living warmth came back into her limbs; she could taste blood on her lips as she finally drew in a deep breath. The bands of ice that had been wrapped around her chest cracked in one place, then two, then melted and were gone. She could breathe again. Her heart was still beating. The black spots vanished to the corners of her vision, and the room was still once more.

Shuddering, she lowered her face to her hands, and for a moment just focused on trying to breathe steadily.

"What is it?" The woman called Erda was kneeling by her side. "Are you all right? Is it something you saw in her? Tell me!"

"I'm all right," she whispered. "And it was not in her." *For a moment I forgot what I was. And almost paid the price for it.* "I'll be fine."

The woman wanted to know more, but clearly sensed that further questions were not going to be answered. That was good. Kamala's focus was on other things now.

Drawing upon the life essence of her consort, gathering power into herself, she looked at the child before her . . . and into her. Deep, deep into the girl's soul she looked, searching for that place where all vital energy was anchored, the wellspring of life from which all natural creatures drew their strength. And she found it, with ease. The girl's soulfire still burned with all the fierce strength of childhood, though it fluttered wildly against the sickly flesh surrounding it, like a candle flame beating against the wind. Clearly she was not a consort at all, to anyone. Which meant this illness was not the result of some Magister's sorcery, but simply a mundane, finite condition. If it could be cured, she might still recover.

With effort Kamala surfaced from her trance just enough to whisper, "It's not the Wasting." Let her mother have that much to calm her. Distantly she heard the woman weeping, though whether it was from gratitude or fear she could not say. Watching a Magister almost obliterate herself was apparently not a reassuring sight.

Deeply she gazed into the child's flesh anew, seeking the source of her illness. Healing was an art she had never been good at, but Ethanus had taught her the basics. In fact, no great skill was required in this case. The culprit was not some secretive disease, or an imbalance of bodily fluids such as only an experienced healer might detect, but a simple parasite lodged in the child's gut. Yet the word "simple" did not do it justice. From the place where its head had burrowed into the girl's flesh to the last segment of its ghostly white body it was many times her length, and it lay within the convolutions of her intestine, throbbing gently as it stole the food that was intended for her, growing larger and stronger with every meal while its host slowly starved to death.

A healer's potions should have been able to pry it loose and flush it out, she thought. Indeed, she could see in its flesh the signs of past poisonings, but apparently the thing was simply too large or else too strong for normal doses of medicine to have done the job. Or perhaps the child had been too small to endure the kind of dosage that was needed. The same potions that were used to kill such a parasite could also kill its host, if she were weak enough. In this case they seem to have done enough damage to the thing to keep it from shedding egg cases, which is why it had gone undetected, but only that.

Reaching out with her power, Kamala took the noxious thing and tore it loose from the girl's flesh, then sent a wave of molten power coursing down its length, sufficient to sear the life from every segment of its body. The girl cried out in pain and doubled over as the sorcerous flames passed through her, but they did her flesh no damage. In time the charred remnants of the worm would pass from her system by a more natural route, and her body could begin to restore itself.

When she was sure that the job was done, Kamala withdrew her senses from the child's body. For a moment she was silent, gathering her strength, restoring her composure. Her battle to keep hold of her consort had left her body filmed with sweat and all her muscles aching with exhaustion. She bound enough power to cleanse herself, deftly removing the filth from her skin without affecting the stains that were on her clothing.

"I have killed the thing that was stealing your child's life," she said quietly, not meeting the mother's eyes. "Feed her often, in small portions, as much as she can accept. She will need strength to recover."

The woman blinked her eyes. There were tears coursing down both cheeks. "She is going to live?" she whispered.

"She will live. She will be fine." The words seemed a distant thing, almost as if someone else was speaking them.

With effort, Kamala stood. The room swam about her for a moment, then was still. Apparently she, too, would recover.

Erda's hand fell on her arm. "You saved her life."

She shrugged stiffly. "I did what I could." The bands of linen about her breasts began to slip out of position as she moved, so she bound a bit of power to hold them in place. "As I said I would." *I have drained one morati to save another. Such is the power the gods have given us, to use as we see fit.*

"You will let me feed you dinner? As I promised? My husband will be home soon. He will . . ." The words trailed off into fresh tears. "He will want to thank you himself," she whispered. "He had given up hope."

Kamala shook her head. "I must move on, I am afraid. Spare me what you can for the road, if you like; I require no more. My apologies to your husband, we shall have to meet some other time."

"But the bed you spoke of—"

Kamala's gaze was resolute. "I am sorry. I need to go."

She did not even try to give the woman reasons. There were none that she would understand, and Kamala was too tired to weave convincing lies for her. Only a Magister would understand the need she felt to put as much distance between her and this place as possible, as quickly as she could, along with all the memories it contained.

You were right, my master. I should have heeded your warning. In the future I will, I promise you.

When Erda was finally convinced that Kamala simply would not stay longer, she scurried about the cabin, gathering up enough food to sustain a small army: loaves of bread, slabs of cheese, slices of salted meat and fish. She probably would have given Kamala everything she had in her stores had the Magister not stopped her; even so, when her generous offering was tied in a bundle for travel, and a fine woolen blanket had been added to it for good measure, she was clearly distressed that Kamala would accept nothing more.

"It is enough," Kamala assured her.

Anything else that I need, sorcery can supply. There was a strange peace in the thought. *I, too, have been cleansed tonight.*

Night was falling as Kamala left the small cabin. She looked back only once. Long enough to see the mother cradling her child in her arms, tears running down her face as she whispered promises of eternal love and protection. Kamala felt a brief pang in her heart, a vague and uncomfortable envy which she refused to acknowledge. Then she looked past the mother, past the child, into the child's flesh, to that place where the wormlike parasite had once lodged its assault. Nothing was left now but a charred length of flesh, which the natural tides of the girl's body had already begun to force out. Soon it would be gone.

Farewell, brother, she thought to it.

Hoisting her pack to her shoulder, binding enough sorcery to ease the soreness in her muscles, she let the door fall shut behind her.

Chapter 25

A HAWK flew over Gansang.

It was an unusually large bird, though its distance from the ground disguised that fact. Its wings gleamed like fire against the orange skies of sunset, and the few other birds who saw it backed away warily, not certain what it was, but sensing that nothing so large could be natural.

It let out a cry. To most human ears—and to other birds—it was simply the keening of a hawk. Witches in Gansang looked up, however, wondering what it was that had just pricked their supernatural senses. And those for whom the message was intended heard it yet more clearly, and after a few seconds their answer came, in tones only the bird could hear.

It circled down lower over the city, following the directions it had been given, and in time came to a tower set apart from the rest. There were no merchants crowding around the base of this one, nor any sign of a door, nor any windows save for a row in the topmost story. There was no glass in those, nor curtains, nor anything to bar passage. The hawk landed on a sill, studied the place for a moment or two, then ducked inside.

A few minutes later an oversized falcon followed the same path. By the time it entered the tower Colivar had reclaimed his human shape, and was waiting for him.

The room within the tower was a large one, with chairs enough to seat perhaps a dozen men, and dust enough upon them to indicate the place was not used often. There were neither decorations nor other comforts, and as with the tower itself, no sign of entrance save the windows.

"Interesting meeting place," Colivar commented, as the last of the other's feathers faded into flesh. "I do like the privacy of it."

"A city with so many Magisters requires some sort of neutral ground."

Colivar nodded. "Of course. Will more be coming?"

"If your business requires it."

"Very well." He looked about the room. "You must forgive me, I have never before been in a city that had so many Magisters living shoulder to shoulder, and with equal claim to the greater territory. You must have customs worked out as to who does what that are quite . . . labyrinthine."

His host smiled slightly. "It is not always harmonious, but it never fails to be . . . interesting." He bowed his head a mere fraction of an inch, a gesture of polite acknowledgment to an equal. "Colivar, yes? I remember you from Ramirus' little soiree. Magister Royal of Anshasa, as I recall? I am Tirstan. We do not bear such pretty titles here, but I serve House Iabresa."

"Masters of the local silk trade, yes?"

He nodded. "You do your research."

"Always."

Tirstan waved his hand over the table; the air shimmered briefly, then a pewter goblet and two matching cups appeared. "You are far from home, Magister Royal Colivar. Shall I guess at the reason?" He poured both cups full of a deep-hued ale; a cold sweat was beginning to condense on the pitcher even as he set it down.

"Hardly a challenge, given the recent news here."

Again the faint smile. "I do cling to hope that some visitor will surprise me." He waved absently toward two of the chairs, binding enough power to clean the dust off them first. "Please, sit, relax." He offered him one of the pewter cups. "We are a far flight from Anshasa, and travel is dusty business."

Colivar accepted the cup but did not drink from it. "A good helping of news is all the refreshment I seek. The death of a Magister is not a common occurrence."

"No, thank the gods, it is not."

"Who was it?"

"He called himself Raven. Yes, after the carrion bird. I think he used other names before that, but he was the secretive sort and rarely shared information about himself. And in Gansang we have learned not to pry into each other's affairs." He sipped from his own cup, and nodded his approval of the chilled ale within. "Some say the name captured his essence. I believe it fell short."

"I know the man. And I've heard him called much worse things."

"At any rate, the true ravens have him now, or at least his ashes."

Colivar looked startled. "You burned him?"

"Had to. Otherwise we'd have had every treasure hunter this side of Sankara scouring the city for his bones. Did you not know that the secret of a Magister lies in his magical flesh, and that after death his powers can be claimed by any witch who—well, I will spare you the process. Those are the tales, anyway, and since a dead Magister only comes along once in a lifetime, we decided not to test how many might believe in them."

Colivar nodded. "Wise."

"He fell from a bridge," he said, gesturing with his cup, "a curiously mundane end for one of our kind. He was following a woman at the time, some witch that Lord Ravi had found in the foulest district of the city, cleaned up, and was passing off as a lady. He introduced her as Sidra. No information has been found regarding the woman or the name, apart from what little bit Ravi himself knew; it is as if she appeared out of nowhere."

"Where is she now?"

Tirstan's eyes glittered darkly. "If you were alone with a Magister and he died, would you remain in that place one minute longer than you had to? Whatever sort of witch she is, she had enough power to call all her personal possessions to her when she left, so we have nothing to trace her with." He took another swallow of the ale. "All this we learned afterward, of course; that night, all anyone knew was that she was a mystery and Ravi believed she had power. Those were reasons enough for any Magister to show interest in her. There are also rivalries between the great houses here in which some of us have vested interest; Lord Ravi showing up with some sort of magical prize on his arm was a direct challenge to those who did not wish him moving up in the ranks." He sipped from his cup again. "And witches, of course, must be taught their place. Many reasons for a Magister like Raven to show an interest in her. None of them shed any light on the matter of his death."

"You questioned Ravi about her, I assume?"

"Of course. The information I give you comes from him. Apparently he heard news of some fight a witch was involved in down in the Quarter and took the chance that anyone who would throw her power around like that might also be interested in a little social advancement. For a price."

"Only a fool barters his life force to another, for any price."

"Yes, well, that is a safe statement from our perspective, yes? Not everyone has the option of bartering other men's life-force instead."

"So tell me of this Raven's death."

He shrugged. "Apparently he stepped out onto one of the city's bridges during a fete, either for a moment of fresh air—these city affairs are stifling—or specifically to seek this woman out. We know she was there, for we have found traces of her presence on the bridge. Much power seems to have been thrown about, some of which shattered the railing near to him, but none of it looks like witchery, so it must all have been his. I myself believe that Raven was having his sport with her."

"And she did not respond in kind? Even to defend herself?" Colivar's eyes narrowed suspiciously. "If she were truly a witch, I find that hard to believe."

"You are welcome to look for yourself, though by now most of the important traces have been muddled past recognition. And of course Raven's body is dust. But I assure you, we found no signs of witchery having been used on the bridge, on the rail, or upon Raven's person."

"Nothing to explain why he fell?"

"Oh, we know why he fell." His tone was dry. "A fitting end, if you do not mind my saying so."

"Go on."

"He was . . . ah . . . how shall I say . . ." He bit his lip for a moment as if considering. "Well, he was kicked in the balls."

Colivar blinked. "I'm sorry?"

"His nether regions were bruised. Dramatically so. It was the only wound on him."

Colivar sat back in his chair. "So you are telling me you believe she struck him, and he . . . fell? Just like that?"

"Well, we are assuming he entered Transition during the fall, and thus could not muster power in time to save himself. If he was throwing that much power around, it is not an unreasonable theory. Of course, you are welcome to offer a better one if you like."

He shook his head. "There must be more to it."

"You would think so, yes? Yet there is no evidence of anything more than I have told you . . . you are welcome to inspect the site yourself, if you doubt me."

Colivar waved off the suggestion. "I am sure you have been quite thorough."

"Mind you, there are those who have suggested that his death was not necessarily a bad thing; he was not, how shall I say, the most personable of our kind—"

"He was a prick," Colivar said shortly.

Tirstan sighed. "Yes, but he was an *immortal* prick, and that entails certain obligations on our part."

"You will avenge him?"

"The death of a Magister cannot go unpunished."

"Even if it was his own foolishness that got him killed?"

Tirstan shrugged. "If the morati see that a Magister is killed and we do not punish the offender, they may begin to wonder where our limits lie. A bad question for any man to be asking."

"You must find the woman, then."

"With such a dearth of clues? Every day we spend trying to locate her would cost us more in reputation than the hunt is worth." He chuckled darkly. "It is hard to appear omnipotent when one cannot track down a single witch." He reached for the pitcher and poured himself some more ale, chilling it anew with a touch. "No, we put the blame where it rightfully belongs, on the man who brought her into our company. A shame, that; Pahdman Ravi had his uses. But an example had to be made of someone, yes?" He sipped from his cup. "So now the morati see that we are swift and merciless in our vengeance, and they will tremble at the mere thought of displeasing us, which is far more important in the long run than hunting down one terrified witch."

"You will not seek her?"

He waved expansively. "Please, search for her if you like. Bearing in mind that we have no personal objects to serve as a link to her, or any knowledge of her true identity. By now I expect she has taken a new name, wears a new face, and if she has half a brain she is so far from this place that one must learn a foreign language to ask after her." He shrugged and drank deeply from his cup, emptying it. "At least, that is what I would do if I were in her shoes."

"She left nothing behind?"

"She had a room in Ravi's tower. I can show it to you if you like. I believed she lived there for all of a week before this incident."

"I should like to see that, yes."

Tirstan raised an eyebrow. "You find her . . . interesting?"

Colivar was careful to keep his face impassive. "Let us say I enjoy a good mystery."

Tirstan stood with a sigh, dropping his pewter cup; it disappeared before it hit the ground, and the pitcher followed soon after. "As you wish. Though I fear you will find the visit unenlightening. So many others have, you know."

———

It was twilight by the time the two Magisters reached Tower Ravi, and they wrapped the shadows of early night around them so that none might see or hear them as they slipped past the gauze curtains and through the half-open window into what had once been Kamala's room.

Inside, Tirstan set the lamps alight with an easy gesture, and waved for Colivar to inspect whatever he liked. "There is nothing of hers here that we could find, save for those gifts that Ravi had given her." Even though his sorcery would keep their voices from being heard outside the room, or the light from being seen, still his voice had instinctively dropped to a whisper. "Nothing she identified with herself, that might be of use in reading her. Or in calling her."

The room was a rich one, whose furnishings spoke eloquently of how much Ravi had wished to please its resident, but it was clear that most of his efforts had gone unappreciated. The fine gold toilet items on the marble-topped vanity were untouched, bottles of unguent unopened, flasks of perfume still sealed. Colivar picked up a comb and studied it closely.

"Not a single hair of hers anywhere," Tirstan informed him. "As I said, she either destroyed such things as might be used against her, or else she called them to her later that night. Nothing was here by the time we came to search."

A pile of finely embroidered silk garments lay neatly folded on a chair near the window, probably in the same position they were in when they were first delivered; she had never even looked at them, Colivar guessed. "Not as vain as her host assumed she would be," he said quietly. Then he looked up at Tirstan. "Do you know where she might have kept her personal things while she was here?"

He indicated a leather-bound trunk set in the darkest corner of the room. Colivar went to it and lifted the heavy lid. It was empty.

"Not so much as a speck of lint left behind," Tirstan said. "You're not the first to look, you know. What do you hope to find that we did not?"

Colivar knelt by the trunk. Propping the lid open, he reached down into the dark space within until his hands pressed against the bottom of it. "If she called her things to her, as you suggest, there should be some trace of her witchery here."

"Yes," Tirstan agreed. "And there is not."

Colivar looked for it himself, drawing enough athra from his consort to alter his senses so that he could detect such things. But the interior of the trunk was dark. His questing hands felt nothing. As Tirstan had said, there was not the faintest trace of witchery present. If she did indeed have the power, it had clearly never been used on anything inside the trunk.

Tirstan picked up a perfume bottle from the vanity, took note of the fact that the seal was intact, and put it back down. "Magister Tamil has suggested that perhaps she was not a witch at all, but secretly served one of our kind. That the power she had called upon in the Quarter was not her own witchery, but rather the sorcery of her patron. Perhaps it was not even an accident that she was attacked that night, he has suggested, but rather the whole scene was staged, to draw the right kind of notice and win her noble patronage. As it did." He shrugged. "It is a curious theory, and not the kind of game a Magister usually plays, but it would explain why she left no signs of her own power behind her."

No witchery had been used on the bridge either. Colivar recalled him saying that. Only sorcery, pure sorcery.

"That is one possibility," he agreed.

There was another one, but he would not speak its name yet. Not until he was sure.

Slowly he reached his hands into the trunk again, running them along the bottom. This time he did not look for witchery, but for something more subtle. Not for the hot, fiery residue of mortal magic, but for the cold, whispery touch of true sorcery. Not for life force sacrificed in passion or need but power coldly stolen, wielded by men who were no longer alive in their own right, who could no longer leave the kind of hot imprint on the mortal world that was the birthright of living creatures. To the morati world, the powers of witches and Magisters seemed all but identical; to one who truly understood them, however, they were as distinct from one another as life and death.

After a moment he leaned back on his heels. He stared into the darkness without words, trying to gather his thoughts.

"Colivar?"

"Tamil may well be right," he said at last. "There are traces of sorcery here as well."

"Magister Kant has suggested she might even have been a Magister herself, shapechanged to pass as a woman." Tirstan shrugged. "I find that theory hard to credit, myself. It is difficult to imagine a Magister willing to pass as a woman for any length of time."

Colivar nodded his agreement. Technically it was possible, of course— a Magister might alter his appearance however he liked—but the kind of man who survived First Transition was unlikely to find the social station of women a comfortable refuge. Those few instances Colivar had heard of where sorcerers had tried such a thing, they had been quickly unmasked; Magisters could make their bodies appear female easily enough, but they could rarely play the role that went with it.

"No doubt it was your first suggestion," he said. "She served a Magister."

There is one other possibility, he thought, *but it is so foreign a concept that you do not even think to name it.*

What if the woman were a sorcerer in her own right, he wondered. That would not only explain the signs she had left behind in Gansang, but it might shed light on Andovan's situation as well. Or perhaps she was not a sorcerer proper, but some new sort of creature that had no name yet.

More than a witch, but less than a Magister. An equally intriguing possibility.

Tirstan came to his side and inspected the trunk's interior himself, as Colivar had done. After a moment he too sat back on his heels, looking thoughtful. "You may think this is mad, but I have thought that this woman may be linked to that prince Ramirus called us in to study."

He kept his voice carefully neutral, devoid of any emotion. "How so?"

"If her patron was the Magister that had claimed him as consort, so that she had an indirect connection to that bond, it might explain the prophecy Andovan was given, yes?"

He did not trust himself to speak, but simply nodded. It was a respectable theory. It might even be true.

There was a time when the world had no Magisters at all, and it was unthinkable that anything like us would ever exist. Now we are here, and no man dares question us. Who are we to say that nothing new will come after us, or that a new kind of woman might not arise, one could master the old forms?

How much did he *want* that to be the answer, he wondered suddenly, rather than some more mundane explanation? How much did he hunger to believe that there was something truly new in the world, a puzzle worth exploring? Life was long for a Magister, with few real challenges; like most of his kind he hungered for novelty. Was this mysterious woman truly worth his efforts, or was he weaving theories out of moonbeams to convince himself that she was?

He would know soon enough. The spell he had cast on Andovan was beginning to have its desired effect; the young man was being drawn toward the source of his illness. Sooner or later the prince would reach his target, and while Andovan might not recognize a sorceress if he saw one, Colivar would. Then he would know if the same woman was responsible for both incidents. Until then, it was best to leave the others following false trails that suited them, so that they stayed out of the way of his own investigation.

He walked back to the pile of silk garments that the witch had so meticulously ignored, and lifted up a gold scarf from the top of the pile. "May I take this with me?"

Tirstan looked confused. "It holds no trace of her. She never identified with it—"

"I understand all that." He held it up. "Call it a whim. May I?"

For a moment there was silence. It was the kind of silence Magisters suffered often: one of them hinting at secrets, the other hungering to share them . . . but never being trusted to share, because that was not the way of their kind.

"I will tell you what I discover," Colivar promised.

"I will not hold my breath waiting for that," Tirstan said with a wry smile, "but you may take whatever you like."

. . . and he chuckled darkly and added, "It is not like Ravi will be taking inventory any time soon."

Chapter 26

THE DREAM was a desolate one, set on a landscape swept clean of life by wind and hail, chill in the way the northern wastelands are chill with the coming of winter, so that the lungs grow colder with each breath. For a moment Ramirus considered turning back and waiting for a more auspicious night, a better dream. Normally he could mold a morati dream to his needs with little effort, but such sorcery was not subtle and was likely to be noticed. And that would be bad for the dreamer. This time, alas, he had to work with what his subject provided.

He fingered the object in his hand and considered. Carrion birds circled overhead, screeching their hunger as they looked for fresh meat, and finally spiraled away into the distance, having found nothing.

No, he decided at last. He would talk to her now. The link was strong, the dream was clear, and if its tenor was a bit on the ominous side, that only reflected the mind-set of the dreamer. His subject was restless and did not sleep that often; already he had wasted a week trying to establish himself in her dreams, and each time he did so he risked discovery anew. There was no guarantee that if he left now he would do better next time, and meanwhile the risk would only increase with each new attempt. No, this was the night it must be done, and this was the dream he must use.

There were stormclouds ahead, pregnant with thunder, that cast long shadows upon the earth beneath them. Given the dreamer's dark mood he guessed that she would be there, where things were darkest. He headed that way quietly, gathering soulfire about him as he walked, drawing upon bits and pieces of dreamstuff to mask his presence from other men of power. It was little more than a token effort, really; any Magister who looked her way right now would sense the presence of another of his kind, as clearly as if Ramirus had trumpeted his arrival. But one who was not looking directly at her might miss the signs if they were well camouflaged, and so he made the effort. He owed her that much.

A short while later he saw the ring of stones ahead of him; aged, pitted, crumbling. Not the Spears as they were in the real world, nor in Gwynofar's courtyard simulacrum, but as her fears had sculpted them. Time and weather had reduced these dreamstones by half to mounds of gravel, and he knew that in the eyes of her faith it meant they had lost an equivalent amount of their power. He understood enough of the legends of her people to understand just what kind of a warning that was, and how she must fear to see them thus.

The High Queen knelt in that circle, centered among the wounded stones, eyes shut, perhaps praying. He approached slowly, silently, and for a moment just watched her. She seemed a thing too fragile to survive in this place, but he had done enough research into the Protectors' bloodlines before Danton's marriage to know that was just an illusion; her family line was renowned for its strength, both physical and spiritual, and she was no exception. That was the one thing Danton had never fully appreciated about her, and other men rarely thought to question. Most men were such shallow creatures at heart, he mused, and when you set before them such a delicate waif, with her soft voice and slender hands and skin the color of moonlight, they assumed her to be fragile in truth, and thus easily dominated. With luck that would play in her favor now, and whatever Magister served the High King would never think to check on her while she slept, or search through her waking mind for signs of betrayal.

For it would be that in Danton's eyes if he knew she had contacted me, Ramirus thought. *Gods help her if he ever finds out.*

He waited a few minutes to see if she would notice him, and when she did not, bound a wisp of soulfire to alert her to his presence, and to let her understand that it was in fact a dream they were sharing. Sometimes when one contacted dreamers they were so lost in the landscapes of their own imagining that they never realized that someone from the outside was really speaking to them. Any information given to them in that case was likely to be forgotten by morning's light, along with their own fantasies.

Though nothing in the surrounding landscape changed she looked up suddenly, and rose to her feet as soon as she saw him. He could see immediately that she had been stressed near to the breaking point by something; given that she'd spent years dealing successfully with Danton and his moods, that was an ominous sign indeed.

She is no longer your queen, he reminded himself. *It is no longer your job to worry about her.*

"Ramirus!" The look of relief gave way to one of confusion. "This dream then, is it of your making?"

"No, Lady Protector. It is your own. I merely use the tools at hand." He held forth the token her servant had given him—a golden ring with a silken scarf knotted around its band —and scowled at her. "You were foolish to send such a personal object into unknown places. Even a witch can bind enough power to harm you with such a focus."

"I knew of no other way to contact you—."

"Then perhaps you should not have tried," he said curtly. "By your husband's own words I am enemy to your House. Banished from your realm, forbidden any contact with the royal family. Are you so sure it is wise to seek out such an enemy, much less place your essence into his hands?"

She said it softly. "You are no enemy of mine, Ramirus."

"Your husband would beg to differ."

"My husband—" She bit her lip. "Is a fool, sometimes."

He nodded shortly. "On that we are agreed, at least."

She sighed heavily; one hand fluttered up to her stomach and remained there, resting against the silk of her gown as if guarding some secret pain. "I have need of answers, Ramirus. For questions I cannot entrust to strangers. What would you have me do?"

"You believe I can be trusted?"

The blue eyes fixed on him, their depths pleading. He wanted to hate her as he hated Danton, he wanted to make her part of that bitterness and dismiss her as callously as Danton had once dismissed him, but he couldn't. She didn't deserve his hate. He might not be a compassionate man—no Magister was—but he prided himself on being just. And it would be unjust to turn his wrath upon this woman merely because her husband had offended him.

"You are a foolish woman," he said at last, and he sighed. "One should never trust a Magister. Didn't I teach you that much?"

"I am foolish," she agreed. "And stubborn, as you often noted."

"Indeed. Though so beguiling in your stubbornness that few men ever object to it."

She smiled faintly, sadly, an expression edged with shadows. "Will you aid me then, Ramirus? For I tell you truly, if you deny me in this, I have nowhere else to turn."

"There is risk in it," he warned her. "Do not mistake that. In making contact with your spirit I am trespassing upon another Magister's territory, and every moment we share this dream increases the chance of discovery tenfold. If Danton were to find out about it . . . you will lose your head, milady. At the very least."

"I know that," she whispered. "I knew it when I sent out men to search for you."

"You are that desperate for aid?"

"Yes," she breathed. "Yes, Ramirus, I am."

If she had made one move to pressure him then, if she had hinted through gesture or tone that he owed her the service somehow, perhaps in memory of past affection, he would have blasted the dreamscape to a smoking ruin and left her to find her way out of it alone. Indeed, that was what he had half intended when he had first entered her dream. But there was no pride in her manner now, no regal authority, no sense of entitlement such as a High Queen was taught to have, only humility. And that was as it should be. He had known her for twenty years, since the day she first came to the High King as a virgin bride, he had seen to her education in all things royal, had watched with almost a father's pride as she proved herself a true queen in every sense of the word—but the day Danton had banished him all that was swept from the record. Magisters did not cling to past affections. Clearly she understood that. Clearly she respected it.

She's worth more than Danton will ever understand, he thought. *And is ten times more woman than he deserves.*

"Very well," he said at last. "I will hear you."

The clouds overhead lightened a bit as he spoke; her dream was responding to her mood. The increased bit of sunlight let him see clearly just how drawn and pale she was. A morati would have felt great concern for her.

"What do you know of the Magister named Kostas?" she asked him.

He frowned. "Danton's new Royal? Next to nothing. His name isn't recognized by others of my kind; I know, for I've asked after him. The face he wears is not one any Magister has seen before. Which means either he is a very new Magister . . . or perhaps very old, and he has changed those things because he wishes not to be recognized."

"You could not see through such a spell?"

He scowled. "Were I to look upon him directly, perhaps. Are you suggesting I do that? He would surely know if I tried, and then we should become embarked upon the sort of relationship I do not relish."

It was not quite true—a good adversarial relationship was as sweet to a Magister as the finest of wines—but that was not something he was going to reveal to a morati.

"There is a darkness in him, Ramirus. I don't know its name, but I can sense it. Not like the darkness in other Magisters I have seen. Not like anything human." She shuddered, wrapping her arms about herself as if guarding against sudden chill. "He plays my husband like a puppet, encouraging all that is worst in him to come to the surface . . . I do not know toward what end."

All princes are our puppets, dear Gwynofar. The only question is how openly we pluck their strings, and how much effort we will expend to maintain our puppets once we tire of them.

"He is a Magister Royal," Ramirus said quietly. "The one that Danton has chosen to support his throne. If you are asking me for help in protecting him from the consequences of that choice . . . I am sorry, Lady, that service is not being offered."

She whispered, "I would not ask that of you."

"Then tell me what it is you wish."

She told him then, in halting words, of her husband's last visit to her. Of what she had sensed in him that night, the frightening power that attended his assault. Of her fear that this unnamed sorcery had affected her newly made child, perhaps even altered it into something less than human.

"Who else could I turn to for answers?" she whispered finally. "What witch could I ask to search my flesh for signs of a Magister's curse, that would give me the truth, while keeping it a secret from all others? Or what Magister could I ask for help, when by custom all are rivals to Kostas, and will not hesitate to lie if it gains them political advantage over him? Only you, Ramirus. No one else would give me the truth. But you will do that for me, yes? Even if it is something I do not wish to hear."

There was a long pause. The clouds overhead stirred darkly, and in the distance on all sides of them a thin veil of rain began to descend to the earth. Only within the circle of crumbling Spears was the rain held at bay . . . for the moment.

"What you ask," he said slowly, "will put you at great risk."

She nodded. "I know."

"No, I don't think you do." He drew in a deep breath, choosing his words with care. "Lady, in order for me to enter this dream I needed only to touch your spirit with my own. If this Kostas is watching your dreams he may detect the invasion, but otherwise it could well pass beneath his notice. What you ask for now requires considerably more effort. You ask me to read the truth of what is in your flesh, and in the flesh of your child, and to do that I must extend my sorcery to actually touch your body where it lies, in Danton's own keep. If Kostas is watching you . . . I can disguise the fact that the sorcery is mine, I can try to hide its purpose, but he will be aware that something has been attempted. And that will not be good for you, Lady."

If his words had caused her to have second thoughts she gave no sign of it. Which was little surprise, really. Other women might whine and wring their hands and beg for mercy with tears in their eyes; Gwynofar was made of stronger stuff.

That is why men are willing to serve you, he thought, *even when they are not obliged to do so.*

"Kostas is arrogant," she said, "as my husband is arrogant. He will not be watching me."

"Arrogance does not mean carelessness," he warned her. "And your husband keeps close watch upon friends and enemies alike."

"Kostas has no reason to suspect I know of his sorcery, and my husband will assume that if I had the power to defy him I would have done so that night. Neither has any reason to watch me now. After all . . ." Her tone was bitter. "I am merely a weak woman, easily raped into submission."

"Are you willing to bet your life on that assessment?"

"Ramirus . . ." Her gaze was clear, compelling. "My life is more threatened by ignorance right now than by the risk you describe."

He sighed. *Fair enough.*

First he focused his Sight upon her person, looking for any overt sign of sorcerous taint in the athra surrounding her. It was a bleak aura, that trembled with fear and despair, but there was nothing unnatural about it. Nothing that came from an outside source. He told her so and then commanded, "Lay bare that place where the child resides."

She hesitated, then began to unbutton the front of her gown where it lay over her belly. She opened that and then pulled her chemise aside, until the skin beneath was bare.

He put his hand upon her flesh within the dream, and in the real world he reached much farther with his power, to that canopied bed where her true body lay. It was a feat he probably could not have managed without her token to aid him, but with that in his hand it was as if he was truly standing in the room beside her. He hoped for her sake Kostas did not sense his power entering the keep. When Ramirus had been Magister Royal he was always alert for the tricks of his fellow Magisters, but perhaps Kostas was different.

Gwynofar's body, like her aura, was pure of any sorcerous manipulation. He did find a few lingering wisps of soulfire apparently left over from some spell that had been worked upon her in the past, but the source was now safely expired. If Kostas had indeed used sorcery to influence her child's conception it might have left just such a trace. There was nothing active within her now, which was good, but that also meant there was no way to discover what the purpose of that spell had been. Not enough had been left behind to analyze.

He told her that as well, and could feel the relief pass through her body in a shudder.

Then he began to look for the child.

Tiny . . . it was so very tiny. . . . A normal woman would not even have known she was pregnant yet, but the women of the Protectors' bloodlines were unique in that regard, and seemed to know instinctively when they were with child. In the north it was believed that the gods of the Wrath had given the Protectors the ability to control their reproductive arts in ways that normal women could not. Having watched Gwynofar manage her own births with ease, unconsciously manipulating when and how each child would be born, bringing them to term in relative comfort and safety, Ramirus saw no reason to doubt it.

Now, searching deep within her flesh, he focused his senses upon the whispering flame that was her child, that tentative flickering of soulfire which was the first sign of a new life being created. At this point the child's athra could hardly be distinguished from that of the mother, and looking for it was not unlike trying to focus on a candleflame in the midst of a blazing fire. But he had experience in this matter, and knew how to search. Unbeknownst to Gwynofar he had watched each of her pregnancies closely, curious about the innate magic her bloodline was rumored to have. It was in fact the real reason he had suggested that Danton take a bride from a Protector's line—he had wanted one to study.

As far as he knew, neither Gwynofar or Danton had ever suspected that. Which was as it should be.

At last he found the tiny thing, close against its mother's flesh, weaving the nest of blood and tissue that would secure it for the next nine months. It was neither male nor female in body yet nor even remotely human in form, but that was no hindrance to his sorcery. He had learned long ago that the mere seed of a human coupling contained all of its potential, and by observing that seed closely one might gain a hint of what the adult would become. So he did now to this child, studying the ebb and flow of its tiny life, marking the tenor of its fledgling aura, and plucking at the tapestry of Fate that surrounded it, seeking insight into its unique patterns.

He spoke as he did so, though his voice seemed to him a distant thing, echoing as if in a cave. "I see no sign of foreign sorcery in your child's flesh, Lady. Nor any sign that sorcery has altered his flesh or spirit. Whatever spells might have accompanied his conception, they have not changed his identity, nor wedded any power to him that you should fear."

"Thank the gods!" she breathed. And then she whispered, "You say 'he.' Is it a boy? Can you tell?"

"It will be a boy, when such things are determined."

"Can you—can you tell me more?"

Ramirus hesitated. Normally he regarded divination as an art better left to fortune-tellers in the marketplace. Most divination was simply an illusion, the wishful thinking of witches applied creatively to earn a few coins. Men did not like the fact that the future was uncertain, and so were willing to invest money in any proclamation that would allow them to pretend it was otherwise.

Nevertheless, a child's flesh bore within it clear signs of what it might become. And there were greater fates that had been set in motion by the very fact of its conception. A skilled Magister might observe such things and take counsel from them. A truly skilled Magister might weave them into a story reflecting the child's possible future.

He did not do it often, but for this woman he would try.

And so he opened himself up to the tides of power surrounding the child. Not only Gwynofar's own athra but all the strands of consciousness that were present in her castle, those emanating from Danton and Kostas and far beyond . . . all the thoughts and intents that touched upon this child and his future. There were some Magisters who believed that in doing so one enjoined oneself to some sort of universal consciousness, while others claimed to commune with a god who himself knew everything the future would hold. Ramirus was much more down-to-earth, and simply believed that every thought and action in the world left behind ripples in the tides of fate, which one might observe and interpret if one looked closely enough.

With that in mind, he studied the child. It was strong and healthy in its substance, and likely to come to term safely. That was no surprise, given its mother's heritage. The boy would take after Gwynofar in coloring and temperament, as Andovan had. He paused to tell her both those things, and could observe the mixture of love and sorrow that coursed through her at the reminder of her lost son.

Then he steeled himself for greater effort and reached out to touch the boy's future. A flood tide of raw potential washed over him, and he struggled to make sense of it all. Such strange images! There was nothing in them that reflected a normal life, nor even a Magister's twisted existence—it was as if the boy was fated for something else entirely, so powerfully that all the normal signs of a future were swallowed up and lost.

He felt himself speaking and let the words come, sorcerous instinct bringing phrases to his lips without conscious thought. "He will not be a hero himself, though he will help bring a hero into existence. His strength will never be measured, but he will test the strength of others. He will attend upon Death without seeing it, change the fate of the world without knowing it, and inspire sacrifice without understanding it."

Slowly he opened his eyes. Gwynofar was gazing at him with frank astonishment and not a little bit of fear. He was no less surprised, though he hid his emotions better. *No, High Queen, I do not know myself what all that means, only that it is true.*

She was about to speak when he suddenly caught sight of something dark in the sky coming swiftly toward them. He waved her to silence and focused his sight upon it, willing the soulfire to sharpen his senses so that he could see what it was.

When he did so he drew in his breath sharply.

"Ramirus? What is it?"

"This is your dream," he breathed. "So it is something drawn from your spirit . . . or from *his*. You tell me."

The darkness was coming closer now, and resolving into individual winged shapes arrayed in a triangular formation, like birds. But they were not birds. Their wings were not shaped right, their motion was all wrong, and the essence of the creatures besides was somehow . . . foul. Ramirus could sense the *wrongness* of them in his flesh, a repellent knowledge, as if he had swallowed something poisonous and needed to vomit it up. A wave of raw terror washed over him—terror!—and knew it came from the creatures overhead, for nothing that resided upon the earth could inspire such fear in him. He found suddenly that he wanted to flee, but could not do so. He could not even move, save to put his arm around Gwynofar as she moved closer to him. It was as if the presence of the creatures had frozen him in place, and not all of his sorcery could countermand it.

What in all the hells are those things?

Vast they were, vast creatures with wings too long to measure, powerful wings that stirred the stormclouds into eddies and funnels as they passed. Where a fleeting bit of sunlight fell upon them it was quickly absorbed, their skin glistening like ice for a moment before it passed into darkness again. Rain came in their wake, as if the beating of their wings had torn the stormclouds open, and he could hear it pounding along the ground as they approached. To fall into the shadow of their wings was death, he knew that as certainly as the hare knew there was danger in the shadow of a hawk, yet he could not run from them, nor even gather the power to defend himself. It was as if the mere presence of the creatures turned him to stone.

Gwynofar screamed then. It was more than a mere sound, it was a howl of anguish such as an animal might make while predators slowly tore it to pieces. His arm about her tightened instinctively, and with a herculean effort he managed to bind enough power to confirm that their appearance was no more real than the rest of the landscape, however terrifying they might be.

"It's your dream," he whispered fiercely. "Take control of it."

She shut her eyes and nodded. He could feel a shudder pass though her body as she struggled to shut the creatures out, to deny them existence. It did not seem to help. The shadow of their wings were nearly upon the two of them now, and Ramirus instinctively lent her strength, not wishing to discover what would happen if they fell prey to such creatures, even while dreaming.

Were these the ikati that legends spoke of? Had they truly been that fearsome when they lived? Could they have overcome a Magister's power as easily as these did? The thought was a chilling one, yet not half so chilling as the question that followed: what were these ancient creatures, supposedly extinct, doing in the High Queen's dream?

Then, with a shriek that made the very air shiver, the first of the great creatures wheeled in its flight, turning back the way it had come. Others followed, likewise keening their rage at the power that was forcing them back. The movement of their wings struck up a black funnel that touched the ground briefly just outside the circle of stones, then disappeared. And in another few seconds they were swallowed up by the clouds overhead, and were gone. Ramirus felt himself breathe a sigh of relief, and forced his hand to release its death grip on Gwynofar's shoulder. Where the clouds were parting now there was a glimpse of a bloody, swollen sunset, as if the sky itself had been bruised by the creatures' passage.

A tremor passed through Gwynofar as Ramirus released her. Her eyes met his; he wondered if his own expression looked as fearful as hers. It was a strangely naked feeling.

"*Souleaters,*" she whispered.

"I would guess so." The air felt strangely crisp, like it did just after a storm. "Though I have never seen one myself, so I cannot say for sure."

"The bards of my land say that at the end of the Dark Ages they would fill the sky like that, until the sun could no longer be seen . . . that men turned to stone in their shadow and could not even run away to save themselves."

With effort he forced his tone to become something more like its accustomed self: controlled, unemotional, authoritative. "The songs of bards may reflect some truth, but they also exaggerate it. In that the Lord Protectors established their rule in the name of protecting mankind from such creatures, it stands to reason they would encourage stories that made men cringe in terror at the thought of their return."

She looked at him sharply. "And is that all you think it is, Ramirus?"

"The last ikati was killed a thousand years ago, Lady. The skies have been free of them ever since. Do you not think that if any had survived, we would know it by now? In all the human lands there is not one creature remaining that feeds the way they did, for all were hunted down and destroyed following the Great War. Had they not been, we would be barbarians still, and the Second Age of Kings could never have begun."

She hesitated, then breathed, "My people believe they will return someday. You know that."

His nod was solemn. "I know."

She sighed heavily. "Danton has utter scorn for such beliefs. He says the Lord Protectors invented those tales to claim power long ago, and were foolish enough to forget that and to fall for their own lies."

"Danton . . ." his expression darkened, ". . . is an ass."

"What if this dream is some kind of omen?"

He shrugged stiffly. "I don't know, Lady. For now, let us hope it is merely a dream. Your mind has been filled with tales of these creatures since your birth, it is not unreasonable they might make an appearance in your nightmares. Or even leave images appended to the fate of your son. He is half a Protector as well."

She gazed out at the bruised horizon and said quietly, "The northern skies looked like that, this past winter. Rhys wrote me about it. There were many who took it for an ill omen, but then nothing came of it, and in a few months things seemed mostly normal again. But he said that for a few months it was as if the sky itself were bleeding, and the sunsets were the most terrible and beautiful thing he had ever seen."

Ramirus nodded "I remember the color of the northern sky being odd for a time, though not to that degree. The witches and fortune-tellers were delighted, of course. They made a fortune peddling doom and gloom to the rich and gullible."

"And the Magisters? What did they make of it?"

He chose his words carefully. "They determined that it was a wholly natural phenomenon. The sea too turns red in some places, and that is only an illusion brought about by the profusion of plant life near the surface. Something similar may well have occurred in the skies, far enough north that we could not see the cause from here."

She said it quietly. "That would mean it came from beyond the Wrath."

He said nothing, just nodded.

"Do you believe there is really something out there? Do you believe that—that it is linked to us somehow, like the legends say?" She did not meet his eyes, fearing what might be in them. "What do you think of my line, Ramirus? I have never asked you directly before, but now, with these omens . . . I must know. Danton scorns the Protectorate legends, Kostas listened to my tales as if I were a child reciting nursery rhymes. Yet you—you never laughed at me. You asked me of my bloodline, and I told you the truth, and you never ridiculed my answers."

Ah, my Queen, that was because I brought you here to teach me these things, and it would have been poor return on such a service to laugh at your lessons.

"I believe that your line is imbued with special gifts," he said quietly, "but I also observe there are no witches among the Protectors, none at all, nor any who have ever become Magisters. The combination is . . . intriguing. I did not lie to Danton when I told him you were not a witch, for you have no control over your own soulfire, nor even a conscious awareness of it, I am guessing. But if the legends speak true, and the ikati do return . . . perhaps that will change."

"You believe that the gods gave us power for that day," she breathed. "Like the legends say."

"That, or simply that the army of witches who traveled north for the final battle left behind enough survivors to found a unique bloodline—one that has inherited their potential for power, but not the ability to master it. That is . . ." He smiled slightly, ". . . outside of matters of childbearing, in which some manner of instinctive control seems to come into play. But you have told me yourself you are not aware of that."

She had not meant to ask, but now that the moment presented itself she had to. "The birth of my children—did you affect that at all?" She tried to keep her voice steady, but even she could hear the emotion in it. "Danton accused me of seeking your help."

He met her eyes with a rare frankness. "A Lady Protector needs no help in begetting or bearing children," he said quietly. "Only a fool would think otherwise."

She flushed.

"Now, Majesty, you have business to get back to and I . . . I have some things that need looking into."

"The Souleaters."

He nodded solemnly. "If this dream has true significance, I will discover it."

"And you will tell me what you find out?"

He hesitated. There was no reason not to lie to her. It shouldn't have mattered to him if he did. *Just tell her yes,* an inner voice urged. *It is the answer she wants to hear.*

"As much as I can," he promised at last. *As much as the Magisters are willing to share.*

He held out his hand to her. The silken scarf in it had been crushed by his fisted grip when the creatures approached; it eased slowly open as he released it now, like the wings of a newborn butterfly spreading to meet the wind. "I cannot return this to you here. The real items are over a thousand miles away from here, where my true body lies. I am sorry."

"Keep it," she said. "I may have need of you again someday, yes? Or perhaps . . ." her pale eyes glittered, ". . . you will have need of me."

"I hope that will never be the case, Lady Protector." His expression was solemn. "For both our sakes."

It occurred to him then that there was something else he should say to her. A warning he should give her, before they parted ways. But as he saw her rest her hand upon her belly again, as he saw her face soften in anticipation of the child to come, one cast in her beloved Andovan's mold, he kept his silence. Let her have this moment, this silent communion, without his adding new fears into the mix.

It is not needed yet, he told himself.

And an inner voice added, *Let us hope it never is.*

Chapter 27

IN THE tower that had no doors, upon a table of unpolished oak, a
body lay.

"Where did she turn up?"

It had once been a woman, though warm days submerged in the river
had taken their toll upon her flesh. The face was unrecognizable, its softer
parts gone to feed the denizens of the river. Several fingers were missing.
The heavy silk of its green gown had proven too much for the scavengers,
but the fabric along the neckline was damaged in several places where
metal adornments appeared to have been torn loose, and tiny creatures
stirred behind the holes, apparently unaware that they were being
observed.

The body was wrapped in a shroud of sorcery, which trapped the worst
of the smell inside it. Without that precaution it would surely have made
the room unbearable.

"Up the river, by several miles. One of my men heard word of it and
brought it here." Tirstan paused. "It's the gown she wore that night, there
is no question of that."

The forest green silk was coated with muck and soaked in blood and
very little of its original color was visible, but where it was, the hue could
not be mistaken.

"Gemstones stolen, you think?"

"No doubt. We are lucky whoever took them did not just bury her to hide the evidence."

"Do we know for a fact it is this . . . what was her name . . . this Sidra?" Magister Kant asked.

Tirstan shrugged. "The flesh is too long dead to garner any living trace from it. The dress appears to belong to her, though; they both bear the same resonance. So it seems likely."

"How did she die?" Tamil asked.

"Fell from a height, crushed several bones, drowned." Tirstan's expression was grim. "There is a distinct impression of suicide, though it is hard to make out details at this point. My guess is that she threw herself off the cliffs north of Tonnard, onto the rocks below. The river must have washed her downstream."

"There is sorcery about the body," Tamil said quietly.

The other two narrowed their eyes, focusing their special senses upon the rotting flesh. Tirstan cursed softly under his breath as he caught sight of the trace Tamil was referring to, a residue of sorcery that clung to the body so faintly, it took all his skill to make it out. "It is not what killed her," he said at last.

"No, but it may be what caused her to kill herself."

Kant drew in a sharp breath. "You are saying one of our kind forced her to commit suicide?"

"So it would appear."

Tirstan looked up at Tamil. "Your mystery Magister, perhaps?"

Tamil's dark eyes, lidded with the parchment skin of great age, returned the stare. "It seems certain now, does it not? She escaped our justice only to find a harsher master waiting at home."

"Falling to her death," Kant mused. "There is irony in that, no?"

"Her master is subject to the same Law that we are," Tamil pointed out. "What she did in Tower Savresi was an offense to all the brotherhood."

"Yes, well." Tirstan sighed. "She has paid for it now. And the morati jackals have had their entertainment, in Ravi's death. Shall we say this matter is ended?"

"Save for not knowing the name of her master," Tamil said quietly.

"The body came straight down the river toward us," Kant pointed out.

"Which means that he meant for us to have it. I would call that an apology."

The aged eyes fixed on him. "And if there is a Magister still at large who would use a morati thus, to invade our city? To insert his spy in our midst, to undermine our houses, perhaps even to claim what is rightfully ours?"

"It is not against the Law," Kant pointed out.

"Actually," Tirstan offered, "it was rather creative."

"However," Kant added, "if you would like to leave Gansang to go search for this individual, by all means, please do so. Tirstan and I will be happy to care for the city in your absence."

Tamil glared.

Tirstan carefully did not smile.

After a moment Kant passed his hand over the corpse, muttering words of binding under his breath. The flesh seemed to quiver for a moment, then contracted. Water poured forth from it, first in a trickle and then in a torrent, raining down the sides of the table onto the floor. When the flood finally ended there was only a pile of ash left upon the oaken table.

Tirstan banished the sorcerous shell that had enclosed it, releasing a noxious mist that was quickly dispelled by the breeze. With a gesture, Tamil conjured stronger wind that picked up the ash and carried it out through the window, out over the city, and away.

"We are done here?" he asked.

Moments later, three great birds left the high tower, winging their way back to various posts within the city.

If any morati noticed, they did not comment upon it.

———

In a forest that had no name, in a circle carefully cleared of brush, a fire burned.

Kamala stared into its depths for a few long minutes, then drew out a leather pouch from beneath her cloak. Opening it, she spilled a handful of gems into her palm: cabochons of star sapphire, square-cut diamonds, and a single golden brooch set with marsh pearls.

For a moment she hesitated. A lifetime of poverty did not prepare one to discard such wealth, no matter the cause. Briefly she entertained the thought of keeping the gemstones, if only as a souvenir.

But they were dangerous. Too dangerous. She had worn them that night—used her power while wearing them—and so they bore her trace as well as Ravi's. The dress was another thing; soaking it in the blood of her peasant sacrifice, she had impressed it with traces of its wearer's death, so strongly that her own mark was all but obliterated. Gemstones defied such treatment.

It had been a true suicide, anyway. If they studied the body closely they would see that much, yes?

It is all wasted effort if you do not let the gemstones go.

Muttering words of power under her breath, she closed her hand about the precious gems. When she opened it again there was nothing in her hand but sand. She cast it onto the fire and summoned enough power to force it to burn; when the fire finally died there was nothing left but ash, indistinguishable from the remains of any other fire set for any other purpose.

Not until the embers were cold and dark did she leave the clearing behind, and with it the city of her childhood.

Chapter 28

"WELCOME, MY teacher."

Colivar brushed the long black hair out of his eyes, where the wind had blown it, and looked over the place that his former student had chosen for a landing point. From the hilltop where they stood he could see northern wilderness on one side, stark granite mountains with a stubble of pine trees clinging to their lower slopes, peaks capped in glistening snow. On the other side was a valley with a river coursing down its center, in which a small town was nestled. Narrow windows, multiple chimneys, and steeply canted roofs spoke of a region where snow and the omnipresent cold ruled every human concern. Yet there were places even farther north than this forsaken place, he knew, and even more inhospitable . . . places where it was said only Magisters and witches might survive.

He banished that thought with effort. Too many memories within him responded to that vision, including things he had promised himself he would not remember. That was the problem with living as long as Magisters did. After too many centuries the walls between memories grew thin and were easily compromised, letting the thoughts bleed into one another.

Sometimes that was dangerous.

He took a deep breath of the chill, bracing air, and forced himself out of the past and into the present. "You said it was important, Sulah. There are few I would trust to call me across the nations like this, but as you have not ever wasted my time yet, I give you the benefit of the doubt."

"You do me great honor, my teacher."

A brief sweep of his hand dismissed the honorific. "I am not that any more."

The younger Magister shrugged, acknowledging the denial without accepting it. He was one of the few apprentices Colivar had ever taken, and he had never quite internalized the tradition which said that a Magister who had been released should be a rival to his teacher, not an ally. Colivar kept him at arm's length most of the time to drive the lesson home, but there was no denying that his loyalty was . . . intriguing. Such emotions rarely survived Transition, and almost never survived the immersion in Magister politics that quickly followed. Sulah was unique.

The politics of immortals, Colivar mused. After the first few centuries of life one came to commiserate with the ancient gods, who were said to have bickered and connived and cheated like a household of spoiled children. Why should a mere human do better than they? There came a time when all your lovers had died, your family was long gone, and your most treasured projects had sparked briefly and then descended into the abyss of the forgotten, and all that was left was those who were equally powerful, equally immortal, and equally bored.

Had Sulah's teacher been anyone but Colivar, his loyalty would have been seen as a weakness and he would have been used, abused, and discarded in his first few centuries. But Colivar preferred more constructive projects, and was faintly amused by the fact that his idealistic young charge had managed to survive with his optimism intact for so long. Setting obstacles in his way—a traditional Magister sport—would have been poor answer for such a rare accomplishment.

"There was a boy you wanted me to see?"

Sulah nodded. He was a blond man, light-skinned in the way of the north, tall and lean but with a strength and agility that defied the Magister stereotype. Of course he might look like whatever he wanted, now that he had the power of the athra to draw upon, but he had always preferred his natural appearance. Yet another facet of his varity.

"In the town," he said, nodding toward the settlement below them. "Easier to bring you to him than to bring him out."

"Very well." Colivar nodded. "Lead on."

Sulah didn't wear black, Colivar noted. Not that it was needed here. The chill northern wind posed a dangerous trial for merely morati flesh; only someone with the power of souls to draw upon for heat would dare to walk in it as they did, protected by no more than a single layer of clothing. The simplicity of Sulah's garb was as much a sign of power and rank as any trick of color.

Still, it was . . . disconcerting.

There were houses scattered along the valley. Sulah led him to one of the larger ones and knocked on the door. A man passing by looked up at the sound of the noise, saw who had made it, and managed a hurried bow that nearly had him tripping over his feet.

How quick they are, Colivar thought wryly, *to grant respect to those who feed upon them.*

The door opened partway and a ruddy-face woman peered out. She held a ladle in her hand, and it was clear she was less than pleased at having been interrupted. "Yes? What do you—" Then she realized who—and what—stood before her. "Oh—" She drew in a quick breath. "Forgive me, my lord, I didn't realize it was you. And with Magister company, too! Come in, please."

The house was pleasantly warm, with a low-banked fire in the common room to sustain the heat. Cooking smells wafted toward them as their hostess shut the door: nutmeg, cinnamon, the aroma of fresh bread. "You weren't waiting long, I hope? I'd never forgive myself if I kept a Magister waiting." She was trying to look straight at Sulah, to ignore Colivar until he was introduced. It must be some local custom, the Magister mused. Nonetheless her curiosity was evident, and the bright blue eyes, rimmed with lines of age and hard work, kept sneaking glances at the black-haired visitor.

"Not long at all, Mother." Sulah said the word as if it was some kind of official title, and Colivar took note. "I hope we do not disturb you."

"Never a disturbance, never a one!" Another glance at Colivar. "I've got fresh bread coming out of the oven, if you want some . . . you and your visitor . . ."

Sulah nodded. "Colivar, Magister Royal of Anshasa."

The woman's eyes grew. "Oh my. I am . . . honored, sir. Will you break bread with me? My husband is out working or I would call him in to meet you, and the children all off on errands . . . what can I do for two such distinguished guests? Please forgive my humble abode, and I've no table set for you . . ." The worry lines about her eyes scrunched in dismay. "Magister Sulah, how could you bring me such a guest without any warning?"

The blond Magister smiled. There was a genuine warmth behind the expression but the edge was forced; whatever had moved him to call Colivar to this place, it did not lend itself to congeniality. "Your house is fine, Mistress Tally, and your table is not what we came for." He glanced toward the farther reaches of the house, hidden behind closed doors. "I should like to show Magister Colivar the boy, if that is all right with you."

The color fled from the woman's face, as did her smile. She recovered quickly and forced the smile back into place, but the paleness remained. "Of course, my lords, of course. Whatever you want." She fumbled with flour-stained hands at her apron, withdrawing a key at last from somewhere in its depths. "Maybe you can do the boy some good—the gods know we have tried, I tell you that. Tried over and over again, my husband and I, and he not a patient one on the best of days . . ."

She seemed to be chattering to herself, Colivar noted, not to them, and so he was silent as she led the two to a narrow door at the back of the house. "We would have kept him upstairs if we could," she went on, fumbling with her key in the lock, "but you see he tried to break out again and again, so it was really this or a closet. Or make him a room of his own without windows, to which my husband said no, this is too much for such a mad creature—"

The door swung open. Beyond it, steps led down into the earth. A dim light glittered from somewhere below, not a pleasant light but enough to see by. The smells were earthy and damp, but clean; whatever was in the cellar, the place was well maintained. There was something else besides, in the scent of the place, that it took Colivar a moment to identify. A human smell, normally masked by other things, but a clear note here, rising up from the depths.

Fear.

He glanced at Sulah, who nodded grimly and moved to lead the way down. Colivar followed him. The woman muttered something about how she would follow them were the bread not rising, but the oven needed tending to . . . and there was fear in her as well, Colivar observed, though this time he heard it in the voice rather than smelling it.

"Danger?" He said it in Sulah's native tongue, which the locals would not understand.

"Not for us." The blond Magister drew in a sharp breath. "Not yet, anyway."

At the bottom of the staircase was an oddly shaped room that seemed to extend under much of the house. Supplies were stacked along several walls, and they had once filled the entire space—or so the pattern of dust suggested. Currently the boxes and sacks and racks of tools were pushed back from one corner, clearing a small square area not much larger than a pantry. In that space a small bed had been made up and piled with blankets, clean but worn. A chamberpot stood beside it, and a small table on which sat the remnants of a meal, untouched. There were a few other amenities as well, but Colivar had less interest in them than in the thing that was huddled under the covers, keening softly in terror as they approached.

"It's all right," Sulah said softly. He spoke to the mound of blankets in a northern dialect that Colivar had known ages ago. "We're friends. Come out, it's all right."

A moment passed with no response. A lesser Magister might have used his power to press the issue, but Colivar knew Sulah and did not believe in using his power when other means would suffice. Sure enough, after a few moments had passed, the mound of blankets stirred. Something wriggled beneath them. A tiny hand came out, grimy and with broken fingernails, as if testing the air. Then the blanket's edge was folded back and the whole of a small boy was revealed . . . pale, trembling, and clearly half mad with terror.

"That's it, my boy. You see? No danger here." Sulah sat down on the edge of the bed, and Colivar wondered if the boy might not shy away from him. But it didn't seem as if he was afraid of men. Rather, his eyes flitted nervously about the room as if seeking something else in its shadows, and only when he had looked everywhere twice and found nothing did he relax a tiny bit and dare to look at his guests.

His eyes were terrible things to look at, young in their freshness and color but aged whole centuries in whatever they had gazed upon.

"Not here?" he whispered.

"None of them here," Sulah assured him. "They can't get in here, remember? Mother Tally has seen to that."

He nodded slowly. The motion was painful to watch.

"This is my friend. His name is Colivar. He wanted to meet you."

The haunted eyes studied the black-haired visitor.

"Colivar, this is Kaiden."

"I am pleased to meet you," the Magister said.

The boy said nothing.

"I told him how brave you were," Sulah offered.

A tear rolled down the boy's cheek, to join the sheen of dried salt already there. "Not brave," he whispered. "I ran away."

"Kaiden—" Colivar began to reach out to him, but the sudden motion startled the boy and he backed hurredly into the corner, as far as he could go, jerking the worn blankets tightly about him. Colivar's hand froze in place, but he did not lower it. After a moment had passed, he waited until the boy's eyes met his own, and then said softly, "Sleep."

The tortured eyes closed. The muscles of the face relaxed a bit, though the channels etched by tears remained the same. The hand holding the blanket opened slightly, but not enough to let it fall.

"He cannot tell anything useful," Colivar mused. "That much is clear."

Sulah nodded. "His mind is gone. Sometimes he speaks fragments of things that hint at the cause . . . enough that I was called here to see him. But mostly he is like this."

Colivar drew in a deep breath, willing the power to come to him and do his bidding. It took a moment before the athra responded; his current consort was likely near the end of his or her life, and not able to fuel many more endeavors. He would have to take care in the future, lest he be caught between consorts at an awkward moment.

For now, however, it was enough. He willed his power to wrap itself around the young boy, and then to reflect, like a mirror, the cause of his fear.

The athra-born force came into view slowly, at first in tendrils of hesitant mist, which then it solidified into a thicker fog. In front of the boy's eyes it gathered together then, until all of it was in that one place, and a picture began to take shape. Bits and pieces of things flickered in and out of existence, as if the power was struggling to choose a focus. Feces. Dead flies. Rats. Bodies draped over a table. Then at last it seemed to fix on something, and the image that it formed became truly solid . . . so much so that it seemed one could pluck it from the air and set it free in the real world.

Black it was, with shimmers of purple and blue along its body and wings, and it hung in the air like a dragonfly, though it was nothing like a dragonfly in truth.

Sulah's reaction was immediate, instinctive. With a gasp he took a step back, and sketched a sign of one of the higher gods over his chest. "Is that . . . is that what I think it is?"

When Colivar did not respond to him right away, Sulah turned to look at him. The black-haired Magister's expression was grim, and dark in a way that his former student had never seen before. The look in his eyes was daunting—ominous, fierce, haunted—as if some terrible memory had surfaced, and for the moment he could not see past it.

Then slowly his attention returned to the room, to Sulah and to the boy. For a long moment he said nothing. Then, "Yes. So it would seem."

"I thought they were all dead. Destroyed in the Dark Ages. Isn't that what you taught me?"

"No," he said quietly. "Not destroyed. Gone, yes . . . but not destroyed."

Colivar put out a hand slowly, as if to touch the thing. The illusion scattered when he touched it. Of course. Real and unreal could not be combined.

Sulah drew in a sharp breath. "It's so small . . ."

"It will grow larger," Colivar said quietly. "And change again. This is not its final form."

Sulah looked at him sharply. "You've seen one of them. Fully grown."

Colivar said nothing. After a moment he rose up and turned away from the boy and Sulah both, so that his student could no longer see his face.

At last he said, "The Black Sleep will come here, if this things has . . . brothers."

"It is already here, my teacher."

"Where?"

"Up north, a day's travel. This boy's home, I gather. I've gotten it out of him in bits and pieces over the past few weeks . . . not an easy task. His soul struggles to forget."

He whispered, "Tell me."

"The whole town is dead." Sulah's voice sounded hollow in his own ears as remembered the boy screaming out details of the event, fevered bits of rememberance interspersed with raw animal terror. "He was away from home for a time, and when he came back . . . that's how he found them."

Colivar turned back to him. "All the people? Or . . . everything?"

"People, animals . . . everything alive that was there at the time. Rumor has it a few other inhabitants survived, who were abroad when it happened, but either they can't be found, or they simply aren't talking."

Colivar's expression had become a terrible thing to behold. "And those who went there after this took place. What did they find?"

Sulah shook his head. "The town has been declared cursed, and no man will go near it. Or at least no man will admit to having gone near it."

"But you have gone."

"Yes." He said it quietly. "I have gone."

"And?"

"It was as the boy described. A town of death. Where I found bodies undisturbed, it was as if they had simply lay down to sleep and died." His bright eyes fixed on Colivar. "Like the tales you told me of the Black Sleep, the Devil's Sleep . . . only this was more than sleep."

"The Black Sleep doesn't kill. Not that many. This is something else." He shook his head; his expression was grim. "It *must* be."

"You're going to want to go there yourself, aren't you?"

It was a moment before he answered. "There is no other choice, is there? I must know what happened."

"I have horses ready, if you want to ride."

"Yes." He thought of his failing consort, and how unpleasant it would be to be caught in Transition while transporting himself. He had made that mistake once before and almost been killed. "Horses will do."

Sulah reached down to wrap the blanket more tightly around the sleeping boy. It was an oddly human gesture, the sort of casual compassion that most Magisters lost touch with by the end of their first lifetime. An odd quirk of this particular student, which Colivar alternately disdained and marveled at. Magisters who could feel for others rarely survived the ages; sooner or later their natural compassion warred with the necessary inhumanity of their survival, and one or the other lost the battle. Yet Sulah had been through a handful of Transitions successfully, there was no denying that. And the human side of him was still strong enough to surface now and then. It was . . . interesting.

They climbed up the narrow stairs silently, each lost in his own thoughts. Mother Tally greeted them at the top, chittering about poor manners and how they must forgive her for not having bread ready, or perhaps they would wait? Colivar left it to Sulah to fend off her aggressive hospitality; he was lost in his own thoughts, barely cognizant of the world around them.

After they left the house it was but a short walk to where Sulah's horses were stabled. And a very short time to get them ready for travel, since Sulah had prepared everything well in advance.

As they led the horses out of the stable and turned them toward the northern road, Sulah finally broke the silence that had reigned since they'd left Mother Tally's house. "How do you know all these things, from times that even the history books have forgotten? When was the last time there was a living ikata, that you could take its measure?"

Colivar did not look at him, but yanked on one of the buckles holding a worn leather pack in place, to make sure it was tight enough. "You should have asked me that when you were still my student, Sulah. I might have answered you then."

"Truly?"

"No." With a practiced motion he slipped his foot into a stirrup and hoisted himself into the saddle. "Now no more questions, until we have seen what there is to see, yes? I am wanting answers myself."

Sulah nodded shortly as he mounted his own horse, then turned him to lead the way out of town.

He would not forget, he promised himself. Some questions needed to be asked.

———

It was quiet, in the way that unwholesome things were quiet. Colivar noticed that right away. A place that the beasts of the surrounding forest might visit, but they clearly did not want to remain in.

He reined up his horse at the edge of the small town and sat there for a minute, studying the place. Sulah waited quietly by his side, patting his horse once as the beast snuffled its own discomfort with the unhealthy aura of the place.

"How long has it been?" Colivar asked finally.

"A month, as near as I can tell. The boy has no real sense of time."

Colivar nodded. Another moment passed in silence, then he dismounted. Sulah followed suit. There was no need to hitch the animals to any tree or man-made contrivance; if they wandered off, two Magisters could call them back easily enough when they were needed.

Slowly, his eyes taking in every detail, Colivar began to walk through the town. Dark things skittered back into the shadows as he did so, save for a few that had courage enough to stand their ground. Rats. One of them stood guard over a prize he was clearly willing to defend against the intruders. A bone of some sort. Human. Colivar looked about and saw other bones in shadows, near doorways, and some just out in the middle of the street. "The beasts of the forest have been here." he mused, and Sulah nodded. A town full of corpses might seem a fearsome thing to human beings, but to the wild things that inhabited the surrounding woods it was no more nor less than an invitation to a feast.

Sulah remembered what Colivar had taught him about the balance of nature, and wondered about the effect this tragedy would have on local animal populations. Would more meat eaters be born in the time following such bounty, only to be brought into a world that offered no more such feasts? Would they be forced out of the forest by their increased numbers, to brave the towns of men in search of sustenance? Would men die five years down the line in some distant town, not knowing what had prompted the assault?

All these things were related, Colivar had taught him. Nothing changed in the world without fostering changes itself. The difference between the art of the Magisters and the magic worked by witches, he said, was that the former took such things into account, both in the planning and the execution.

As well we must, Sulah had once mused. A witch might create a sizeable disturbance before she died, but only that. A Magister could, in theory, change the world itself. Though the gods alone knew how many people would have to die to provide the power for such a thing, or what a Magister's soul would look like after he had done it.

Moderation and restraint are what will keep you human, Colivar had taught him. *Never forget that.*

Sulah had asked him many times why being "human" was so important, since it seemed to him that many Magisters were not. It was among the many questions his teacher had never answered.

Slowly the two of them walked through the small town, reading its story in the bones that were scattered along the street. Once Colivar stopped and opened the door of a small house, to see what there was in places the beasts could not go. A putrid smell greeted their nostrils, and he bade the breeze sweep it away before they entered.

The bones of those inside were stripped equally clean, but eerily so, as they were still more or less in the posture in which they had died. The discarded husks of maggots lay in thousands upon the floor and crunched underfoot as Colivar inspected the place. A handful of insects buzzed about his head, but most had clearly found their way out by the same means they had come in. And of course there were rat droppings. Always rat droppings.

Sulah was silent while his teacher inspected the place, his expression grim. He had been to the town before, for the same sort of inspection, and knew what would be found.

Finally Colivar nodded for them to leave. The fresh air outside was welcome, with a brisk wind from the north that scoured the town clean of its rotten smells. Colivar took a deep breath of it and said, "What is there in the surrounding area?"

"Woods, mostly. A river down that way." He pointed.

"No clearings? There should be one somewhere, not far beyond the borders of men."

"I do not know. I did not think to search for one."

Colivar nodded. With an almost casual gesture he called up a bit of soulfire and bade it gather before him. A foggy map that seemed to reflect the landscape surrounding the small town appeared. There appeared to be a few places nearby that were bereft of trees, the majority of them cultivated lands, circumscribed by low stone walls built when they were cleared. There was a wilder place farther off, a narrow strip where the earth was not deep enough for trees to take root, but evidently not well suited to farming.

"There," Colivar whispered. "That will be it."

"What?" Sulah asked him. "What are you looking for?"

"What I hope not to find," Colivar said quietly, "but fear that I will."

He would answer no more questions after that, but called the horses to them and mounted his own in silence, his expression as dark as a storm-cloud about to break. And Sulah, who had been his student, knew him well enough not to press for answers.

———

Wild the land was, in the place surrounding the narrow clearing, and wild things chittered and chirruped in the shadows as Colivar and Sulah made their way through the thick brush at its border into the open.

For a moment then Colivar just stood still, studying the landscape. His aspect reminded Sulah of a wild beast just come into the open, eyeing the surrounding woods for predators . . . or perhaps prey. But whatever Colivar sought it was not so simple a thing as wolves or deer, that was clear. Sulah had never seen him in such a dark mood as now, and as he watched his elder take the measure of the land, he could almost taste on his lips the aura of foreboding that surrounded him.

The strip of land was a narrow one, but long, that twisted between jutting granite slabs near the rise of a mountain. Some quirk of earthly creation had made its soil shallow enough that trees could not anchor themselves comfortably, and the place was too rocky and irregular to draw human interest, so it had been left for grasses and scraggly low bushes to colonize despite its proximity to the town.

"This is the place," Colivar said quietly. His expression was grim as he looked about the area, searching for something as yet unseen. "If it is anywhere to be found, it will be here . . ."

Having learned from the preceding hours that Colivar was not in a mood for answering questions, Sulah followed patiently behind him as he slowly walked the length of the clearing, his sharp black eyes taking in everything. Then suddenly he hissed, and stopped. The sound was sudden enough that Sulah found his hand going for his knife . . . as if what had killed all the people in that town might be stopped by simple steel.

What had drawn Colivar's attention was a mound of rocks near one edge of the clearing. All around it the land was barren, stripped even of its sparse grasses. As Sulah looked more closely he could see that the area was scored by what might be claw marks, as if some huge thing had been digging there. In such a context, the mound of rocks at its center seemed distinctly unnatural.

Colivar cursed vividly, and the dialect he used was so foreign—or so ancient—that Sulah could only understand half of it.

"What is it?" he asked.

Colivar did not answer him. He no longer seemed to be aware of Sulah's existence, or indeed of anything else surrounding him.

With steady steps he moved to the rock pile and began to remove stones from it, one after the other, casting them aside with little concern for where they might fall. Sulah had to dodge one as he scrambled to his side to watch. Now that he was closer to the mound he could see clearly that it was no natural thing; the stones had been placed so as to interlock closely, providing a sound shelter for whatever lay beneath. A burial mound, perhaps? It didn't seem to him that the size was quite right, unless it was that of a child. . . .

And then Colivar seemed to find whatever he was searching for, and he cursed again, this time in a language Sulah did understand. The nature of that curse made his blood run cold.

"Look," his teacher commanded.

He leaned forward to look down into the hole that Colivar had made. In its shadows he could see a layer of dried grass that his teacher had broken through, and could just make out beneath that some off-white fragments of something. It took him a moment to identify them.

"Eggshells?"

Colivar nodded, and then resumed his digging. This time Sulah helped him. Now that he had some sense of what they were digging toward he was able to do so without ruining the find, and soon they had laid bare a collection of what appeared to be broken eggs, all gathered neatly in a bowl-shaped depression that had been scraped into the shallow earth.

They would have been large eggs, about the size of a fist, and like nothing Sulah had ever seen before. The outside was a dull white but the inside glistened with color, and as he turned a fragment up to catch the sunlight it flashed a deep blue where something had caught on the shell and stuck there. He pried it loose with his fingernail and held it close to his eye to examine. Reptile skin, it looked like, though of the most unusual color.

"Is this where it came from?" he asked. "The thing the boy saw?"

Colivar nodded grimly.

Sulah put the shell fragment down. The nest—if that's what it was—was a large one. There must have been dozens of eggs in it once, though most were now shattered.

"Are there then . . . this many? Of those things?"

Colivar shook his head. "They fight each other when they first hatch, so that only the strongest survive. They don't leave the nest until much later. Sometimes a dozen will survive that stage. Sometimes only one." He studied the part of the nest that still lay buried, as if trying to calculate how many were born, and how few of those might have survived. "Even one is not good," he said at last.

Sulah dared to ask it, finally. "This is what killed the town?"

Colivar hesitated. "This is the cause of the Black Sleep," he said finally. "So many of these making their transformation at the same time . . . once they cease to feed on one another they need another source of food. But this one nest should not have killed a whole town . . ."

"Are these what the ancients called Souleaters, then?"

Colivar nodded. "Men used to hunt the nests, trying to kill them before they came forth. But it was hard. The presence of that many, even in their hatching form, acts as a kind of sorcerous barrier; one can stand right on top of a nest and not realize it is there." He looked at the fragment of shell he held in one hand. Then crushed it. "Only witches could find them, back then. And the effort cost them many years of life. Few would risk it, in the early days."

"And after that?" Sulah asked the question softy, as if afraid that sound would scatter his teacher's thoughts. In all the years that he had been with Colivar the man had never spoken so openly of what took place in the Dark Ages, when mankind had waged a losing war against the beasts that fed upon human souls, and lost everything that was precious to them as a result.

"Then the hunting flight of the ikati darkened the skies, and all that was within man that was intelligent, or creative, or civilized, died." His voice had dropped to a mere whisper, hardly louder than the breeze stirring the trees nearby. "They had come to prefer men for food, you see, and from that time onward, it was said there could be no peace between the two races—one or the other must die.

"So the witches finally came together and hunted them down—or drove them out—until there were none left . . . on either side." He turned his hand over and dropped the crushed bits of eggshell to the ground. "Their blood was the purchase price for the Second Age of Kings."

"The witches all died?"

"If not in battle, soon after."

"You never told me that."

Colivar looked at the younger man. "You are not a witch. And there were no ikati when we spoke. Why remember things that have no purpose?"

"So where did the first Magisters come from?"

"Later. They came later." He brushed his hand against his breeches, dislodging the crushed bits of eggshell. "Now, it seems, we must learn these things anew."

He stood up beside the mound, slowly, as if the weight of all those stones was upon his shoulders. Then he turned north and gazed at the cold skies as if answers might be found in them. Sulah did the same, but found no enlightenment in the pattern of clouds—whatever his teacher was gazing at had clearly more to do with memory than with the current situation—and he finally brought his gaze back down to earth—

And gasped.

Colivar looked down at him sharply. "What is it?"

He couldn't speak, for a moment. So he pointed. To the mound of rocks perhaps ten yards away, almost hidden from view by the tall grasses between them.

With a muttered curse Colivar strode to the place. It was smaller than the first nest but similar in structure, and this time he didn't pick it apart with care. A quick gesture served to bind enough soulfire to blow it apart, sending the small rocks hurtling toward the forest, baring the pile of broken shells beneath.

"It can't be," he whispered, staring at the fragments. "They would never do this . . ."

Now that he knew what to look for, Sulah could make out another bare spot some yards beyond them. It, too, seemed to host one of the great nests, stones just visible in the shafts of cloud-filtered sunlight.

"Another, my teacher." He said it quietly, but the words had great effect; a shudder seemed to run through Colivar's body as he turned to regard the newest find, and a new emotion stirred in the black depths of his eyes that Sulah had never seen there before.

Fear.

"They are hostile creatures," he whispered, "even to their own kind. If they had been otherwise, if they had been capable of gathering together in great numbers, and of acting in a unified manner, mankind would have stood no chance at all. For the females to share a nesting site . . . it is . . . *was* . . . unthinkable."

"They have changed, then."

Covilar didn't respond. He turned to the north and gazed into the skies as if somehow answers could be found there.

"This is what killed the town, isn't it?" Sulah pressed. "So many of them at once, all drawing their strength from the nearest source of life."

Colivar nodded. "Yes. So many at once . . . more than a human settlement could handle."

Without further word Colivar began to walk back to where they had left the horses. Sulah attempted a few more questions, but they went unanswered; the elder Magister was clearly too lost in dark thoughts of his own to play the teacher's role any longer.

There was only one more thing he offered, as he mounted his horse, and as he shot one last look toward the nesting ground and the tone of it made Sulah's blood run cold.

"May the gods save us all . . ." Colivar whispered.

Reckoning

Chapter 29

IT WAS a moonless night, and a fog hung low over the High Queen's courtyard. The ancestor trees were shadowed and ghostly, lit only by the flickering light of a half-hooded lantern set upon a marble bench, and her spears glistened wetly in the damp night air. It reminded Gwynofar of how the real Spears appeared back home, when morning's moisture condensed on the chilled stone; the sight of them made her ache with homesickness.

She was spending more and more time here of late. There was no other place in the castle she could go to escape Kostas but her own chambers, and she refused to let him make her a prisoner in her own rooms. Once she could have sought refuge in her husband's presence, taking comfort from his obvious devotion to her but now that had changed, too. It was hard to be in Danton's presence without remembering what he had done to her. Hard to remember that act and forgive.

With a sigh she offered up drops of her blood to the Spears, placing one on each glistening surface, praying to the gods of the Wrath as she did so that they would lend some kind of peace to her soul. They were gods of war and generally did not oversee such gentle tasks, but she had nowhere else to turn. Her family was too far away for comfort, her memories of home were fading in the face of her long absence from the northlands, and the one member of Danton's household who had brought her real joy had taken his own life.

Suddenly there was a rustling behind her. With a terrible sinking feeling in her heart she turned to see who it was, half expecting Kostas to be standing there, or perhaps her husband. But it was neither of them, though in the flickering shadows her visitor might have been mistaken for the High King.

"Mother." It was Rurick, her firstborn. "I don't disturb your prayers, do I?"

"You are never a disturbance." She reached out a hand to welcome him; he took it and kissed it with rough grace. "But I thought you did not care for this place."

Rurick shrugged. In the darkness he was the spitting image of his father, from his heavy brow and narrow black eyes to his hawklike nose. He was not as stout as Danton—yet—but had the same solidity of frame that lent the High King an aura of uncompromising substance. In truth, it was sometimes hard to believe that a creature so utterly unlike her had come out of her womb, but that was the way of it with Danton's sons. All of them except Andovan.

The sudden reminder of her loss threatened to bring tears to her eyes, and she lifted up a hand to brush a lock of hair from her face, wiping the corners of her eyes before moisture could gather there. Even in front of her sons she hated to look weak.

"Not my favorite place," Rurick allowed, "but there are others who like it less. And so it has its uses. Are we alone here?"

"No servants come here, by my order. And your father does not, by his own choice."

"And Kostas hasn't the balls to. From what I hear."

She bit back on her first response. "No," she said quietly. "He does not come here."

He nodded. "Good enough."

He was an impressive figure, dressed in a rich knee-length gown, with the Aurelius double-headed hawk repeated in gold upon a velvet background. The fabric was too heavy for the season, but that never mattered to Rurick. Strutting about in fine clothes and being feared and admired by all within eyeshot was very important to him. In that he differed greatly from his father, who only cared about the "feared" part.

He looked over the area surrounding the Spears, peering into the shadows as if making sure that no one was hidden there. Was he really so worried about eavesdroppers, or was his message so unpleasant that he was stalling its delivery? Neither explanation was reassuring to her. She waited silently for him to broach his business, dreading the worst.

Finally he sighed heavily, and rested one foot upon the end of a pale marble bench. "Frankly, I am afraid that if I tell you what is going on in my mind, you will judge me mad."

She smiled faintly, with a mother's eternal indulgence. "Never, my son."

"Or that I merely desire the throne before my time. That I seek signs of trouble in House Aurelius, to make that come about."

She kept the maternal smile carefully in place. "No, Rurick. I know you better than that." In truth it was very possible that he lusted after the throne, and had possibly even harbored dreams of claming it ahead of his time—what ambitious young prince would not?—but he was not a creature of great subtlety, and was unlikely to weave some complicated plot to undermine his father, if only out of certainty that Danton would catch him at it.

She came to the bench and sat on the other end. After a moment she took his hand in hers. His was a large hand, as heavy and coarse as Danton's own, but it returned her grip with a warmth that made her heart ache. There was a time when her husband had touched her with similar affection. Now the last memory she had of Danton's touch was the night he had come to her bedchamber. A very different relationship.

"Your words are sacrosanct here," she promised him. "I will neither judge you for them nor share them with others, unless you allow it. This I promise you, by the gods that watch over this place."

He nodded, his expression grim, and squeezed her hand tightly. Rurick was not the most eloquent of her sons, and she sensed now how hard it was for him to find the words he wanted. She did not try to urge him onward, but simply waited until he was ready.

"Things have changed," he said at last. "It's like–like the very air in this place is different, somehow. Unhealthy." He shook his head, clearly frustrated with his own verbal inadequacy. "Father is changing. Not for the better. The things that once brought him pleasure no longer do. The political gestures that once satisfied him now only whet his appetite for violence. His temper—it grows shorter and shorter, with his sons, with his ministers, with everyone that surrounds him. And every day he is more of a hermit, locking himself in his rooms with his accursed *Magister* for hours at a time" —he fairly spit out the title—"while his court whispers in the shadows of his growing madness, and wonders where he will lead the kingdom. Such rumors can bring down a ruler, mother. You know that. Yet he seems oblivious to it all. That's not like my father at all."

No, she thought, her husband was uniquely sensitive to such things. She sometimes thought that not one word passed in the castle without his hearing it, not one piece of gossip was traded but that he knew the source. That he should no longer pay attention to such things was yet another sign of how much was wrong with him.

"What is my duty as firstborn?" Rurick asked. "To let the High King do as he wishes, even if that leads to the loss of his empire? To stand by his side and try to show him where his folly lies and hope he listens to me?" He laughed shortly, bitterly. "You know what he would think of that effort, mother. 'Vulture, son of a vulture', he once called me. He certainly wouldn't take advice from me, even if I knew how to offer it. And perhaps for good reason." Once more he looked into the area surrounding them, as if searching for eavesdroppers. His voice was low and hoarse. "If it comes to the point where he cannot maintain his throne," he whispered, "what is my duty then?"

"We have not yet come to that point," she said evenly. Wondering, even as she spoke the words, if they were true.

The thin lips tightened. "I've heard of his plans for Corialanus. Plans the old Danton would never have countenanced. Now he seems to take pleasure in bloodshed for its own sake. As if something in him hungers for violence, above and beyond the call of political necessity." He paused for a moment, his eyes gazing deep into her own. Deep into her soul. "You've seen this change in him too, yes?" His voice was a whisper. "I can see it in your eyes."

"That he hungers for violence?" she asked. The words caught in her throat. "That he is ruled by rage now, rather than reason?" Slowly, sadly, she nodded. "It is as you say."

More than you can imagine, my son.

He sat down on the bench beside her. "Why, Mother? Was it Andovan's suicide that caused this? Or something else? A man doesn't change so much without good cause."

She bit her lip for a moment, wondering how much she dared to say. At last she said, very quietly, "Sometimes he may, if he falls under the influence of another."

"You mean Kostas?" Rurick spat upon the ground. "I wouldn't trust that foul creature to wash my codpiece. Father needs someone who cares about him, to help him keep to his center. You are the only one who can do that. But you—you withdraw from him. The court never sees you anymore. Once you were always by his side, now you are little more than a stranger to this court. And in your absence that vile sorcerer has complete control over him. Why do you allow it?"

She looked away from him. A tiny knot lodged in her stomach. "Some things I cannot change."

"There was a time you would have tried."

"There was a time . . ." The words caught in her throat. "Things are different now."

"What do you fear? Kostas?" He snorted derisively. "He's more afraid of you than you are of him, mother."

"Of *me*?" A faint, sad smile flickered across her face. "Now I do think you are mad, in truth. Why would a Magister fear *me*?"

"I can't say why, but I've seen it in his eyes. Trust me. Whenever your name comes up, it's like—like . . . you know how when a dog doesn't like the smell of something, how its hackles rise? Like that." He snorted. "Though he is not one to be complaining about bad smells, in my opinion."

She felt her heart suddenly skip a beat. "What do you mean?"

He sighed. "Now I know you will think me mad, mother. I am sorry, but the man smells to me like rotting meat. And not only do I smell him when he is around, oh no, but he leaves his stink trailing behind him like a skunk. The very halls reek of it sometimes when he has passed. And yet . . . it's not really a smell." His brow furrowed in perplexity. "The wind doesn't spread it like true smells are spread. And it doesn't ever seem to fade. And mother, here is the odd part . . ." Something dark and fearful flickered in the backs of his eyes. "I've mentioned this to other people, and they look at me like I'm mad. Only a few others can smell it; the rest—the rest think I have lost all reason."

She was glad he could not hear the pounding of her heart; she tried to keep her voice steady as she asked him, "Which others?"

"Valemar. Salvator. Perhaps Tiresia. She said something about 'the foulness of Kostas' presence' when she last visited here. I didn't ask if she meant it literally. At that time it didn't occur to me it was anything worth asking about." He shook his head. "No one else can smell it, Mother. Not the servants, not other nobles, not even children . . . they stare at me as if I am daft when I ask. To the rest of the world, Kostas is no more odiferous than any other sorcerer."

Valemar. Salvator. Tiresia. Those were all Gwynofar's children. Would Andovan have smelled that curious odor too, had he lived? Would his skin have crawled like Gwynofar's every time Danton's foul Magister passed by?

All of her bloodline sensed this thing. None but her bloodline could.

The air in the courtyard suddenly seemed very cold.

"Mother?"

It meant something, that much was clear. But she was suddenly not sure she wanted to know what that *something* was.

Rurick's hand on her shoulder startled her out of her reverie. "You all right?"

"Yes." She whispered it. "Yes. Only . . ." She looked up at him. "I've smelled it too. And worse. I can *feel* his presence, as if an icy wind blew across my flesh." She wrapped her arms about herself and shivered. "I thought it was a kind of madness. My hatred for him made manifest. But if all of my children are experiencing it as well . . . then there must be more to it than that."

Rhys would know, she thought. Rhys knew all the ancient legends; he would know how to read meaning into all of this.

Gods, how she wished he were here now.

"Mother." Rurick's hand on her shoulder squeezed tightly. "You need to talk to him."

"Who?"

"Father."

She drew in a sharp breath and turned away from him.

"You're the only one who can. The only one he will listen to."

"He doesn't listen to me any longer."

"He *trusts* you, Mother. Only you."

The memory came back to her in a rush, unbidden. Danton's accusation, his assault upon her flesh, the foulness of Kostas' magic as it clung to him. "What other man has had input into my line?" he had cried.

She turned away from her son, unwilling to let him see her tears. "Things have changed," she whispered.

"Surely not that much."

She said nothing.

He came before her, then, and knelt, waiting until she met his eyes before speaking. "I don't know what happened between you and my father. And it's not my business to ask. I only know that you told me once, when I was a boy, that you were queen first and a woman second. That all other things must come second to royal duty, for one who wore a crown. I believed in you then." He paused. "I still do."

She did not trust herself to speak.

Rising up again, he leaned over and gently kissed her on her cheek, then whispered in her ear, "If you forsake him, Gwynofar Keirdwyn Aurelius, then he is truly lost."

She could not meet his eyes again, but stared off into the night. "I will see if it is possible," she promised him. Even to her own ears, the words sounded weak and insufficient.

From their perches atop the mist-dampened Spears, the northern gods watched in silence.

—————

Dawn's light spread slowly over the castle, turret by turret, drawing out dew from the cracks and crevices of its ancient walls. It was a peaceful and silent dawn, with few witnesses. One guard passed quietly below, walking his rounds. A handful of birds rustled in their nests. A single figure atop the roof, dressed in tattered black silk, watched the sunrise.

Gwynofar's face was dry of tears now, but streaked with salt from a long night's weeping. In one hand she held a tiny note, curled tightly into a tube. In the other she held a plump homing pigeon, taken from the royal dovecote. Its wings were banded with white in the manner of northern pigeons, and she could feel in the rapid beating of its heart against her palm its hunger to be home again, to leave this hot and dreadful place for the cool, clear skies of the northern Protectorates.

Would I could go with you, she mourned.

There was a tiny leather tube harnessed to the bird's leg. She slid the note inside and made sure the closure was secure. It would not do for her message to fall out somewhere along the journey.

Then she cast the bird up into the dawn's sweet light, and watched as it headed north.

Rhys, the note said, *I need your counsel. G.*

He would know what it meant. He would come if he could.

She stayed on the roof for a time, watching until the bird was out of sight and the sun had finished rising, and then, with a sigh, returned below to greet the trials of a new day.

Chapter 30

*S*AFE. SHE *is safe at last. Thank the gods.*

All senses alert, Kamala tries to hear if her pursuer is still right behind her. But for once she seems to be truly alone. Every other time she has tried to rest, every time she has even slowed down to catch her breath, it was just behind her. And she can't allow it to catch her. She hasn't seen its face, she doesn't even know what it is, but she knows with a kind of raw animal instinct that she must not let it catch up to her or terrible things will happen.

Now—now it seems she has left it behind. For the moment.

Gasping for air, she bends forward, her legs trembling and weak from fatigue. She doesn't dare use sorcery to steady them. The thing that is hunting her can smell her magic every time she casts a spell; the only hope she has to lose it lies in simple morati-style flight.

Running.

The forest behind her rustles suddenly, as something parts the brush. It's here now! It's coming for her! Desperately she straightens up, gulps down one last lungful of air, and then starts to run again. It is a hopeless, faltering effort, on legs that are past the point of exhaustion. Even as she starts to run she knows it is too already late. She has let it get too close to her. She can feel it reaching out for her—

She whips about, expecting to see the bulk of some demonic predator bearing down on her, or something else equally fearsome. But there is nothing there. For a moment she thinks that maybe she was wrong, that she is still alone, and her heart begins to ease its wild pounding. But then the darkness surrounding her begins to transform itself, and she realizes it is not simply the shadows of night she is seeing, but something black and fearsome and utterly malignant that means to swallow her whole. She turns and tries to run again, but the ground beneath her feet is crumbling, falling away beneath her, and she can find no purchase. Quicksand. The earth melts into liquid and then begins to rotate—first slowly, as she sinks into it, and then with greater and greater speed—until a whirlpool has formed with her at its center. Vast and powerful, it is sucking the whole of the landscape into itself, devouring trees and birds and even the very stars. Downward, it is dragging her downward, into an unnamed and terrible darkness. Desperately she tries at last to summon her power, but it will not come. The whirlpool closes over her head. Beyond it, beneath it, is nothingness, utter nothingness. She screams—

———————

Awake.

Her heart was pounding. Her skin was covered in a film of sweat. But she was awake. The nightmare was gone.

For a long time she lay still in the darkness. The air was hot and humid, the worst sort of summer night. Finally she raised one hand and called forth a bit of power, weaving it with her fingers as one might weave a cat's cradle. The air cooled and a fresh breeze blew across her face, drying her skin.

The nightmares had started soon after she left Gansang, but only recently had they grown so unnerving. The first ones had simply reflected her fears while she was in the city, and she had accepted them as the inevitable price of what she had done. But now . . . now they were becoming something more. Now there was the distinct sense of another presence in her dreams, as if some Magister were trying to enter them, but failing.

She wished she knew more about dreamcasting. She wished she had stayed with Ethanus another year—another ten years—and learned all he knew about every kind of sorcery, before going off on her own.

This was the price one paid for impatience.

With a sigh she got out of bed and stretched her limbs. Her legs felt as though she had been running in truth and the muscles across her back

were a tightly knotted mass that hurt when she moved. She bound a bit
of power to ease them, remembering what little Ethanus had taught her
about the nature of dreams.

*Do not trust people or objects that you see. The sleeping mind often substitutes
one thing for another, or distorts the measure of a thing until it is barely recog-
nizable. Trust to your feelings, for those are genuine. Emotions are your sign-
posts to understanding.*

Valid advice, but not very helpful. Her dreaming self feared that something was chasing after her. Did that mean something really *was* pursuing
her, or was the dream simply reflecting her fear of the Magisters' wrath?
Was something truly so close behind her now that it was about to catch
her, or did she only fear it was so? Kamala's mother had believed that
dreams might accurately predict events to come, in which case this was
bad. Briefly she considered conjuring enough power to remember what
her mother had told her about premonitions, but decided against it. If the
woman had chanced upon a shred of genuine wisdom it was surely accidental. Besides which Kamala didn't want to see her again. Not even in a
sorcerous vision.

Emotions were what mattered, Ethanus had taught her. Emotions provided a guidepost to meaning, when all else was chaos. Focus on emotions.

*You fear that something will catch up to you, and that when it does, a whirlpool
will form beneath your feet, and it will suck you down into an abyss. You feel as
if doom is impending, and perhaps inescapable.*

Ah, hells.

Perhaps the power was warning her not to go to Bandoa. She had only
just made the decision to do so. Perhaps it was responding to that.

But if so, the power would not confirm it, and at last she was forced to
lie down again without answers, dreading the nightmares that would
surely come.

———

The Third Moon was a sizeable inn just outside the port city of Bandoa
with a reputation for catering to foreigners. It was especially popular with
merchants, who often scheduled a visit as they traveled up and down the
western coast. So the gossips told Kamala, anyway. It was said to be an odd
place, where odd stories were told and odd men encountered.

For Kamala it seemed the perfect hunting ground.

Since the night she left Gansang she had tormented herself over what path to follow next. Painfully, she had acknowledged a hard truth: that she had no long term plans, nor any goals greater than "learn to use magic without dying" and "go to the city where you suffered as a child and show them you can't be pushed around any more." Now she had gone through First Transition and had her adventure in Gansang and . . . what next? She might have sought out other Magisters had she not just killed one of their kind, but she had, and so probably it would be best to let the dust settle on that little story before she approached any of them again. So, where was she going now? What did she want? What did she hope to become?

She didn't know.

The contract she'd had with Ravi had been promising. Comforting. Let a morati take care of one's daily needs, so that one might focus upon larger issues. She thought that perhaps she would like to set up something like that again, but not with a landed lord this time. No, she needed to find a man of wealth who traveled, whose retinue would benefit from a witch's service, and see the world at his expense, without needing to conjure food each night or steal clothing from peasants. Maybe somewhere in that world she would find a place for herself. Until then, she would at least be comfortable.

Her search for such a patron had brought her to Bandoa . . . and to the Third Moon Inn.

At first glance the owner did not welcome her. She was still dressed like a peasant youth—though she had added a doublet and several accessories to the shirt she'd once stolen, and so no longer appeared wholly destitute—but she drew out a small purse from inside her shirt and spilled a handful of silver into the man's palm, assuming it would assuage his suspicions. It did not. Apparently he had an eye out for the kind of vultures that might prey upon his more prosperous guests, and a lone boy coming from nowhere, going nowhere, with a purse full of unexplained silver, fit the bill. In the end she had to bind a bit of sorcery to get him to admit her, and she made him send extra pillows and a flagon of wine up to her room, gratis, in compensation.

That night she slept on a real bed, beneath a roof that morati had built, and ate food and drank wine that had not been conjured, but rather farmed and fermented in the morati way, without a hint of sorcery. It was refreshing.

At night the merchants came.

Some of them were travelers, tired and dusty and brusque with their servants after a long day on the road. Some had come by sea, and were taking advantage of a night's berth in Bandoa to seek a bed that did not rock with every wave. There were at least a dozen true foreigners present when Kamala arrived, not counting the servants and retainers who gathered in shadowy corners to await their need, and the locals who had come to hear their tales. A charcoal-skinned man from Durbana, whose ears gleamed with golden hoops, as elegant and exotic as a jet statue. A fair-skinned Eynkar from the Protectorates, whose pale blond hair gleamed albino-white in the lamplight. A swarthy Anshasan wrapped in desert-style robes, with indigo tribal markings tattooed upon his face, who called for a round of some fermented mint drink for all those who would tell tales of foreign places, then settled back quietly to listen as the stories flowed.

Whatever these men asked for, Three Moons supplied. Never mind if it was a rare honey wine from the Free Lands, sour-spice cake from Calash, or bread baked in the style of some obscure town at the edge of nowhere; even a half-jesting call for the flesh of some rare beast from the Forest of Midnight resulted in half a dozen dried strips of flesh being supplied, that had been donated to the Inn by a traveler from the Dark Lands. It cost them a pretty penny to have such things served up, of course, but these were men who had money to spare, and they seemed to consider it a kind of competition to see who would spend the most for some foreign treat . . . all the while eyeing one another like wolves over a fresh kill, knowing that tonight's drinking mate was tomorrow's business rival. While the same proprietor who had given Kamala such a hard time beamed with sweaty pride as the tables of his inn were piled high with rare delicacies, knowing that no other establishment could rival his offerings.

Well, it explained the prices, anyway.

Not a woman was among the crowd save for an occasional servant, and of course the whores who came from Bandoa to court the favor of these wealthy men. Kamala sank into the shadows in her corner of the room and pretended not to notice the various expanses of flesh they bared in their attempts to seduce one merchant or another. The sight of them brought back memories that made her stomach churn, but she didn't blame them for it. A woman alone in the world had very few options open to her. Kamala would have had few options, and might be baring her breasts in rivalry with the rest of them right now, had not her special gift pointed the way to a different fate.

She wanted to do something for them. Change their fate—change the world that had shaped them—change the very nature of mankind, perhaps. But she couldn't. Not all the sorcery in the world could alter the forces that had made these women what they were.

There was food in front of her, but her appetite was gone. Every time one of the men ran a hand up the skirt of one of the women, or fumbled drunkenly at half-bared breasts, she flinched inside. The pain was hypnotic in its intensity, freezing her in place. Dark-skinned hands reached out of the past to stroke between her legs, leaving a slug's trail of scented oil in their wake—

"A tale of Sankara!" someone called.

There was laughter. Kamala shook her head and tried to shut out the images of past abusers that gathered around her like a wolf pack. Why had she come here? This was a mistake—

"Ah, the Free Lands!" A stout man with red hair almost as bright as Kamala's own rubbed his greasy hands together lustily. "A dozen prosperous cities within a day's ride, and all with rivalries enough to make any man's fortune."

"I hear the Summer Feast in Deshkala nearly caused the island itself to sink beneath the weight of the food."

"Or the weight of the guests," the Eynkar chuckled.

"Well of course, they must outdo the Spring Feast of Orula."

"And the Winter Feast of Lundosa."

The man with the ebony skin stood, a tankard in his hand. He swayed a bit as he did so; the whores on both sides reached out to steady him.

"An ode to Sankara," he said, bowing slightly. The whores applauded as he cleared his throat and began to sing, in a tenor of surprising clarity:

> *Oh tempt me not to pleasure, lass,*
> *For I have been where bliss resides*
> *And kissed, beneath an azure sky,*
> *That secret place where lust abides.*

And tempt me not to travel, lass,
For I have traveled far and wide
And found within a witch's grasp
The key to earthly paradise.

Oh, tempt me not to warm embrace
Within your arms, however blessed,
For I have known a Witch-Queen's grace
And cannot bed the second best.

So tempt me not to speak of love.
My heart's entranced by witchery
I will not love, save by her spell,
Nor dream of my soul's liberty.

The brief performance ended with a bow and received much laughter and applause. One of the whores tried to kiss him on the mouth as he fell into his seat, but his tankard got their first.

"Aye, that's Sankara," said the redhead. "I remember the Witch-Queen's midsummer feast. There were fireworks enough to fill the sky, and she made them dance as if to music."

"I'm surprised she did not dance among them," the Eynkar said.

The redhead chuckled. "She could have if she had wanted to."

"Aye, and died young for it."

"Die?" The redhead snorted. "Didn't you hear? She has the favor of the gods. They won't let her die." He winked. "She is lover to all of them."

"The women too?"

"Aye, goddesses most of all. They are frustrated creatures, you know."

"Too often ignored by their husbands for thunderbolts, or chariot races across the sky."

"Just so."

Quietly Kamala said, "Tell us more of this Witch-Queen."

A few of the merchants turned about to see where the new voice was coming from, but most were too busy drinking or fondling their whores to care. "What do you wish to know?" the Durbanan asked, without turning around. His accent was liquid, foreign, exotic.

Is she real? Kamala wanted to demand. *Is there truly reason to think she is not dying of her witchery, as others do, but has found some other way?* But she dared not ask those things. These men were well traveled and educated and knew much of the world; she was an ex-whore, a hermit's student, who knew nothing of current affairs in distant lands. If the depth of her ignorance became obvious, they might not accord her respect enough to answer her questions.

Or they might, if they sensed the intensity of her need, ask too many questions of their own.

She tired to keep her voice casual as she said, "How much of the story is legend, and how much truth? Do you know?"

Now the dark-skinned merchant looked back, scanning the room for the speaker, but Kamala had drawn the shadows around her so that she could not be found. "It is truth that her palace overlooks the port of Sankara. I know this, for I have been there myself. And that she holds parties to which not only the rich and the noble are invited, but anyone who amuses her, where all manner of foreign entertainments are offered. These things also I have seen. Whether she beds those men as well . . ." he shrugged. "Who can say when a monarch's flirtations are meaningful, and when they are merely . . . diplomacy?"

"And her power?" This time she made the words seem to come from somewhere else, and in a more familiar voice, so that she would not draw attention to herself. "Tell us of that."

"What of it? She is a witch, renowned for her skill. No drought has ever come to Sankara that she has not transformed to rain. No enemy has ever laid siege to her lands, but some great disaster laid them low before armies even met. Plagues travel around her city rather than through it, and likewise avoid the lands of her allies. Winds blow when the merchant ships in her port have need of them. Her fireworks are more magnificent than any I have seen a Magister produce . . . and I have seen many."

"Yet she does not die," Kamala's fake voice mused softly.

"Not yet. Kantele be praised."

"For how long?"

"Who knows?" He chuckled, and chucked a whore gently under the chin. "A woman does not tell her age."

"She's been in power forty years," the redhead offered. "No one seems to know where she was before that."

"Birthed full grown from a giant clam shell, no doubt." The Eynkar chuckled. "Isn't that the kind of thing the southern gods like to do?"

Forty years!

Kamala asked nothing more, but let the men go back to their own drunken chatter. Leaning back in the shadows, she exhaled sharply. Forty years! If one assumed this woman was not a child when she claimed her throne—could not have been younger than the age of majority, or legends would surely have immortalized that fact—that meant she had already lived a respectable lifetime, nearly as many years as morati were ever given. Yet if these reports were true, she used her power more freely than any Magister.

Is she perhaps a Magister herself? she wondered. *Or is there some other path for women that is possible, that this one has found?*

Somewhere deep inside her, a cold ache reminded her of the price she had paid to be become what she was. What would it be like to face eternity without the need to murder an endless succession of innocents? The thought brought with it sharp recall of the dream-child she had murdered, and a sudden wave of nausea that reminded her of the cost of human compassion.

You dare not regret what you are. Not even for a moment. Human sympathy is anathema to the power that keeps you alive.

Quietly she shut her eyes and tried to center herself anew. The murmuring voices of the merchants rose and fell in the distance, unheard, as she envisioned herself back in the forest with Ethanus. Remembering that first day when she had come to him, so determined to become his apprentice, so utterly intolerant of the suggestion that a woman would not, *could* not, be a Magister. She had sworn back then that she would let nothing stand in her way. Now there were hints that another woman had found an answer—perhaps a different answer than the one Ethanus had provided—and Kamala knew she could not rest until she learned the truth.

When her heartbeat was steady again and the feeling of nausea had safely subsided, Kamala got up silently and left the common room, binding enough power that no one saw the front door open as she passed through it, nor heard it as it fell shut behind her.

———————

The inn had been built upon the rise of a hill facing Bandoa. The stables where guests' mounts might be sheltered, the open fields where wagons and tents might be pitched for the night, as well as more the prosaic accommodations that all men require, were over the rise of the hill, out of sight of passing travelers. There were guards present, no doubt, but they could not be seen by any casual observer, and Kamala doubted they would make their presence known unless some thief or vagrant decided to test their readiness.

Standing at the top of the hill, Kamala gazed at the lights below. A caravan had parked its wagons on the lee side of the slope and torches still burned outside several of them, no doubt to hold thieves at bay. From one dark corner of the camp she could hear soft singing, too distant for her to make out if the singer were male or female. The merchants within the inn had partied their way to a far later hour than their servants had kept, apparently, and all but the guards and a few stragglers seemed to be soundly asleep.

She waited in silence a few moments, drinking in the quiet and the darkness. After a few minutes she saw a figure approaching. His black face was invisible in the darkness, but the gold hoops in his ears and the shimmer of his garments shone like fire in the moonlight.

He passed by where she stood, saw her, and stopped. The scent of ale and whore's perfume clung to his silken robes.

"You have a fine voice," Kamala said.

He cocked his head to one side. "You are the one who asked after Sankara."

"Your ear is good."

"Your accent is a strange mix. Western Delta, perhaps, overlaid by something more northern. Hard to mistake."

A faint smile twitched her lips. "Your ear is *very* good."

"My business rewards those who are observant."

"And you travel much."

He inclined his head. "That is also true."

"I was intrigued by your tales of Sankara. Do you go there often?"

He was silent for a moment. His black eyes studied her, seeking . . . what? She did not know enough of the standards being applied to use sorcery to convince him he had found it.

At last he said, "It is a place where I occasionally have business. Why do you ask?"

"Your tales intrigue me. I would like to see that city for myself."

"Truly?" Now it was he who smiled dryly. "Now, see, I would never have guessed that."

Gently she twisted the threads of his consciousness, cutting short those which were wary of strangers, strengthening those which responded well to novelty and challenge. It thrilled her down to her toes to feel her spells take hold of him, to sense his very soul being reshaped at her command. Ethanus had taught her the skill in a theoretical sense, but she had never had the opportunity to use it before. One did not practice such arts upon one's own master.

"I wish to see the world," she said. "You would be valuable to me as a guide."

If not for her sorcery he might have been displeased by her forwardness, but as it was his eyes narrowed thoughtfully, as if considering whether the youth he saw before him might actually serve some purpose. "You must have something of great value to offer," he said at last, "or you would not speak to me thus. Judging from your attire, I would guess it is not money."

"Again, you are insightful."

"What, then?"

She raised up her hand before him, and in her palm made small lights appear and dance. It was a child's trick, but it had the desired effect.

He looked at her sharply. "You are a witch?"

She nodded silently. And held her breath. There was no way now to guess what he was thinking now, which made it dangerous to try to influence him. Altering the threads of a man's consciousness when you did not know what they were to start with was bound to cause a terrible tangle. If your assumptions were wrong enough you could destroy a man's mind entirely.

She settled for binding a whisper of power to support her disguise. It would not do to have him guess her true gender. Merchants rarely took women into their retinue unless it was to see to their more private needs, and Kamala had no desire to play that role again.

Finally he said, "You are offering . . . what? I do not wish to mistake you."

"Fair winds if you sail. Safe roads if you ride."

His black eyes gleamed in the moonlight. "That is a lot of witchery to expend upon one journey."

"I expect to travel comfortably."

The night was silent, but for crickets. The singing in the distance had stopped.

"I travel by land," he said. "And, as it happens, I am headed to the Free Lands. Though not directly."

"I am in no rush," she said casually. A necessary lie; she did not wish anyone to start asking questions about why this journey was of such pressing interest to her. "I am sure I could amuse myself along the way . . . shopping, perhaps."

"No doubt." He reached up a hand to stroke his chin thoughtfully; his gold earrings shimmered in the moonlight. "And if there were a business deal along the way that was not going as well as it should. . . ."

"That is a more difficult art," she said, "and costly." The corner of her mouth twitched slightly. "The shopping would have to be *very* good."

"Of course."

"So we have a deal?"

He shook his head and made a *tsk-tsk* noise, smiling ever so slightly. "A wise man never signs a contract after a night of drinking. Lesson number one if you mean to be part of my business. Now, I am going to do something I should have done a long time ago, and seek my bed. In three days' time I will be done with my business in Bandoa and prepared to move on. If you come to the Third Moon on that night and ask for Netando, then we can discuss our terms. Is that acceptable?"

She nodded.

"And here." He reached into his robe and pulled out a small purse; red silk embroidered with gold. He threw it to her. "Buy yourself some decent clothing. A man is judged by the company he keeps, yes?"

"My name is Kovan," she told him.

He chuckled. "And I am sure I shall forget that by morning. Do remind me, will you?"

Without a further word he turned toward the inn once more. Even that place was quieter, now. Even the whores had fallen silent.

Three days.

Did she dare remain in one place for that long? What if some unnamed power really was pursuing her? Could this be what her dreams had been trying to warn her about, the danger of slowing down to rest, of giving it time to catch up with her?

Downward, the whirlpool is dragging her downward, into an unnamed and terrible darkness . . . the whirlpool closes over her head . . . beyond it, beneath it, is nothingness, utter nothingness—

Three days.

"Her fireworks are more magnificent than any I have seen a Magister produce," Netando had said, and another had added: *"She does not die."*

The purse was full of silver. She stared at it for a long while, weighing her options. Then she, too, returned to the inn, and used some of it to arrange for a room for the next two nights. The rest she would spend on a proper young man's clothing.

If indeed she would have to do battle with an unnamed darkness, she might as well be well dressed for the occasion.

Chapter 31

THE FEAST hall in the Witch-Queen's palace was full, and spirits were high. At the center of the U-shaped arrangement of couches and low tables Siderea reclined, her dark eyes glittering as she directed the gathering with subtle gestures: a finger lifted to order that flagons of mint wine be refilled over *here,* a delicate twist of the wrist to indicate that a tray of sweets should be delivered over *there.* When she laughed it was with a sound like wind chimes tinkling in the breeze, and the men surrounding her leaned close as they whispered choice secrets in her ear, hoping to win that laughter as a sign of her favor.

Into this gathering a servant came, unlike the others who were so festively attired in colorful silks and golden ornaments. This one was in plain woolen attire, and looked as if he had just been toiling in the gardens, or some other dirty place. The guests were inebriated enough that they did not notice his arrival—or did not care to acknowledge it if they did—but Siderea always kept close watch upon the business of her palace, even when her guests were not aware of it. A moment or two after the servant entered she glanced up at him, took his measure quickly, and then whispered apologies in the ears of the two men closest to her, and in a flurry of scarlet veils and tinkling jewelry, withdrew herself from their company.

"Send in the dancing girls," she whispered to another servant as she passed, and he scurried off to obey.

The one who was waiting by the door shifted his weight nervously as she approached. This close to him she could see that his brown woolen doublet was spattered with something dark. "Not here," she said quickly, and nodded for him to back out the way he had come. She followed him into the outer hallway, and from there indicated a side chamber where they might speak in private.

"Forgive me for interrupting you—" he said breathlessly, as soon as the door was shut.

"I assume you would not do so if you did not have good reason."

He nodded. "I am sorry to say so, Majesty. I have heard word . . . there is someone here . . ." He seemed uncertain how to begin, and twisted his woolen hat in his hands as he struggled for words.

"Just say it," she said quietly. "The manner of delivery does not concern me."

"We have a visitor from Corialanus," he said. "From the Western Reaches. He says . . . he says the whole of some city has been destroyed . . . everyone killed . . . there was some sort of great monster there. . . . You must hear the details from him, Lady, they are too terrible to repeat."

An ice-cold serpent stirred in the Witch-Queen's heart. *That will be Danton's doing.*

"Take me," she commanded.

She stopped briefly in the hall outside the feast chamber to give orders for more entertainment, and to make sure the guests' flagons would be refilled with mint wine each time they emptied them; they would be less likely to notice her absence that way. She also called for a servant to run to her chambers and fetch her a somber kaftan that she might wear over her festive attire. If there had truly been a slaughter in Corialanus, it was not appropriate to hear the news in the silks and jewels of a celebratory costume. She pulled off her earrings as well and shed her necklace, dropping them into the hands of other servants as she walked; by the time they reached the chamber where the messenger was waiting, the only adornment remaining upon her was a slender anklet with tiny coins hanging from it, that jingled softly as she walked, and an opulent comb she could not easily dislodge.

Servants threw the doors open before her, revealing a room with yet more of her people inside. On the bed lay the man they were attending to, himself a figure covered in dirt and dried blood and even less pleasant substances. The smell coming forth from him was akin to the reek of an outhouse, and she was pleased to see that her people had already drawn a bath for him, though they would not move him into it until she gave the order.

She came to the side of the bed and looked down upon him; he did not seem to notice her. His skin was scored with many scratchmarks and also with one deep gouge, which her physician was trying to clean and dress, even as the man turned from side to side, moaning in the grip of some nightmare. Every now and then he would try to bat the physician away and another servant would come and pin him down, until he just lay there sobbing, exhausted, trapped in some remembrance that left him only half-aware of where he was, unaware of who was surrounding him.

She watched him for a moment, wishing she had one of her Magisters present to assist her. If Danton had made some move on Corialanus, that was the kind of news any one of them would wish to hear. But the price of relying upon the power of others was that sometimes they were just not around when you needed them.

A bowl of water had been set by the bed. With a silent gesture she ordered one of the servants to wet a cloth in it, wring it out, and give it to her. She sat down by the side of the visitor then, shushed the physician for a moment, and applied the cool cloth to the man's burning head with all the delicacy of a butterfly's wing.

The soothing motion seemed to break through some barrier in his mind; he grew still beneath her ministrations, slowly, and then looked up at her with eyes that seemed to contain a spark of awareness. They were encrusted from dried tears and perhaps worse, red-rimmed and bloodshot, and swollen from his repeated attempts to rub them clean.

"Dead," he whispered. "They are all dead. Take care, Lady! It will come to this place too."

Then a fit of coughing wracked his body, so powerfully that he shook from head to toe for struggling to contain it. When it was over Siderea gently wiped the phlegm from his lips, noting the fine threads of blood that seeped from his cracked, dry lips. The brief moment of lucidity had passed, however, and his eyes slowly ceased to focus on her and focused instead on some distant, unknown vista. She spoke to him softly, trying to rouse his interest, but he only stared into the distance, seemingly unaware that anyone had spoken to him.

Finally she stood, and gave the compress over to the hands of a servant. "How did he come here?" she asked.

"He was found on the Great Road, just north of the city. The rider who brought him in said he was raving about monsters, or something like that. Evidently he had walked from Corialanus . . . or so he claims."

Very likely, she thought. His leather boots were worn through at the sole in several places, scored and pitted from gravel and thorns and stained with mud. Corialanus was not close by, and until one reached the Great Road, the way was not easy. He must have been traveling on foot for at least a week. No wonder his condition was so wretched.

She thought with a sudden chill: *Hadrian is in the Western Reaches.*

She needed counsel, badly. And the kind of counsel she needed was not currently available within her domain. Silently she cursed her reliance upon foreign powers, but that of course had been her choice; the price of independent power was simply not acceptable.

"Can you bring him around?" she asked the physician. "Will he be able to speak?"

He hesitated. "In time, Majesty. But he is on the edge of physical collapse, as you see. You may get a clearer report from him if you allow him a few hours of sleep first."

"So be it, then." She nodded to two of the servants who were clustered around the bed. "See him cleaned up, so that any wounds may be found." To another she directed, "Bring him food and water; the doctor will tell you what is best." To the physician she said, "Treat the wounds that require immediate treatment, and if you find nothing more urgent on him, let him sleep. I will hear his tale when his mind is restored to him."

"As you command, Majesty."

It was hard to sound calm when she was anything but that. But she could not allow her attendants to see just how badly she wanted the news this man carried, for then they would wonder why she, a renowned witch, did not simply use her power to take his knowledge from him. Or else heal him with her power, so that he might speak sooner.

Oh, there were a thousand things she wanted to know, was desperate to know, but the men who might gather that information for her were not present, and so that meant a holding game, a mask of calm applied over fevered concern, and patience feigned with royal perfection. Certainly it was a game she was accustomed to. The Witch-Queen of Sankara was nothing if not a consummate actress.

"Call me if there is any change," she commanded. "In the meantime I must see to my guests. They must catch no hint of this disturbance."

They are all dead. Take care, Lady! It will come to this place too.

She shuddered inwardly as she left the chamber.

———

Power. Coiled within her; untapped, unfocused. She could feel it inside like she could feel her own heartbeat, the pounding of blood in her veins, the passage of air in her lungs.

Not for the first time, she hungered to set the power free. She hungered to know sorcery as the Magisters knew it, that glorious moment when will became magic, when a single thought might set the very heavens to trembling. Sometimes at night, when she lay very still, she thought she could sense the soulfire yearning within her, as if it, too, hungered for freedom.

But the price of that kind of power was death, and she had decided long ago she was not willing to pay it.

Her guests were leaving now. She could hear the palace growing quiet, and it was as if the walls themselves were breathing a sigh of relief. The final hour had been interminable. One could not bring guests into the house only to order them suddenly from it, or rumors of all sorts would follow. One must court them into leaving—seduce them into exit—so that each man thought he had chosen the single most perfect moment to take his leave. Anything else was politically unthinkable.

It was a game she excelled at, but it was a tiring one, and she was glad it was finally over.

Now, secure in her private chamber, within that secret closet which no servant was ever allowed to enter, she bound enough power to open the lock of the chest that had no key. It only required a whisper of power; hardly a second's worth of life, surely. It was her one concession to witchhood, to guard her secrets thus . . . or perhaps, her one concession to the Magisters. For if ever their secrets were lost to another merely because she valued her own life more than theirs, they would be quick to let her know the cost of her error. She had no illusion about that. Even as they lay beside her on silken coverlets, even as they breathed their sweet lovers' lies into her ear, she never forgot the difference between them, and she was sure they did not, either.

Inside the small chest were her most precious tokens, things entrusted to her by the kind of men who generally trusted no one . . . or else in some cases, things they had left behind unknowing. A fallen eyelash, abandoned on a pillow. The scent of sweat on a linen towel. They were each packaged neatly, wrapped in silk—for it was said that silk could insulate such things against spiritual pollution—and stored without names on them, so that only she would know which token belonged to which Magister.

In a small silk bag at one side of the chest were the tokens they had given her knowingly. Not permanent items, these things, that could be turned against their makers, but a mere kiss of each Magister's personal essence upon fine paper, folded like a lover's note. As with all her other tokens, there were no names upon them. She kept these in the order that she had first met their owners, which no other witch could guess at. Thus did she safeguard an arsenal which was, in raw potential, more dangerous than any mundane armory.

Slowly, thoughtfully, she rifled through the notes, at last selecting three that were connected to the more sociable of her lovers. It was a compromise between contacting only one, who might not be able to respond in a timely manner, and calling them all, which was guaranteed to make for a uniquely hostile meeting, and would only be an option in the direst of emergencies. She chose three Magisters that were unlikely to take offense if others were also summoned; not an easy task at the best of times. Some of the black-robed sorcerers could not share space with their own kind for more than an hour without getting caught up in a magical pissing match, and while that had only happened a few times in Sankara, the clean-up afterward had been expensive enough that she did not relish the thought of a repeat performance.

Not to mention they were all her lovers, and a woman should never bring more than two of those into a room without first hiding all the breakables.

Carefully locking the chest and then securing the room it was hidden in, she ordered a servant to bring her a small brazier and flint. Her staff was accustomed to such requests and she soon had what she needed.

Then she drew in a deep breath and tried to still her soul so that the athra would flow freely from it, as her witch father had taught her to do so long ago. She rarely used her own power these days—rarely needed to—but sometimes it could not be avoided. The tokens the Magisters had left with her would help provide focus for her efforts, but if she wanted to use that focus to contact them, her own soul must provide the power.

It will only cost me a minute's worth of life, she told herself. *Surely it is worth the sacrifice, to call someone here who can do greater things.*

When her spirit was still and she felt ready to shape the athra to her will, she struck a flame and set fire to the tokens. The smoke was fragrant and clean, and she shut her eyes as she breathed it in, taking the Magister's spiritual signatures into herself, weaving a message to bind to them, sending it forth along that channel. The task was strangely difficult, almost as if her life force did not wish to be bound, and when the message finally went out it felt weaker than it should be. Was she too tired—or perhaps too stressed—to cast a simple communication spell properly? If so, it was the first time such a thing had ever happened to her. She was a natural in witching terms, had been so since her childhood, and the single greatest struggle of her life had been how to learn *not* to use the power. This was an odd sensation, almost as if her soul did not want to release the athra she required. Curious . . . and troubling.

Come look through my eyes, she whispered into the smoke, to the distant Magisters receiving her message. *See what is here.*

What manner of message the Magisters perceived would depend upon their mental state when it arrived, of course. Those who were awake would probably be aware that visions were being sent to them, and from whom they came. Those who were asleep, however, might simply incorporate her offerings into their natural dreamscape, and not realize that this handful of images had any special significance. Yet another reason why calling to the Magisters did not always produce results.

Shutting her eyes, she envisioned the traveler as she had seen him, bloodstained and filthy. Then she replayed in her mind his chilling explanation she had been given, and his own dismal prophecy. *The whole of his land has been destroyed . . . everyone killed . . . there was some sort of great mon-ster there . . . it will come here too . . .*

He is delirious, she thought into the smoke. *I cannot tame his mind or know his secrets without assistance.*

At last it was done. She bowed her head before the brazier for a moment, wondering why she felt so weak. On those rare occasions when she used her own witchery it generally invigorated her, causing her body and soul to feel abuzz with vital energies. This sensation was exactly the opposite. It was as if accessing her power had opened some wound that was bleeding out her energy into the night, weakening her more with every moment that passed.

The message has been sent. That is all that matters. If there is something wrong with me, those who can help with it will be here soon enough.

She settled down upon her couch and tried to shut her eyes and sleep for a while, aware that once her Magisters arrived there might be little time to rest.

———

Three of them came, though not the three she had invited. Colivar was first, stepping through the intervening miles between *here* and *there* without warning or fanfare. To her surprise he brought Sulah with him, a pleasant-looking young man with the fair skin and blond hair of the northern races, who had visited her once before. "He has an interest in this matter," Colivar said mysteriously, and would not explain further. That was fine. This Magister shared things with her in his own time, which was sometimes frustrating, but she was certain he would not leave her ignorant in any matter that impacted the safety of her realm.

Fadir arrived shortly after, clothed in his usual husky, red-haired body; charms and talismans hung from the coarse braids of his long hair like barbarian trophies. She watched with some interest as he and Colivar took each other's measure like wary dogs; evidently neither man had assumed other Magisters would be present. It was a small thing but it pleased her, as did any happenstance which managed to surprise her sorcerous lovers. She knew enough of their natures to understand that *novelty* was the most precious commodity in their universe, and it pleased her to know she had provided it.

Briefly she outlined the situation for her guests. Colivar's expression was dark as he listened; Fadir's was simply wary. Sulah seemed as curious and receptive as a young morati, so much so that she wondered if he had only recently gained his immortality. Then again, that might be an aspect he feigned to set rivals off their guard. If her years with the Magisters had taught her nothing else, it was that there was no perceivable limit to the games these men might play with one another. A young-seeming Magister was as likely to be one thousand years old in truth as he was likely to be twenty.

Colivar nodded when she was done speaking; his expression was grim. "Take us to him." Sulah started to whisper something to him but Colivar shushed him; with a pang of jealousy in her heart, Siderea realized they had not truly fallen silent, merely moved the conversation to realms of unvoiced thought that she could not share. She did not protest their privacy, but led the three of them in silence to the chamber where her guest lay. By the time they arrived there, Sulah's expression was as grim as Colivar's.

The man was asleep, but he did not look peaceful. He stirred fitfully as if in the grip of some nightmare, and moaned softly as they approached, as a wounded animal might.

"I have given him something for the fever," the physician said. "His outer wounds are cleansed and dressed but I can only guess at the wounds inside him. He needs your skill, Majesty."

A Magister's voice inside Siderea's head told her, *The sickness is in his mind, not his flesh.*

She spoke the same words aloud, as though she had determined the fact herself. The physician nodded, trusting to her power, and backed away to give the newcomers room to come close. They did so, Fadir coming to the foot of the bed, Colivar and Sulah to one side of it, and Siderea sitting down on the edge of the mattress on the other side. The servants had peeled the man's foul clothing off him and managed to get him clean enough that the bruises and cuts which covered his upper body were plainly revealed. Blankets covered the rest of him, but she was willing to bet that the view down there was much the same.

She waited a moment for the Magisters to study him with their invisible sorceries, then gently put a hand upon the man's cheek. He jerked upright in his sleep and began to pull away from her hand—and then something seemed to take hold of him, freezing him in place. His brow furrowed as if in pain, and then, after a moment, slowly relaxed . . . and his body relaxed as well, falling back onto the bed with a creak of weary bones as his eyes slowly opened.

There was no pain in his gaze now, nor fear, nor was there anything that might rightly be called human consciousness. Whoever had taken control of him had clearly brought him to a state where he might answer their questions without being driven to madness by the memories those questions might arouse.

"Who are you?" she asked it softly, in the tone one might use to calm a wounded animal. It was probably unnecessary, given what the Magisters had done to him, but it would encourage those of her people who were present to believe that she was the one who had brought him to this calm, if not by witchery then by the simple power of her presence.

"Halman Antuas." His voice was equally quiet, but without human inflection of any sort.

"Where do you come from?"

His brow furrowed; he seemed to struggle with the question.

"Permit me, Majesty." It was Fadir.

"Of course." She nodded graciously for him to proceed.

"Where did you travel from last, to come here?" Fadir asked.

This time there was no hesitation. "The western reaches. Corialanus."

She had to ask it. "Lord Hadrian's land?"

"Aye."

She shut her eyes for a moment and shuddered inwardly, wondering if the slaughter he had hinted at had included one of her favorites.

"Why were you there?" Colivar asked.

"We were bringing supplies to the men stationed at King's Pass." As he spoke the name of the place he flinched; Siderea could almost see the Magister's sorcery struggling to maintain control of the man as memories began to return to him. "I had two dozen with me, strong guards, good fighters. All gone now . . ."

She said quietly to the Magisters, "King's Pass is a lesser road leading from Danton's territory southward. It is narrow and treacherous, not an ideal route for armies, but still a potential road for conquerors, if they wished to avoid the more heavily fortified regions. The Lords of the Western Reaches take turns outfitting a guard post at the neck of the pass to have warning if such a move were launched."

"So," the man whispered feverishly. "Just so. All gone now. The Dark Ones have returned—we are all doomed—"

"Tell us what you saw," Fadir commanded. "Start to finish, as it was that day."

Sweat was breaking out on the man's brow, but as Siderea reached forth to pat it dry with a cloth she found it was a cold sweat. If the fear was a fever inside him, Fadir's power was not allowing it to surface.

"I came with a team on horseback, carrying supplies into the mountains." His voice was hoarse, strained and halting, as if each word had to be forced out individually. "The guard who was supposed to meet us on the way, to guide us the last mile, did not. It made our captain wary. He sent out a scout into the woods ahead, to see if there was trouble."

His voice dropped to a whisper. "The scout returned . . . in body . . . but his spirit was gone. His eyes were filled with a terrible madness. Even I could not break through it."

"You are a witch?" Siderea asked.

He nodded. His skin had drained to a ghastly color, like that of dead flesh, and his head began to jerk from side to side as unwelcome memories came pouring back into him. "Couldn't help—didn't have enough power—it would have eaten me alive—" He shut his eyes; a violent shudder ran through his body. *"Where were the gods?"* he choked out. *"Why did they let this happen?"*

She had no answer for him, but bit her lip as Fadir's sorcery took hold of the man once more. This time, however, even sorcery was not enough to quiet him; in the end the Magister reached out, touched a finger to his forehead, and commanded, "Sleep." The man's body sagged immediately, as it did earlier, all the strength seemingly drained out of it; his head rolled limply to one side, the lids half open but the eyes unseeing.

"Clearly he has told us all that he can," Colivar said quietly. "So we shall view the past as he saw it."

He walked to the head of the bed and passed his hand over the man's face. A tremor ran through the witch's body, but he did not awaken. Then, slowly, mist began to coalesce over the man's face, colors drew together, and a vision began to take shape over him.

Dark it was, very dark. The sun was shining but the man's fear obscured it like black stormclouds; only in the center of the vision did light shine clearly. The substance of the conjuring was a fine-colored mist that shivered in eddies and currents as it responded to the man's memories, and details were unclear about the edges, but in the center of the field the mist soon resolved into a company of men on horseback leading several narrow wagons, with a pair of men arguing at the head of it. Near them on the ground sat another figure, uniformed, with the aspect of an idiot; a thin line of drool trickled down his chin as he stared off, trembling, into vistas no one else could share.

And then one of the men left the company—Antuas himself—and began to hike into the woods. He made an odd gesture about himself as he did so, such as witches sometimes used to bind power, and Siderea guessed that he was making sure that any sentries would be looking in another direction when he passed by.

What was it like to use the power so freely, she wondered. To feel the power surging through one's soul from within in such deliberate quantity, instead of being portioned out in dribs and drabs for fear of an untimely death?

As the witch Antuas walked through the woods and then passed through them and beyond, they faded, became shadow. A settlement took shape before him. Empty. It likewise was left behind as he continued to walk. Houses came into view. Empty. Weapons were missing from their racks. Doors were left open. Dark stains were splashed upon a threshold, across the earth, trampled into the mud. The images passed in and out of focus like a dream, each fading into mist in turn as the viewer turned his attention to the next detail. That the witch in the vision was terrified was painfully clear. He was clearly no soldier himself, Siderea thought, merely a villager who had been paid to join the company of soldiers "in case of emergency." Now the emergency had come, and it was clearly more than he could handle.

Then the trees gave way to open ground, and he saw what was waiting there for him.

He fell to his knees.

Siderea gasped.

All about him, as far as the eye could see, were bodies. Each was hoisted up upon the point of a towering stake, which had been set vertically into the ground. The bodies had clearly been there a while, and scavengers had plucked much of the flesh from the bones, but from their position it was clear that they had been impaled while alive, and thus condemned to a slow and terrible death.

There were dozens of them. Maybe even hundreds. Seen through the lens of the visitor's memory the number was uncertain, as if the sheer horror of the scene made clear focus impossible. Already details of the scene were bleeding out around the edges of the vision; even Colivar's sorcery could not keep such terrible images from being swallowed up by the man's madness.

The witch in the vision fell to his knees and vomited.

"Is this Danton's doing?" Siderea whispered. It was all she could think of. No other ruler seemed capable of such atrocities.

And then, as they watched, a dark shape began to arise from behind the forest of spears. Something with wings that had been hidden behind a rocky outcrop, that was now taking to the air.

The vision wavered. The witch moaned. His lips were a cold blue now, and where his eyes showed there were only whites.

It was a great beast, winged but not like a bird in its form, nor like a bat, nor any other flying creature she might name. Its vast wingspan stretched across the field of spears and cast the rows of rotting bodies into shadow as it rose. Fear-shrouded sunlight played through its wings as if through painted glass, glittering along veins and tendons as it might through the wings of a locust.

It was terrible. It was fearsome beyond words. And yet . . . it was beautiful. Siderea could sense its beauty even through the mists of Colivar's vision, could feel the power of that beauty wrapping itself around her soul as she stared at the creature, transfixing her as a hare must be transfixed in that terrible moment just before a hawk strikes. An ecstasy of helplessness. How much more powerful must it have seemed in that place and time, in the creature's actual presence? It was clear now why this man could not endure the memory of it, nor even narrate details of his story without being overwhelmed by what he had seen.

"Make it clearer," Colivar commanded. His tone was strange, unlike anything she had ever heard from him before. "Look upon it more closely, we need the details. . . ."

Higher and higher the great beast rose, its wings beating the air with a force that made the bodies tremble upon their stakes. Though there was no smell coming forth from the vision, Siderea sensed the moment at which the witch's bladder gave way in sheer terror. The creature turned its great head in his direction then, as if that had drawn its notice. She saw the man bind his power again, as much of it as he dared, and he used it to disguise his aspect, so that when the creature looked his way he would appear to be no more than another body upon a stake. The subterfuge was visible in the vision as a misty overlay, beneath which his true shape was apparent, but apparently the real spell had been effective. The creature looked over the field of bodies once, twice, three times . . . and then vaulted higher into the heavens, moving quickly toward the south.

The vision began to fragment, then, and all of Colivar's power could not make it do otherwise. Images flashed through the sorcerous mists like scenes glimpsed during a lightning storm at night: suddenly illuminated, quickly gone. The witch running through the woods. A camp littered with dead bodies. The witch tripping over the nearest one and landing face-down in the dirt. Screaming. Shadows of wings overhead. Crouching down among the corpses, binding power to appear as one of them. The rising of a reddened, swollen sun. Staggering through the woods toward the only hope of safety. . . .

Faster and faster new images came, the visitor's body beneath them now shuddering as if each one was a blow to his flesh. They were losing all coherency now, scenes from memory fading into nightmare, and from nightmare into simple madness, in less than a heartbeat. From the man's ghostly pale lips came a strangled cry, as the air above the bed suddenly became filled with winged creatures, eyes burning like crimson stars. "They're coming!" he gasped. "They will come here!" Then his body convulsed, chest thrust outward, blank eyes bulging—and with a terrible final cry it collapsed suddenly, arms and legs askew like the limbs of a broken doll.

The vision faded. The sorcerous mists dispersed. From someplace near the door, the physician whispered a prayer to his gods.

Then there was only silence.

Finally the young one, Sulah, dared, "Was that . . . ?"

Colivar nodded grimly. All the color was gone from his face, and in his eyes a terrible black fire burned. It made Siderea tremble just to look at him.

"Souleaters," he whispered.

"I thought they were all killed," Siderea offered. "Long ago."

"Driven away. Not killed." He looked up at her. She could not bear what was in his eyes, and quickly looked away. "An important distinction, my queen."

Then he looked to the other two Magisters. "We must go to this place. There are questions that need answers, and we will only find them there."

"Do you know where it is?" Fadir indicated the body on the bed, now patently lifeless. "He can hardly lead us now. Or even anchor enough sorcery to show us the way."

Colivar considered for a moment, then asked Siderea, "Do you have the clothes he wore when he arrived?"

She nodded.

"Have them brought."

She gestured for a serving girl to do so. The three of them waited in silence as the frightened girl scurried off to obey. After a moment she returned with a pile of clothing wrapped in linen that reeked even through its bindings. Atop it sat the few simple items the man had possessed: a knife, a small purse, a worn belt, a leather cap. Colivar picked up the last. There was a band around the edge adorned with small brass studs; he ran his fingernail under the frontmost part of the design, where it would have sat upon the man's forehead. Then he held his finger up to the light, showing them the grains of dirt he had dislodged.

"The earth he picked up when he fell will guide us to the place," he said.

"What will you do there?" Siderea asked.

The black eyes fixed on her. It was a terrible, hollow gaze. She shivered inwardly but did not look away.

"You have called other Magisters?" he asked.

She nodded.

"If they come, tell them to follow us." He lowered his hand down over the sheets and rubbed off a bit of the dirt, so that it fell upon the coverlet. "I leave them this to facilitate the journey."

"Colivar—"

He reached over the bed, across the twisted body, and caught up her hand. "Do not ask to accompany us. Please, my queen. I would be loathe to deny you anything, but even more loathe to bring you into the middle of what we may find there."

She shut her eyes for a moment. Sighed. Then, slowly, nodded. "You will tell me what you learn?" she breathed. "Everything?"

He kissed her hand. "Of course, my queen."

Then he released her and stepped back from the bed. Sulah and Fadir came to his side.

Colivar looked over at the servants. The physician was huddled white-faced against the door frame. The girl who had brought the clothing cowered in a far corner. "You will forget what you have seen here," the Magister said quietly. Siderea saw them stiffen slightly as the power in his words took hold of them. "No news of this man's journey nor his message shall pass your lips until your mistress commands it be so. His death was a natural thing, the consequence of simple exhaustion. Any stories he told before dying must have been from the madness of that state. You understand?"

The girl whispered, "Yes, my lord." The physician simply nodded.

Colivar shut his eyes for a moment, gathering his power. Then he whispered words of binding . . . and slowly the air surrounding the three Magisters began to shimmer, like waves of summer heat over desert sands. Their features grew hazy to Siderea's vision, then insubstantial, then faded out into the air like the substance of ghosts. Until nothing was left in the room but the Witch-Queen and her servants, the slowly cooling body upon the bed, and the lingering scent of fear. And silence.

Chapter 32

IT WAS strange, Andovan thought, that his moments of greatest strength were fueled by his moments of direst frustration. But so it was.

Gods knew, there was enough frustration to last him a while. His dreams no longer guided him clearly, which meant that every step he took might be taking him farther from his quarry, rather than toward her. He had no way to know. Some nights he had no dreams at all, and it was as if Colivar's spells had lost all their power, leaving him stranded in the middle of nowhere without guidance, without focus, without oversight. If that was the case, then he was exactly what strangers on the road perceived him to be, a wanderer without destination or purpose. A pitiful thing for a royal prince to become, for sure.

The only thing he knew for certain now was that if his quarry had left Gansang just ahead of him the night the dream-towers fell, then every day in which he failed to find her increased the likelihood she would pass beyond his reach forever, and that made him rage inside against the gods, the stars, or whatever forces of Fate seemed nearest. There were rare moments when something suffused his veins that was almost his accustomed strength, and the weakness that was the Wasting seemed to loosen its stranglehold upon his spirit. But only for a brief while. Sooner or later it returned again, a suffocating shroud of enfeeblement that sapped his hope even as it sapped his physical strength. It was all he could do to keep moving each night, and to pray that Colivar's spells were still active, even though he no longer sensed them. If his dreams would no longer guide his steps, perhaps instinct would.

The dreams themselves had become chaotic, with strange images that seemed to have no rhyme or reason. Burning gems. Bales of wool. A beheaded infant. The images were like pieces of a puzzle—or ten different puzzles—and he could not manage to assemble them into a meaningful whole. Did that mean Colivar's power was failing him, or was he simply going mad? Or maybe the machinations of the foreign Magister had intended that all along, to separate him from his father's house and then play with his mind—

Don't think like that, he told himself. *You* will *go mad for certain if you do.*

Because she was almost certainly traveling, he traveled as well. Nameless villages provided him with fresh supplies and sometimes a bit of excitement as one local or another chose to challenge him . . . and then they passed into the mists behind him as though they had never existed. Dream stuff. All of his life felt like a dream now. It was a disconcerting sensation, and he feared more than anything it heralded some new and weaker stage in the progression of his illness. And so he forced himself to pay the price of a night's room and board at various inns along the way, and listened from the shadows to the tales of other travelers, always hoping to hear some bit of news or gossip that would give him focus again. But there was none. He listened to tales with an empty heart well into the night, and left in the morning with no more sense of direction than he'd had when he arrived.

I will not die in bed! he raged at the gods. But they were cold and silent. And the more he traveled, the less and less certain he was that he was heading toward anything other than an empty, meaningless death.

———

Kamala's dreams had been bad enough that she hadn't gotten more than an hour's sleep the night before. Each time she put her head down on the pillow it seemed she was transported into the depths of the abyss again, and those few times when utter exhaustion took hold and she would actually slumber for a few moments, she awakened soon after with a film of cold sweat upon her skin, her heart pounding as if it might burst from her chest.

Whatever it was that was after her, it was coming closer. Or at least she feared that it was, so much so that her mind was becoming unhinged. Which possibility was more terrifying?

Two days had passed since she had spoken to Netando. One more and she would be on the road again, able to lose herself among his retinue of servants and guards. But could she bring herself to wait that long? The nightmares were running her ragged. They might stop if she left this place, if she put enough miles between herself and . . . what? What refuge was safe enough? She didn't even know what it was that was coming after her, much less how to avoid it.

One thing was certain, and that was that hiding in her room only made things worse. In the great room at least she could distract herself, and perhaps learn a bit about the world she was now set loose in. Kamala the whore had known nothing about the lands outside her own city, and Ethanus the hermit had been more interested in teaching her the ins and outs of sorcery than the rise and fall of morati governments. Now, in this place, for the first time, the whole world was being laid out before her, but in bits and pieces that she must fit together like fragments of a vast, confusing puzzle. Nations and wars and monarchs and treaties and political triumphs and social travesties were paraded before her in dizzying array, and she struggled to assemble some kind of mental map to give them all context. She could never ask for a real map, of course, or any kind of help in understanding the shards of knowledge that were being thrown about so freely. If her youth in Gansang had taught her one thing, it was that a show of ignorance attracted trouble like rotting meat attracted flies. In this company, so conspicuously worldly, any request for help would surely draw attention to her. And attention was what she must avoid at all costs, if someone or something were truly hunting her.

Now and then she caught a glimpse of some other customer keeping quiet in the shadows of the room, as she was, and she wondered if they were equally lost, equally struggling. The men who filled the center stage did not seem to notice their audience. Or perhaps they simply did not care. Boisterous as they were, self-absorbed and progressively drunk as the night wore on, they probably imagined they were being admired by all who saw them.

When at last it seemed to Kamala that her head had absorbed as many random facts about the world that night as it might contain without bursting, and that sheer lack of sleep would soon overcome her no matter where she was, she rose from her chair and began to move toward the stairs that led to her room. The darkness waiting for her there was uninviting, to be sure, but it was preferable to falling asleep in this public place and suffering her nightmares here. Or worse.

But as she moved through the main area of the room, trying to be as inconspicuous as possible, a young girl entered who froze her in her tracks.

Maybe it was the girl's age. Maybe it was the look in her eyes, half fear and half determination. Maybe it was the awkward way in which she approached the crowd of drunken men, as if she knew in words what she wanted from them, but had not yet convinced her body to support the mission. Ten years old, perhaps twelve at the most, but Kamala could feel the tension rising from her flesh like heat from an oven.

It was like looking in a mirror. No, more accurately: it was like looking through a distorting lens, not at the present but at the past.

The girl was clean in the way that peasants were clean when they expected to be in good company: hair washed, face scrubbed, hands pink and raw, but with telltale lines of ingrained dirt any place that water did not easily reach. Had Kamala looked like that once? A lump caught in her throat as she saw the girl's fingernails, each with a thin line of dirt tucked down tight against the flesh, where a casual washing could not easily reach. No doubt she thought herself truly clean. Kamala had once, when she had achieved such a state.

The girl came hesitantly into the great room, like a deer might enter an unfamiliar meadow, watching on all sides for predators. Yet unlike a deer she would not run, Kamala knew that. She had come to meet the wolves.

Go back! she thought to her. Unable to move or even speak, simply staring at her in pained empathy. *There is nothing here worth what this will cost you. Trust me!*

The girl was wearing a simple linen gown; it was probably the finest thing she owned. A line of rings had been sewn down both sides and a cord laced through them so that, by drawing it tightly, she might impose a more adult curve upon her waist. It was an unnatural illusion on so young a child, but it brought her the notice she desired. Several of the men turned to watch her as she threaded her way through their company, and the inn's owner, normally so protective of his patrons, kept his distance as she approached, having not yet decided if she was a creature to be welcomed or expelled.

Finally she came to where all could see her, and in a voice that seemed surprisingly steady to Kamala (but how one struggled to sound fearless, when one was most afraid!) "I am looking for Master Beltorres, please."

Some of the men laughed and some of the whores whispered, but a bearded man in an eastern-style doublet looked up at her words. "I am Beltorres. Who and what are you?"

The girl bit her lip as she curtseyed. Pain lanced through Kamala's heart as she watched the motion. Had she looked this awkward herself when she had tried to impress Ethanus, aping noble mannerisms that so obviously did not come naturally to her?

"I am called Selti, sir, if it please you." Again the awkward curtsey. "I have a message for you from Master Hurara." She took a piece of carefully folded vellum out of her sleeve and offered it to him. With a smile he took it from her, brushing against her hand briefly but suggestively as he did so. The girl blushed but smiled, and did not back away. The lump in Kamala's throat turned to a burning ember. She could feel the power inside her, angry and indignant, urging her to act in the girl's defense. *This is her moment,* she told it. *Her choice to make, not mine.* The power was not convinced, and it roiled molten in her gut. She knew what the girl intended. She could smell it on her. She also knew where it would lead.

"Well then," Beltorres grunted. "I suppose I may have to visit the harbor after all." With a hearty laugh he threw the paper into the fire. "Business is as business does, eh?" He grinned at the girl; it was the kind of expression one might see on a hungry hyena. "Stay about a bit, I may want to send an answer back."

Kamala drew in a sharp breath as one of the whores reached out for the girl, laughing softly as she did so. How many times had she looked back on her own life, wondering what single moment she could have changed to make it into something different? This was the girl's moment. Clearly she knew it, too. Kamala could see it in her eyes. She could smell it in the room's thick air, the fear of a girl not yet past the threshold of womanhood, the perfumed amusement of whores surrounding her, and the eager sweat of the men watching . . . it was all she could do to keep hold of the power inside her. Gods alone knew if she released it now it might do what it had done in the streets of Gansang, only ten times worse. Not because killing these men was qualitatively worse than killing a handful of ruffians, but because these men were far more likely to be avenged.

But she wanted to kill them. She really did. She wanted to kill any man that would put his hands upon a child, whether she was willing or not. And with him any woman that would draw such a girl down into a circle of whores, as these were now doing, plucking at her coarse linen dress and the body beneath with whispered laughter as one of the men reached over to feel for himself what was beneath the homespun packaging—and the girl stared at them in a daze, trembling, wanting their favor and the coin that might come of it but too young to know how to handle such attention.

"Let her go."

The words came from behind her, shattering her mood like glass. Kamala turned about just in time to see the owner of the voice approaching. He was a young man dressed in a woodsman's costume, simple in cut, but made of the kind of quality cloth only the richest men could afford. He was blond and fair-skinned and passably handsome, with piercing blue eyes that shone like ice as he stared at the tableau before him. They were all frozen now, looking back at him, merchants and mercenary captains and whores and serving girls and the one little girl in the center of it all, her face now leached of all color.

"Let her go," he repeated.

The one man who had been reaching out toward the girl paused in his motion, but did not withdraw. "This is not your business."

"It is now. Let her go."

The man spread his hands, palms upwards, and grinned. "No one has put shackles on her. Or forced her to join us in the first place." He looked at the girl. "You are here of your own will, yes?"

Kamala held her breath. At that age, she remembered, the only way one could deal with some things was by denying they were happening. By asking the girl to acknowledge her situation in words, to give him permission to use her as a whore, this man had just laid waste to all her defenses.

Kamala saw the girl begin to tremble. For all the accustomed hardness of her heart, it was more than she could handle. But the blond stranger moved again before she could act, crossing in front of her and spoiling her view of the group. Breath held, she watched as he waded into the midst of the painted women, reaching out to the child's arm and pulling her out from among them. A couple of the men jumped angrily to their feet and the one that had been fondling the girl cursed loudly. But the stranger stared them down. There was fury in his eyes, and death, and in the end none of the pampered crowd had the courage to test him.

Kamala released her breath in a long, soft hiss as he passed by her again, taking the child with him. While all the eyes of the place were upon him she gathered the shadows of the room about her so that she might follow him unobserved. She also conjured a vague cloud of foreboding to gather by the door itself, and to prevent the men inside the inn from choosing to do the same. Simple spells of little substance, but sometimes those were enough.

By the time she left the inn the stranger had gone some distance from it, and had just released the girl from his grasp. She looked more angry than afraid right now, and was staring at him with angry, hollow eyes.

"Go home," he was saying. "This kind of place is not for you."

But she didn't move. The small eyes were filled with tears. "They would have paid for me," she protested. The words were voiced in a tone of desperation that twisted like a knife in Kamala's gut. It seemed to have a similar affect upon the stranger. For a moment he shut his eyes, and his jaw clenched visibly as he struggled to rein in his emotions. "You want to be paid?" he said. "Is that the only problem? You weren't paid? Here." He fumbled for his purse. "Here. I'm paying for you. Is that good enough?" He spilled out a handful of coins into his palm and held it out to her; his hand was trembling. "Take it," he urged, and when she still did not respond he cried out, "Take it all!"

He cast the money out from him, in the direction of the road. The girl stared at him for a moment, then ran to where the coins had fallen and got down on her hands and knees to gather them up. He turned from her, too pained to watch. Kamala saw him waver slightly as he did so, and he reached out to a nearby tree to steady himself. So he was not nearly as strong as he seemed. That was interesting. The scene in the great room must have been a bluff, albeit a fierce one. The man Kamala was looking at now could not hold his own in a brawl against so many.

Which spoke eloquently for his courage in confronting them, she thought. Or else his lunacy.

She waited until the girl had collected her prize and run off toward the road to Bandoa, then stepped quietly out of the shadows. She waited until the stranger saw her there before speaking. It was a long moment of waiting, for his thoughts were clearly elsewhere.

When at last he noticed her standing there she asked him quietly, "Why did you do that?"

"Do what? With the child?"

She nodded.

He suddenly looked very weary. "What business is it of yours, boy?"

"Few men care about such things."

A corner of his mouth twitched. It was almost a smile. "Well then, I suppose I am not like most men."

Kamala took a few steps closer. "You can't help her, you know. She will just come back here tomorrow. Or find another place like it."

The truth of her words seemed to settle like a weight upon his shoulders. He sighed heavily. "I know. The words of one man mean very little in this world, don't they?"

Something about the tone of his voice made Kamala catch her breath. *He is accustomed to his words having more weight than this,* she thought. *Accustomed to having the power to change things.*

Intrigued, she reached out to touch the fabric of his sleeve. He looked at her curiously but did not move away. The fabric was fine and smooth to the touch, such as only master weavers could produce, and clinging to it were echoes of its owner's past history. She tasted status, wealth, and a fierce independence. *He has argued with someone in authority while wearing this,* she observed. *Often.* Beyond that were more subtle traces, unfamiliar to her, that she had to work to unravel. When she finally realized their source, the breath caught in her throat. Not even Ravi's possessions had hinted at such a birthright of authority. There was only one possible explanation for it, and that one so outlandish, given the circumstances, she was hard pressed to believe it.

"You are not what you seem," she said at last.

"Nor you," he said quietly. He had been studying her while she did him, she realized. And she had been too preoccupied to take her usual precautions. Her heart skipped a beat as he reached up to the woolen cap she wore, but she made no move to stop him. He removed it. Wild red hair fell out into a fiery cloud about her face, not the long feminine locks he had expected, perhaps, but still not a boy's style by any means.

"Now perhaps it is my turn for questions," he said. "I shall begin with . . . what gives you such interest in the girl's fate?" When she did not answer he said, "On the other hand, a woman traveling in boy's attire . . . shall I guess?

She flushed. It was something she had never done in response to any man other than Ethanus, and she raged at herself for letting her guard down that much. "Guessing is a dangerous pastime."

"Is it?" The blue eyes were no longer icy, but warm, like a mountain lake in summer. "The deer in the forest that has never known man does not fear the crossbow. While the one that has been hunted before, and wounded, warns young ones to flee at the first sign of human presence." Again a faint smile flickered across his lips; not a leering expression, or a cruel one, but oddly compassionate. "Am I wrong?"

For a moment she was speechless. "Are you likening me to a deer?"

"A wolf, then." He chuckled. "The observation is still valid, yes? Even though in the latter case the mother would also rip out the throat of anyone trying to hunt her."

Regaining something of her composure, she raised an eyebrow. "Am I a deer then, or a wolf? Make up your mind."

"Women can be both at once." He grinned. "That is why men go mad trying to understand them."

She was about to respond when the door to the inn swung open. She saw the stranger's expression harden and she turned around quickly to see what new trouble was looming.

It was the owner of the place. He looked about himself nervously, as if expecting trouble, which at least confirmed that her spell was working. In one hand he held a travel pack, woolen blankets bound around a bundle of supplies that had clearly been hurriedly and inexpertly tied; in the other was a small leather purse.

He glared at the stranger, then cleared his throat and spat upon the ground. "I think it best you leave now." He hefted the bundle and threw it toward them; it raised a small cloud of dust as it fell to the ground just

short of the blond man's feet. "I pride myself on maintaining a peaceful establishment; remember that if you come here again in the future." He
threw the purse to him as well, and this time it made the distance. "Your
money, minus last night's room and board. And a small commission for
my trouble this afternoon."

His eyes narrowed in warning as he glanced at Kamala, then he went
back inside the inn. The traveler hefted the purse in his hand as the door
slammed shut, as if remarking upon its light weight. "I suppose it is just as
well I have this back, given that I threw most of what I had at that girl."
He looked at Kamala. "I do hope I haven't gotten you in trouble here."

She shrugged. "If so, I can deal with it." The owner could not fail to
offer her hospitality, with her sorcery wrapped around his heart, any more
than the sun could fail to rise in the morning. But she was not about to
tell him that.

"My name is Talesin," he offered.

She mused upon that for a moment, wondering just how much she
wished to reveal to him, then said, "I am called Kovan."

"A boy's name."

She took her cap back from him and put it back on, tucking her wild
red hair back into it. "Well, I am a boy, yes?"

His blue eyes sparkled in the sunlight. "And what would you call yourself if you masqueraded as a girl, Kovan?"

She hesitated. The open warmth of his manner was hard to resist, but
not so intoxicating that she forgot the position she was in. Magisters were
hunting her, probably the nobles of Gansang were as well, and then there
were her dreams to consider. Might this pleasant young man, so far out of
his accustomed noble element, perhaps connected to one of those forces?
It was a chilling thought.

"I cannot decide," she said, masking her unease with a flirtatious tone.
"Choose something for me, Talesin."

"Well, then." He made a show of considering the question. While he
did so, she reached out with a tendril of sorcery to take the measure of his
soul. If he had secrets she would know them soon enough.

But the moment she touched him she knew that something was wrong.
It was not just that there was sorcery wrapped around him like a cocoon,
though there was. Men of rank often had Magisters' spells cast upon them

for one purpose or another, and the fact that this man had one only confirmed her suspicions about his true social station. But beneath that . . . beneath that was a soul like nothing she had ever known before. Touching it with her power was like grasping hot embers. The moment she made contact with him a searing magical heat shot up her arm and into her flesh, and she could no more analyze it in that moment than she could have kept her hand in a blazing fire to count the embers.

It took every ounce of strength in her soul to keep her surprise from showing on her face, and to fight the instinct to step back from him. Was his soulfire so much stronger than that of other men? Or was it simply so unfettered that it roared like wildfire along any magical conduit she gave it? In all her years with Ethanus he had never even hinted at such a phenomenon. She did not know what to make of it.

"Lianna," he said, bringing her back to the present moment. "In the land of my ancestors is it the name of a goddess of great beauty, with a spirit like fire. Her touch shatters the ice on the great rivers, so that spring can come again. Will you bear that name, when you pretend to be a woman?"

She managed to smile calmly, though her heart was pounding fiercely. "A fine name. I will try to do it justice." Gently she drew her hand from his grasp; his warm fingers were like velvet to her touch.

"So where are you from, most lovely pretender?" His tone was casual, but she sensed with instinctive certainty the question was anything but that. "If you do not wish to share your origins, then perhaps . . . tales of recent travels?" The answer mattered to him, she realized. It mattered very much.

He is connected to my nightmares somehow. He must be. The thought chilled her, especially as she was afraid to try to read him again with sorcery. Instead she reached out with a tendril of power—carefully, this time, oh so carefully—and wound the strands of a new spell about him. Not trying to break through the spells that were already there, simply adding one more to the cocoon. *If you are searching for someone, I am not her. If you seek the answer to a mystery, I will not provide it.* It was a simple safeguard, but it would suffice. Unless he was a Magister himself he would not be able to think past it . . . and she knew from the touch of his soul that he was not that. Magisters were chill in their soul's essence, more like a corpse than the fire of a living man. Stolen life might fuel a Magister's power, but it could not warm the ice which was at his core.

Once that precaution was taken, she found she could breathe again.

What are you? she wondered. *Born to wealth but lacking more than a handful of coins, born to power but traveling like a mendicant, born to a blood-line of great renown yet unwilling to use your own name for fear it would be recognized . . . or am I misreading all those signs? Are you something else entirely, that sorcery has obscured?*

She wished she dared use her power to investigate the matter. But she feared establishing any sorcerous contact that would make her vulnerable to his heat again. Not because she thought it would hurt her. It was clearly not a malign power. But because even the memory of it now stirred a strange longing in her, almost a hunger, and that frightened her. This was surely what a moth must feel like, she thought, just before it cast itself into a flame. Fluttering about the dancing light, feeling that blissful warmth upon its wings, an ecstasy of heat . . . and then, suddenly, unexpectedly, consumed.

"My past travels are of little interest," she told him.

"And the future ones?"

I could lie to you. I could weave a spell that would convince you you'd heard my answer and found it of no interest. I could drive you away from me with a thought, and make you forget we had ever met.

Perhaps the last option would be wisest. Ethanus would certainly counsel her in that direction. But then she would never have a chance to learn what this stranger's true purpose was, or why the touch of his soul was like fire to her. And besides, if he was truly connected to the presence that haunted her nightmares, might he not be more dangerous to her lost in the shadows, where she could not watch over him, than in plain sight nearby?

"I have taken up with a caravan," she said. "Tomorrow we head south and east, toward the Free Lands. And yourself?"

His blue eyes fixed on hers. What depths they guarded, what mysteries! With enough time she could surely unravel them.

Careful, Kamala. This mystery can burn you.

"I have not yet chosen my next road," he answered her.

"Indeed?" Kamala's own eyes sparkled. "I hear the shores of the Inner Sea are quite temperate this season."

"Are they?" He reached out toward her—she drew back, startled—but it was only to tuck a loose strand of hair up into her cap. His hand was warm against her skin, and lingered for a moment before withdrawing. "Do you suppose such a caravan might have need of an additional escort?"

Ethanus would say she was being foolish. Ethanus would advise that no mystery was worth this kind of risk, especially when unknown powers were involved.

And that, my master, is why I could not learn about the world by your side.

"Come on the morrow, at daybreak," she said. "I will see what I can do about getting you hired."

She left him then, in body at least. But it was a long, long time before the memory of his soul's heat faded from her flesh . . . or from her spirit.

That night, for the first time in many days, Prince Andovan's sleep was peaceful.

Kamala dreamed of moths.

Chapter 33

THE MILITARY settlement overlooking King's Pass was high in the mountains, cold and chill. Yet even colder was the sight that awaited visitors, of which Colivar's conjured images had been but a feeble warning.

The three Magisters stood in a veritable forest of death, overlooked by the staring, vacant eye sockets of twisted skeletons. In the time it had taken Antuas to find his way south the scavengers of the area had finished their work; the impaled bodies were stripped bare of flesh now, and some of them lacked limbs that had been carried off by one predator or another. Fragments of bone lay scattered around the site, where scavengers had cracked them open for marrow. The worst of the smell of death had faded, but one could still taste the memory of foulness on the wind when it blew across the field of stakes. One could only imagine how terrible that smell must have been when Antuas had been here.

Colivar stared at it all with an expression that made Sulah tremble. Not in all their time together had he ever seen his former teacher look thus, or sensed in him such coiled energy that, if it were released, it would surely destroy anything and everything in sight. He knew that Colivar had seen the worst that mortal men could do to each other in wartime, and numerous sorcerous atrocities as well; so if there was something here that was terrible enough to awaken this darkness in him, it must be fearsome indeed.

The three of them had split up briefly: Colivar to inspect the field of stakes, Fadir to hunt down whatever signs of the supply party remained, and Sulah to seek out confirmation of the most disturbing part of the witch's vision, the rising of the great winged beast. Now, as the young Magister returned to his teacher's side, it seemed to him that the Colivar he knew was gone, and in his place was an ashen-faced stranger whose eyes were fixed not upon the field of slaughter surrounding them, but on some distant vision a hundred times more terrible.

"I found marks of one great creature," Sulah reported. "Where the vision showed it rising. So that much at least was true." Colivar turned to him slowly as he spoke, his black eyes hollow, haunted. "No sign of any others."

"There will be no others," Colivar said quietly.

Fadir rejoined them, then. His own expression was grim. "I found the supply party. Most were killed alongside their mounts. A few tried to flee into the woods, it appears, but they did not get far."

"What killed them?" Sulah asked.

"Nothing human. They were torn to pieces while still alive." He shrugged stiffly. "Your guess is as good as mine."

"So the witch's memories were fairly accurate."

"So it would seem." Fadir's jaw clenched tightly as he looked over the field of corpses. "I had hoped he was at least partly delusional." He looked at Colivar. "You think it was a real Souleater he saw? One of these . . . what did you call them . . . ikati?"

"What other purpose can there be for all this?" Colivar waved at the field of stakes, and toward the place beyond it where the supply party had been murdered. "What other motive makes sense?"

"How about a gesture intended to strike fear into the enemies of the High King? This *is* Danton Aurelius we are talking about. His distaste for Corialanus is no secret. Nor is his penchant for brutality. This kind of display is hardly beyond him. A warning to would-be rebels: *disobey me and you will suffer the same fate.*"

Colivar shook his head. "This slaughter was too far from well-traveled roads to serve such a purpose. It was unlikely to be discovered while the bodies were still fresh, which was when the scene was most effective. Danton has better timing than that."

"Not to mention," Sulah offered, "that those who might have served as witnesses were apparently hunted down and killed. That is not what you do when you are trying to send a message to someone."

Colivar walked to the nearest stake, gazed up at its occupant, and then put his hand upon the length of wood. It was an oddly intimate contact, almost a dark caress. "An entire unit of men were made helpless here, condemned to die over the course of a few days, their life force bleeding out along with their blood, from all of them at once, together . . . a Souleater would regard that as nothing short of a feast."

"These stakes were not erected by beasts," Fadir pointed out.

"No," Colivar agreed, "they were not."

"Perhaps these ikati are more than that. Perhaps the legends are right."

Colivar said nothing.

"Some men say they were demons, but I myself have never credited that."

"They are not demons," Colivar said quietly.

"You sound very sure, given as how the last one was dead and gone long before the first Magister was born." Fadir's tone was a challenge. "What makes your versions of the legend more accurate than any other other?"

Colivar gazed out into the distance as if there were some terrible thing to be seen there, so far away he could not quite manage to focus on it, but felt driven to try. "Let us say I remember a time when the legends were young, and a few real facts were still remembered. There were even ikati skeletons to be found back then, kept as trophies of the Great War. I seem to recall a throne being made out of one of them, somewhere in the Northlands, and it was rumored that armor had been made from ikati skin as well." He shrugged. "Truth and fantasy mingle over time, until they can no longer be distinguished from one another. Besides, it is more respectable to claim that humanity was nearly destroyed by demons, than to place the blame upon the shoulders of simple beasts. No matter how fearsome those beasts might have been."

"They ate human souls," Sulah said.

Colivar looked sharply at him. "They fed upon the life essence of their prey. As did many other species, at the time. Now we Magisters are the only ones left who do that." A faint, dry smile flickered about the corners of his lips. "There is irony in that, yes?"

"I wonder if they would see us as rival predators," Fadir mused.

"More to the point—I wonder who it is they see as an *ally.*" Colivar's hand tightened about the stake. "This slaughter was a sacrifice, nothing less. Like the kings of the Dark Ages who left maidens chained on mountaintops, hoping that if the hunger of the Souleaters was sated thus the rest of their people would be spared, the one who did this knew exactly what was here, and what manner of food it hungered for."

"Danton, you think?"

"These lances were made by his people," Colivar said. Stroking the wood of the nearest stake again, letting his sorcerous senses seep down deep into its grain, to read the history of the thing. "The men who placed them here were following his orders. That much is clear."

"But why kill so many?" Fadir demanded. "Surely this is more 'food' than one beast would require."

Colivar shut his eyes. A muscle along the line of his jaw tensed for a moment. Again Sulah caught the sense of coiled energy within him, some black and terrible instinct that he was struggling to control. "Assuming an ikati was here," he said at last, "and that someone made arrangements to feed it this many lives, all at once . . ." he looked at Sulah. "What would you expect to find, if you searched for it properly? And where would you look for it?"

For a moment the younger Magister stared at him, not comprehending. Then his face went even paler—if such a thing were possible—as he realized what Colivar was suggesting.

"A nest," he whispered.

He looked out over the landscape, though the field of stakes, across the top of the gorge that was the King's Pass, and to the granite-faced cliffs on the other side. After a moment he located a broad shelf strewn with rubble, set in a place that no man could reach without risking his neck climbing up to it. A winged creature, on the other hand, would find it a comfortable and convenient perch. Even a very large winged creature. "There," he said.

Colivar nodded. "Go. Confirm it."

It was rare that one Magister gave orders to another, and for a moment Sulah hesitated. But the look in Fadir's eyes made it clear that Colivar's knowledge of these matters had won him a kind of implied authority in this instance, so he nodded at last, and exchanged his human flesh for a winged shape that might fly the distance.

The wind slowly grew colder as the sun began to slip down behind the mountains. It was hard to find what he was looking for, but Colivar had trained him well, and Sulah uncovered the nest just before sunset's shadows claimed that part of the ledge.

For a moment he just stared at the broken fragments and tried to gather his thoughts. Colivar seemed to take all this in stride, somehow, but he could not. The Souleaters were creatures out of legend, and when they last flew above the earth, it was said, mankind had been reduced to utter barbarism. All the proud monuments and civilizations of the First Age of Kings were gone now, lost to that terrible assault. Beasts the Souleaters might be—even natural beasts, perhaps—but their legendary status was well-deserved. And the thought that they might now be returning was terrifying.

The Magisters will manage to survive, he thought, *but what is the value of one man's survival when the very world he belongs to is destroyed?*

Finally he pulled himself together, picked up a fragment of a shell to bring back with him, and returned to where the other two Magisters were waiting. The object that was grasped in his talons appeared in his palm as he reclaimed his human form, and he held it out silently, grimly, for inspection. It was the size of a man's fist, dull white on the outside, with an inner surface that gleamed a darker hue, blue-black, like the heavens at twilight.

A muscle along the line of Colivar's jaw tightened for a moment. "How many?"

"One nest on the ledge. Many eggs, all broken. There . . ." he hesitated. "There could still be others. Elsewhere. Yes?"

"What is this?" Fadir asked.

"Why so many had to die." Colivar took the shell from Sulah, looked it over, then handed it to the red-haired Magister. "This place was used as a breeding ground for ikati. These were—" he indicated the forest of impaled bodies "—food for their young."

Fadir's thick brow furrowed. "So whoever killed all these people was doing it to feed a Souleater? To help it breed?" He breathed in sharply. "Do you realize what you are suggesting?"

Colivar nodded grimly.

"Who would be mad enough to do that? Knowing that the last time these creatures roamed free, human civilization was nearly obliterated?"

"I have heard the High King is mad," Sulah offered. "That the death of his son unhinged him, awakening a hunger for bloodshed that no amount of violence can slake."

"He was always mad," Colivar said, "but for a while he had a man of reason to guide him. Now that man is gone."

"Ramirus?" Fadir asked. Colivar nodded.

"I rather had the impression you did not approve of him."

"I despised his master. That is not the same thing."

"Do you think Danton is fool enough to do something like this? To invite these . . . these abominations, to return?"

Colivar's eyes narrowed; the black gaze was unreadable. "The High King is a fool, but not that kind of fool. It takes no genius to understand that if the Dark Ages come again, it will affect all domains, all princes . . . all Magisters." His hand unconsciously stroked the stake beside him, as if trying to coax more information out of its bloodstained wood. "My guess is that someone is using him. Someone who knows what these things are, and thinks they can serve his purpose."

"Or someone who only *thinks* he knows what they are about," Fadir offered, "and therefore imagines he can control them."

"Just so," Colivar whispered. Once more his gaze unfocused, fixing on some dark and distant horizon.

"Can we tell him?" Sulah asked. "Tell Danton? Or his Magister, perhaps? If, as you say, he would never support such a plan, maybe knowing what these creatures really are would cause him to rethink his plan."

"And who will tell him that?" Colivar asked sharply. "I am counted among his enemies for my alliance with Anshasa; most of the other Magisters who might dare to tell him the truth were banished from his realm when Andovan died. Who do you imagine can go to this High King bearing words he does not wish to hear, and make him listen?"

"Ramirus knows him," Fadir said quietly. "He would know how to get through to him."

Colivar exhaled sharply. "Yet another one who treasures my counsel."

"The reason for your conflict with him is over now. And there are others who can make that journey in your place."

Colivar looked up at him. "You are offering?"

"I will seek out Ramirus, yes. And tell him what is happening, and ask him how Danton is best handled."

"He is best simply killed," Colivar muttered, "but our Law does not allow that."

Fadir nodded. It was customary among the Magisters that once one of them had made a contract with a prince, that prince was not to be assaulted directly by any other of their kind. It was a frustrating handicap, at times like this, but one that had been proven necessary back in the days when there were no rules. "Who serves him now?"

"Someone named Kostas. There is no history to the name, at least not that anyone has been able to discover. Rumor has it he has a nature as bloodthirsty as Danton's, which, if true, is only going to make things worse."

"Is it possible he is behind all this?"

Colivar's eyes narrowed. "How would a Magister benefit from the return of the Souleaters? If the spirit of man is devoured, this is not going to be a pleasant world to inhabit. Not to mention—"

He hesitated for a moment. Sulah held his breath, sensing they were at the threshold of secrets, wondering how much his mentor would reveal.

"We may be food to them," Colivar said at last. "You do realize that, don't you? They were drawn to mankind because the soulfire burned more brightly in him than in any other species. And we . . . we steal that fire, we concentrate it inside ourselves. They could feed off a Magister's athra for years, and their prey would never die. . . ."

Sulah shuddered. "You don't know that. You can't know that."

"No, I can't." The dark eyes met his own; something in their depths made a cold chill run down Sulah's spine. "No one can know that. Souleaters and Magisters have never met. Correct?"

The word *yes* lodged in Sulah's throat and would not come out.

Colivar turned to Fadir. "Go to Ramirus, see if he has any insight to add to this. For all that he can be a pretentious bastard, he has more innate wisdom than most other Magisters combined. And he knows Danton better than any other man alive." He shut his eyes briefly, considering. "We will need to tell the Magisters about this. All of them. We need to share news of any disturbance that might be linked to this . . . campaign. And either get witches to search for new nests, or do it ourselves if we must. Common men cannot find them. We *cannot* let these things continue to breed."

"How likely do you think it is that there will be others?" Fadir asked.

"There have already been others. Up north. Far from Danton's influence. So whatever is going on . . ." His expression tightened. "It is not simply morati politics that is causing this."

Fadir nodded. "Siderea has contact information for many of us, we can ask her to—

"—Siderea is dying," Colivar said abruptly.

Fadir's mouth hung open briefly, then closed soundlessly. "How? Is it—"

"The natural end of her life. Disguised by our art, but no more than that."

Fadir exhaled slowly. "Does she know?"

"I don't think so. Not yet. But she only has so much life left in her, and every act of witchery we ask her to perform will lessen that meager store. When she is gone we are going to lose a vital link in our network. Perhaps an irreplaceable one." He looked at Fadir. "If you feel that asking her to help with this is worth the cost, I will listen to your argument."

"No. No." He shook his head slowly; his expression was grim. "You are right. We need her too much for other things." He hesitated. "We should spread that news as well, I suppose."

Colivar nodded. "To her lovers." Again the dry, pained smile flickered across his lips briefly. "What a strange society we have formed, bound together by a morati woman. And by nothing else, save perhaps an instinctive distrust for one another."

"If you are right about what these things are," Sulah said, "and how they operate, the Magisters will have to ally. As the witches did in the Great War."

"I can think of quite a few Magisters who would rather fornicate with a Souleater than work with others of their kind," Colivar said dryly. "Let us hope we do not need to test them. As for the Great War . . . I will remind you that what the witches did was offer up their lives in sacrifice. Every last one of them was lost."

Fadir nodded. "Not likely they will be willing to do the same again, now that *we* are here."

"And not likely that any Magisters will offer to take their place, given that the one quality we all have in common is an unwillingness to die. So we need to see that matters never reach that point, yes?" Colivar wrapped his arms around himself; it was a strangely morati gesture. "I for one have no desire to see the Dark Ages return. And do not mistake it, that is the cost if we fail."

"I will spread the word," Fadir promised. He stepped back from the other two and raised his hand as if to bind enough power to leave their company, but suddenly Colivar stopped him.

"Tell them to kill their consorts," he told him. "They will understand."

The red-headed Magister bowed his assent and then called his power to him. The night air shimmered briefly about him . . . and then there was nothing in the place where he had stood save a chill breeze, which quickly dispersed.

For a moment there was only silence, and the deep ruddy shadows of the setting sun.

Then: "Your observations?" Colivar asked. "I am . . . curious."

"You know more than you are telling us," the younger man said bluntly. "Quite a bit more, I suspect. And I have as much chance of getting the rest out of you as these skeletons have of coming down off their posts and dancing, if you are not ready to talk."

Colivar chuckled darkly. "You were always an insightful student. . . ."

"Am I wrong?" He waited a moment for an answer, and when none was offered, pressed, "What did you mean, 'tell them to kill their consorts?' "

"A custom of war, among Magisters Royal. On the eve of battle one drains one's consort dry, to force Transition to take place, so that one has a fresh consort when the battle begins, and needs not worry about having to hunt down a new one at an inopportune moment."

"Are we going into battle, then? Or just taking precautions?

For a moment Colivar did not answer him. He gazed out into the night, and once more Sulah had the feeling that his thoughts were elsewhere. Remembering past battles, perhaps, or envisioning future ones. Finally he said, "It is possible, I suppose, that a handful of ikati escaped the hunt at the end of the Great War. Possible that they and their descendants kept a low enough profile that we did not realize any had survived until now."

"And if not?"

The black eyes fixed on him. "Then the ones we are seeing came from the North. From beyond those boundaries which were supposed to hold them prisoner forever. And if that is the case, Sulah, if that barrier has truly been breached, then the war has already begun. On very different terms than the last time we fought them."

He gazed out across the field of stakes; Sulah thought he saw him shudder. It was so uncharacteristic that the sight of it made Sulah's skin crawl.

"Last time they did not have allies," Colivar whispered.

Chapter 34

IT WAS late at night when Gwynofar returned to her chambers, and she was weary. She hoped that was because of her pregnancy, and not any more significant problem. Not the fact that the whole building seemed to reek of Danton's foul Magister now, and merely breathing air that carried his scent made her stomach churn. Once, mere days ago, she would have tried to deny the sensation, telling herself that the stink was no more than her imagination . . . but now that Rurick had made it clear that was not the case, and others could smell it as well, it seemed ten times more sickening.

At the door to her chamber Merian paused. The maidservant looked back the way they had come as if listening for something. When she did not move after a moment, Gwynofar asked, "What is it?"

"I thought I heard voices, milady. It would be odd, for anyone to be here so late at night."

Gwynofar doubted that anyone would be passing by her chamber at such an hour, but she knew from experience that her maidservant would not be at ease until she had investigated the matter. "Go," she said. "I will wait for you."

She took the lamp from the woman's hands, listened to the obligatory apologies for her running off when she should be by milady's side, and watched with a half-smile as Merian finally went off down the corridor, back the way they had come. Woe betide any man who she decided was responsible for disturbing the queen's peace, Gwynofar thought.

With a sigh she opened the heavy doors of the bedchamber herself and stepped inside. Setting the lamp down beside the bed, she wondered if she should just undress herself and go to sleep rather than waiting for her servant to return to help her. But no, that would just upset the woman more, and Gwynofar would have to reassure her ten times over that she had not failed in her duty to her queen by leaving her to undress herself. With a heavy sigh Gwynofar decided just to wait for her, and settled for pulling the long pins out of her hair and then turning to the bed—

—and she stumbled backward with a low cry, upsetting the sideboard and nearly knocking the lamp over.

There was something on the bed. It was small and still, and there was some kind of liquid spreading outward from it, wet and dark as it pooled upon the coverlet.

Leaning against the wall for support, she picked up the lamp again. Her hand was trembling, and the lamp sent shadows dancing across the walls. Slowly she approached the bed, raising it up so that it would cast its light directly on the object.

It was a messenger pigeon.

Her messenger pigeon.

Its neck had been torn open, a wound from which its last blood now dripped, staining the coverlet crimson. The tiny leather case that had been strapped to its leg was still there, but it had been opened, and the message she had placed within it was gone. The flesh was still warm, she noted with a trembling touch, the blood still fluid . . . which meant that it had only just been killed. Perhaps even while she and Merian were talking in the corridor.

She stared at it in horror and wanted to scream, but when she tried the sound caught in her throat and nothing would come out.

"Your bird, I believe."

The voice came from behind her. She whirled about and suddenly found the speaker so close to her that she nearly fell onto the bed trying to back away from him.

Kostas.

"Merian!" she yelled. Or tried to yell. But though she did all the things one normally did to make a sound, no sound came out.

"She will not hear you, Majesty. No one will hear you, until I allow it."

For a moment she was so weak with fear she could hardly stand. The sickness she felt in the Magister's presence was nigh on overwhelming, and for one terrible moment she wondered if she might faint before him. Then anger took spark within her, setting fire to her soul . . . and she was queen once more.

"Get out of my room," she commanded.

The lizardlike eyes fixed on her: unblinking, inhuman. "I suggest you listen to what I have to say, Majesty. Until now you have simply annoyed me, and it has cost you a messenger. But I would not like to think that some foolish act in the future might bring us to greater conflict."

Her heart was pounding wildly, but she refused to let him see her fear. "I am your queen," she said in her most imperious tone. "For as long as you are bound in contract to Danton, you are bound to my service as well."

"But to him first and foremost, Lady. And if those two interests should conflict . . . let us say it would not be a good thing for you."

Her voice was like steel. "I am his wife. I rule over his household. I share his throne. It is not for you to judge the manner in which I do those things."

He reached out to touch her, to cup his hand under her chin; it was the sort of condescending gesture one might make with a child. She hissed softly as his fingers came near to her face, and could feel something within her self about to snap. It was a dark and terrible something, like nothing she had ever felt before.

But just as he was about to make contact with her, he stopped. It was not by choice, it seemed to her, but almost as if some unseen barrier had stopped the motion short. A strange look came over his face. For a fleeting moment she saw something in his eyes that was neither arrogance nor disdain. Could it be fear?

"You cannot plot against me," he said quietly. "You understand that? I will know it if you do. Any thought you may have of interfering with my plans, or of turning your husband against me, I will know of it as soon as you begin. When you walk into a room where I am present, I will understand all your plots and connivings as certainly as if you had explained them to me. Your allies will be as clear to my Sight as if they wore your mark plainly upon their foreheads . . . and their thoughts, also, shall be known to me." His eyes narrowed. "You have no secrets from me, Majesty."

She did not trust herself to speak. She hoped he could not hear the wild pounding of her heart.

"Your husband is High King," he told her. "I know what lies before him and I am guiding him to his destiny. That is my duty. You are his queen. That is a different role. Bear him heirs, pleasure his flesh, run his household if you please. Stay out of his business otherwise."

That something which was inside her finally snapped. Willing authority into her voice, drawing energy from that place within her soul where terror and fury both raged, she could feel her expression harden.

"*You will leave my room,*" she said. "*NOW.*"

For a long moment he just stared at her. Perhaps waiting to see if she would back down. But she drew strength from the power of her hatred for him, and did not even blink. If he was reading her mind now, she thought, let him drink in that hatred and drown in it. *My spirit is poison to you, Magister.* The words seemed to come out of nowhere, but she suddenly knew them for the truth.

"Call upon your ancestral power if you like," he said between gritted teeth. "But know that the cost will be the life of your unborn child."

With no further word he turned and left her. Not until the door had swung shut behind him did the strength finally drain from her limbs. With a short cry of anguish she fell to the floor, and the tears she had fought so hard not to shed in front of him began to flow freely. Her body shook violently as all the emotions she had struggled to control in his presence were let loose. Ice-cold terror, molten rage, confusion . . . what had his final words meant? What power was he referring to? How was it a threat to her child?

"Milady? Milady!"

It was Merian. She was kneeling by the queen's side an instant, cradling Gwynofar in her arms as one would a fallen child, drying her tears with the end of one sleeve. "What is it, what happened? What's wrong? Did he hurt you?"

"He cannot hurt me." The words tasted strange on her lips, but somehow she knew they were true. "He lacks the power."

"I will kill him if he tries, I swear it, milady—"

"Shh. Shh. There is no need." It was oddly comforting to focus on the other woman's fear instead of her own. "He is gone now."

He had not been able to touch her. He had tried to, he had reached out to her with his hand . . . and he had not made contact. What had stopped him?

"Find me a room he has never been in," she whispered. "Have my things moved there tonight. I will not sleep in a place that creature has befouled with his presence, not ever again."

"But milady . . ." Merian glanced back nervously toward the door, no doubt imagining how well it would be received when she started waking up servants to see to the task. "I do not know—"

"And a new bed. There must be a new bed. I will not sleep in this one again."

She sighed. "Yes, milady. As you wish."

Gwynofar would wait in the garden, by the Spears, while a new room was prepared. She would sleep there if necessary. Kostas would never approach the Spears, she knew that now. Maybe that was the power he had referred to. Maybe he feared her family's gods, and because of them, feared her. But why would the gods hurt her child?

My spirit is poison to you, Magister. I do not know how yet, or why, but I saw the truth of it in your eyes.

I will not forget.

Chapter 35

OF ALL the sorcerous obstacles Fadir encountered, the fifth one was the most annoying of all. It appeared to be a garden maze of the sort one might find outside a grand manor house, the kind of thing that rich men created to show off how much money they had. The walls of the maze were made of cropped hedges taller than a man, so that once entered the way out could not be seen. Presumably one was supposed to wend one's way through the labyrinthine pattern of the maze, admiring its botanical display with a lady on one's arm, perhaps, and feeling no particular urgency about reaching one's destination.

It should have been easy enough to divine a way out, but apparently the owner had taken safeguards against such an action, and the best of Fadir's sorcery only brought him visions of more hedges. He had wandered about for almost an hour, wasting precious time, when finally he decided enough was enough. He gathered up his power into a ball of seething, molten athra, and loosed it in the direction he thought he should be traveling. As it crashed into each viridian wall it seared a hole through the tangled leaves and branches, leaving a black, charred path in its wake. So much for parlor games.

He was not in a good mood when he finally climbed through the last hole and reached the house that lay beyond. Fortunately there were no more games to be endured. No doubt the series of obstacles had accomplished its true purpose, causing him to waste enough power that he would be more hesitant to summon vast displays of sorcery while he was here. Either that, or Ramirus' exile had unhinged his mind.

Right now he was willing to bet on the latter.

No servants scurried to meet him as he approached the house, or any other manner of living creature. He bound a wisp of soulfire to locate Ramirus and exhaled a sigh of relief when it worked. He didn't have any more patience for games. He followed the sorcerous trail into the house, up a vast curving staircase, and to a library of sorts, that overlooked the gardens he had just been in. Through the diamond-paned window he could see the black path of his rage cutting through the maze like a carriage road. Ramirus could see it too. He was standing by the window as Fadir entered, gazing out at the ravaged gardens.

"You could have levitated," Ramirus pointed out. "It would have been simpler, though arguably less dramatic."

"I felt I had to destroy something," Fadir replied shortly. "Be glad it was only shrubbery."

Ramirus chuckled and turned from the window. He appeared much as he had when he had called them all to Danton's palace a small eternity ago. If the stress of recent events weighed upon his soul, it did not show.

"I do not get many visitors here," he said. "Though the ones that do come rarely make it as far as the gardens. Usually by the time they discover my giant monitor lizards they are having second thoughts about bothering me."

"And the morati?"

The piercing blue eyes fixed on Fadir. "When I have need of morati I seek them out. Otherwise they know better than to come here."

"Yes, speaking of which . . . where is 'here,' exactly?" Fadir looked about him as if expecting that a map might be pinned to the wall somewhere; the primitive ornaments in his hair clattered and tinkled as he moved. He looked extraordinarily out of place in this polished, sophisticated environment, but that was an image he enjoyed. In fact it had been many mortal lifetimes since he had been rightfully called *barbarian*, but some things were hard to leave behind.

"Does it matter? You sought me out, I allowed you to come. Now do sit down and tell me what this visit is about." He waved to a pair of leather-covered chairs flanking a mahogany desk; there were books and manuscripts strewn across the latter, as if he had just been interrupted in the midst of some complicated research project. "I assume you can conjure any refreshments you desire." Ramirus waved one hand and a glass of red wine appeared in it. "Make yourself at home."

Yes, like I am going to waste one more bit of power in this place than I have to. Fadir was irritated, but only that. By Magister standards Ramirus was being downright hospitable.

The chair creaked as he sat down in it. After a moment he did indeed conjure himself a tankard of ale, despite the cost. The waxed leather vessel he created was better suited to a rustic tavern than this polished sitting room, which he hoped would annoy his host.

"I hear you have not taken patronage again," Fadir said. "Any truth to that rumor?"

"I hear you are developing an unhealthy interest in other men's affairs," Ramirus responded pleasantly. "Any truth to that one?"

The visitor sighed. *So much for small talk.*

He put his tankard down on the table—a sorcerous breeze moved several papers out of the way just in time—and then said simply, without prelude, "The Souleaters are back."

The wine glass that was halfway to Ramirus' lips stopped there, frozen in place.

"And Danton is going mad."

"Danton was always mad," Ramirus said quietly. "Tell me about the Souleaters."

So he did. All of it. The appearance of the witch Antuas in Sankara, the interrogation that had followed, the slaughter in Corialanus, the nest, the bodies, Colivar's theories . . . all of it. Ramirus was silent and still as he listened; he moved only once—to let go of the wine glass, which vanished from sight before it could hit the floor—and then steepled his fingers thoughtfully, his white brows furrowed above eyes that had suddenly become colder than human eyes should ever be.

When Fadir was finally finished, Ramirus said quietly, "Colivar always did have a taste for offering up fantastic tales—

"Do not mock what you know nothing about," Fadir warned. "I was there and I saw—"

The white-haired Magister held up a hand to silence him. "As I was about to say . . . he also knows more of these matters than any man alive."

"You believe him, then."

"No man would lie about such creatures." He smiled darkly, an expression without warmth or mirth. "Not even Colivar."

He rose up from his chair and walked to the window again. For a long while he just stood there, gazing out at his ravaged gardens.

Finally Fadir said, "They have allies, Ramirus. Human allies. Danton may be one of them."

He said nothing.

"It has been suggested that if he understood what the Souleaters really were, he would surely keep his distance from them." Still the white-haired Magister said nothing. "Colivar said that you were the only one who would know how to reach him."

"It takes no great art to know how Danton should be 'reached.'" Ramirus' expression was grim. "But our Law dictates we cannot harm him directly while one of us is bound to his service. So what would you have me do? Show up at his door and offer him counsel? Send him flowers, perhaps, wrapped in some spell that will make him a gentler, kinder king?" His tone was harsh. "Danton is a ruthless bastard, who wants one thing and one thing only. Power. If a Souleater showed up at his door I do not doubt that his first thought would be how to bind it to his purpose . . . and if any morati could accomplish that, it would be Danton Aurelius."

Fadir exhaled sharply. "Surely he would understand that the return of such creatures puts the whole world at risk—"

"—and he will not live long enough to see it happen. That is both the gift and the curse of the morati, is it not? What does a man like Danton care if five hundred years in the future someone else must do battle with these creatures again?" He turned back to his guest; there was a blackness in his eyes that was terrible to behold. "If the monsters will serve him now, if they can help him strengthen his empire, let future generations worry about the consequences."

"Do you really believe that?" Fadir demanded. "Conquerors like Danton care passionately about what kind of legacy they will leave behind. You tell me this High King is different, you tell me the future means nothing to him, that he would sell out the world in which his own son would be

High King for some fleeting military gain . . . and I will say, you know him better than any other Magister. From you alone I will accept those words. But they strike me as wrong, by all of my own experience with kings."

For a long time Ramirus just stared at him. His expression was unreadable. "No," he said at last. "The Danton I knew would never make such a bargain. Not because he was unwilling to pay the price. Because he would not trust that anything so powerful, so innately malevolent as a Souleater is said to be, could be controlled indefinitely." He shook his head. "He is many things, Danton Aurelius, but above all else, he likes to be in control."

"He appears to be losing control," Fadir said quietly.

Ramirus said nothing.

"Those who know him best say his manner is becoming more and more erratic. Violent fits of anger are more commonplace, provoked by the most innocent cause. Allies whisper of him being ruled now by impulse and emotion, rather than ruthlessness and reason. They fear that his judgment is floundering because of it. They whisper he has even turned on his own family." He saw Ramirus stiffen at that suggestion, and paused to give him a chance to comment, but the white-haired Magister said nothing. "Is it not possible that in such a state of mind Danton might do the unthinkable? Perhaps cross the line between ambition and recklessness, where he has always backed down from it before?"

For a moment Ramirus shut his eyes; his brow furrowed briefly as if in pain. "I've heard these things," he said at last. "From one who would not lie to me. Yes, Danton is changing, and not for the better."

"What can be done?"

"Nothing. He is Danton Aurelius." His eyes flickered open; their depths glittered like ice. "And he has a new Magister Royal, so our Law dictates that none of us may work sorcery upon him directly. Not my favorite rule, granted, but I understand why it was enacted. So what do you propose we do?"

"Surely his Magister Royal understands the danger of allying with Souleaters."

"Why? No Magister existed back when they ruled the skies; our time came later. We know of them in the same way the morati do: from legends and songs created long after they were gone. All after the fact, as they say.

Man did not have the spirit to write songs or create legends when they ruled the earth." He shook his head. "Still, a Magister should know the risk, at least in theory. And if Danton is serving these creatures in any way, even unknowingly . . . that is bad, very bad."

"Will you help, then?"

Ramirus looked up sharply. "Help with what?"

"Colivar suggested that if Danton could be made to understand the larger picture, he might change his course."

"Colivar is a fool," he said shortly. "Danton 'changes course' for no man." He came back to his chair and sat down in it once more, stroking the carved wooden arm like he might the soft skin of a lover. "There were once three people in the world who could broach such a matter to Danton Aurelius without suffering his wrath for their honesty. I was among them. My counsel is no longer welcome, for obvious reasons. The second was his wife, the High Queen Gwynofar." A muscle along the line of his jaw tightened briefly. "I have reason to believe that their relationship is . . . let us say, it has changed. So she cannot help."

"And the third?"

"The third was Prince Andovan. Gods alone know why Danton valued his word so much, but he did. Perhaps because the boy had no great desire for political power, and thus could never be a rival to his father. Perhaps it was simply because he had his mother's eyes. Who can say what manner of sentiment rules the heart of a tyrant? A prince who does not desire his father's throne can say things straight from the heart without the worry that his every word will be dissected for motive."

"Andovan is the dead one, yes?"

"Oh, yes. Quite dead. And Danton's other sons all have agendas of their own that their father is wary of . . . even that mad recluse Salvator. So they could sermonize about the dangers of Souleaters for a fortnight, and all Danton would ever hear were the echoes of their own ambition. He'd likely do the opposite of whatever it was they advised." He shook his head sadly. "I'm sorry, Fadir. That's not the answer you came for, I know, but it is the truth."

"Then there is no one to counsel him."

"Not unless this Kostas can. And I suspect—" He drew in a sharp breath and did not finish the thought.

"Suspect what?"

For a long time again he was silent. Weighing a Magister's love of secret knowledge against the need for cooperation in this case? If so, there was nothing Fadir could do but wait for him to decide.

Finally Ramirus said, "Some time ago, I experimented with the effects of sorcery upon a morati mind. Specifically, when we wrap our spells around the spirit of a man, so that his thoughts are more in keeping with what we desire, does this change him in other ways? It is well known that a misstep in such arts can cost a subject his sanity, but are there more subtle changes, perhaps cumulative, that might normally pass beneath our notice?" He steepled his fingers before him as he spoke. "The answer is yes. Over time the natural barriers of a morati soul can weaken, until he begins to absorb more than simple orders from his master. In time, he may even take on something of the sorcerer's own aspect . . . a sort of spiritual contamination." He paused. "It was an impressive experiment, and in this case, I think you will agree, most relevant."

For a moment Fadir was speechless. Had Ramirus really just shared with him the kind of knowledge that might give a Magister sorcerous advantage over his peers? To do so was almost unheard of among their brotherhood. Magisters were rivals first and foremost, and everything else came second.

It is a measure of how serious he thinks this matter is. The thought sent a shiver up his spine. *What extremes he thinks we may have to go to, to deal with this threat.* "So you think Danton suffers from too much sorcerous manipulation? That his seeming madness is the result of someone toying with his mind?"

Ramirus' eyes glittered darkly as they fixed on Fadir. "You miss the point, my brother. Kostas did not cause his madness. Kostas *is* his madness."

He rose again, and walked back to the window. The sun was just beginning to set. Orange rays speared through the line of charred holes in the maze, setting their edges alight. "Now the only question is how does Colivar imagine he will deal with a Magister who may have passed beyond the bounds of sanity, and a king who may soon do the same, without breaking the Law that binds us all?"

Chapter 36

THE GIRL/boy/goddess was a witch.

Once he finally figured that out, Andovan was roundly embarrassed that he had not guessed the truth earlier. What else would explain
the casual way she had spoken of adding him to Netando's retinue, as if
any request she made would of course be granted? Who else but a witch
would dare to make such an assumption? A woman of rank might have
done so, but Lianna did not have the manner of one born to noble blood,
he thought. Despite occasional hints of a pride that would have done the
Aurelius line proud.

True, there had been an awkward moment when she had first spoken
to Netando about his coming along. Certainly it was not helped by the
fact that Andovan had refused to give Netando any information on his
background. Any merchant worth his salt would have considered such a
cipher a high risk on the best of days. Rival merchants would be all too
happy to plant a spy in such a prosperous company, and as for bandits, the
havoc they could wreak with an agent on the inside to feed them information did not bear thinking about. Yet, despite all this, the caravan leader
accepted Andovan into his company, with little argument. Only a witch
could have caused that great a turn of heart.

Yet it had not occurred to Andovan to ask about such things, or even to suspect that she might have power, until the first long day of travel was over. There was enough to think about before that point. He had agreed to serve as scout, a position which suited his natural talents well, but it had him riding ahead of the caravan most of the time, so there was little opportunity to focus on the mystery he had named Lianna. Or to strike up a closer relationship with her, for whatever that might lead to.

The caravan was a large one, comprised of the companies of two experienced men: Netando's retinue—flanked by black-skinned warriors from his homeland who looked fierce enough not only to take on an army of bandits, but to tear the flesh from their bones with their very teeth—and that of a Sudlander named Ursti, whose cargo of spices permeated the air surrounding the company with an odd and often distracting combination of smells. He also had guards, but they were disguised as simple servants, and drove the wagons and handled the goods as if they were no more than common workmen delivering a load of wood or stone to the nearest building site. Hopefully anyone observing the company would underestimate the true force it had at its disposal, Andovan thought, and if bandits attacked, they would walk into a trap. It was a strategy noticeably at odds with Netando's own, which was designed for a deterrent effect, and he wondered that the two had made arrangements to travel together, given the disparity.

But they were heading into the highlands, a dangerous area by any measure, and no doubt the company of another well-armed merchant along the trip was worth overlooking a few points of disagreement. Roving bands of thieves were a danger in any realm, but in the twisting mountain roads of the Highlands travelers had to be doubly wary. Indeed, if both Netando and Ursti had not had trade goods they wished to purchase which were only available in that region, they would likely not travel there at all.

But they did, and so Andovan spent the first few day of the journey ranging far ahead with the other scouts, looking for signs that someone was taking an interest in the caravan. It was exhausting work, given his condition, and made all the more exhausting by the fact that he was determined to let no man see his weakness. But it was also a task that played to his strengths as a woodsman, and several times he was able to read meaning into patterns of scraped bark and trampled earth, where his companions could only point and say, "Look, something has been here."

Thus far there was no trouble, and all the signs of human passage in the lands surrounding them were old. Perhaps the goddess Lianna was watching over him?

He hadn't told the witch Lianna the whole of the goddess' myth; he wondered if she knew it. Each spring, it was said, Lianna came down to earth to do battle with her half-brother Umbar, who claimed dominion over the world during the winter months. The sheer force of their confrontation shook the very ground men stood upon, and the northlands resounded with the agonized groans of Umbar's ice as it was split into shards by the convulsions of the earth beneath and carried away in pieces by chill, swift-running rivers. Yet even so Lianna's triumph was not complete, for the earth was still cold, and in the end she must come to her half-brother's bed and seduce him, so that the heat of their passion might warm the earth, and allow the bright summer sun to claim the sky for a season.

Personally, Andovan suspected that the god of winter had long ago resigned himself to his yearly defeat, and kept up the fight at this point simply because it won him the lady's sexual favors . . . but that was another story.

What a mystery this mortal Lianna was! How she obsessed him, in the hours they traveled! And when he finally heard Netando make mention of her witchery the force of his obsession trebled. Who was she, really? Why was she part of this odd company? At first he had thought that she was somehow connected to the mystery of his illness, but no, his gut instinct assured him that was not the case. Wouldn't Colivar's spell have alerted him if it were? Then for a short while he had thought that she and Netando might be lovers (and he'd felt a surprising spark of jealousy over the matter), but now that he'd had a chance to observe them more closely he did not think that was so either. Did she have an interest in Andovan? His masculine ego would have been happy to believe it, but he was never quite sure. Not that there weren't moments he knew such a thing was on her mind. He could tell it by the brief flash of heat in her eyes when she spoke to him, the lingering of her touch upon his arm, and the thousand and one other nuances of a woman's desire that an attractive young prince learned to read at an early age. Yet, just as clearly, no door was being opened for him. She might spark his interest with a brief hint of fire, but then it was as quickly gone, and all the walls of her spirit were like fortified steel again.

She had been hurt badly, at least once. He had seen it before in women and knew the signs. And if his guess about the child in the Third Moon was right, and this witch had also been manhandled at a young age . . . it was little wonder she did not trust men. Or take lightly the thought of bedding one of them.

That in itself was enticing, in a strange and somewhat disturbing way. He had grown up in a world where women were easy conquests, if not falling for his masculine charms outright, then to the dual seductions of wealth and power that he embodied. He could probably have bedded any woman he chose, save perhaps those princesses of such high rank that their marital favors could alter the fates of nations . . . and even in those cases there was often room to maneuver, providing the outward signs of chastity remained undisturbed.

Yet here was a woman he could not even court openly as a woman, lest he be labeled a sodomite . . . a woman who was clearly intrigued by him, but not necessarily in a way he comprehended or desired . . . a woman who had been injured in the past, so that one wrong move might cause her to withdraw into herself, behind such barriers as no mere prince could ever breach. It was all strangely enticing. Energizing, even. It even seemed to him that when she touched him something of his accustomed strength flowed back into his limbs, and his skin tingled with a mysterious heat. Was that witchery? Or just his overactive imagination? All he knew was that he had not had any real interest in a woman since his illness had begun, and feeling all those instincts come alive again inside him was like emerging from a dark, dank cave into the blinding light of day.

Not that he had much of a chance to explore such possibilities. She apparently did not know how to ride, and so established a perch for herself upon the driver's seat of Netando's own carriage, from which she commanded a view of the entire caravan. When the scouts were being briefed she caught Andovan's eye, and an enigmatic smile hinted at secrets that might be revealed if only there were a private place to share such things. But there wasn't, and she knew it. Maddening.

They spent the first day traveling hard, making progress as quickly as they could through the rocky foothills, anxious to reach the heights before nightfall. The road grew narrower and steeper by the hour, and the air grew colder as well as they moved up into higher latitudes. After the stifling heat of the shoreline, it was a relief to all but the black-skinned Durbanas, who gathered cloaks around themselves tightly and muttered invectives about the "northlands." As if they had any real idea what the northlands were truly like, Andovan thought.

Thus far there was no real danger of ambush, as the terrain did not favor concealment, but Netando was not a man to take chances, and so Andovan and the other scouts were ordered to ride on ahead of the party, spreading out on all sides to inspect the nearby terrain while the caravan laboriously followed. The road was precarious and narrow and bent back on itself more times than Andovan cared to count, but the scouts on their horses forged directly up the slope and thus secured the heights well before the rest of the caravan caught up to them. There they rested, surrounded by the charred circles of dozens of past campfires, and the ruins of an inn which had apparently been burned to the ground after its owner was caught passing information on to the bandits of the region. The ruins had been left in their current state as a warning to those who might follow him, which was all very well and good as a dramatic statement but it did not make for convenient traveling. A caravan entering the highlands in summertime was hard pressed to make it to the first shelter along the route by sunfall; a caravan in any other season would not stand a chance of it.

How beautiful the sunset was, viewed from the crest of the mountains! Here there was no screen of trees to mask the horizon, only barren, windswept ridges, over whose western edge the full glory of the sun god's descent could be appreciated. It was much more stunning than the view approaching Gansang. Or perhaps he had simply not bothered to appreciate the beauty of Gansang's sunsets, with Colivar's spells driving him to distraction. Now . . . either those spells were gone or they had somehow been transformed into a subtler power that was satisfied to see him moving in the right direction without the need for constant prodding. That should be a relief to him. Shouldn't it? Or was his strange attraction to the redhead "boy" witch making him lose sight of his true purpose?

Colivar said his spell would guide me for as long as I needed it. If it has faded now, then I no longer need it. Which means my quarry is likely in Sankara, or somewhere on the route there. So I am heading in the right direction.

What if his quarry was the Witch-Queen herself? Now that was a chilling thought. Colivar had assured him she was not the one behind his

sickness, but Colivar was his father's enemy and could only be trusted so
far. The political tension between Danton and Siderea was well known, as
was Danton's hunger to extend his influence into the prosperous Free
Lands, and the latter's determination to keep him out. Could the Witch-
Queen have used her power to weaken Andovan as part of some byzan-
tine plot to bring Danton down? Or perhaps simply to distract him, so
that he wasted his royal energies seeking a cure for his son instead of plot-
ting the annexation of Sankara?

If so, Andovan would know it as soon as he saw her. He was sure of that
now. He remembered how strong Colivar's power had been outside
Gansang, the last time his quarry was close by, and had no doubt that
when the day came when he actually stood before the source of his disease
he would recognize her instinctively, as certainly as a salmon knew the
pool in which it was spawned.

And then what? he wondered.

It was still a long way to Sankara. There would be plenty of time to
come up with a plan before he got there, he told himself. Though it made
his blood run cold to think that his adversary might not only command
witchery, but political power as well. Still he was a prince himself, and not
without his resources if he chose to reclaim them, and once he knew who
and what he was fighting he could make the appropriate choices.

The sun was nearly gone by the time they reached their destination,
and Andovan's strength was nearly gone as well. The inn Netando had
brought them to was a far cry from a warm, welcoming lodge like the
Third Moon. This stone hostel was perched on the crest of a bare granite
ridge overlooking a cliffside so steep that only a few scraggly bushes had
managed to cling to its surface. A wide stone wall with a fortified gate secured the southern side of the property, but only that side; in all other directions the ground was so treacherous that approach by armed men
would have been all but impossible.

Nevertheless, Andovan took note of the high watchtower that commanded a view of the entire crest and its surroundings, and a low, crenellated barricade running along the cliff's edge, which would offer
protection for archers should they be required.

That the caravan was expected was obvious. A servant opened the
heavy gate for them as soon as their name was given, and Netando showed

some papers to the armed men who guarded it. After a moment they waved the whole company into the courtyard, and horse by horse, wagon by wagon, the company passed between the narrow gates.

Inside was a courtyard flanked by stables and barracks, clearly designed to accommodate such groups as this. The hostel itself was built out of stone, and seemed to rise out of the granite slabs beneath it like some natural protrusion. With his father's eye Andovan assessed its defensive capacity, and nodded his approval to see the slate tiles that guarded its roof, the narrow windows that faced the courtyard, and a pair of main doors heavy enough to keep all but the most determined intruders from entering. The owners did not expect trouble to breach the outer wall, but if it did, they were prepared to deal with it. Andovan was willing to bet there were siege tunnels as well, probably ending up somewhere far down the side of that cliff, out of sight of the walled property.

All of which did not come cheaply. He saw Netando and Ursti turn over sizeable purses to the owner, who accepted them without counting their contents. Of course. No experienced merchant would dare to cheat this man, not if he wanted such shelter available to him on future journeys.

Then he tried to dismount from his horse, and that took enough effort that everything else faded from view. He nearly stumbled when he hit the ground and was forced to lean against the animal's flank for a brief moment, catching his breath, before he could move on.

Be grateful for small things, he told himself. *You did not black out during the ride. You still have enough strength to stand upright. You made a reasonable show of strength while out on patrol, so that the others will not know you for the sickly, pitiful creature you are.*

He managed to get through the motions of stabling his mount, though his feet were so numb that he stumbled several times. Someone said something about food being laid out in the main building soon. Someone else said something about a billet being provided for him in the barracks. It was all a blur.

Then *she* walked by, and somehow his stubborn Aurelius pride managed to stiffen his backbone enough that for a brief moment he looked like the hearty and healthy young man he was pretending to be.

"The heat has faded, it seems." Her smile was a thing of shadows and secrets.

"Some heat never fades," he responded, and he managed to keep what he hoped was an equally enigmatic smile upon his face until she had passed him by and disappeared into the inn . . . at which point he would have fallen to the ground had not a passing Durbana caught him by the arm and held him upright.

"Taste for boys, eh?" The guard's grin gleamed whitely in the gathering darkness; the sweet scent of sardo root spiced his breath. "Or only witches?"

Before Andovan could get over his surprise and answer, another guard clapped that one on the shoulder. "What do you care? I hear your father sodomizes pigs."

"I hear your mother suckles them."

"I'm all right," Andovan told them. "Really."

The black man snorted. "Demons feed on liars, s'maar. You look like death. Go sleep for an hour, you will thank me. Food will not come for at least that long."

He had other things to do, he wanted to say. A woman to follow. Enticements to whisper. A private corner to be found somewhere where he and she could talk quietly, without half the caravan gathering round to listen and make ribald jokes about it.

But even thinking about doing those things made his head hurt. The man was right. He needed to rest a bit before doing anything else. An hour would do it.

Somehow he found the place he had been assigned to sleep, and the worn straw mattress that had been set aside for him. Then he lay down and shut his eyes and finally, gratefully, surrendered to exhaustion.

Someone woke him up later in the night to bring him food and drink. One of the black men. He couldn't see which one it was, in the darkness, but he was grateful.

He dreamed strange dreams in which he was surrounded by men from the caravan. He was standing naked among them, but no one seemed to notice. For some odd reason that pleased him.

He did not awaken again until morning.

———

It was wet and dreary when they left the next day, with a fine mist that hung heavy in the air, soaking everything that was exposed to it. Kamala thought Netando might ask her to banish it, which would have put her in the awkward position of refusing his first request. Ethanus had taught her to have a healthy respect for the long-term ramifications of weather-work, and besides, no real witch would be willing to expend the kind of energy it took to banish rain, especially just to make traveling more comfortable. But apparently Netando understood that, for though he looked pointedly at the dismal landscape ahead and then at her, as if giving her the opportunity to volunteer her services, he said nothing about it.

In such conditions the scouts and the guards had less than perfect visibility, so Kamala took up her station beside the driver of Netando's coach rather than inside, where it was dry. She could have caused the rain to pass to either side of the coach, leaving her and the driver protected, but again, no real witch would waste her power like that. So she settled for a subtle spell to keep the wool of her cloak dry while she drew the hood forward over her head, a one-time application of sorcery that was minimal in its cost, and focused her special senses on the road ahead.

Talesin looked miserable, though he was trying hard to hide it. The dreary weather seemed to sap his energy even more than usual, and she could see what a strain it was for him to maintain a façade of strength in front of the other guards. She had wanted to take him aside the night before and seek the cause of his weakness—there were few things she could not cure for him, if she set her mind to it—but Fate had been unobliging. *Tonight*, she promised him silently. *Whatever your illness is, I will find the cause and deal with it.* She owed him that much for the little girl he had saved . . . especially now that she understood he had not been strong enough to defend himself in the Third Moon, should any of the men have chosen to challenge him. It was, all things considered, a rather remarkable display of courage.

He was not a man used to being weak, she guessed that much. He had the instinctive body language of one who was accustomed to his own strength and took that strength for granted. She was intrigued by the contradictory mystery of it, and oddly pleased by the sparkle in his eye as he touched a finger to his forehead in leave-taking as a gentleman might, before riding off into the mists ahead. Why had he not sought her out the night before? Had she misread his intentions? She had waited for hours to see him, had stayed up long into the night amid interminable tales of battles won and financial markets conquered, just on the chance he might come to the inn to find her, but he never appeared. Later she took a walk in the courtyard to see if he was there, in the shadows, but the shadows were empty, too.

She could not ask after him without revealing more about the two of them than she wanted the others to know, so in the end she had simply retired to the room she'd been assigned. There were several other men from the company in it. Netando had seemed less than certain she would accept that, but she knew the hostel was being strained to capacity by the double caravan, and besides, it meant very little to her who was sleeping in what room. She had wrapped such spells around her person that the others would persist in seeing her as a boy even if she suckled a babe in front of them. She even tested the matter by taking off all her clothes and standing in the middle of the room when it was her turn at the wash basin. One of the men made a crude joke about the pubic hair of young men— it made no sense to her but was clearly some kind of traditional male humor—but no one else even looked at her twice. It was an odd rush of power to fool them so easily, trivial but pleasing.

In the morning there was no chance to seek out a private rendezvous, only time to eat, cast a quick divining to see if anything was waiting outside the gates to devour them (nothing was), and then each man took up his station again, with her at one end of the company and Talesin at the other.

They followed a road along the crest of the ridge for several hours, while ahead of them the thickening mist obscured any sight of the coming terrain. After a time Netando ordered the scouts in close, knowing there was not much that human eyes could accomplish in such a fog. Witchery was another thing. Kamala knew from the maps Netando had shown her that they would soon be flanked by steep mountains, at which point their road would turn downward, into a network of valleys and seasonal riverbeds that connected the few navigable passes. It was in this region that the danger of assault was highest, particularly in those narrow passages where the caravan must spread out thinly, and where the danger of flash floods was as pressing in this season as any threat bandits had to offer. Checking for the floods was an easy thing for her, as the the one that might threaten them in an afternoon was clearly in the making that morning, and might easily be detected. Not so with human intentions. Divination was the most difficult of all the sorcerous arts, as one could only foresee the possible outcome of fates that had already been set in motion, but she made a good show of it. If someone was planning to strike at Netando's caravan in specific, and had made plans accordingly, she might be able to catch wind of that. If it was anything less specific she was not so sure . . . but there was no reason Netando had to know that.

They stopped for a brief rest break at midday. Netando's retainers quickly erected a few large canopies, so that the travelers might have a break from the incessant drizzle. At least the surrounding mountains now offered a partial shield against the wind. Ursti's men made doubly sure of the oilskin covers over his wagons, beneath which precious spices and perfume stuffs huddled in their wax-sealed caskets, aromas dampened by the fog.

Soon they were moving again, and as if to mark the event, rain began in earnest. Kamala kept one sorcerous ear attuned to the movement of distant groundwater, and at one point suggested Netando lead the caravan to higher ground. He obeyed her without question. It was an odd feeling of power, to direct the lives of men so casually. But it was also tiring to need to be so perpetually alert to everything around her, not only the possible movements of men in the distance but the fall of rain, the shifting of mud . . . after hours of travel she had to fight to keep her focus.

She almost missed the light when it appeared.

At first she blinked, not quite sure what she had seen. The rain was a silver curtain ahead of her, which made it hard to pick out details of anything more than a few yards away. But it seemed to her that there was something in the road ahead of them, not so much a solid construct as . . . well, light. A strange light, that seemed to come from nowhere, and cast no shadows.

She hesitated a moment, then banged on the side of the carriage to alert Netando. "Stop the horses," she said. The driver looked over at her, startled, but he wouldn't stop the carriage until his master commanded it. "Stop them!" she cried, loudly enough to carry clearly even in the rain-drenched air.

Netando opened the shutters and leaned out to look at her. Either his respect for her powers was very high, or perhaps it was the expression on her face that moved him to urgency. He called out some words in an unknown tongue and his driver reined up the horses suddenly, nearly throwing Kamala from her seat. The black-skinned guards did the same, as the order passed through their ranks like a wave. Ursti's men followed suit, wooden wheels churning up mud as the ponderous wagons ground to a halt.

"What is it?" Netando asked her.

"I am not sure yet." Eyes still fixed on the strange light ahead of them, she climbed down from her perch. The ground beneath her feet was the consistency of swamp muck, making her reflect upon the fact that this was yet another good day not to be wearing women's clothing. Carefully she wended her way to the front of the line, all her senses focused upon a place some ten yards beyond the lead riders. Their horses stamped nervously as she passed them by, sensing something was wrong, but not sure how to deal with it.

By the time she reached the place where the ground was alight, she had figured out that the others could not see what she did. That should not have been a surprise to her, really. Since her earliest days she had been gifted with the Sight, and even before she had begun to study sorcery with Ethanus, she had been able to see traces of power where witches and Magisters had practiced their arts.

She was looking at such traces now.

The muddy ground glowed with power. The trees surrounding were marked by it also, as if some phosphorescent moss had sheathed their trunks. Even the leaves overhead glistened with something more luminous than raindrops, though it was hard to make out details through the omnipresent mist. Clearly some kind of spell had been cast in this place, probably upon the ground itself, though it had later saturated much of the surrounding plant life as well. Who would do such a thing in the middle of nowhere? What was its purpose?

Hesitantly—aware that the guards were all watching her now—she reached out a hand into the affected area. The power was warm to her touch, and tasted of witchery. Otherwise it had no effect upon her. Perhaps some kind of alarm would be raised when someone entered it? She took a step forward, all her sorcerous senses alert, ready to strike down any outgoing power before it could reach its destination. But there was no response. The mud beneath her feet felt just like the mud near Netando's carriage. The rain was the same. Whatever spells had been woven here had clearly served their purpose long ago; no active power remained that should be of any concern to those she was protecting.

She took another few minutes to inspect the place thoroughly, warning the morati not to follow her—Netando had come up to the front of the line now, with Ursti scurrying close behind—but she could find no cause for concern. The affected area apparently continued on for another hundred yards or so and then ended, as suddenly and inexplicably as it had begun. Nowhere along the length of that distance was any active power triggered by her presence. In fact, as far as she could tell, there was no threat of *any* kind in the immediate vicinity, including that of bandits. Netando's fears about this stretch of road had clearly been unfounded. The caravan would be safe until nightfall, when the walls of another hostel would shelter it, and in the morning they would put both the rain and this treacherous passage behind them.

She turned back to the company and gave them a reassuring nod. The guards—who had watched her exploring nothing for quite some time now—did not look very reassured. She caught Talesin's eye—he was watching her with frank fascination—and then, as she exited the enchanted area, Netando's own.

"Old witchery," she told him. She reached up a hand to wave the company on—

And froze.

"What is it?" Ursti asked. "What's wrong?"

There was power glowing faintly along her own skin. It was a subtle thing that even a Magister's eyes might have missed, but Kamala had grown up with the Sight and could not mistake it.

It is nothing to worry about, an inner voice whispered.

Whatever that strange enchantment was that had seemed so inert when she inspected it, it had left its mark upon her. But how? For a moment the question concerned her, and then . . . then all worry faded from her mind, and a strange but compelling conviction took its place. This was nothing to worry about. Really. It was no more than the whispering vestige of a spell long since depleted, incapable of doing any damage to current travelers.

"Kovan?" It was Netando. He sounded worried. He shouldn't be worried. Everything was exactly as it should be. She would tell him that.

She stared at her hand for a moment, blinking hard. Alien power. What had Ethanus taught her? *Any time you see evidence that a foreign power has touched you, cleanse yourself immediately. Even if you do not feel the need. Make it so fixed a habit that no reason or emotion can dissuade you. The best spells will always include a component to effect your judgment.*

It was not needed, she told herself. There was nothing wrong.

"Kovan? Is something amiss?" Netando was coming toward her now. She waved him back. Still staring at her hand.

Do it even if you do not feel the need, Ethanus had taught her.

He knew sorcery better than she did, she told herself. And more important, he knew *her.*

Make it a fixed habit.

Closing her eyes, she drew forth power from her soul—which in turn was drawn from her consort's soul, in some distant, unnamed place—and let it flow outward through her flesh, driving out the vestiges of this foreign power. It did not work as easily as she had expected. The spell had affixed itself to her like a second skin and did not wish to be dislodged. In another time and place that might have alarmed her—and she knew in the back of her mind that it would have alarmed Ethanus, had he been witness to it—but still she was sure the power was not malevolent, merely . . . tenacious. She exerted more effort, but still the foreign power held true. *You are upset over nothing,* an inner voice chided. *It will fade in time on its own. You saw for yourself it has no current purpose.*

But she knew what Ethanus would say to that—*When you doubt the need the most it is when the need is greatest*—and so she persisted. In the end she had to send a wave of power surging down her limbs that burned so fiercely in her flesh it was visible even to the morati. Her eyes half-open now, she could see the morati company standing slack-jawed as they watched her, her arms extended as if to welcome them, sorcerous flames lapping at her skin, seemingly unaffected by the rain now pouring down upon her.

Then at last she was done. Cleansed. Thoughts that a moment ago had seemed impossible raced through her head with sudden clarity. She let her own power fade.

She looked at Netando. His eyes, too, were wide with wonder, even perhaps fear. Considering how many strange things he must have seen in his travels, it was an odd sort of compliment to her power.

"There is a spell upon this place," she said. "Any who pass through it will be blinded to danger, no matter what form it takes." *Most certainly not inert,* she thought. *How could I have been fooled so easily?* "The purpose of such a thing is obvious, yes?"

Netando nodded shortly. "So you think there is a reception committee waiting on the opposite side?"

She thought she knew the answer to that, but tested it anyway, casting her power in a net around the affected area, rather than through it. "No," she said at last. "Not right there. They will want to be farther on down the road, so that the whole of a caravan can pass through this area without any chance of detecting them. After that, even the most obvious signs of trouble would be missed, and as for the effect of this witchery upon warriors . . ." She shrugged suggestively.

Ursti's expression was a dark and terrible thing. Netando cursed under his breath.

"Too late to turn aside," the spice merchant said. "We're well past any place where the road divides."

Netando nodded, and studied the rising slopes on both sides of them. They were steep and rocky, and now covered with patches of slippery mud as well. "The horses and men can flank this area, with effort." He looked at Kamala. "How far does the enchantment extend?"

"About a hundred paces forward. Half that in width, I would judge. Add a bit more to be on the safe side."

"The wagons cannot climb that hill," Ursti pointed out.

"Can you banish it?" Netando asked. "Or, how do they say . . . unweave it?"

Kamala hesitated. As a Magister she could. A witch, however, would not admit to such capacity. The cost of such a cleansing would be high, too high, measured in whole days of life, even weeks, rather than minutes. Netando would know that. Any man with a brain would know that.

"I cannot," she lied. "It is too deeply entrenched. I am sorry."

Netando nodded again.

"The wagons must go straight through," Ursti said. "The horses should as well; they will not like the ground in this condition."

"Both those things require men to guide them," Netando pointed out.

"I can protect a few men," Kamala said. "Not the whole company, but a few."

Netando studied the road ahead with narrowed eyes. For all he knew the place was utterly devoid of power, and Kamala was just playing them all for fools. Except he would not think anything like that. The spell she had cast upon him did not allow for him to doubt her.

I was almost entrapped by such a spell myself. The thought was chilling. For the first time now she understood the purpose of lessons Ethanus had drilled into her that had seemed like wasted effort at the time. In a world where sorcery so easily reshaped the world, one's own mind might be turned to an enemy's purpose. No Magister would do that to another—it was against their Law—but witches were not bound by any such contract.

"Very well," Netando said at last. "The guards will go around on foot. The rest will stay on the road. It won't hurt the horses to be less afraid of danger . . . nothing depends upon their judgment." To the scouts he said, "Fan out, and see to the high ground. There will be an ambush waiting for us beyond this, probably not far down the road. I want to find them before they find us."

The drivers were not all that happy about that plan, but they followed their masters' orders. Some muttered prayers or fingered protective amulets while Kamala wove her own spells about them. They were even less happy about entering an enchanted area. Kamala mused dryly that she should have made her spells less than perfect, so that the power in the place would calm their nerves.

"You understand what this implies," she said quietly to Netando, as he stood beside her to oversee the operation.

He looked at her, eyebrow raised.

"They may have a witch present."

She saw him grind his teeth slowly as he digested that new piece of information. "I did not bring you here to enjoin battle," he said finally, "but rather to avoid it."

She said nothing.

At the end of the column of guards came Talesin. His face was a pasty white and his hands trembled where he held the reins. It looked like whatever fragile strength had sustained him thus far was finally waning. *Just make it through this day,* she thought to him. *I will take you aside tonight and heal you, I promise. Forgive me that it was not yesterday.*

How strange it was, to care if someone lived or died. Even before her apprenticeship she had not invested much energy in caring about people. It hurt too much when they left her. The last time she had truly mourned a death was when her brother died, and even back then her tears had been mixed with rage at all the people and things that had caused it. This was a quieter feeling. Haunting. Unfamiliar.

You cannot afford to care for any morati. You know that.

She saw him struggle up the muddy slope, his stubborn pride refusing to let him accept any aid along the way. And then he was lost to her sight in the mists, and she had to climb the slope as well, and for a while that took all her attention.

———

The crest of the ridge was more solid than its flank, thank the gods. Andovan stopped there for a moment, bent over double as he struggled to catch his breath. He had felt reasonably good that morning, after his long night's sleep, and that made it doubly frustrating that now his strength was leaving him again. Just when it looked like they might be heading into a fight, too. Not good at all.

When he thought he could stand upright without passing out he joined the others once more. Netando's guards had been sent ahead to clear out trouble before the caravan got there. Ursti's men had remained behind in case some secondary assault targeted the wagons. Andovan could probably have stayed with the latter group if he'd asked—he hadn't signed on as warrior, after all—but that meant letting Lianna see how utterly enfeebled he had become.

No, he thought dryly, *much better to march into battle in such a state.*

Damn the Aurelius pride!

He'd been all right that morning. He'd even felt somewhat optimistic about the journey when they first started out. The Wasting gave him good days and bad days, and this had promised to be one of the good ones.

But then when they had stopped so that Lianna could inspect the road the strength had run out of his veins like ale from a punctured keg, until it was all he could do to stand upright. He didn't want her to see him like that. So instead he was clambering up this rocky, muddy slope, to a place where he could slink through a rain-drenched forest to sneak up on well-armed brigands who might or might not have a witch with them. Much, much better choice.

You're an idiot, Andovan, you know that?

Lianna had located the brigands with her witchery, and had used Netando's maps of the region to show the captain of the guard where they were likely to be hiding. He in turn had sketched out various avenues of approach based upon what little they could observe of the terrain from their vantage point. His plan was for a force to come up behind the outlaws and engage them, in the hopes that their rear was unguarded. If they chose to withdraw to safety, it would most likely be along a narrow trail leading south from their current position, in which case a second team would pick them off as they fled.

Which all sounded very well and good, but when you added a witch into the equation just about anything could happen.

Including the fact that he might leave his allies to flounder, Andovan reminded himself. The difference between a witch and a Magister was that the former had to expend a portion of his own life essence for every single spell. How likely was it that the same person who had set up the enchantment on the road would be crouching in the rain now, ready to trade a few more days of his life for another handful of foreign coins? If it was Andovan, he'd be relaxing in a tavern in Sankara right now with what he'd been paid for the first enchantment, not crouching in the mud tempting fate.

They asked him to follow along the crest of the ridge and seek out any sentries that had been assigned to the highest watch points. He was fortunate and there were none to be found. He did not want to admit to the other men that he no longer had strength enough to take down a single man, though he feared that was the truth. But the gods, for once, were merciful to him, and it was one of the black Durbana that located the brigands' sentries and dispatched them. The killing was swift and silent; any signs of disturbance that might otherwise have been noticed were swallowed up by the wind and the rain.

Watching Netando's men at work, Andovan began to wonder if their master was simply the wandering merchant he appeared to be, or whether this whole expedition had been staged to draw out the thieves of the region so they could be dealt with for once and for all. That would also explain Ursti's men, who were so perfectly outfitted to remain with the caravan and make it look unprotected. They had not had need of such a ruse with Lianna along, since she was able to pinpoint the enemy's position, but without her they would have needed such tricks to draw the enemy to them.

Of course if she had not been with them, if they had stayed on the road, they would have ignored all signs of danger up until the minute their throats were cut. No matter how skilled they were.

Lightning flashed across the sky overhead, and thunder rumbled hard enough to shake the ground as the small company of guards moved into position surrounding their targets. The ambush site the brigands had chosen was a steep slope spotted with ancient pines and tangled brush that offered a combination of excellent cover and clear access to the road below. Granite ridges shouldered through the earth here and there, and it was behind such barriers that the thieves crouched now, waiting for their quarry to come into range. On the far side of the road the ground dropped away precipitously, disappearing into the mists of a narrow ravine; if the route were blockaded up ahead, the travelers would have nowhere to run. With a chill, Andovan realized that these thieves did not merely intend to drive off the merchants and claim their goods, but to kill off the whole of the company so that no one might report their fate.

Little wonder the hostels in the area were so well fortified.

Black-faced, dressed in garments the color of the surrounding forest, Netando's men were all but invisible as they took up their positions surrounding the brigands. The latter were clearly focused upon the coming caravan now, no doubt trusting to their sentries to warn them if there was trouble. A fatal mistake. One could hear the horses approaching in the distance, and Ursti's men were making the kind of noise that men did when they had no reason to be quiet. With a lurching feeling in his gut, Andovan realized that Lianna was probably still with them on the road, riding into the ambush even now.

She is a witch, he told himself. *She can take care of herself.*

The rain was growing heavier now, with gusts of wind that threatened to throw off Andovan's aim. He breathed in deeply as he focused his eye upon the targets before him, telling himself that at this close range he should be able to take down a thief as easily as he had once felled deer. But these were not deer, were they? Andovan wondered if the thought of killing men as casually as he had once hunted game should bother him, but he did not allow his aim to waver. What was it his father had taught him, back when he was a boy? *Being born to royal blood means having the power of life or death over other men. Being worthy of royal blood means accepting that burden.*

Are you proud of me now, my father? he wondered, with a sudden pang of homesickness. *Is this how you would wish me tested?*

Lightning flashed again, so close this time he could feel it tingle along his scalp. Andovan watched as one brigand raised up a hand to warn his fellows back, maybe giving them some kind of instruction, and chose him for his target. He was a tall man, black-haired, dressed in a loose woolen shirt that might be layered over some kind of armor. Not a problem. Andovan fixed his aim upon the back of the man's head, confident in his ability to make the shot even under these conditions. Now there was only the captain's signal to wait for, and he would take his first human life.

Thunder rumbled in the distance.

The voices from the caravan below were closer now.

A brigand raised his hand to signal his men to begin their fire—

—and a quarrel flew from out of the trees, taking that man squarely in the back. A dozen more shots followed. Andovan let fly his own quarrel, clean into his chosen target, with enough force to crack open bone and pierce the brain beneath.

Or so he thought. But instead the wooden bolt shattered as it touched the man, as if it had impacted against some impenetrable armor. The man whipped about even before the last splinters of it had fallen to the ground, seeking the source of the assault, and as Andovan crouched behind his cover, he realized that the eyes that were seeking him out in the rain-dimmed light were something more than human.

He had found the brigands' witch.

Most of the thieves had been hit hard by the first volley, and two were lying facedown in the mud. A few whipped about and fired into the brush behind them, but the majority of the ones that still had their mobility bolted for cover amid the surrounding trees. It was a fatal choice. As soon as they moved from their hiding place they were visible to the caravan below, and Ursti's men, ready and waiting, opened fire upon them. Andovan saw one man spin about as a quarrel took him square in the chest, clean through the heart. But the one Andovan had fired at stood safely in the midst of all that, uninjured. His black eyes burned with hatred as he scanned the surrounding brush, as quarrel after quarrel dashed itself to pieces against the spell that protected him. Each time that happened, Andovan realized, it cost him a moment of life. Little wonder he was seeking out the assailant that had brought such trouble to him.

And then he saw Andovan. It was as if the bushes between them did not even exist. Lightning filled the clearing with molten light, but still those black and terrible eyes remained fixed upon him. The prince could see the man whispering, now, and with a sinking feeling in his gut he realized the witch was gathering his power for an assault. How could he stand up to such a thing, in his weakened state? In better days he might have hurtled toward the man in a desperate attempt to bring him down before his spell was completed, but that was not an option in his current state. He backed away, looking desperately for cover—

And then *she* appeared.

Her cap had fallen off and her red hair spread out like a fiery corona, despite the rain. She walked amid the fallen thieves as if they did not even exist, and when one of them tried to strike out at her, the sharp crack of breaking bone was so loud that Andovan could hear it from where he stood. The man cried out and fell back, clutching his arm in agony. Unexpectedly, Andovan felt her witchery in his own gut, as if a red-hot knife had rent open his stomach at the same moment. For a moment he doubled over, and the world rushed dizzily around him as he struggled not to vomit. Was her power so strong that it was affecting more than her targets? Fighting to focus upon the scene before him, Andovan saw that the black-haired man had summoned his power, which swirled like a maelstrom about his fingertips, and was about to strike—

—and *her* eyes burned as she raised her hand, reaching upward toward the stormy skies as if directing some greater power to assist—

—and lightning crashed down into the clearing with deafening force, throwing Andovan back upon the muddy earth. The whole of the world blazed white-hot for an instant, and the ground shook beneath him as he discovered he could no longer move; the last of his strength had finally left him. For one brief and terrible moment images flashed before him, seared into his brain: the brigands' witch reduced to a pile of charred flesh. Lianna's eyes fixed upon him with a terrible intensity. Netando's men rushing forward, swords drawn, to finish the job they had started.

But the feeling faded from his limbs even as the light faded from his eyes, and despite his best efforts to hold onto consciousness, he could sense the world losing substance about him and a cold, nameless darkness taking its place. What if this was the last time? What if he never awakened?

Lianna!

———————

"Bring him over here."

The guard who was carrying Talesin down the hill almost lost his footing in the blood-slicked mud, but Kamala did not use her power to help him. She stood like a statue, watching in silence. She would not use sorcery again until she was sure what had just happened.

A chill ran down her spine as she remembered the look in Talesin's eyes. The way his strength had left his body at the exact moment she had drawn upon her power. Surely she was wrong about what had caused it. Surely it was . . . something else.

"Is that all of them?" Netando asked her. The guards had been hunting down the last of the thieves; bodies were being piled up beside the road.

She nodded without looking, not wishing to be distracted. Let him assume that she had divined the answer, as opposed to merely guessing. They were still awed by the magnitude of power she had unleashed on their behalf, and not likely to question her. Foolish morati! The lightning had already been in the making, thanks to the weather; the only "witchery" required was to attune one man to it, so that the coming bolt chose him for a target.

Darkness flickered about the boundaries of her soul as she remembered Talesin's collapse. She recognized that darkness from her dreams, and the blood ran cold in her veins. It was the touch of the abyss. Hungry for her, as it was for all Magisters. Waiting to devour her the moment she doubted her chosen path.

You should help search for any thieves who escaped this trap. Focus on the future. Let him die.

But she was only guessing what had felled him. She needed to know for sure. Even if that brought her to the very edge of the abyss, even if it threatened to push her over the edge . . . she needed to *know*.

"I see no blood on him," said one of the guards. The whole of Talesin's body was dripping with mud, but there was but no red in it that Kamala could see either. "But he's out cold, that's for sure."

"I will see to him," Kamala said. She looked around for a place to have him put the body down, so that she could inspect it. But there was nothing surrounding her except a chaos of men cleaning their weapons, tending to the wounded, stripping the enemy dead. No private corner in which to seek enlightenment.

"Over there." It was Ursti. "You can use the last wagon, there's some room in it."

She looked to where he was pointing, then nodded for the guard carrying Talesin to follow her. The wagon was far down the line, indistinguishable from half a dozen others piled high with Ursti's trade goods. She loosened the back of the oilcloth cover and lifted it up, revealing an open channel between tightly bound stacks of wooden crates. The smell of saffron and cassia was strong in the confined space.

"Put him in there," she said. It was a narrow area, but large enough to shelter two people so long as no one tried to stand up. She watched as the guard slid Talesin's body gently inside, between the crates, then climbed in after him, affixing the oilcloth cover back in place so that the rain would not splash in on them. There was little light coming in once she had done that . . . but the Sight she needed now did not depend on earthly light.

There were no visible wounds on him, not anywhere. She felt in his mud-soaked hair for the warmth of flowing blood and found none. His limbs were whole and uninjured. No matter how she searched, she could find no sign of what had struck him down.

Only one thing was possible.

She remembered him standing there, when she had summoned the lightning. He'd been watching her. She remembered the look on his face as the color had drained from him suddenly, as his eyes went blank and then fell shut . . . as the very life in his veins had been squeezed out of him by some giant fist, and then what was left had crumpled to the ground, an empty shell.

Carefully, fearfully, she summoned her sorcerous senses again, begrudging herself the power it took to do even that much. Then she looked inside him: past his blood, past his flesh, past all the organs that were laboring to sustain his life . . . into the heart of his soul. The place where his spirit should be blazing. The core of his mortal strength.

Dying embers.

Darkness swirled about her soul as she saw the truth before her. She took a moment to still her heart, to catch her breath, to try to think. *He is a consort,* she told herself. *That does not mean he is necessarily* my *consort.*

But no words could make the truth go away. She had seen the life go out of him when she had conjured her power. She *knew.*

Tentatively, fearfully, she looked within him again. The soulfire that was barely strong enough to sustain a morati life was still hot to her sorcerous touch, and it drew her in like a fire drew in fresh fuel. His living heat flowed into her . . . and she knew in that moment that if she wished to devour him, if she wished to drink in every last bit of his heat in one vast, indulgent, bloody feast, that nothing could stop her. She had that power.

"Lianna?"

His eyes were open now, and fixed on her with an intensity that made her shiver. "What happened?" His voice was a whisper, hardly louder than the pattering of rain on the oilcloth overhead. "Are we . . . did we . . ."

"They're all dead. No casualties on our side, though a few were wounded. Netando's men are cleaning up now."

He tried to sit up. He was weak, very weak. But there was no visible cause for such weakness.

No cause, save that for a short while I drew upon more of his strength than he could spare.

He looked about the small space, a puzzled expression on his face.

"Ursti's wagon," she said.

"Ah. I should have guessed from the smell." He looked up at her again. "Am I wounded?" He said it as if he feared to hear the answer.

Slowly she shook her head. "No." *Not wounded, not by mortal weapons.*

The answer did not seem to comfort him. He laid back his head with a sigh of resignation. "I am sorry," he whispered. "I should have told you. . . ."

She said nothing. It seemed she could hear his heart pounding . . . or perhaps that was her own.

"I suppose I should have told Netando, too, back at the Third Moon . . . but then he would not have let me come with you." He sighed again. "You should know the truth, Lianna, since you saved me. The reason I fell—"

She put a finger to his lips to silence him. "Quiet," she whispered. "Do not say it. I know."

His lips were warm to her touch, so very warm. Was that because of the living soulfire inside him, or did he simply seem warm in contrast to the chill of the abyss that had taken root in her own soul? One wrong thought, one moment of regret over his dying, and she would plummet down into that darkness forever. A terrifying thought.

Her heart was pounding. His life fueled every beat. She could feel it inside her, his strength rushing through her veins, warming her flesh, supporting each breath. She could feel it inside him as well.

His reached up to take her hand from his lips, and whispered, "Were you a woman to the others, as well?"

For a moment she did not realize what he meant. Then she glanced down and saw that the wrappings which normally constrained her breasts had come loose during the battle. The neck of her doublet was open, and as she leaned down over him the natural curves of her body were undisguised. "It doesn't matter," she said softly. "I use spells . . ."

. . . *born of your life force.* She couldn't bring herself to say it.

He reached with his free hand to the edge of her doublet, and ran a finger along the inner curve of her breast. His rain-drenched touch was cold against the warmth of her skin . . . but that was surely not why she shivered. "Yet you use no spells with me."

"No," she whispered. Mesmerized by his voice, his touch. "Not with you."

His hand slipped inside the neck of her doublet, stroking the fullness of her breast. She should have protested—wanted to protest—but she couldn't. It was *his* heat rushing through her veins now. *His* desire making her legs feel weak. His hand caressed her lightly, suggestively, and then, when she offered no resistance, more firmly; he slid his other arm around her and pulled her close to him.

And then he kissed her. She had never allowed a man that liberty before. With all the indignities she had suffered to satisfy male passions, all the manners of degrading services she had sold at various prices, she had never given any man that. How could she explain what such an intimacy meant to her, or why she guarded it so fiercely? For a moment, as his lips touched hers, she stiffened, and she almost drew back from him . . . but then she heard him sigh softly in pleasure, and she tasted the sweat and the sweetness on his lips, and she knew that this was different than anything which men had asked of her before.

"Netando," she breathed. "He will come looking for us—"

"Let him look," he whispered, and he kissed her again. There was an urgency to his touch that could not be denied. Little wonder. He had faced death tonight, and needed to reinforce his ties to life. She could taste the need in him, as powerful a driving force as the hunger to survive. It flowed into her veins as well, along with his athra. Energizing. Intoxicating.

Together they slid down onto the floor of the wagon, until they lay in the narrow crevice between the close-packed crates of spices and perfumes. A fine dust of some red substance, whose crate had been damaged by the rigors of the road, trickled down the back of her neck. Part of her knew that what she was doing was madness; Magisters did not become intimate with their consorts. But the words were empty things, drowned out by the pounding of her heart, and by the growing spark of her own desire.

Slowly, she peeled the sodden cloth of his shirt back from his torso, and ran her fingers over the smoothly muscled flesh beneath. There were scars that cut across his chest, parallel ridges long since healed; touching her lips to them, she tasted the memories they contained. *The joy of freedom. The exhilaration of the hunt. The rush of hot blood as a great beast comes close, too close, but even that pain is a kind of pleasure, an act of communion with one's prey.* It seemed that memories from his entire life shimmered along his skin, and flowed into her as if they were her own when she touched him. Heady memories, which she savored as she ran her tongue slowly along his wounds, drinking in their energy like a fine wine.

Ah, my prince . . . would we have this pleasure to share if you did not belong to me?

Men's voices sounded near the wagon suddenly. For a moment she thought of using her sorcery to make sure no one tried to look in on them, but that would be a poor answer to his passion. Let it be enough that every breath she took was stolen from him, that every heartbeat which re-sounded in her chest meant one less beat would sound in his, that the very heat in her loins was drawn from his own hunger. She would take no more from him than that. Not now.

The owners passed by on their own and the sounds faded. Kamala had not realized until that moment that she'd been holding her breath. Talesin caressed her lips softly as she exhaled and then kissed her again.

"It doesn't matter," he whispered.

They think I am a boy . . . they cannot find us like this . . . Then his hand slid between her thighs, his touch leaving rivers of hunger flowing across her skin. She moaned despite herself and shut her eyes, transported by the sensation. Let the rest of the world be damned. She would drink in this moment for what it was worth, and worry later about the consequences.

Sliding his hands up to her waist, he tried to untie the cords that held her leggings in place. It was a difficult task in such cramped quarters, but boy's wear did not allow the kind of freedom a woman required for love-making, and so they must be taken off. For perhaps the first time in her life Kamala found she regretted not wearing women's clothing; the thought was so unexpected that she laughed softly at herself. Talesin looked up in concern, but she smiled and put a finger to his lips and then followed it with her own kiss, turning his attention back to more pressing issues.

And then the ties at her waist finally came loose, and with trembling hands he slid the leggings down over her hips, over her thighs, free of her legs entirely. She slipped loose the closure of his own breeches, drawing him free from the confining cloth as she parted her thighs to receive him. And then he was quickly inside her, not only his flesh but his spirit as well, his athra surging through her veins anew with every thrust. The sensation was so intense that she almost cried out, but she did not; instead she bit down on her lip so hard that it bled, determined not to make any noise that might draw other people to their hiding place.

And then all those other people ceased to exist, and so did the world they inhabited. And for a short while there was only hunger, and fire, and a pleasure so forbidden it did not even have a name.

———

Peace.

It was a rare and precious thing in his life. A brief time when struggles and fears could be set aside, forgotten. A moment to savor the simple here-and-now of human passion, and drink in the peace that came at the end of it.

The witch Lianna rested against his side, her hand on his chest, breathing in time with his heartbeat as if there was nothing wrong in the world. As if he was not soon to die.

For that one precious moment, he could almost believe it himself.

Thank you, he thought to her. Not knowing how to say the words aloud without feeling foolish. *Thank you for giving me this.*

Voices rose in the distance. He could not say what about them made him suddenly come alert, but Lianna was startled as well. This was not just a few random speakers who happened to be heading in their direction, like before. Some kind of argument was going on, and it was rapidly coming closer.

Quickly he helped her back into her clothing. It wasn't easy in the small space. As they struggled to get her leggings tied back on the voices came closer; with a sinking heart he realized the speakers were heading right towards their wagon. There was no time to restore her disguise, or do anything other than avoid total indecency; if she wanted to convince the men outside she was not a woman she would have to rely upon her witchery for it, for her clothes would no longer serve. Not in their current state.

They will see me coming out of this wagon with a half-dressed boy, he mused, as he pulled his own shirt and breeches back into order. It was darkly amusing.

He didn't loosen the oilcloth cover, but simply slipped out the small opening that Kamala had left. She did the same. Outside, the companies of both merchants seemed to be circling around some new arrival, like nervous hounds that wanted a sniff of a strange new dog but were afraid to get too close. That didn't bother Talesin. Taking her hand, he led her through the outer ranks of the group until they were close enough to see the man about whom the circle had formed. He was tall and slender, with the olive skin and almond eyes of the eastern races. His black clothes were dry despite the rain, as was his long, jet-black hair, and when Andovan looked closely he could see that the rain was not falling in the place where he stood. Everywhere else on the road, but not there. It was the kind of display of power that left no doubt as to what he was, and how dangerous he might be to any man that chose to cross him.

The newcomer's eyes fell upon Andovan then, and it was clear that everyone else in the circle had ceased to be of interest to him. "Ah, you are here after all. These fools insisted you were not."

It took him a minute to find his voice. "Colivar? What are you doing here?"

The Magister glanced at Lianna. It was clear from his expression that he was seeing right through whatever witchery she used to disguise herself, and that didn't leave much question about what had been going on between them. He raised a thin eyebrow but said nothing, asked nothing, merely turned his attention to Andovan once more.

"We need to speak," he said quietly. "In private."

He nodded toward Netando's coach. If Netando had any objections to a Magister commandeering his vehicle, he did not voice them. Smart man.

Andovan wanted to look back at Lianna and reassure her, but he didn't. *Never appear weak before a Magister,* his father had taught him. *They are like wolves beneath those black robes, and will tear a man to pieces if he gives them the opening.*

Knowing himself a prince of royal blood, trying to display the kind of confidence a prince should have, he led the way to Netando's carriage, and did not look back.

Chapter 37

THE INTERIOR of the carriage was dark and musty but passably dry, its seats covered with once-opulent silk cushions that had been beaten flat by the rigors of past journeys. Colivar gestured for Andovan to precede him inside, wanting one last look at this witch his wayward prince had found.

How quietly she stood there. How patient. Not gawking, like the morati were. Not nervous, like the guards were. More . . . defiant. Her eyes glittered like cold, hard diamonds, and in truth they were the only part of her that he could see with any clarity; the spells of disguise that were wrapped around her were too tightly woven—too *skillfully* woven—for him to unravel them without considerable effort. Oh, Andovan's own thoughts had revealed her as a woman, and bore witness to their recent intimacy, but trying to read her directly was like trying to read a book that had been sealed shut. All he could do was study the cover and wonder at the contents.

The spell he had cast on Andovan back in Danton's realm was gone now; that much was clear to Colivar the first moment he saw the young prince. Which meant one of two things: either it had accomplished its purpose and expired naturally, or someone had banished it. Which was the more intriguing possibility? Could this diamond-eyed witch wrapped in the seeming of a young man be the one that all the Magisters were hunting? Parasite of princes, killer of Magisters, perhaps even a sorcerer in her own right? Even asking the question was dangerous, Colivar realized. If Andovan was truly her consort, then any attempt to scrutinize the link between them with sorcery might prove a fatal enterprise. Which is why he had not tried to do so yet.

A strange rush of excitement rippled through his veins at the sight of her. Let morati men drink in their fill of undying love and political passions; such things lost their power to affect a human soul after the tenth, hundredth, even thousandth repetition. For a Magister there was nothing more exciting than novelty, nothing more maddening than a mystery not yet explored. How many centuries had it been since Colivar had last seen something new come into the world? He could not even begin to count. Yet here there was something genuinely new, something that appeared to break all the rules of the world he lived in, perhaps the very first creature of its kind—and he was unable to give her the attention she deserved. Maddening.

If the Souleaters return there will soon be no world in which any of this matters, he reminded himself.

At last, with effort, he turned his eyes from the mysterious woman and stepped into the carriage himself. The shutters were already closed against the rain, leaving a small lantern whose wick had been turned down as the only source of light. In the flickering yellow glow he could see how pale Danton's thirdborn son had become, even by normal measure. Colivar guessed Andovan had lost at least ten pounds since he'd seen him last, and the prince hadn't had that much excess flesh on him to start with. The end was very close.

Kill her and it ends, he mused. How simple the words sounded, now that there was a face to attach the pronoun to. How complex they had suddenly become.

"Why have you come here?" Andovan asked. "Have you found the woman who cursed me? Can I end this search now, and deal with her?"

For a moment Colivar was startled. Then he thought, *He doesn't know.* It seemed an incredible thought, from his vantage point. But the prince did not have any knowledge of the kind of parasitic relationship that was responsible for his condition, nor did he have any way to know that Colivar's spell had served its purpose and expired. Furthermore . . . a delicate inspection with a whisper of power confirmed what the Magister should have suspected from the start. There was a spell woven about Andovan with foreign magic, skillfully crafted, that prevented him from feeling any manner of suspicion toward the woman who was traveling with him.

She was thorough, no question of that.

Her spells were sorcery. Though Colivar's blood ran cold to acknowledge that fact, though the universe he inhabited was shaken to its very roots, there was no mistaking the nature of the power. Cold, it was, like a layer of ice in the arctic sea, slick, frigid water over a glittering black core. Witchery did not feel like that. Witchery did not draw the living heat out of a man until his very soul was frozen. Witches did not toy with a man as he was dying, either. Suddenly their recent sexual dalliance was cast in a new light. Even by Magister standards, the implications were chilling.

Concentrate on the moment, Colivar. Do what must be done.

He drew in a deep breath and said, "Forgive me, Prince Andovan. I did not intend to disturb you during your journey. But things have occurred in your homeland that require your attention. I am sorry to be the one that has to bring you word of it."

Andovan stared at him for a moment as if he was out of his mind. "You mean . . . you want me to go home? Now?"

Colivar nodded.

With a huff Andovan leaned back against the carriage wall. "My father told me all Magisters were mad. It seems he spoke the truth."

A faint smile flickered about Colivar's lips, dry and humorless. "Regardless, Highness, my business is very real."

"Well then." He waved a hand in the air, a vaguely regal gesture. "Tell me about it."

So he did. Slowly at first, making sure Andovan understood the potential gravity of the situation before he went into details. He needn't have bothered. As soon as he said the word "Souleater" the prince stiffened in his seat, and he did not relax again for all the rest of the telling.

He hissed softly when Colivar was done, a strangely visceral sound. "So they are not merely legend."

"No, Highness. They are quite real."

"Mother spoke of them. Often. It's part of her religion, you know. She said that her people believed they would come back someday. That a great war would be waged, upon which the fate of mankind would depend." He shook his head. "Who thought it would be in my lifetime?"

"If you know the legends," Colivar said quietly, "then you understand the danger."

Andovan looked up at him. In the shadows of the carriage his eyes seemed black and bottomless. "That Souleaters would devour the world, if they could? Yes. I understand."

Colivar drew in a deep breath. *I can't believe I am about to say this to a morati.* "We believe your father's new Magister may be allied to them somehow. And that your father serves them through that tie, probably without even knowing it. If he understood what was happening, if he grasped the magnitude of the danger . . . some feel he might rethink his course."

Andovan's eyes went wide. For a moment it seemed he could not find his voice. "Is that what you want me for?" He said at last. "To explain all this to my father?"

"Ramirus says you are the only one who can. That he will listen to you."

"Aye, he listened to me. When I was alive!" He tried to rise up in protest, but the close quarters of the carriage didn't allow for such a movement; with a sharp exhalation he sat back down on the bench, his hands rubbing restlessly against one another. "Have you forgotten what we did to him, Colivar? What *you* did? Lianna's veils! You think he will take advice from me after that?"

"He can be told the truth now," Colivar said evenly. "In whatever words will make it acceptable. I will take all the blame if necessary, he can direct his fury at me—"

"What words?" Andovan demanded. "What words will you give me to tell a man like Danton Aurelius that his own son played him for a fool, drove him into mourning when there was no reason for it, cost him his Magister Royal, then drove him to the brink of madness—yes, I've heard the stories!—and for what? So I could take a quick tour of the provinces with no one looking over his shoulder, and then come home again?" He drew in a deep breath. "He will have my head, Colivar. Before I get as far as the second word of whatever speech you have planned. If you do not think so, then you do not know my father."

"Then there is no hope," Colivar said grimly. "Is that what you are telling me?"

"What about the Magisters?" he demanded. "If what you say is true, the real offender is one of your own kind. Can you not get control of him somehow, or even take him down if you have to? I know you have some custom about not fighting one another, but it seems to me this kind of situation should merit an exception. Or is the danger enough for morati kings, but not sufficient to inconvenience Magisters?"

Colivar stiffened. *We have the Law, but you cannot possibly understand what that is to us. Morati have no memory of what Magisters did to this world before the Law was created. If they did then they would fear us far more than they do. They might well have second thoughts about wanting us to share this world with them.*

"We will not act directly against a Magister," he said quietly. "Nor against Danton, while he is contracted to one. Not even for this."

"Well, then." Andovan exhaled noisily and leaned back against the wall. "That is your answer about hope, then." He shut his eyes, rubbing them wearily with his fingertips. "What about my mother? Can she help?"

"Gwynofar?"

"He listens to her counsel. More than he ever did with me. Even Ramirus sought her aid when dealing with Danton on sensitive matters. She calms my father. Always has."

Colivar hesitated. It surprised him to discover that he did not wish to cause the young prince any more pain than he already had. A strangely human feeling. "Danton hurt her," he said gently. "I don't know the details. According to reports, she won't go near him now."

Andovan's face lost the last of its color. "What? What did he do to her? Tell me."

"I don't know," Colivar lied. "I'm sorry."

Andovan turned away from him as much as he could in the small space. Colivar let him withdraw without protest.

"What is happening to him?" the prince said at last. "I don't understand. He was always a harsh man, quick to anger, but Mother brought out the best in him. He told me once she was the one thing in all the kingdom that kept him sane. She and Ramirus." He bit his lower lip. "Now the one is gone and the other afraid to approach him . . . no wonder he is going mad. He is surrounded by rivals and false counselors, with enemies around every corner, and no one to trust. Even the strongest king would have trouble at such a time."

And there is a Magister hovering over him like a vulture, ready to take advantage of it. "You see why he needs you," Colivar said quietly.

"You can say that a thousand times, but it will not keep my head on my shoulders."

Colivar exhaled noisily in exasperation. "Then where is hope? You tell me, Highness. You know the man and you know his court—"

"—And I know you are his enemy, Colivar. Or has that changed? Why would I give an enemy knowledge of his situation?"

Colivar's jaw clenched for a moment. "This is bigger than morati politics," he said at last.

"Yet you did not send Ramirus to me, to make this request. A Magister I would have trusted. So perhaps it is not."

Colivar's expression darkened. "Ramirus hates your father more than the whole of Anshasa put together. He will not do anything to help him."

"That is rather shortsighted, don't you think? Assuming the danger is what you say it is."

"In that one thing Magisters and men are alike, Highness. Both are capable of ignoring bad news when it is something they do not wish to hear." He paused. "Ramirus told us there were only two people who knew Danton well enough to influence him in this matter: your mother and yourself. Both born of Protector's blood. Is it not the duty of your line to deal with these creatures? To whom else shall that duty be given, if you fail to meet it?"

Anger flared briefly in the prince's eyes, but he did not give voice to it. *Because I am right,* Colivar thought, *and he knows it.* Finally he said, in a voice as chill as ice, "You can get me to the palace?"

"To its vicinity. Not inside. Kostas will have woven a network of wards so tightly about the place that any sorcery will draw his immediate attention. Setting you down inside will mean announcing our arrival to him. Not a good idea."

"Location is not an issue. I know a way in."

Colivar nodded. The palace had been a fortified keep once, outfitted for war, and that meant that one or more siege tunnels would have been

carved out of the surrounding countryside to give the royal family a route
to safety if enemies surrounded the place. They were doubtless protected
with enough spells to keep strangers from finding them, but Andovan
would know the way.

"I will go," Andovan said. "I will talk to my mother. I will see what she
has to say about the situation, and urge her to take action if the situation
merits it. Nothing more than that, Colivar. Any other course else is certain death, and while I do not mind dying for a cause, dying for an act of
pointless stupidity is not nearly so appealing."

Colivar let out a breath he had not realized he'd been holding. "I thank
you, Highness."

"Should I ever discover you are using this situation to manipulate me
against my father . . ." He let the sentence trail off into a suggestive silence

If I did you would never know it, Colivar thought darkly. *I would wrap
such spells about your heart that you would beg to serve me, and would cut your
own mother's throat if I told you that I wanted her blood for my dinner table.*

"The Law forbids me to act against Danton," he said quietly. It wasn't
really true—the only action the Law prohibited was killing a Magister's
patron—but the boy didn't have to know that. The less morati understood
of the secretive code of the Magisters, the better.

"We leave now, I take it?"

Colivar nodded. "As soon as you are ready."

Andovan glanced towards the door of the coach and hesitated. Colivar
could guess from his expression what was on his mind.

"There is someone here. A witch. She saved my life. I would ask—"

"She may come with us," Colivar said quickly. "I will transport her as
well. Assuming she agrees."

Andovan blinked. "I expected you to argue with me."

"I have my own reasons."

She will not abandon you willingly, Colivar thought. *Whatever perverse
desire drove her to seduce her food, she will not want to let you go just yet.* He
did not need sorcery to know that; the truth of it had been in her eyes.
They were strange eyes, green and cold, with depths that glittered like diamonds. He remembered the Souleaters having eyes like that. Or maybe
not. It was hard to be sure, with so many years veiling his memories. How
many centuries had it been since he had last seen one up close?

You will see them soon enough if they are returning, he told himself. *And they will know your scent for what it is as soon as they catch wind of you.*

He had no doubt that Andovan's sorceress would accept the invitation. Whatever had driven her to track down and seduce her victim, she would not wish to give up control of him so soon. And Andovan was clearly smitten with her, in that impulsive and sometimes senseless way to which young men were prone. As for Colivar, he could see possible uses for such a creature in Danton's realm, most likely as a prime distraction. If Kostas realized there was a female sorcerer in his realm, he might not pay as close attention to other things. That could be useful.

Those were the reasons he gave himself, and they were good enough that he did not have to ask himself any more precise questions about his own motives, or wonder how many risks he would be willing to take for an opportunity to study her more closely.

Chapter 38

THE MINUTE they arrived in the High Kingdom Kamala could see that something was wrong.

She'd had second thoughts about entrusting herself to a strange Magister's sorcery, but there was no real alternative. She was not about to surrender Talesin a mere hour after discovering what he was, least of all to another sorcerer, and that meant she had to come with him. Either that or do battle with the Magister who had come to fetch him, and stake her territorial claim in terms he could not deny. She was almost angry enough to do that, too. What right did another man have to claim the source of her power?

But confronting him upon the issue meant revealing far more about herself and her consort than she wanted a stranger to know. And as it turned out, Talesin was more than just a noble-born wanderer. He was actually in the direct line of inheritance for the throne of the High Kingdom—arguably the greatest throne in the human lands—and the politics surrounding his lineage apparently now required that he return home.

He explained that to her as well as he could, then asked her to come with him. The black-haired Magister was not within sight at the time—he had walked off a bit to give them a modicum of privacy—but she could sense him in the distance: anxious, impatient. Was he using his sorcerous senses to listen in on their conversation? Kamala would have done so if their positions were reversed.

Colivar. That was the name Talesin had given him. She'd felt a chill go down her spine when he said it, remembering that name from one of Ethanus' lessons. What had her Master said about him? *Colivar is older than most of our kind, and has knowledge of many truths the morati world has forgotten. He is more human than most Magisters in his demeanor, but less human than most in substance, and for that reason he is often underestimated, especially by younger sorcerers.*

I will not make that mistake, she promised her teacher silently.

Under normal circumstances she would have disdained Colivar's aid and simply traveled on her own—if for no other reason than to enjoy the Magister's surprise when she did it—but such a large expenditure of athra would cost her consort dearly. And she was no more ready to magic him to death a mere hour after discovering his true identity than to let some legendary Magister run off with him.

And so, when Colivar wove his spells, she stood silently by and did not weave her own. She allowed him to establish a portal between *here* and *there*, anchoring it to some distant sorcerous mark, and when Talesin offered her his hand, that they might step through together, she took it and went. Ethanus had trained her well enough that she understood the importance of not showing hesitation in front of another Magister, and so she stepped into the spell as casually as if Talesin had invited her for a walk along the beach instead. Never mind that he had told her Colivar was a servant of his father's greatest enemy, so she found the whole relationship suspect. Never mind that she did not have the same confidence he did that this sorcerous portal was exactly what Colivar claimed it to be, or was going to the place he said. Magisters did not display fear of other Magisters.

The sensation of stepping through another Magister's portal was markedly vertiginous, and for a moment she had to shut her eyes and concentrate on steadying her senses just to keep to her feet. Then, slowly, sensing solid ground beneath her once more, she opened her eyes. What she saw was not what she had expected, and for a moment she just stood there, stunned. Beside her she could feel Talesin stiffen as he did the same, and for one terrible moment she thought that Colivar had indeed betrayed them, and had brought his enemy's son to some unknown place. Surely this could not be the ancestral home that Talesin had described to her as they had gathered their belongings, speaking of it with such longing that she knew his very soul ached to return. . . .

But no, there was Danton's palace ahead of them; Talesin pointed to it with a trembling hand, that ancient keep which Danton had adopted as the centerpiece of his sovereignty. (*Call him Andovan,* she reminded herself, tasting his true name secretly as she whispered it to herself.) Surrounding the palace, however, there should have been trees and gardens, walkways roofed in marble and roads paved with glittering stones and a vast marketplace set some distance from the palace gates, shimmering with all the vibrant colors and raucous sounds of life. Or so Andovan had told her.

It was gone. All of it.

Only a wasteland remained.

Andovan's face was white with shock as he took it all in, his eyes wide and uncomprehending. Even Colivar looked surprised when he first saw it, though, being a Magister, he was quick to mask the emotion. Briefly Kamala wondered if he was aware of her standing there as he did so, if he saw her as a potential rival who might take advantage of his weakness. The thought thrilled her, even as she tried to make sense out of the scene that was laid out before them.

You will know you are truly a Magister when the others of your kind fear you, Ethanus had told her.

Against a backdrop of rugged mountains, Danton's palace loomed gray and forbidding. The banners she had been told would be hanging from its outer wall were missing, save for a pair of red flags with a double-headed hawk flanking the main gate. Bereft of other decorations, the cold stone keep looked more like a fortress preparing for siege than a place where foreign envoys were feted. Even the few windows were tiny, narrow things, barely wide enough for an archer to take sight of an enemy through. The building's ancient purpose had become its current purpose once more, as its owner prepared for war.

But if the starkness of the palace itself was remarkable, it paled in comparison to what lay surrounding it. To the west, where Andovan said a great forest had once stood, was only an open plain. The trees nearest the palace walls had been felled and the gardens burned, so that a black ring of devastation surrounded the keep. A fence that had once marked the outer boundary of the royal grounds seemed strangely isolated, trapped between emptiness and more emptiness, bereft of even the illusion of purpose.

Colivar had said they would arrive near a marketplace, close enough that if trouble came their way they might lose themselves in the crowd. But if ever a marketplace had existed in this place there was no sign of it now. All signs of human commerce had been uprooted, leaving only the dry, packed earth as testament to the thousands that must once have scurried back and forth across it. If Kamala had been willing to use her sorcery she might have heard the echoes of vendors long gone, servants chattering as they purchased goods for their master's house, gossip whispered in the shadows. But she cast no spell, and so the earth was silent.

It wasn't that she cared whether Andovan lived or died, she told herself. It was simply that this would be an inconvenient time to be caught in Transition.

"Why?" Andovan whispered hoarsely.

"Like a beast, Danton marks his territory." Colivar's dark eyes glittered. "What better way than this?"

Andovan turned on him; the fury in his eyes made it clear that the Magister had just gone one step too far. "Are you saying my father is a beast?"

"Perhaps not him. Perhaps someone else." He waved a hand out toward the ravaged landscape. "What else explains this, Your Highness? What motive could a man possibly have that would cause him to lay waste to his own lands like this?"

Kamala looked up at him sharply. He knew something he was not saying, that much she could sense in him.

Andovan drew in a deep breath as he gazed out at the devastated landscape. "Defense," he said quietly. His voice was a hollow thing. "My father often spoke of the folly of having wooded lands so close to the palace, saying that enemies could use them for cover, but my mother begged him to keep them . . . she said war would not come this far into the High Kingdom, and she hungered for the comfort of living things. . . ." His voice dropped to a whisper. "That is what he has done. All things that might give shelter to enemies have been removed. Even the crowds that unwelcome visitors might lose themselves in." He looked pointedly at Colivar.

"She was right," the Magister told him. "No army could get this far, not without months of bloody campaigning first. More than enough time for a Magister to level a forest, if the need arose." He shook his head; his expression was grim. "There was no need for this. Not in any *human* sense."

The wind shifted, coming to them from across the battered landscape. The ash was fresh enough that the smell of burning still lingered on the wind . . . and something else.

"What is that?" Kamala said.

It was a musky scent, strangely sweet, like nothing she had ever smelled before. Not an unpleasant odor, but strangely disturbing. She could see Colivar start as the breeze brought it to him, and something flickered in the back of his eyes that might be fear. It was a strangely naked expression, as if for a moment all the strength of the Magister's power had been stripped from him, and with it all his confidence. A second later the expression was gone, but the image of it had been seared into her brain.

"They are here," Colivar whispered.

Andovan seemed about to speak, but instead a fit of coughing suddenly overcame him. More and more violent it became, until at last he was driven to his knees, shaking from the force of it. Kamala knelt by his side, feeling utterly helpless in her inability to help him. Any power she used to heal him would only make things worse.

Colivar simply watched, curious but unmoved.

Doubling over, Andovan vomited upon the packed earth, not once but again and again, until the fluid that he spewed up no longer had any substance to it, save a strange and vile smell. "What is that?" he gasped, as the fit of coughing subsided at last and he was able to breath.

"Your ancestral enemy," Colivar answered. "Legend says that hatred of them is writ deep in the blood of the Protectors. Apparently not even Danton's seed could dilute it enough to matter."

"Then my mother—" He could not complete the thought.

He nodded. "Go to her. Give her strength. Tell her Danton's alliance with these creatures must be severed, or the whole of the High Kingdom will soon look like . . . this." A sweeping gesture encompassed the wasteland before them. "And worse. Much worse. Remember the Dark Ages. They could come again."

Andovan nodded. With effort—and Kamala's assistance—he got to his feet. He wiped a sleeve across his mouth, and spat a few last drops of bile onto the ground. "I know my duty, Colivar." He held out a hand to Kamala. "Come. I will need your protection."

She took his hand.

"She cannot shield you once you are inside," Colivar warned. "Kostas will be alert to the faintest whisper of sorcery within his domain."

"Then she can protect me on the way," Andovan said.

He did not correct Colivar's assumption, Kamala noted. Did not point out to him that his companion was a witch, not a sorcerer. No doubt he was distracted enough not to take note of the fine distinction, or believe that it mattered. But she knew that it did, and she wondered if by not responding to it she was revealing more about herself to Colivar than she should.

Too much to think about now. Deal first with the task ahead, later with this Magister.

"Lianna."

It took Kamala a minute to remember that was her name. When she did she turned back to Colivar.

"I believe this is yours." He held out a folded square of fabric. Golden silk. The dark eyes were fixed on her as she took it, as if seeking to take the very measure of her soul.

Startled, she realized it was one of the scarves that Ravi had given her, back in Gansang. One of many precious gifts that she had never worn.

Her heart skipped a beat in her chest. She did her best not to let her surprise show, but knew from the expression in those piercing dark eyes that she had failed, and that for one brief moment he had read her like a book.

"Your mistake," she said stiffly. "It is not mine."

"Indeed," he said quietly. "My apologies, then." He tucked the scarf into his doublet without looking at it, his dark eyes never leaving her own. "I shall have to seek its true owner some other time."

Cold, those eyes were so cold. Human beings did not have eyes like that.

Shivering inwardly, she turned to follow Andovan across the devastated landscape, toward whatever secret entrance he believed would give them access to the palace.

Chapter 39

GWYNOFAR AWAKENED slowly, not quite sure where she was. She had dreamed so many things in the last few hours, all of them with such frightening intensity, that for a moment it was hard to tell if this was yet another dream, or if sleep was fading at last and she was returning to . . . where?

Trembling, she remembered seeing a sky filled with black-winged Souleaters, a land burned black by sorcery, and strange lizardlike creatures that slithered in the shadows of the palace, leaving trails of slime upon the ancient tapestries. Would that they were only nightmares! But at least one of those images was more than a dream, so who could say how much of the rest might turn out to be likewise? These days she could not rule anything out.

It was a week now since Kostas' sorcery had ignited the royal forest, sending clouds of black smoke high into the heavens for days on end. On the last day the wind had turned toward the palace, as if to admonish those who had sanctioned the destruction, and hot ash had rained down upon the turrets and parapets. It had gathered in gray drifts against the outer walls and gusted in through the narrow windows, and no matter how many servants Gwynofar sent to sweep it away there was always more of it somewhere, waiting to blow in. Kostas could have turned the wind away, but why should he? He clearly took delight in her despair, and no doubt watched from the shadows with pleasure as she stood upon the roof that last day, when the smoke finally cleared, weeping at the sight of the devastation. The forest had been Andovan's favorite refuge, and therefore she had loved it for his sake . . . and like all the things she loved, it must therefore be uprooted or befouled by that creature, for that was his chosen sport.

Only her courtyard was safe from him. Even the ash had not fallen thickly there. Merian had said that was because the bulk of the palace blocked the wind, but Gwynofar preferred to believe that the gods wished to keep this one place sacrosanct. So that there remained one place where she could still find peace, unfouled by Kostas' sorcery.

Now, raising her head up from the needle-strewn earth, she realized she was in that very place. Exhaustion must have overtaken her during her devotions, she thought. Either that, or perhaps she had chosen to rest her head upon the ground for a few moments and shut her eyes, trusting this was the one place in the palace where Kostas would not—perhaps *could* not—intrude. And then sleep had claimed her, the border between waking nightmare and dreaming nightmare so subtle that she never sensed the moment she passed from one to the other.

How far she had fallen, since the days when she had reigned as High Queen beside Danton's throne! These days the rancid odor in the palace was so overwhelming that she could barely stand to remain indoors. Instead she must flee to this place several times a day just to be able to breathe clean air, or Kostas' foulness would surely suffocate her. She could not explain all that to Danton, of course. He would have labeled the whole thing lunacy—or even worse, witchery—and it would have driven yet one more wedge between them. As if they needed anything more.

She rose from the ground unsteadily, brushing dried pine needles from her mourning gown. She wondered if she should call for her maidservant to pick the mess out of her hair as well. But Merian was half mad with worry about her these days, so much so that Gwynofar almost felt guilty letting her see her in this state. Better to brush the dirt and debris out herself, before the woman saw her.

She had barely drawn a lock of golden hair forward over her shoulder and begun to pick at it when suddenly she heard a twig snap behind her.

Her heart skipped a beat. The sound came from a far corner of the courtyard, where the blue pines were crowded so closely together that the sunlight hardly reached the ground; she could not see through the tangled branches to make out the source of the noise. Who would come to this place without announcing himself, and why?

There was no good answer to that question.

Heart pounding, she looked about herself for something which she could use for self-defense, and finally picked up a fallen branch that lay nearby. Her hand was shaking as she hefted it, knowing even as she did so that the effort was futile. It had been too many years since she and Rhys had sported in the meadows as children, waging mock battles with weapons fashioned out of broom handles as they pretended to be Guardians routing out the last defenders of some demonic stronghold. But at least she did not look quite as helpless holding it; perhaps that would be worth something.

Then a figure stepped out from the shadows, and a lean, pale hand pushed back the edge of the woolen hood it was wearing, that she might see its face.

Her legs suddenly grew weak beneath her. The makeshift weapon dropped from her fingers.

"Andovan?" she whispered in disbelief.

For a moment she thought it might be a ghost that stood before her, and not a real man at all. The visitor was pale and drawn, his cheeks hollow, his frame far thinner than Andovan's had ever been. So she moved forward slowly, and raised a hand up to touch his cheek. His skin was dry and taut beneath her fingertips, but it was real. *He* was real.

"Andovan . . ." She could say no more; a mixture of joy and pain too terrible to bear choked off all words. He said nothing, simply took her in his arms and held her tightly. Despite the terrible wasting disease that had sapped his strength his embrace was strong and sure, and it gave comfort to her, body and soul.

Gwynofar wept. From joy, from fear, from sheer emotional exhaustion. She wept for Andovan's death, for the misery of her mourning, and for everything which had followed that loss. She wept for all the nights she had prayed to her gods and seemingly gone unanswered. For all the indignities Kostas had forced her to endure, and the silence with which she had borne them. For the fact that she was High Queen, and being such, might not weep freely, except in such company as this.

At last, emptied of misery, she drew back from him. She looked away for a moment as she wiped her eyes dry, allowing him a moment of privacy to do the same if he required it. Men were not so public about their tears as women were. Then, finally she looked into his eyes—blue, so very blue, like the color of the rivers in the far north when the ice cracked in springtime—and whispered in wonder, "You are not dead."

"No." His smile was so tender it nearly broke her heart. "Not yet, anyway."

"Does Danton know?"

His mouth tightened. "Not yet."

"Then how . . . how is it you are here? Surely the guards must have seen you . . ."

"I used the same tunnels I did when I was a boy. Remember? You and Father would search the palace for me, but I knew all the ancient ways: servants' passages, forgotten spaces between the walls, tunnels carved out in the days when siege threatened. . . ." His fleeting smile reminded her of those days, and of the young prince who would rather play in the woods than attend to his lessons. How her heart ached to be reminded of that time!

"Everything is still the same as it was. Though not quite as spacious as I remembered it." His voice dropped to a whisper. "No one has seen me here save you."

"You faked your death." Her voice caught in her throat; she had to fight to get the words out. "Why, Andovan? Why do such a thing?"

A shadow passed briefly across his face. For a moment he turned away from her, as if he could not meet her eyes while he spoke. "Because I could not bear to die in bed," he said at last. "Because if there was a cause for my condition I wanted to seek it out, and if I could not find it . . . then it would be better to die on the road, I thought, fighting my fate, than swaddled in blankets like a helpless infant."

She shut her eyes and tried to make sense of it all. "Then the note you left—"

"That was truly mine, yes. And I meant every word."

"But the body . . ."

"Not mine, obviously. Though it had that seeming."

"But Ramirus said that it was yours. He said he used sorcery to be sure of it. Did he know the truth as well?"

"No." A pained expression passed across his face. "He knew nothing of it."

"He didn't help you do this?"

"How could I ask that of him? His first duty was to my father, not to me. He would not have lied to Danton for my sake."

"So then who—?" Her eyes grew wide as understanding came. *All the Magisters were here, back then. Enough power to fake a thousand deaths.*

"Which one of them?" she whispered.

For the first time, he seemed to hesitate.

"Tell me, Andovan."

"Colivar," he said. "It was Colivar."

She breathed in sharply. "The Anshasan?"

He cut short her protest with a wave of his hand. "I know what you're going to say—that he serves an enemy of our House—but in this case our goals were identical. The Magisters thought that someone had cursed me, and they were trying to find out who. Colivar said that I had the power within myself to seek her out, if only I had spells to help me focus. No one else could do what I could do. But I knew Father would never let me go on such a quest, and Ramirus would never help, so I did . . . what I did."

She shut her eyes for a moment, trying to absorb it all. *Colivar. Of course.* Now that she understood that piece of the puzzle, all the rest fell into place. How easy it would have been for the foreign Magister to read her son like a book, to know exactly what words would move him to greater and greater frustration . . . until at last he was so desperate to act that he would follow his heart and not his head, embracing the suggestions of his father's enemy without ever questioning where they might lead.

Oh, my son, my foolish, beloved son . . . you were strong and true in your heart and but you never had a head for politics, and now look at what it has cost us.

Of course Ramirus would never have helped Andovan flee the palace, much less fake his own death. Ramirus would have understood that the loss of Danton's son would throw the entire household into turmoil. Perhaps he might even have predicted the events that would come of it: Danton's rage. His own banishment. Kostas moving in like a vulture to feed upon the soft, tender flesh of a kingdom in mourning. Every horror that had come to this kingdom of late had been set in motion by Andovan's death . . . which Colivar had apparently orchestrated. Even by Magister standards, it was a masterwork.

That man is a viper, and through you he has poisoned the very heart of Danton's kingdom.

It took effort not to let all that show in her face. She did not want her son to see anything in her expression other than love and acceptance. It would accomplish nothing to have him understand the magnitude of his error, save to make him feel greater remorse than any human soul could bear. No, this must a secret that she kept up locked in her heart, where no other person could share it.

I will have vengeance for this, Colivar. Someday, somehow, I swear by the Wrath, you will pay for what you did to us.

"Mother." He said it softly, gentling her from her reverie. "I risked Father's wrath to return for a reason."

Wiping new moisture from her eyes, she looked up at him. Something in his expression made a cold shiver run up her spine. "What is it?"

"The demons of the north. The ones they call Souleaters." His expression darkened. "They are back."

She drew in a sharp breath. "Impossible. The Wrath still stands. The Guardians would have told us if it had fallen—"

"They have been seen in the human lands. The young ones, at least. And there are witnesses in Corialanus who testify to having seen one of the adults, or something very much like it, attending upon a field of slaughter."

She shuddered. "Who saw them? Colivar?"

"No. Others."

"But he is the one that told you about them."

His eyes narrowed slightly. "He spoke the truth, Mother. I have a witch traveling with me, I asked her to make sure of his words." He paused. "I am not such a fool as to take that kind of report at face value, not when so much is at stake."

No, she thought bitterly. *Not this time, at least.*

Souleaters. The legends all said they would return someday, for a battle that could bring about the end of the Second Age of Kings. Those same legends promised that ancient magics in the Protectors' bloodlines would be awakened when it was needed. Was that the source of her dreams? Some ancient magic stirring now, responding to this threat, preparing her and her children for roles they were destined to play? If so, shouldn't that same magic make her feel more confident about what was happening, shouldn't it fill her with a sense of purpose, or, of . . . well, destiny? It didn't. She just felt frightened.

"I have had strange dreams of flying beasts," she whispered. "I wondered at their source. Perhaps the gods are showing us what is to come."

"There is more," he warned her.

She looked up at him, bracing herself.

"Colivar says that the Magisters have determined that the Souleaters are somehow allied with men. Men who are feeding them human souls. Serving their purpose. Paving the way for their return."

She opened her mouth and was about to protest that surely no men would do such a foolish thing—

When the truth hit her, with stunning force.

Her mouth opened and closed silently several times. No sound would come out.

Oh, my gods. . . .

She wrapped her arms around herself, trembling, as she remembered the ancient prophecies she'd been taught as a child. *The Protectors shall know them when they return.* The gods had promised her family that, when they set them apart from all other men. That's what the foul essence in the palace was. That cold, clammy feeling of *wrongness* that accompanied Kostas like a rancid wind everywhere he went. The gods had been trying to tell her the truth about him. She hadn't known how to interpret their message.

What a fool I have been!

Her legs were suddenly weak beneath her. She would have fallen had not Andovan reached out and grabbed her; he helped her to the nearest bench, and did not let go of her arm until she was safely seated, her hands grasping its beveled edge for stability.

"Kostas . . ." she whispered.

That was why the new Magister had asked about her lineage. That was why he had wanted to hear the ancient legends. That was why he had done everything possible to separate her from her husband. If the tales of the ancient war were true, if the gods had indeed imbued the blood of the Protectors with secret magics meant to hold the monsters at bay—he wanted her to have no allies when they surfaced, no credibility. No hope.

"But why would a human being serve them?" she whispered. "We are food to them, nothing more."

"Much can change in a thousand years." Andovan's expression was grim. "We sent them north to die. No man has seen them since. Who knows what they may have become in that time?"

"But there is no life up there, no sustenance for them . . . how can they have survived?"

"I don't know the answers to that, Mother. I only bring you what I have been told." He hesitated. "The only other possibility is that Danton himself is assisting them—"

"No," she said sharply. "He would never do that."

"Are you so sure?"

"Of that? Yes. Yes, I am." Her husband might be acting erratically these days, but he was not so mad as to embrace the Souleaters' cause.

Which meant that it had to be Kostas.

Andovan knelt down before her. It was an act that mirrored Rurick's earlier plea to her, which had gone so terribly wrong. She could not meet his eyes because of it.

"What do you want of me?" she said. "That I kill Kostas? That I help set up someone else to do so?" She wrung her hands in her lap as she spoke. "It's not like I haven't thought of it, Andovan. He is twisting my husband's soul against me; there is nothing I would not do to remove him from my life. But it is as he said, he knows every move even as I plan it. One night I dreamed of poisoning him—a mere dream!—and the next night I found a vial of poison in my room, by the bed. He was daring me to try!" Shaking, she drew in a breath. "If he is even within my dreams, watching my every thought, how can I move against him? The moment I begin to plan his murder, he will know every detail. You cannot kill a Magister like that."

"Then Father must be convinced to sever their contract. It is the only way."

She shut her eyes. A shudder ran through her body. "Please tell me you are not going to ask me to talk him into that. Please."

He said nothing.

"Even in the old days that would have stressed our relationship to the breaking point. Now . . . I dare not think what he would do if I told him he should send his new Magister Royal away. He will see me as an enemy of his ambition—"

"You are the only one who can even try," he said quietly. "Ramirus is gone now. I cannot go to him, you know that."

"No," she whispered. "You cannot." Maybe in the old days they could have found a way to tell Danton that his son was alive, but this new king, never more than a hair's breadth away from a killing rage, would not welcome the news. He would hang Andovan's head from the front gate as a warning to any other member of his family that thought they might play him for a fool, and maybe Gwynofar's as well, for encouraging him. And Kostas would laugh at both of them as he plotted his next atrocity.

Danton loved me once, she told herself. *Surely some part of him loves me still. If I can reach out to that part, perhaps he will listen to me.*

"If it is the only thing that can be done, if there truly is no other way . . ." She drew in a deep breath, trembling. "I will speak to him. But whether he will listen to me at all is in the hands of the gods. And they have not been obliging of late."

"The fate of one man is a small thing in their eyes," Andovan told her. "But surely the fate of the whole world is a different matter. If the Magisters are right, if their reports are true, that is what we are talking about." He took her hands in his own and squeezed them, tightly. "No one but you can do this, Mother."

Rurick said the same words to me, once. That meeting is what brought me to Kostas' attention, so that now he watches my every move. Where will this one lead?

"I will talk to him," she promised.

She did not think she would be able to convince Danton to send Kostas away, but if she could even seed doubts in his mind about the man's counsel, that might be enough. The Magister's lies would then lose some power over him, and he might come to his senses. Perhaps in time Danton could even be told the truth about Andovan without flying into a homicidal rage. And then her son could come home again. And they could try to rebuild the lives that Colivar had shattered, and set the High Kingdom on a stable course once more.

Dreams, she thought, *these are only dreams.* But dreams were all she had right now, so she savored them.

As for the Souleaters . . . that possibility was too terrible to contemplate. But if Andovan was right—if the Magisters were right—then there was a greater threat facing them than any living man could remember. And the Protectors like herself would be front and center in dealing with it.

One thing at a time, she told herself. And she embraced her beloved son anew, and held him tightly, trying to forget for one single moment just how great the odds against all of them were.

Chapter 40

ALONE IN her chamber, Siderea Aminestas ran finely manicured fingers along the edges of her secret strongbox. The cover was already unlocked. The Magister's tokens lay inside. It would take little effort to pull them out, and little witchery to use them for what she intended. The cost would be so small that she would hardly notice it. Five minutes of life, perhaps. Maybe less.

Sometimes the price must be paid, she told herself.

Still she hesitated. In the old days she could have been certain that sooner or later a Magister would show up to visit, who could then be convinced to tell her what she needed to know. These days she was not so sure of that. Ever since she had received the visitor from Corialanus things had been different, somehow. Colivar had given her a report of the slaughter up north, as he'd promised to, but she'd sensed he was leaving out important details. Fadir suddenly had business too pressing to allow him to stay overnight, thus robbing her of the venue in which she was most likely to get a Magister to divulge his secrets. Since then, she'd had no visitors of that ilk at all. Was it just coincidence? Or was there something going on that required all their attention?

If so, she needed to know what it was. They were not the only ones directing the fate of the human kingdoms. She might not be their equal in sorcery, but few men were her equal in politics. She would not allow any-one to keep her in the dark—and that included Magisters.

Opening the lid of the chest, she ran her fingertips lightly over the folded bits of paper within it. Such simple tokens. So very powerful. All it would take was a moment of true witchery to allow her to read their own-ers like a book. She was willing to bet not a single one had put up safe-guards against such an effort. Why should they? She had never taken advantage of their offerings before. They would probably not know it if she did so now.

Trust was more powerful than any sorcery.

Slowly, thoughtfully, she leafed through the collection of tokens. If she only used one or two of them then she would only be able to read their owners, and she needed more than that. She needed to establish a con-nection to the entire community of Magisters, so that the secrets they shared with one another would take on a magical substance of their own. Only then would she be able to know what information the Magisters were refusing to share with her.

Because she had their tokens, willingly offered, that would take very lit-tle effort. Though the gods themselves could not save her if they ever found out what she had done.

She remembered the sense of urgency about Colivar when he had re-ported to her, the edgy distraction of Fadir and Sulah, and thought: *I have to know.*

It was impossible to determine which Magisters would know more of these matters than any other, save for the three who had investigated the matter in Corialanus, and two of those tokens had already been burned. Riffling through the ones which remained, she chose a dozen papers at random. It was half of her collection—a priceless store of power—but the kind of knowledge she was after required that level of sacrifice.

And of course, a more visceral sacrifice was required as well . . . but that was what being a witch was all about.

When the half-emptied chest was hidden away once more, she settled herself before her brazier and prepared herself for the task ahead. She found it strangely hard to focus. Frowning, she stroked the tokens her lovers had given her, closed her eyes, and tried to settle her soul to the task.

But it was as if her spirit did not wish to settle down to witchery, and her attention kept flitting away to other things.

Strange, very strange.

Her father had taught her many tricks for taming one's soulfire, and after an hour of focused exercises she felt she was finally ready to begin. The dry papers caught fire quickly, and aromatic smoke rose from the brazier. Wafting it toward herself, she breathed the essence of the Magisters into herself and—

—black whirlpool empty screaming darkness—

Choking, she opened her eyes. The room was spinning. The smoke in her lungs was making it hard to breathe. The power that should have been surging through her veins was—

Absent.

Coughing, she put the cover on the brazier to smother the flames. It was a terrible waste of magical material, but that couldn't be helped. Whatever was wrong with her, it was clear she was not going to be weaving any spells today.

She suddenly remembered the difficulty she'd had the last time she had tried to raise the power, when the Magisters were visiting, and a cold shiver ran up her spine.

Something is wrong.

She knew what it might be. But she refused to name it. Surely, surely, it had to be something else. Anything else!

Trembling, she gathered herself for introspection, and used her supernatural senses to look within her own soul. Deep, deep within, to where the fires that fueled her life should have burned brightly. She had gazed at her own soulfire dozens of times in her youth; it was an exercise her father had taught her, when he was showing her how to focus her power. If there was something so wrong with her that her own athra would no longer respond to her, it would show there first.

Only this time there was no blazing fire within her. This time the sheer heat of her vital essence did not sear her senses. Instead there was only a dim glow of soulfire, that flickered weakly like a dying candle. The essence surrounding it was cold and dark.

NO!!!!!!!!!!

She screamed. That set off another fit of coughing, and for a short while it was all she could do to keep breathing. A servant heard the commotion and came running into the room; seeing her choking for air, she tried to help Siderea the only way she knew how, by pounding her on the back.

"Get out of here!" she screamed. Gasping for breath between the words. "Leave me alone!"

Terrified, the girl backed out of the room. Siderea could hear other servants by the door, drawn by her screaming, but apparently they were now having second thoughts about entering the room. Then she heard the door close again, leaving her alone with the smoke and the fear—

And the truth.

Stunned, she struggled to her feet. The room swirled dizzily around her as she tried to regain her focus. But she managed it, at last. A small victory. Her life was not over yet.

She shouldn't have been surprised by this, she told herself numbly. She had known all along her life would end like this. The Magisters were able to keep her young and beautiful, but that was only a stopgap measure to make her mortal days more comfortable. They could not extend the span of her life by so much as a day, unless she became one of them.

There would be no more witchery for her now, unless she wished to extinguish her life in the act. There would be very few days left at all. The soulfire she had seen had been almost completely exhausted. Soon there would no heat left to sustain her life, and not even sorcery could save her then.

They knew, she realized suddenly.

It was the final blow, realizing that that the Magisters must surely know of her condition and had not told her. Why else would they be keeping their distance now? Her face flushed hot with shame . . . and then the shame became anger. After a lifetime of using her, of taking for granted her efforts to support their paranoid society, this was how they meant to let her end her days? Leaving her to discover the truth herself, to face it alone, to begin her descent into darkness without a single helping hand to steady her way?

With a cry of rage she took up a vase from a nearby table and hurled it with all her might; it hit the far wall and shattered into a thousand fragments. The brazier followed, scattering smoking ashes across the stone floor as it flew. She could hear the servants whispering outside the door, too afraid to come inside as they heard object after object fly across the room. Fools! What did they know of rage? What did they know of shame? They had never had men of power eating out of their hand one day, and abandoning them the next day like some nameless orphan to face their death alone.

Shaking, she lowered herself slowly to the floor. The smoke in the room had dissipated somewhat, but breathing was no easier. The scraps of paper strewn across the floor were charred black, unmarked and meaningless. Only in the hands of a witch would they have any power, and she was no longer that. She was only a morati woman well past her prime who had gazed upon the face of Death.

Overcome by rage and sorrow, the Witch-Queen wept.

Chapter 41

THANK THE gods for paint and powder, Gwynofar thought.

It had taken her an hour, but finally the reflection gazing back at her from the polished silver mirror looked something like her accustomed self. The circles under her eyes had been powdered into oblivion. The pallor of her skin had been warmed with a hint of crushed coral. Her hair had been brushed to a radiant golden sheen, and Merian had seen to it that not even a speck of pine debris or soil adhered to it.

What had made the greatest difference of all was that she had put aside her mourning dress for a gown of garnet silk; the color lent warmth to her flesh and made her look alive again. Now, she raised up her long hair while Merian clasped about her neck a double strand of cream-colored pearls from which depended a delicate rendition of the Aurelius double-headed hawk. Rings that she had not worn for weeks glittered on her fingers. Pearl earrings peeked out from the golden cloud of her hair.

She looked like a queen.

A heavy knock came upon the door. Merian ran over to open it.

Rurick looked about the room as he walked in, then at Gwynofar. His tight-lipped nod assured her that her efforts had been effective . . . even if he had his doubts about how much good they were going to do.

"Kostas is indeed gone," he told her. "Sent out on some sorcerous errand earlier this morning. No idea how long it will take. No one knows his business well, and I cannot press for information without having people guess at why I want it."

"Then it will have to be enough," Gwynofar said. The knowledge that Kostas was not with her husband right now quieted her pounding heart a bit. *That much we have managed,* she thought. *Perhaps it will prove an omen for the rest.*

"Are you ready?" the royal heir asked her.

She let Merian flit about her like an anxious moth one last time, arranging a bit of hair here, a sleeve end there, then waved her away. For a moment she just stood there, breathing deeply, trying to feel as much like a queen as she looked. Danton could smell weakness in others. If she meant to counsel him, she needed to appear confident; he would respect nothing less.

Finally, all was as right as it could be. She nodded to her son. The gesture felt suitably regal.

"Take me to Danton," she told him.

———

The halls of the palace seemed dark and depressing to Kamala; it was not at all what she would have expected of one of the richest and most powerful men in the world. Or perhaps she was just comparing him to Ravi and the other Gansang nobles in her mind, with their gaily decorated towers and their peacock retinues. Perhaps wasting energy on such displays was not an option when the fates of numerous kingdoms were in one's hands.

"Company," Andovan whispered suddenly.

They both fell back into a shadowed alcove as a pair of footsteps approached from around a far corner. Kamala braced herself to use sorcery if she must, to keep their presence a secret, but she hoped it would not be necessary. Not merely because it would weaken Andovan, but because it would almost certainly set off whatever sorts of wards this Kostas had erected to guard the palace, and let him know that a Magister had invaded his turf.

At least that was the situation according to the information Colivar had given her, and she did not feel that right now was a good time to test his assumptions.

They had come in through a long, dark tunnel, its mouth hidden in a deep crevasse in the nearby mountains. There was only the light of a small hooded lantern to guide them underground, but Andovan seemed to know the way so well that it was hardly necessary. He whispered to her about how he had found the tunnel when he was just a boy, despite the fact that it was disguised at both ends not only by the normal tricks of siege design, but by sorcery as well. He was of Danton's blood, however, and Ramirus' spells recognized him as such, so they had done very little to keep him out. The tunnel had been his lifeline thereafter, he said, allowing him to escape the stifling atmosphere of royal life now and then, and thus to keep his sanity.

Once they had arrived underneath the palace itself he led her upward through a veritable maze of passageways. These had been provided when the palace was first built in order that servants might go about their duties without ever being seen, and so not distract their royal masters. Here he could not use his lantern in case it would be seen by servants passing by, so he led her forward by touch, and she marveled at how keen his memory was of all these secret spaces. In another time and place she might have offered up a spark of power to light their way, but even that much sorcery would have given them away to Kostas, according to Colivar.

Had he meant his warning to include all types of power when he said that, she wondered, or was only true sorcery a risk? If the latter, then that meant he knew her for exactly what she was. Kamala felt an icy thrill run up her spine at the thought. The scarf Colivar had offered her showed that he had been following her trail in Gansang; if so, he knew that she had broken the Magisters' Law there. Why had he not acted against her yet, if that was the case? Why did he tempt her with hints and innuendos, like one might tempt a mastiff with fresh meat to see if he would bite?

At last they had come as far as the servants' passageways could take them, and Andovan had brought them out from behind an arras into a large public chamber. It was larger than the passageway they had just come out of, but not much cheerier. They had gone just far enough that they could no longer get back to the passageway for cover when Andovan whispered his warning. And now, pressed back against the wall of a shallow alcove, wishing its shadows were deeper and darker than they were, the two of them could do nothing more than hold their breath and hope that fate favored their subterfuge.

Slowly, two people were coming down the hall toward their hiding place. Kamala could not see them from where she was, but she could hear cultured male voices discussing political matters in the manner of men who might dictate the course of such things. Not guards, then. She held her breath as they passed, but the two well-dressed noblemen who strolled by did not even glance to the side as they walked. Finally they turned a far corner and their voices passed out of hearing. She released her breath in a sigh of relief and heard Andovan do the same.

They had disguised Andovan's features, of course, but given who and what he was it was unlikely that would do any good if people looked at him closely. Kamala had cropped his hair short in the manner of the palace guards and used a whisper of stolen power to change its color to a dark brown—his eyebrows and lashes as well—but without the kind of major spell that might alter the bone structure of his face, it was at best a superficial effort. He was wearing a guard's uniform, which would help him get by the servants if they only glanced at him in passing, but it was a good bet that the members of the guard knew one another, so that subterfuge would only take him so far. And she could not wrap protective magics around him—or herself—without taking the chance that Kostas would sense it. The only way to have a chance at secrecy was to walk unprotected.

He seemed to thrive on the danger of it, though. When he walked now, his footfall was utterly silent. When he dropped back into the shadows to avoid being seen, he was so still she was not even sure he was still breathing. He had the body language of an assassin, she mused. The ultimate hunter.

You are sure you want to go? she had asked him. *You cannot attend her meeting with Danton, or help her in any way once it has begun.*

I will be near enough to help if trouble comes, he had told her proudly. *And I will serve as distraction, if there is need, that others may do their duty.* For a moment the pride in his eyes showed clear and strong, and he was no longer an invalid counting the hours to his death, but a prince defending those who were in his charge. What a fine creature he must have been in the days before the gods decreed he was to end his days as food for a Magister! For a moment she regretted that she would never have the chance to see him in his natural state, but even those few seconds of regret made the air become cold around her, and her lungs suddenly felt bound as if by bands of iron. A warning. She set the speculation aside with effort, and focused upon the present moment. After a few seconds she could breathe again.

Do not care for him. Do not regret. That way lies death.

Finally they reached a small chamber set off the main hallway. There was no door here, but the archway that gave entrance to the space was narrow, and by keeping to the far corner they would be out of sight of any passersby. It was as close as they could come to Gwynofar's meeting, Andovan told her, without being visible to the guards that commonly attended Danton.

He walked over to where a trio of narrow windows offered a fragmented view of the surrounding countryside. Black, it was, all black. The breeze shifted slightly and the smell of stale ash drifted into the room. Andovan's eyes narrowed in anger. To one side it was just possible to see the foothills they had come from, sharp granite bluffs jutting up from the ground as if seeking to escape the devastation. This might have been a beautiful land once when it was lush and green, Kamala thought, but right now it looked like a place the god of the dead might have called home.

To her surprise, Andovan came to her and took her hands in his. He waited until she met his eyes, then said, very quietly, "If I must take action in the next hour, it is because there is no other choice. Which means that Kostas will know we are here, and what we intend . . . there will be nothing left to hide."

She heard the question behind his words . . . a question he would never ask her directly. "I will help you in that case," she promised.

Yes, though you do not know the price.

He nodded, seemingly satisfied, took a seat that was out of the line of sight of the archway, and readied himself to wait.

———

Rurick led Gwynofar to the chamber where Danton was located. While there were guards positioned down the corridor, there were none directly outside the door. That was a good sign, Gwynofar told herself. When Danton was in his paranoid moods he kept his guards close at hand.

Inside, the High King and one of his scribes were deep in discussion over a ledger book. There were several large chests in the room, half a dozen rugs rolled up and bound in one corner, and a small open box on the desk that had strings of pearls hanging over the edge.

Danton looked up as the door opened; it was clear from his expression that he was less than pleased about having his business interrupted. Then that emotion gave way to surprise as he saw who was standing there. For a moment the very air in the room seemed frozen, as no one dared move. Then, with a noisy exhalation, he nodded a dismissal to the scribe. "Leave me."

The small man scurried out of the room as quickly as dignity allowed. Danton's narrowed eyes met Rurick's as he nodded to him as well; his son and heir bowed and backed out of the room, closing the great doors behind him.

Kostas was not there, Gwynofar noted gratefully. She hadn't actually believed that would be the case until she saw it for herself, but now that she did, one of the many knots in her stomach untied itself.

"Well," Danton said gruffly. "The hermit queen graces me with her presence."

She recognized the bait for what it was and simply curtseyed, her eyes lowered respectfully. "If it does not displease you, Sire."

"If it did I'd have thrown you out, and not my scribe. Don't think I wouldn't."

"Of course not, Sire."

He cleared his throat loudly. "You are out of that ridiculous mourning dress, anyway. I approve of that much. The Queen of the High Kingdom should not be walking around in rags. I don't care who died."

She drew in a deep breath, steadying herself. "Yes, Sire."

"Well, then. You are not here simply for the charm of my company, I am sure. So what brings you here? Are your Spears not keeping you content? Do you wish me to have the servants carve more trees for you?"

Anger flared hotly inside her . . . which of course was exactly what he wanted. She drew in another deep breath, counting silently to ten as she settled her spirit. "Is it not my duty to attend upon my king and husband?"

"Is it? I did not think you still remembered that duty."

"My mourning is over now."

"Indeed. Is that why you have avoided me? For Andovan's sake?"

She had to fight hard not to let any hint of the truth show in her face; if he guessed that his son was truly alive, no room could contain his rage. "I am a mother, Sire, and mothers must mourn as their hearts move them to do. Surely you would not deny us that."

The narrow lips tightened. "No, my queen. I deny nothing to mothers."

"Then I may remain here?"

His dark eyes narrowed as he tried to read her intentions; she was accustomed to such scrutiny and gave him nothing.

"You may stay," he said at last. "Provided you tell me what business brings you to my side. I have little patience for puzzles these days."

She drew in a deep breath, and tried to still the sudden pounding of her heart. "Your Majesty knows me well."

"We have been married for a long time," he said. "So? What is it?"

She looked him over carefully, taking his measure. *He is not ready to hear about the Souleaters,* she decided. *And he is likely to reject any hint that someone else has manipulated him, no matter how true it is. I must tread this ground with care.*

She made her voice a soft thing, more that of a worried wife than that of a queen. "I am concerned for you, Sire. Concerned for changes I have seen of late. You are a man of strong habit, and I am seeing habits change. I cannot help but wonder at the cause."

"Little has changed," he said shortly, "save that my queen no longer rules by my side."

Did he honestly not understand what had caused that? Or was he merely baiting her, to see how she would respond? "Well, now I am here, Sire." She bowed her head respectfully. "And I welcome any manner of chastisement you see fit to direct at me, for that time in which I failed you."

For a moment he was silent. His black eyes stared at her as if they would pierce through to her very soul. "There is no need at the current time," he said at last. "I will let you know if that changes."

She bowed her head. "I thank you, Sire."

"And I thank you for your concern, but I am as I have always been. Nothing has changed, save that I exchanged one servant for another."

She felt her heart skip a beat. "That is no small thing, when the servant is the king's counselor."

His expression darkened; she knew him well enough to recognize it for a warning. "Perhaps those who imagine they deserve the title better are not capable of being wholly objective in this matter."

"Perhaps those who are most devoted to you understand the importance of objectivity in this case, and would not misdirect you."

He sputtered something unintelligible under his breath and turned away from her.

She waited, heart pounding.

"I have not sent you away," he said at last. "You may speak your mind."

She drew in a deep breath, praying to her gods for the courage to say what was needed and the wisdom to say it properly. "You are a builder, Sire. A creator, a unifier. I watched as you took a dozen kingdoms that had never known anything but war, and melded them into the world's greatest empire. Under your governance men now travel safely on roads that did not exist a generation before. Trade prospers. Some say for the first time that perhaps the Second Age of Kings will rival the original."

He exhaled noisily, clearly wary of where she was heading, but said nothing.

"Some who would counsel you to violence do not understand all that. They see you not as builder, but destroyer. They note the severity of your justice, and do not see it as the tool that has built a great peace, but simply a sword to destroy other nations. They see—"

"Do you mean Corialanus?" he demanded. "If so, then just say it."

Her heart fluttered wildly. "It is not only Corialanus, Sire. Or even this." She nodded toward the destruction visible outside the window. "It is all those things, and more. It is a sense of who you are, and where your true greatness lies."

"You speak like Ramirus," he said angrily, "and in the end he showed us all how much his loyalty was worth. I am tired of his song. I am ready for change." He looked around the room. "Do you wish to see where my *greatness* lies? Do you wish to see what blood has brought me? Here!"

He walked over to one of the large chests, reached down, and slammed its lid open. Inside were stacked plates of beaten gold, goblets with jewels set about the lip, and half a dozen candelabra with double-headed hawks at their center. Walking a few steps more, he threw open the second box. Rolls of fabric glittered against a velvet lining, samite and cloth-of-gold and a lustrous brocade worked in purple and gold, in the pattern of the Aurelius arms. Then he moved to the third. It was a long box, almost the length of a coffin, and as he threw the lid open she saw a full suit of armor fitted inside, its surface richly etched with the patterns of Danton's ancestry. A pair of gold-hilted broadswords were lashed to the inside of the lid, each with a shield upon its crosspiece that bore the double-headed hawk. Even as a noncombatant she could recognize the quality of the manufacture, the obvious expense of the materials. The three chests together were worth a small fortune.

"These were all sent from Corialanus, with the king's humble apologies for recent 'misunderstandings.'" He snorted derisively. "He also sent me half a dozen human heads, supposedly of the traitors who had foolishly counseled their king to rebellion, when it was clear all along that his duty lay in obedience to me. Look at this!" His sweeping gesture encompassed all that was in the room. "More goods than I ever had from common tithe, delivered with such cowardly subservience that you'd think I buggered the poor fool, instead of just killing a handful of his troops. Pah!" He spat again on the floor. "Kostas understands the way of such things. He is a fit counselor for what the High Kingdom must become, an empire whose very name makes men tremble in terror. Then and only then we will have no more need of correctional displays . . . such as in Corialanus."

For a moment she could not find her voice. All the arguments she had planned seemed insubstantial things now, and doomed to failure. She knew her husband well enough to understand that this new wealth translated to raw power in his eyes, and that not even a queen dared counsel Danton Aurelius to abandon a path which promised him greater power.

But she had to speak. She had to say something. If she gave up this battle no one would take her place, and if Kostas were truly allied to the Souleaters . . . that could not be allowed to continue. Danton had to be made to understand.

Suddenly she heard Rurick's voice raised outside the heavy wooden doors, loud enough that she knew he was speaking for her benefit.

"Good day, Lord Magister. I fear His Majesty is occupied right now."

Her heart sank. *Gods of the northlands, could you not have given me five minutes more?*

The wide doors swung open without any human hand to push them and Kostas entered. Rurick was right behind him, and it was clear that he did not intend to leave his mother alone in the room with the foul-smelling Magister. Filled with gratitude, Gwynofar backed away as far from Kostas as she could. She almost tripped over one of the great chests in doing so, and at last took up position between two of them . . . as if such riches could protect her from the malignancy that hung about the man like a cloud.

The Magister looked at the tableau before him, and no doubt expended a bit of sorcery to know what had just taken place. The filmy lizard eyes met Gwynofar's own and his thin lips quirked into a mocking smile. "Your Majesty is out of confinement, I see. You do us great honor with your presence." He looked at Danton. "Do I interrupt something . . . private?"

Danton dismissed the question with a short wave of his hand. "Not at all. In fact I was just about to call for you. These offerings came in from Corialanus . . . as you said they would." He glanced at Gwynofar as he spoke the last words, to drive home the point. She flinched inwardly.

Kostas nodded his approval. "You wish to know they are not cursed."

"That, or any other manner of treachery. The whole of that court has only one ball between them, but that doesn't mean someone with more courage than sense didn't tamper with the shipment en route."

Rurick pulled the doors shut behind him, closing out the guards. What did he have planned? "A fine tribute indeed, Sire. And I am sure it is quite clean. No man in that kingdom would be so foolish as to tempt your ire again, after the last lesson you gave them."

"So you approve now, do you?" Danton's smile was utterly without warmth. "This is the first I am hearing of it."

"This is the first I have learned of your success."

"Well, it seems my family approves of me today." His narrow eyes glittered coldly. "How very comforting, eh, Kostas?"

"A veritable reunion," the Magister said dryly. He walked near to Gwynofar, ostensibly to run his hand along the edge of one of the chests as he admired its contents but she knew that the real reason was that he wanted to move nearer to her, to make it clear that he understood just how helpless she felt right now. She could not back away from him without tripping over the offering boxes; she could not elude him by any other means without running into her husband. Rurick met her eyes from across the room, trying to lend her strength, but unable to help her at all. Danton alone seemed unaware of the dance of tensions taking place before him. But that was appropriate, Gwynofar thought darkly. It was the blood of the Protectors that made her hackles and Rurick's rise like cornered wolves with Kostas in the room.

And then he did the unthinkable, and reached out to touch her. The gesture would have been insufferably condescending if he were a normal man, or even a normal Magister. But he was more than that, and the thought that he would once more attempt to set his hand upon the face of a Lady Protector, and in front of her husband the king, evoked such fury in her that for a moment her composure cracked, and she knew he could see the raw hatred in her eyes. She could just as easily see the triumph in his, as he reached out to stroke her cheek in a mockery of human affection, knowing it was one offense she could never tolerate and that she would surely snap—

But she would not. She *could* not. She stumbled backward against one of the offering chests, steadying herself against its lid as he approached, whispering a prayer to her gods, begging them to give her the strength to stand her ground if this creature attempted to violate her again—

Rurick cried, "Magister Kostas!"

The moment shattered like glass. The Magister looked back at Rurick. Gwynofar managed to draw in a deep breath, her first in several moments. Her hand slid along the lid of the chest as she tried to regain her balance. Maybe if the Magister's attention remained upon Rurick for a moment she could manage to get clear of him somehow.

Kostas' tone was civil as he answered Rurick, but barely that. "Highness?"

"I challenge your counsel to my father," Rurick said imperiously.

Gwynofar's heart skipped a beat. She dared not look at Danton, only watched the back of the Magister with horrified fascination. He had gone rigid with rage.

"What nonsense is this?" Kostas demanded. "You dare to challenge me?"

Pride and arrogance were the qualities Rurick excelled in, and he resonated both those qualities as he announced, "I do not believe you truly serve this kingdom. Or my father."

He is distracting Kostas for my sake, she realized suddenly. What terrible, foolish courage! Kostas would surely destroy him for it, or if he did not, then Danton certainly would. This act would amount to insurrection in both their eyes—

And then her hand fell upon cold steel, and she understood.

Rurick did not meet her eyes. He dared not. Kostas would read him like a book if tried.

The Magister hissed softly.

And she grabbed the thing that was beneath her hand, and prayed for the gods to give her strength as she wrenched it free. For a moment it seemed that even her desperate strength was not enough . . . and then the bindings snapped and the sword came free, polished steel gleaming as she pulled it back, a prayer upon her breath—

—And Kostas sensed suddenly that something was amiss, but it was too late. Not even a Magister could foresee an act that had never been planned.

She swung the sword with all her strength, with all her soul, with all her prayers. She swung it knowing she would have one blow and one blow only, and after that her life would be forfeit. Her blood would be spilled in vengeance by the Magisters and her head perhaps dressed on a pike outside the main gates, but that was all right because she would have served her purpose; the Souleaters could not be allowed to control her husband, and she was willing to give her life if that was the cost of freeing him. Such was a Protector's duty.

The steel struck flesh. Kostas' neck was slender, and offered little resistance.

Bone snapped. Blood sprayed her face, her hair, her gown.

Something heavy went flying off to one side. The Magister's body, headless, collapsed like a bloody rag doll to the floor. The sword went flying from Gwynofar's hands and clattered onto the bloodstained floor halfway across the room. And she followed, falling to her knees, gasping for breath as the enormity of what had just happened set her whole body to shaking.

For a brief eternity there was silence. Then:

"What have you done?" Danton whispered hoarsely as he came around the table, as he knelt down in the pool of blood by Kostas' side. *"What have you done?"* He looked at her then, and she saw nothing but madness in his eyes. He looked about for the sword she had dropped; she moved back from him as well as she could, while Rurick came running over to protect her.

And then suddenly a screech split the air, of such terrible volume and tenor that all three of them froze in place. It was an unearthly sound, unlike anything that human or animal throat had ever issued. And it was coming from outside the palace.

Danton moved toward the nearest window. Rurick came to Gwynofar and helped her to her feet. For a moment she just stood there, swaying. Not moving toward the window. Not needing to. She knew what was out there.

"Souleaters," she whispered.

———

"What in the hells was that?" Kamala said.

"Outside," Andovan whispered. His face was white. "It came from outside."

They moved quickly to one of the windows. The narrow opening did not make for good visibility, and for a moment they both scanned the surrounding landscape anxiously, searching for anything that might explain the strange noise.

And then they saw it.

It rose up from the mountains in the distance, a great winged creature whose skin glittered like jewels in the sunlight. Even from this far away Kamala could see that it was immense, and it cast a shadow on the ground so large that the charred remnants of whole trees were swallowed by darkness as it passed. Its body was snakelike, and the long tail cracked once like a whip as it rose from concealment, the sound echoing across the devastated landscape. And those wings! They were unlike anything Kamala had ever seen before, or ever dreamed possible. Vast layered wings, as fine and fragile-seeming as panels of stained glass, a deep blue-black that transformed in color as it flew. Black one moment in the shadow of a cloud, and glistening the next with overtones of cobalt, violet, and green, as sunlight lanced through them.

It was fearsome. It was beautiful.

It was riveting.

Andovan put a hand on her shoulder; she could feel him trembling. Not from fear, though. She could feel his fingers biting into her flesh, could hear him mutter some curse under his breath; his voice sounded far more hate-filled than afraid. As for herself, she could not take her eyes off the creature. Its movement was hypnotic, compelling. It made her want to go outside and take a closer look at the beast, even if that meant climbing out the window and down the palace wall to do so. She wanted to be in the shadow of those wings, to feel their colors dancing across her face, to smell whatever scent that strange flesh carried and hear its alien cry resonating within her own flesh. She wanted—

Andovan pulled her sharply away from the window. "Lianna!"

She blinked. For a moment it seemed she could not focus on anything inside the room. Then, with effort, she was able to master her senses once more, and Andovan's face slowly came into focus.

"What is that thing?" she whispered.

His voice was like edged steel. "The ancients called it a Souleater. No man has looked upon one since the Dark Ages. The legends say they have the power to mesmerize their prey."

The beast was rising higher into the sky now, and was clearly turning toward the palace. Not good. Not good at all.

"We have to stop it," Andovan whispered hoarsely.

"How?"

Tight-lipped, he shook his head in frustration. "There are warriors in the north who know the way of such things, but I do not think anyone in this kingdom has that knowledge. If it is even still valid, after ten centuries."

Then he met her eyes.

"They are beasts," he said quietly. "They breathe, they bleed, they die."

She felt her heart skip a beat at the unspoken question.

Outside, the great beast shrieked again. There was rage in the sound, and madness. Whatever it intended to do when it reached the palace, there was surely going to be bloodshed involved.

"You are not of my people," he said to her. "I have no right to ask you to expend your vital energy in any cause. Least of all in service to ancient legends."

"You want me to kill it," she whispered. Trembling inwardly at the thought.

"Can you do such a thing? Is that possible?"

She looked out the window again. Now that she knew the nature of the creature's power she was able to keep from being mesmerized simply by the sight of it, but it took effort. Focusing sorcery upon the creature would be even harder, and would increase the threat of entrancement a hundred-fold. And she could not do it from here. There was no question of that. In another moment the creature would pass out of sight of this vantage point, and while she might run from window to window throughout the palace trying to keep sight of it, that sort of behavior was not conducive to well-focused sorcery.

And then of course, there was . . .

The obvious.

She needed no sorcery to read the creature's emotional state. That was a gift of her Sight, which made the creature's spiritual aura plainly visible. The beast was maddened with pain and with rage, and so frenzied in its bloodthirst that all other emotions had ceased to exist. No animal was ever more dangerous than one in such a state.

Nor any man, she thought.

Andovan was waiting for her answer. She looked into his eyes and weighed all the lies she might tell him, all the half-truths designed for subterfuge and obscurity . . . and then discarded them. This man deserved better than that. Even if she had to break the Law to give it to him.

"If I do this," she told him, "you will die."

Her words clearly took him aback. His mouth opened as if he would question her, but no sound came out. For a moment he just stared at her.

And then something flickered in his eyes that might be understanding. Or perhaps simply acceptance.

"I am of the Protector's line," he said quietly. Proudly. "If I could raise up my sword and charge this thing on my own, I would, even knowing that death would surely come of it." He took her face in his hands; a strange tenderness filled his eyes. "Do it for me, Lianna."

She felt tears coming to her eyes. She fought them back with stubborn pride. *I knew all along he must die, and by my hand. Why does it bother me now?*

He kissed her. She shut her eyes and for one bittersweet moment smelled saffron and cassia bark again, and heard the patter of a warm mountain rain overhead. Then the memory was gone and there was only the Souleater overhead, screaming out his challenge to the skies, and the source of power that was standing there before her.

"Go," he said.

And she did. She drew the power from out of his soul and transformed into a great bird, even while he staggered back against the wall, gasping as the athra left him. But he was still standing, she noted. That was good. That meant there was probably enough life left in him to sustain her through the course of battle, and she need not fear Transition would claim her in midflight.

With that thought, and a hawk's cry of challenge voiced to the heavens, she slid her new body through the narrow window and launched herself into the air.

———

Standing alone on the blackened earth, Colivar watched the ikati take to the sky.

It screamed in pain as it rose, a piercing sound that echoed across the length and breadth of the ravaged plain. Colivar had only heard a cry like that once before, but it was something he had never forgotten. Thus did the Souleater scream when its guiding intelligence was suddenly ripped out of its soul, when fury and fear so consumed its heart that rational thought was impossible, even by animal standards. It was never more dangerous than at such a moment, he recalled, particularly if the source of its pain was within reach. In this case, Colivar was willing to bet the source was within the palace . . . and apparently the creature thought so as well, for it circled once in its flight as if getting its bearings, and then headed straight for the keep.

Once, long ago, he had heard a man scream like that. Sometimes in his nightmares he heard it still.

Swiftly the creature flew, its vast stained-glass wings filtering the sunlight into rainbow-colored shards. So much beauty, in such a lethal form! It was almost a pity such a proud creature had to die, he thought. But that was the way of war, even one that was stretched out over the course of centuries. This Souleater had made its home in territory where its presence simply could not be tolerated, especially in its current state of mind. If it did not know when it came here that every human hand would be turned against it, its allies certainly did, and they had accepted that risk. Colivar was merely helping the creature to fulfill the destiny it had chosen.

As the beast passed overhead, he gathered his power to him. He reflected upon the weaknesses of the beast, the places where a simple wound might do the worst damage. The knowledge was so deeply buried inside him, underneath so many half-forgotten memories, that he had to work to dig it out. Some of the memories he disturbed were not pleasant ones; he would have to work hard at forgetting them again later. Sometimes a man's sanity depended upon such tricks.

When the soulfire burned along his fingertips, when whirlwinds of power gathered spontaneously about him, when all the force of a lightning strike was contained within his body, he looked up towards his enemy and focused all his senses upon the Souleater, sorcerous and material—

But he did not strike.

He could not strike.

And then the moment passed and the Souleater had passed him by, its shadow racing along the ground like some ghostly predator. A scent came to him on the breeze in its wake: sweet, so sweet, more enticing than any man-made perfume could be, more intoxicating than the finest of wines. He tried to put the smell out of his mind, but it was impossible. He could feel a dam inside his soul shattering in response it, and a flood tide of memories came crashing into his mind, so suddenly and so powerfully that he reeled from the impact.

—*Young women cast into the boiling hot springs in sacrifice, to die oh so slowly*—

—*Mountaintops rising from a sea of clouds, stark and white in the arctic sunlight*—

—*Winged monsters rending each other with tail and claw, frozen blood raining down upon the earth like ruby crystals*—

Gasping for breath, he fell to his knees. The shadow of the great beast had passed beyond him now, and he shivered as if it had stolen the very warmth from his flesh. How fortunate he was, that the Souleater had not seen him! What a fool he had been, to think that he would be capable of attacking it!

This is not your battle, he told himself. The thought was bitter, and cut to the heart of his pride. *Others must take up that banner now.*

Then he saw the great hawk launch itself into the air from a window of the palace, and he realized that someone intended to do just that.

———

The rush of air across her wings was invigorating to Kamala, and—surprisingly—the sense of danger was also. Had Ethanus ever imagined in his wildest dreams that she would come to this point, readying herself to fight one of the most fearsome creatures that had ever existed? What stories she would tell him if she survived this!

It was clear the Souleater was heading toward the palace, and since the last thing she wanted to do was to be trapped between it and its target, she set off toward the open air to one side of its course. It did not appear to even notice her. Its black eyes were fixed wholly on the palace ahead, and waves of fury and hatred that resonated from it like heat from desert sands left little doubt as to its intentions.

Clearly something had triggered its frenzy. But what?

Its eyes glittered like black jewels in the sunlight, but when she looked at them for more than a moment a wave of weakness overcame her, and she had to look away. She discovered she could not study the creature directly at all for more than a second or two without its mind-numbing power wrapping itself around her brain. Once when she tried to test that limit her wings lost their natural rhythm, and she hurtled many feet toward the ground before she was able to save herself.

Not good. Not good at all.

She had only so much power to spare, she knew that. If she drew too much life from her consort he would die prematurely, which was the worst possible thing that could happen in the midst of a battle. This time there was no natural force nearby that she could manipulate to her advantage, as she had used lightning in the Highlands; the only power available to her was what she could draw from Andovan, until that supply ran out. Com-

plex spells must all be set aside, then, in favor of a simple assault, hopefully with enough good planning behind it that it would take the creature
down.

The only problem was that there was no time to plan anything.

Desperately she tried to assemble her peripheral impressions of the
creature into enough of a unified picture that she could pinpoint some
weakness. The body appeared to be covered in overlapping scales, which
might be some kind of natural armor. The wings . . . they seemed fragile,
as if fashioned from glass, but she was not so much a fool as to believe they
were weak in truth if they were supporting such a creature. Wave after
wave of its strange mesmeric power washed over her as she struggled to
pinpoint an appropriate target area. Part of her wanted to destroy the
beast, but part of her wanted to lay down on the earth, belly-up, and invite it to devour her. Half her energy had to be expended just convincing
herself that she did not truly wish to die.

Where is an armored knight most vulnerable? she asked herself, desperately. Trying to focus on the problem.

And then she realized the answer.

Summoning up all the power she could—*Forgive me, Andovan!*—she
paused only long enough to gather it into one hot, blazing bolt of energy,
then cast it toward the beast. It struck exactly where she had intended, in
the soft flesh at the base of one wing, and it pierced the great body like a
red-hot lance, searing skin and flesh from the inside out. The Souleater
screamed in agony and wheeled in its flight, its flesh smoking blackly from
the assault. It had noticed her now, and its mesmeric power increased tenfold as it focused its attention directly upon her. But its flight was unsteady, and it clearly had to struggle to keep itself aloft. That gave Kamala
one more second in which to act, but only that. After that she must flee,
or the beast would be upon her.

Avoiding its eyes—what a prime target they would have been if she
could look at them directly!—she quickly drew upon her consort's soulfire
again, molding it into a bolt of fiery power ten times more powerful than
the last. Apparently Andovan was still strong enough to fuel such efforts;
perhaps he might even survive this battle, if she could kill this thing quickly
enough. She had to look directly at the creature again to take aim, and
braced herself to resist its hypnotic power. This close, she had no trouble

seeing the narrow patches of softer skin that covered its joints, a marked contrast from the armored shell that seemed to protect the rest of its body. So it was with human armor, Ethanus had taught her; the need for freedom of movement meant that joints were always the weakest point.

Drawing in a deep breath, she focused her will upon the creature—

And the world went black

And the abyss screamed in hunger.

And there was no sorcery.

———

For one brief moment, time itself seemed frozen. Danton stared out the window as if unable to absorb what he was seeing. Gwynofar knelt in Kostas' blood, staring at the headless body before her as if expecting it to rise up at any moment. Rurick . . . Rurick knelt by her side, speechless, wary, not yet sure what his part was to be in all this.

Then the beast shrieked yet again, and the tableau shattered.

Danton turned from the window. There was madness in his eyes. "This is what you have brought to my kingdom!" he roared. A wild wave of his hand encompassed the entire situation, from the carnage in the room to the unnamed monster rising beyond the palace walls. "My Magister dead and now a Souleater in my realm—if that is what that thing truly is—you will bring us low before all our enemies—"

"Sire," she began, "please let me explain—"

"*Silence!*" His voice was shaking with rage. "You have betrayed my kingdom. Betrayed *me*. There is nothing to explain!"

He looked over the room as if searching for something in particular; after a moment his eyes lit upon the sword, wet with the Magister's blood. Gwynofar shrank back, trembling, as he walked to where it lay and picked it up.

Outside, the Souleater shrieked again. The sound was like ragged fingernails playing along Gwynofar's spine.

"It is your last betrayal," Danton proclaimed. His dark eyes gleamed with a fury she knew all too well. Alas, it was not possible to blame such madness on Kostas. While the Magister might have encouraged Danton's more violent side, the raw material had been there before he arrived and clearly it had survived his death.

Rurick stood. "Father, please, don't do this. Let her explain—"

"You, too? Also a traitor?" The High King's eyes narrowed in fury. "Is my whole family turning on me now?"

"Your family only wishes to protect you—"

"Protect me? *This* is protecting me?" He gesticulated wildly at Kostas' body, then toward the window. "Summoning a Souleater to my realm is protecting me?"

"Kostas did that," Gwynofar whispered hoarsely. "Kostas fed him human souls from your kingdom. And in Corialanus. He *used* you, my husband. That"—she nodded toward the window—"that creature out there is what it was all about."

But it was clear that Danton was not listening to her words any longer; madness had taken possession of him, and no mere morati could reason with it. With a sinking in her heart Gwynofar realized that whatever spell Kostas had worked upon the High King, it was too deeply ingrained now to be banished by a handful of words. Her husband was lost to her.

Proudly, she stood. She would not die kneeling.

Growling deep his throat, Danton drew the sword back and stepped forward—

And Rurick stepped in front of her. Gwynofar held her breath. Her son was clearly banking on the fact that Danton would not be so mad as to kill his own heir.

He was wrong.

His face black with fury, Danton thrust the sword through his son's body. Rurick was so surprised he did not even cry out, merely stared at him in astonishment as his lifeblood began to seep out. Danton twisted the sword once, then yanked it out. The trickle of blood became a river, and then a flood.

Gwynofar screamed.

Rurick put a hand to the gaping wound, not so much trying to staunch the flow of blood—that was hopeless—as if trying to convince himself the wound was real. When he withdrew his hand and saw it covered in blood, he stared at his father in astonishment.

"You are a fool," he whispered. "May the gods have mercy upon this kingdom."

He swayed once, and for a moment it seemed he would be able to keep

to his feet, but then his legs folded beneath him. Gwynofar caught him
from behind, but his weight forced her down to one knee again, struggling
to support him. Tears streamed down her face as she whispered his name,
pleading with him to live. But the river of blood was thinning now, and
slowly his eyes glazed over.

Lowering her head to his shoulder, she wept.

"No need to mourn," her husband told her. "You will not be parted
long."

———

Gwynofar's scream cut through Andovan's awareness like a knife. The fog
of weakness that had slowly been enveloping him was suddenly gone. Or
rather, it was still present, but he was no longer was willing to submit to
it.

Pushing himself away from the wall, he took a few seconds to fight
back a wave of dizziness that threatened his balance, then took off at a run
down the hallway. Sheer determination took the place of physical
strength, sustaining him at a speed he could not have managed for any
other purpose.

Other guards were coming, but they had not been as close to where
Gwynofar was, so they fell in behind him. He was grateful for the uniform
he wore, not only because it meant they would not question him, but because he was armed. He pulled out his sword as he ran, not knowing what
to expect, but preparing for the worst.

He slammed open the doors which separated him from Gwynofar, not
caring who or what was on the other side, so long as he reached her in
time.

The tableau which greeted him was horrific. A headless body in Magister's robes lay in a pool of blood on the floor. Gwynofar knelt in the
blood, cradling the body of Rurick in her arms, weeping. The royal heir
appeared to be dead. And Danton stood over them both with a sword in
his hands and madness in his eyes. Even as Andovan entered he was
preparing another blow, this one directed at the High Queen.

Something in Andovan snapped. Too many months of feeling helpless while other people determined his fate had finally brought him to
the breaking point. A sudden rush of strength suffused his limbs, not

unlike the kind of desperate fortitude that allowed a mother to lift a fallen boulder off her child. With a cry of fury he threw himself at Danton. Maybe if he had been anyone else the High King could have responded in time to save himself, but because he was Andovan Aurelius, he did not. Danton looked up as the doors slammed open, he prepared to defend himself against this unexpected assault—from one of his own guards!—and then he realized who his attacker was. His eyes went wide. His mouth hung open. For a crucial second, his sword did not move quickly enough.

Andovan ran his own sword through his father to the hilt and held it there. For a moment they were face to face. Andovan stared into his father's eyes, mourning the madness he saw there but regretting nothing. For a brief moment something else flickered in the royal gaze, that might have been sanity, or perhaps understanding . . . and then the High King slumped against Andovan, as the strength left his limbs along with his blood.

"No!" Gwynofar screamed. "Don't! He is the prince—"

Something sharp and cold thrust into Andovan's body from behind. Another thrust followed.

He could feel the breath leave his body in a hot cloud as his lung was pierced. Then another thrust. His brief moment of fortitude flowed out of him with his blood, and he sank to his knees. His eyes met his mother's. *I am sorry,* he mouthed. Unable to find the strength to voice the words.

The guards did not know who he was, of course. All they had seen was a stranger in a uniform attacking their king. They had never seen his face. And they had to strike him down to protect their queen. Of course. He understood that. The assassin had to die so that Gwynofar might live. It all made perfect sense.

Then those thoughts left him, along with any others. Death, who had dogged his footsteps for so long, finally stepped forward to claim his due. It was almost a relief, Andovan discovered. No more pretending to be strong. No more fear of being unmanned by his final incapacity. He had fought to the end. Now it was time to quit the field of battle in honor.

Take care of the kingdom, my mother.

In his last moment of consciousness he was dimly aware of Lianna. It was almost as if they were connected, somehow.

Then that connection snapped, and all that was left was darkness.

Black, black, the universe is black, and so cold that thoughts shatter like ice even as they are formed.

Andovan is dead! the darkness screams. Life is gone! Find more!

Regret is lethal! the darkness warns. Do not mourn, do not mourn, DO NOT MOURN!

Bright shining prince, so full of honor

Blue eyes

Hope

Such resolve

Such strength

Willing to die for a cause

Are you?

Cold, cold, the place where a Magister's soul goes to die. Warm, the world surrounding. Latch onto that warmth. Infect it with cold, with death. Suck the life from its veins until your own veins are full. If a whole world must die to sustain you, then you must kill it.

Never regret.

Mourning is death

Do you care enough to live, knowing the cost?

Is this the existence you want, for the rest of eternity?

Decide!

Gwynofar knelt by Andovan's body. Slowly she turned it over so that she might see his face one last time . . . and in that moment the guards knew what they had done.

She heard their whispered prayers and curses, but it was as if they were a great distance away from her. There was nothing in Gwynofar's universe save her and her child—her children—and the husband she had tried so hard to save.

Dead. All dead.

She wept.

One by one, with silent solemnity, the guards knelt before her, awaiting her word as High Queen, prepared to submit to whatever judgment she saw fit to pronounce.

She did not even know they were there.

Colivar saw the hawk fall. It dropped like a stone from the sky, and he realized as it did what must surely have happened . . . and what that would mean to the Magisters, if the hawk was indeed Lianna.

Transition.

Thus far he had avoided giving a name to what she was, but if it really was Transition that had just snuffed out her consciousness, there was no longer any question about that. Only whether she would survive the next few minutes or not to face the Magisters who would judge her.

He summoned up a whirlwind to break the bird's fall, and while he could not bring the hawk down perfectly he did manage to divert some of its downward velocity into lateral movement. It rolled violently as it hit the ground, crashing into the charred remnants of fallen trees with all the force of a speeding boulder, snapping more delicate bones in its wings at every turn. When it finally stopped, Colivar's sorcery assured him that the hawk was still alive, though not much more than that. It did not seem to be stirring, which was a bad sign. For all that Transition was terrifying when it came on at such moments, it did not usually last more than a few seconds. If she had taken enough damage in the fall that she was now genuinely unconscious, her life was still very much in danger.

But though he could save the bird from being killed by its fall, he could not save it from the ikati. The creature clearly had no intention of letting its attacker go free, and began its descent before the body had stopped its movement. Even on a good day Colivar would have been hard pressed to stop it. Given that he could not seem to attack the Souleater at all, he was forced to back away helplessly as it descended to claim the unconscious Magister.

She would not have lasted long anyway, he told himself. *Not after breaking our Law.* Nevertheless he regretted that a genuine mystery should be destroyed at the very moment he had begun to unravel it. There were few enough diversions worthy of his attention these days, and the loss of one as promising as this was something to be mourned.

Suddenly there was a cry from behind him. It was a strange sound, human and inhuman all at once, and it stirred memories in Colivar so ancient, so compelling, that for a moment all present concerns faded from his awareness. The sound played like fingers along his spine, it made the blood rush hotly to his loins, it made him want to cry out in response with all the volume his lungs could muster, until his very soul was exhausted from screaming . . . and then, as suddenly as it had begun, it was gone.

Shaken, Colivar turned back to locate the source, and saw a man standing atop a nearby rise. He was a tall man, pale and blond in the manner of the northern races, and well armed. As Colivar watched he raised his hands to his lips and made the strange noise once again. Its effect upon the Souleater was immediate and dramatic. The creature no longer had an interest in the fallen Magister, but wheeled in midair to head directly toward the stranger instead.

Colivar watched in amazement as the man went down on one knee, bringing up a crossbow to bear upon the beast. He was so still then that Colivar thought the Souleater's power of entrancement had overcome him. Closer and closer the beast came—and then the stranger let fly his quarrel, and to Colivar's amazement he managed a well-aimed shot into one of the wing joints. The Souleater screamed in pain, and though its wings remained extended, it began to lose altitude. *Of course*, Colivar thought, admiring the move. *Bring it down first. Deny it mobility.* Whoever this stranger was, he appeared to know what he was doing.

Given how long it had been since any man had last fought an ikati, that in and of itself cried out for explanation.

With a cry of bestial frustration the ikati hit the ground, beating its damaged wings upon the earth. The motion raised a thick cloud of black dust that spread quickly on the wind, and would have set Colivar to coughing had he not summoned a breeze to keep it away from him. Now one must concentrate even harder to see it clearly, which meant that its power would be more effective. This was becoming an interesting contest.

Knowing how dangerous it still was, Colivar watched with interest as the man took up his lance and approached the thing. Certainly he seemed unaffected by the creature's mesmeric power, and that was half the battle.

He appeared to be chanting something as he walked forward, low enough that Colivar could not make out the words. Perhaps it was some kind of protective spell, he mused. It was something to ask about later if the man survived.

As he approached the beast drew itself up to its full height, trying to intimidate him into retreat. It was a mating display pure and simple, and little wonder; the man's strange cry, Colivar realized, had been a mating challenge. The ikati bared a mouthful of razor-sharp teeth, stretching its jaw in the same odd, disjointed way that a snake might, and the stranger watched it closely. Too closely. Evidently for all his knowledge of such creatures, he was not prepared for reality of what was in its arsenal.

The long tail whipped about, low to the ground, and cracked with stunning force against his side. If he had been a few steps farther away the sharp plates on the tail's end would have gutted him like a fish, but as it was, the ikati merely broke a host of bones and sent him reeling to the ground. *Give the man credit for being well-trained enough that he did not drop the spear,* Colivar mused. The man was lying still now, and it was very possible that the creature had knocked him unconscious. Either that, or the blow had stunned him hard enough that the ikati's power could finally take hold of him.

The Souleater opened its jaws and stretched forward, clearly intending to claim its enemy as dinner—

And the man moved suddenly. Bringing up the spear in both hands, he thrust it into the creature's mouth and upward, into the brain beyond. The ikati let out a bellow of rage and pulled back, snapping the spear free of the stranger's hands, but it was too late. Blood gushed out of its mouth and the great wings spasmed against the ground as it struggled to save itself. Its tail whipped about wildly, with no conscious control behind it; once by sheer luck it hit the blond man again, and Colivar could hear his cry of pain as it connected.

Then, slowly, the great beast stopped moving. Its glassy wings fell limp from its sides and lay upon the ground, black against black, all their colors gone. The ground beneath it was soaked with blood, as was the man who lay before it. Everything was still.

Colivar found that he could breathe again.

With one glance at the hawk that lay behind him, to assure himself that it was still alive, he moved to the side of the fallen warrior. The man's wounds were severe, but nothing sorcery could not heal. He knit the broken ribs back together and repaired the bruised organs, including one collapsed lung. The stranger said nothing through it all, just coughed up blood now and then as he struggled to get enough air to remain conscious to the end of the treatment.

When at last his breathing steadied, and nothing inside his body was about to fail him, Colivar stood back and looked at him. A dry, pained smile spread across the warrior's face. "Well, I see the legends did not exaggerate, anyway."

Colivar helped him to his feet. "I take it this is the first time you have seen one?"

"Oh, yes." He brushed at the dirt on his clothes out of habit; in fact there was way too much blood and ash adhering to him for any simple gesture to dislodge it. "First time anyone has seen one, as far as I know."

Colivar said nothing.

"Well." The voice came from behind them. "That was quite impressive."

Colivar did not turn around. "You could have helped."

"And miss the chance to see a Guardian tested? I think not." Ramirus looked over the body as he joined them. "Besides, I am a scholar, not a warrior. But introductions are in order, yes?" He nodded toward the blood-stained Guardian. "Rhys nas Keirdwyn, Guardian of the Wrath, this is Colivar, Magister Royal of some little state down south, I forget the name of it."

"Anshasa," Colivar muttered. He nodded a curt greeting to Rhys. "May I say you have . . . remarkable timing?"

"Serendipity," Ramirus assured him. "Rhys is Queen Gwynofar's brother, and perhaps her most trusted confidant. I was bringing him here to see if he could inspire her to the task required, when we saw this . . . thing."

He stepped over to the side of the great creature and put his hand upon its flank. "Is it what it appears to be?" he breathed. "Truly?"

"I am afraid so," Colivar said.

"Then they have returned?"

Rhys cursed softly under his breath as Colivar joined Ramirus at the ikati's flank. Its skin was cold and smooth, like a serpent's. Down its spine ran a series of sharp spikes, many longer than a man's hand. Colivar pulled the heavy body toward him, to where they could see a place where several of the spikes had been removed. The hide where they had once been anchored was covered over with scars; the surgery had taken place long ago.

"This one is from the north," he said quietly. Even speaking the words made a shiver run up his own spine. "Beyond the Wrath. So . . ." He looked at Rhys. "They have found a way through it."

The warrior's expression was grim. "Then we must discover a way to repair the breach before more can follow."

Colivar did not say what he already knew, that the move would come too late. Ikati were already nesting in the human lands, which meant that sooner or later there would be a flock of them to deal with. But the warrior who had just defeated a Souleater deserved his moment of hope. For now.

The world is at war, he thought grimly.

He wanted more than anything to ask Ramirus if he had felt the creature's power himself, as Colivar had. The Magisters must know if they were stronger than morati in resisting these creatures, or perhaps doubly susceptible for being such choice prey. But he could not ask that question without inviting others that he himself was unwilling to answer, so he kept his silence.

Rhys stroked the wings in wonder. "I have heard they once made armor out of layers of this stuff," he said, "and from the hide as well."

"They did once," Colivar confirmed. "There are few substances that can protect a man as well. But it requires special treatment in the first few hours after death, and I suspect you did not come here prepared for that." He nodded toward the end of the tail, where it lay some yards away from them. "There are sharp plates in the tip, there. Take them as trophy. Make blades of them, and spearheads as well. They will pierce the hide of these creatures as nothing man-made can."

Rhys nodded and began to walk down the length of the tail, pulling out his knife as he went. Colivar was about to speak to Ramirus when a commotion sounded in the distance behind them. Glancing that way, he could see a small phalanx of guards leaving the palace, no doubt to investigate what had just occurred.

"There was a hawk," Ramirus said quietly.

"A witch," he answered, equally quietly. "I tracked her from Gansang, where she killed one of our kind. Apparently she was particularly susceptible to the beast's power. Which should come as no great surprise, given how much hatred that species must have for witches." He shrugged. "Justice is done, if not by our hand."

"Indeed."

"Well, if you will excuse me." He nodded toward the coming crowd. "I really do not think it the best thing if I stay around to wait for the reception committee. Nor should you, for that matter."

Ramirus looked toward the palace; his white brow furrowed as he concentrated. "Danton is dead," he said finally. "And Rurick also. And . . . and Andovan." His thin mouth tightened. "Not a good day for the throne of the High Kingdom."

"That is your affair, not mine, Ramirus." Colivar's tone was dry. "I rule over sand dunes and tents, remember? Take control of the whole continent if you like, I have no plans for it."

Ramirus put a hand on his shoulder. He waited until Colivar met his eyes. "We will have to cooperate on this matter. All of us. Anything less than that could get us all killed."

And trying to work together could get us all killed even faster, Colivar thought. But he merely nodded.

He made himself the body of a red-winged falcon and took off across the field, low to the ground, hoping that Ramirus did not take note of his direction. He wanted to collect the fallen hawk before the palace guards reached that spot, preferably without Ramirus noticing. He had no desire to share his precious mystery with anyone.

But the hawk was gone. Traces of sorcery clung to the ground where it had rested. Apparently she had left under her own power.

Keening his frustration into the air, the falcon circled higher and higher . . . then the air surrounding it shimmered, and it was gone.

———

Halfway across the world, in a field being readied for harvest, one of the workers paused.

"Liam?" another worker asked him. "Are you all right?"

"Yes, just . . . just a moment of dizziness. But it's gone now."

He waited a moment longer to see if the strange feeling of weakness would come over him again, and when it did not, shrugged and returned to his work.

Chapter 42

THE FIELDS in the monastery had just come into bloom, and a half-dozen monks in coarse linen robes were picking the precious medicinal blossoms and gathering them into wicker baskets. In the distance several others had tucked up their long shirts into their belts in order to wade among close-set rows of gosberry bushes, and their bare legs were splotched with juice. Farther still, the hum of bees resonated in the warm summer air.

The messenger pulled up his horse at the main gate and dismounted. He was a young man, well dressed, and he walked with the stiffness of one who had been in the saddle too many hours for his liking.

"I seek the one you know as Father Constance," he called out to the first monk that noticed him. A hand waved him toward the stone cloister beyond the fields, then the monk went back to his work.

The messenger walked toward the building as fast as his stiff legs would carry him. His somber expression caused several of the monks to look up from their work long enough to take his measure, but none asked him any questions, and he did not stop to invite any.

Inside the building he had to ask two more times after the one he sought, and at last was directed to a small chamber in the back of the cloister, a plain cell with minimal furnishings in which a young man sat reading.

"Are you the one they call Father Constance?" the messenger asked.

He shut his book. "I am. What is your business?"

The messenger pulled out a flattened scroll from his doublet and went down on one knee to read from it. "Prince Salvator Aurelius, son of Danton Aurelius, I bring to you the words of the Queen Mother Gwynofar, called the Fair. She informs you, with great regret, that the High King has passed from this earth, and his firstborn son and heir has also, and thus by our customs the throne of the High Kingdom falls to you. She bids you come as priest to preside over their funerals, and then if you will, set aside your priestly robes and take your rightful place at the head of Danton's empire, that you may guide her people in their time of mourning and provide them with justice and leadership afterward."

The messenger rolled up the scroll again, and waited.

Bells tolled in the distance, signaling the end of one task and the beginning of another.

For a few minutes the monk did not answer. Then he stood.

"Tell the Queen Mother," he said, "Salvator will come."

Epilogue

NO ONE noticed when the Witch-Queen slipped away from her guests. Wine was flowing, music was playing, and the carefully chosen guests were keeping each other occupied, mostly with ribald tales of previous gatherings. If one chose the right mix of guests to begin with, such things took care of themselves.

Quietly she slipped out of the great hall. The closeness of so many people was giving her a headache, and she needed a moment to herself. Such bouts of introversion had been rare things once, but now, toward the end of her days, they were becoming more and more common.

Or perhaps that was simply the natural result of discovering that one was soon to die, and that there was nothing any living man could do to change it.

No one knew the truth yet. No one saw any change in her. A few faint lines that the Magisters' sorcery could no longer conquer had begun to creep across her face, but no one noticed them. A vague lethargy enveloped her at seemingly random moments, but she covered for it well.

The effort was exhausting, though. As was playing the perfect hostess when what she really wanted to do was stand up on a table and scream out her fury at the world, for the cruel trick it had played on her.

And the Magisters. Never forget the Magisters.

Wrapping her arms about her as if it were the depths of winter rather than a balmy summer evening, she slipped out onto one of the wide terraces that overlooked the harbor. Hundreds of boats bobbed on the water below, waiting for the morning's tide, and lanterns lit the piers and walkways like rows of fireflies. From where she stood she could hear the drunken laughter of sailors, the wheedling promises of women, the thousand and one sounds of life as usual in Sankara. In the morning the sun would rise once more and merchants would make their deals, fisherman would set out with their nets, stray dogs would nuzzle strangers in the hopes of handouts. Life as usual.

How easy it would be, to cast herself off the balcony and end it all. One single, slow dive into the darkness, a brief kiss of midnight waters as they closed over her head, and then she might live on forever young in memory, a creature of legend.

Tempting. So tempting. But she had not become monarch of a keystone state of the Free Lands by giving up on things before their time, and she would not do so now. No, until the very end she would fight this thing and rail at her fate, and deny Death his due by every means she could, until that due could no longer be denied by any means.

With a sigh, she turned back from the view and prepared to return to her guests.

"It is a sad thing when a woman must leave the world in her prime," a male voice whispered.

Despite the sudden pounding of her heart she turned about calmly, with true regal composure; in such situations proper demeanor could make the difference between life and death. "Who are you, that you speak to me thus?"

There was a figure in the shadows, and as it moved forward the shadows moved with it. In another time and place she could have banished those shadows and forced the speaker to reveal himself, but no longer.

"One who watches. One who understands. One who sees an ally discarded by those who should have valued her more." The whispering voice was strangely accented; she could not place its origin. "But being a Magister does not make a man less of a fool, does it? Only a more powerful one."

"What is it you want?" she said sharply.

"Only to inform you that their way is not the only way. And that not all allies are as fickle and inconstant as your black-robed lovers."

Her heart was pounding so loudly she was afraid he might hear it, but she kept her voice steady and calm. "You have another way to offer, then?"

He reached out suddenly; she backed away quickly, wary of his purpose. But the move had simply been to cast something small upon the floor of the terrace. It glinted in the moonlight and rolled a few feet away before it stopped.

"We will speak again," the visitor promised. "In the meantime, a token to remember my words. So that those who bear similar signs will be known, and welcomed." He paused. "You are worthy of much more than your current allies have given you, my queen. Others will not be so miserly with their power."

He disappeared then, or seemed to. More likely he was still on the terrace, simply cloaked from her sight. In her current state there was nothing she could do to affect such sorcery, or even to detect it.

She waited for a time in silence, to see if some other surprise would manifest itself, but nothing did. At last she knelt down, wary, to retrieve the small object the visitor had left behind. It was a narrow silver ring, unremarkable save for the odd stone set in it: a cabochon gem of the deepest blue, that swirled with rainbow sparks when the light fell upon it.

Was there really hope for her? Or was this some new and cruel game of the Magisters? There was no way to know.

Cursing softly, praying secretly, the Witch-Queen returned to her guests, uncomfortably aware that a spark of hope had taken root with her . . . and dreading to find out what might be required to nourish it.